W9-DDC-495

FORGE BOOKS BY JAMES SWALLOW

24: Deadline

Nomad

Exile

Ghost

Shadow

SHADOW

JAMES SWALLOW

A TOM DOHERTY ASSOCIATES BOOK

NEW YORK

This is a work of fiction. All of the characters, organizations, and events portrayed in this novel are either products of the author's imagination or are used fictitiously.

SHADOW

Copyright © by 2019 by James Swallow

A Forge Book
Published by Tom Doherty Associates
120 Broadway
New York, NY 10271

www.tor-forge.com

Forge® is a registered trademark of Macmillan Publishing Group, LLC.

ISBN 978-1-250-75080-8

Our books may be purchased in bulk for promotional, educational, or business use. Please contact your local bookseller or the Macmillan Corporate and Premium Sales Department at 1-800-221-7945, extension 5442, or by email at MacmillanSpecialMarkets@macmillan.com.

First U.S. Edition: August 2021
First U.S. Mass Market Edition: March 2022

Printed in the United States of America

0 9 8 7 6 5 4 3 2 1

For *the Hopeful and the* Noble.

SHADOW

— ONE —

Through the window of the carriage, the close ranks of the fir trees crowded in along the sides of the railway line. The green of their foliage was dark enough to be almost black in the splash of light spilling from the fast-moving train. They blurred into a single mass, a wall of gloom supporting a heavy night sky that threatened rain.

Jakobs turned away, rubbing the bridge of his nose, deliberately blinking to force away his growing fatigue. The repetitive pattern of the view would have a soporific effect if he allowed it, lulling him, robbing him of his necessary edge.

It was important to stay absolutely focused. Too much was at stake to let his attention slide now, even for the briefest of instants.

He rocked with the motion of the train, standing in the vestibule that connected this carriage to the next. He considered the locked door in front of him and the cargo in the compartment beyond it.

How long had it taken to get to here? How many man-hours, how many false leads and failures, how many deaths? The bill coming due was lengthy and Nils Jakobs knew every last detail of it by heart. He carried those losses on his shoulders—not that he would ever have been allowed to forget them. His commanders in the Federal Police, in their comfortable offices in Brussels, would not permit that.

For years, they had said that the singular dedication Jakobs showed toward his quarry was barely on the right side of obsessive, but they tolerated him because he got the job done. His fixation meant that he would never rise above the rank of *aspirant-inspecteur principal,* but the men in Brussels told him that as if they thought it was a criticism. Jakobs didn't care. All he had ever wanted was the job, and his job was to catch the worst men in the world.

The one Jakobs wanted the most was on the other side of that door, in manacles. Marking off the hours until they crossed into Belgian territory and he became property of the nation he was born in. The nation he had shamed.

The quality of the light through the window changed suddenly as the train thundered through a rural station—Jakobs caught sight of the name *Východná* as it flashed past at speed—and then the dark treeline was back in place. The train wouldn't stop until it reached the border with Austria several hours from now, moving swiftly through the Slovakian countryside, following the northern edge of the Low Tatra mountain range and then down toward Bratislava. Jakobs would have to get a little sleep at some point, but that thought was disconnected and vague. He couldn't shake the sense that something would be missed if he wasn't there to observe every second of the prisoner transfer.

Without warning, the sliding door leading to the passenger carriages juddered open and a civilian was revealed in the connecting tunnel, a man of narrow build with an oily black beard and a rumpled jacket. He almost bumped into Jakobs and held up his hands apologetically.

"Sorry! Sorry! Looking for the toilet . . ."

Stale breath that smelled of cheap tobacco wafted up, and Jakobs thought of how long it had been since his last cigarette. He'd quit six years ago, on his fortieth birthday, but the urge for a smoke was suddenly right there, testing his resolve.

Jakobs deliberately stepped across to block the man's path. He'd picked up a little Slovak during a secondment to Interpol, enough to warn the civilian that this car was off-limits. To underline the point, he peeled back the lapel of his jacket to reveal his police badge hanging from a chain around his neck. The action also exposed the butt of the Smith & Wesson semi-automatic pistol in Jakobs' belt holster, and the man's eyes widened as he caught sight of it.

From behind Jakobs, through the locked door, someone let out a noise that was half-laughter, half-snarl. It was an animal sound, full of threat and hate, and it startled the civilian even more than the sight of the handgun.

He made a show of looking past Jakobs' broad-shouldered frame toward the door, giving a nervous chuckle.

"What do you have in there, a dangerous animal?"

Jakobs gave a solemn nod. "In a way."

He gestured toward the front of the train and the civilian got the message, retreating through the sliding doors. He waited until the bearded man was out of sight, then turned back and used the thick metal key the train conductor had given him to open the locked door.

His prisoner looked up at him as he entered, but Jakobs didn't return the courtesy. Briss and Stodola, the two escorting officers from the Slovak Republic's National Police, met his gaze and said nothing. Still,

Jakobs couldn't miss the way that Stodola was nursing his knuckles, or the new bruising on the face of the man in the steel chair bolted to the floor of the otherwise empty cargo wagon.

"I stopped a civilian coming up," he told the two cops. "That shouldn't happen." He jerked a thumb at the door and nodded to Stodola. "Stand your post out there. Discourage anyone else who wants to take a look, yes?"

"Sir."

Stodola straightened up and did as he was told.

Jakobs waited for the door to slide shut and the key to turn in the lock before he finally graced his captive with his direct attention.

"Your boy is easy to needle." The man in the chair deliberately spoke in Dutch, a language he knew the Slovaks didn't understand, and his face split in a wide grin.

Jakobs had always thought the prisoner had too many teeth in his head, as if it unbalanced the hard, rectangular shape of his aspect. The ones at the front were uneven, chipped in street brawls and prison fights. The man's hands came up to run over his shorn scalp and scratch at the blue-black tattoos poking up over the collar of his featureless penal jumpsuit. The handcuffs holding his wrists together and the chain fixing them to the floor jangled with each movement.

The prisoner's grin held firm. "Not like you, Nils. You don't crack a smile. Not even when you and I were part of the team."

"You were *never* part of the team," Jakobs replied without thinking, then cursed inwardly, annoyed at himself for allowing the man to goad him into a reply.

"This says different."

The prisoner pulled up a sleeve to show the tattoo of

a winged dagger above a scroll that read *Geef Nooit Op*: "Never Surrender" in Dutch. The symbol of the Belgian Special Forces Group was surrounded by larger, showier designs, bellicose imagery of lightning bolts, lions and spindly Norse runes.

"Any idiot could get that kind of ink," Jakobs replied. "But no real soldier ever would."

That touched a nerve, and the prisoner scowled. But this man had been, if only for a short time, a member of Belgium's most elite soldier corps, as repellent as that truth was. Jakobs remembered the day that Noah Verbeke had joined his unit, grinning that cocky predator's grin, winning over the top brass with his obvious skill and cunning, even though he was a complete fucking prick.

That had been years ago, and a lot had changed since then. Now Jakobs was an officer in an anti-terrorist police unit and Verbeke . . . well, he was still a fucking prick. But no one had realized how ruthless and hateful he was until it was too late.

There was a trail of death and terror across Europe, and a slick of poisonous ideology that wound back and forth in Verbeke's wake. Not a day passed when Jakobs didn't wish that he could turn back the clock to that day in the barracks, to step into the moment and use it to snap the other man's neck.

"You have always been a miserable shit," Verbeke told him, meeting his gaze. "Even now, after your Slovak friends caught me, you still cannot be happy about something. It is not in you." He made a back-and-forth motion with his fingers. "When this is the other way around, I will smile and smile."

"You will not slip away this time," Jakobs countered. He nodded toward the walls of the train carriage. "Did you wonder why we are transporting you by rail in the dead of the night, instead of by road or by plane? Interpol knows about your network of white power hooligans and alt-right sympathizers. We made sure they didn't get word of your transfer." He leaned in. "No one will know where you are until we trot you out like a whipped dog, in front of the General Commissioner's office for the TV cameras." Jakobs considered that for a second. "I might smile then."

"That is a pretty little fantasy," replied Verbeke. "But you and the rest of these worthless mongrels are never going to get what you want." He snorted loudly. "When are you going to wake up, Nils? How deep does the tide of immigrant rapists and foreign parasites have to get before you finally accept that we are at war?" He jabbed a finger in his direction. "You are the whipped dog, but you will not accept it. You are a race traitor." He shook his head. "It is actually very sad. You could be—"

Jakobs came forward and snatched at the chain, jerking it so Verbeke jolted forward, choking off his words in mid-sentence.

"If you try that *we are not so different* bullshit on me, you will regret it."

"My mistake."

Verbeke recovered quickly, shrugging off the moment, but there was a murderous glitter in his eyes. Jakobs had seen footage of his prisoner at rallies, whipping up his supporters with the same words—and other images too, of him beating people with bricks and kicking a helpless man into a gory mess.

Noah Verbeke was crafty, but he had a thug's manner and the morality of a violent child. In the end, that had been what allowed the Slovaks to arrest him. A night of sinking beers in a drinking pit in Košice had spilled out into a fight on the street, and Verbeke would have slipped away, if he'd been able to resist the urge to get his hands bloody.

But that's not in him, thought the police officer, silently echoing the other man's statement. *He can't see weakness without wanting to stamp on it.*

"When we are done with you," Jakobs began, savoring the thought as he spoke, "daylight will be a distant memory. You will spend the rest of your wretched life in a tiny concrete box. It will be much more than you deserve."

Verbeke showed his teeth again.

"That is not going to happen."

Behind them, something heavy—like a body—slammed into the locked door, making it judder on its slides.

It had rained the night before, and the humidity hanging in the air convinced Susan Lam to wear a baggy cotton dress to work over her underclothes. Soon enough, she would be in her lab coat and work trousers, inside the perfectly climate-controlled environment of the research laboratory, but the industrial campus where it was located was a good drive from her home in Dempsey Road, skirting around the traffic flooding into the city core of Singapore.

She would be hot and sweaty if the journey caught her in the wrong place, and that was no way to start her day. Today they were going to start the trials of the newest drug batch, with the modified T-lymphocyte structure, and she was eager to get started. Months of preparation and incremental advances had brought Susan and her team to this point. If this test series performed well, it would be a major milestone in the project.

She paused over the cup of black tea in her hand, inhaling the aroma and considering the situation. A part of her—the clinical, reductionist element of her persona that was the unemotional scientist—weighed the value of her work against the rewards it had brought her. The other part of Susan Lam—the wife and stepmother, the woman in her late forties with her cozy life and her nice, colonial-era home—basked in the feeling.

A decade ago, she would have dismissed the life she had now as a foolish pipe dream. She would have rejected it outright as worthless and decadent.

So much has changed, she thought.

Bare feet slapped on the tile floor of the kitchen and Susan turned to hear a stifled yawn. Michael wandered in from the living room, the child rubbing at his face with one hand, feeling his way along the countertop with another. Her stepson had slept badly the night before, recovering from a stomach bug spread to him by one of the other boys at his school.

"Hello, drowsy," she said gently.

He looked better, still a little dehydrated, but nowhere near the same bundle of tears and vomiting he had been a day ago. Susan boxed up the annoyance she felt and crouched so she was at eye level with the ten-year-old. For all the money they paid to that expensive private school, she expected them to take better care of the children. Susan made a mental note to talk to her husband about formulating a sternly worded complaint for the next parent-teacher meeting.

"Can I have juice?" Michael peered up at her, blinking in the morning light.

"You can," she agreed, watering down some straw-colored apple concentrate for him.

"Do I have to go to school today?"

"No. Rest up."

She handed him a plastic beaker and he sipped at it. Michael was definitely not his usual self. Under any other circumstances, such an admission would have made him clap his hands with glee.

"Okay."

The boy shuffled dolefully back across the room, pausing to meet his father as he entered.

Simon paused to ruffle his son's dark hair and Susan felt a pang of joy at the simple warmth of the moment. Father and son shared the same pleasant moon-face and brown eyes, the same openness that had drawn her to the man she had decided to marry. Every day she was quietly thankful that fate had fallen in her favor, that it had opened up a path to lead her to this new life. Susan never felt quite as happy as she did in Simon's arms. And while Michael wasn't her child, having lost his mother before he could walk and talk, the boy treated her as if he was.

"What?" Simon was looking at her, one eyebrow quirked upward.

"Nothing," she said, around a smile.

"All right." He shrugged. "I'm going to work from home today. Keep an eye on . . ." He patted Michael's head again. "I have some lecture notes to prepare. We don't need to call the nanny."

Simon taught in the degree program on Law and Life Sciences at the National University of Singapore, where he and Susan had first met at a faculty mixer event, but his son always took precedence over his job.

Michael wandered away, out into the cavernous hallway, as Simon came to Susan's side, offering her a good-morning kiss.

"He'll be fine," she told her husband.

"I know." Simon rolled his eyes. "Such drama." He

poured himself a cup of tea. "Today's the new trial set, right? Are you going to celebrate?"

"It's just test tubes and Petri dishes. It's not a party."

She automatically downplayed the importance of the work. It was a reflex she had never been able to break.

He smirked at her, trying to draw her out.

"Are you kidding? You keep telling me, if MaxaBio make this work it could mean—"

"Don't jinx it."

The words came out more harshly than she intended them to. But that non-scientist part of Susan Lam didn't want to say it aloud, in case the act of doing so changed the way everything would play out.

Simon hugged her.

"Things aren't as fragile as you think they are," he said, with a baseless confidence.

"Hey . . ." Michael called from the hallway, his voice echoing, and a note of worry in it. "C-can you come here a second?"

"I'll go," she said. "He might have thrown up again."

"I can call the maid in early," Simon said, smiling widely.

"It's fine."

But as it turned out, that was a long way from the truth. Susan was three steps into the hallway before she saw what the problem was.

"What's the matter . . . ?"

She never finished the sentence, the words turning to bitter ash in her mouth.

Michael was frozen, shrunk up against the dresser by the wall like a cornered cat, still clutching the plastic cup in his hands. He was staring fixedly at the intruder standing inside the front door, who held it open a few degrees.

The stranger was a white woman. *Very* white in

fact, to the point that she seemed to have deliberately enhanced her paleness through the use of cosmetics. Slender and angular, she wore a simple black pantsuit, matching flat shoes and matte gloves. She was in the process of pulling down a dark muslin scarf to the neck of her collarless jacket, as if she had been wearing it like a mask before Susan appeared. Her lips were red like fire and she had hard, searching eyes that swept over Susan in an instant, measuring her for purpose.

That was a familiar look, an experience Susan knew too well from her old life. Through the half-open door she could see movement out in front of the house, men in black outfits similar to the woman's emerging from a pair of windowless blue vans, walking up the drive. They carried guns and their heads were lost under shapeless muslin masks that stole away every definition of their features.

All the hope and joy and goodness in Susan's life dropped out of her in a single bleak instant, swallowed into the earth like floodwater rushing down a sluice.

How many times had she dreamed of this, or something like it? How many times had she bolted awake in the darkness, her heart thudding against her rib cage? How many times had Simon held her as she cried, as she lied to him about the reasons for her nightmares?

The white woman raised a gloved finger to her lips.

"What happens next," she said quietly, the words issuing out in a French accent made of brittle glass, "that's up to you."

Jakobs had his pistol drawn and held down at his side, his finger resting on the Smith & Wesson's trigger guard, as Briss stepped forward. The Slovakian had not pulled his own gun, opting instead for a collapsible baton which snapped out to its full length with a flick of his wrist.

The two men exchanged glances and an unspoken question: *Could Verbeke have someone on the train?*

Every possible precaution had been taken to avoid the details of the prisoner transfer from getting out. Interpol's circle of information was tiny, just a few of the Slovakians and some of the men in Jakobs' unit. He had personally vetted them, making sure to pick people with an axe to grind against the prisoner. His biggest fear had been that one of them might exercise their grudge and kill the man before they made it to Belgium, but never that there would be a leak.

"Knock knock," said Verbeke, as if he was reciting a nursery rhyme. "Who is at the door?"

Jakobs had a hand-held radio in an inside pocket, and raised it to his lips, squeezing the push-to-talk button.

"Stodola. Answer me." When he got no reply he tried again, this time trying to raise the man he had brought with him from Brussels. "Gatan. You there?"

"Not them," continued Verbeke.

"Open it," said Jakobs, nodding to Briss and taking aim at the door with the pistol.

He was thinking about the man with the smoker's breath who had blundered up the train. That seemed less and less like a coincidence with each passing second. He stiffened and put his finger on the trigger.

"Yes!"

Verbeke shouted out the word as Briss put his hand on the lock, and the mechanism exploded inward, blasted from the other side by a shotgun shell. The Slovakian cop was showered with splinters of wood and hot metal fragments that tore up his arm.

Briss reeled back, clutching his ruined hand, as the

door slammed open on its runners and a figure lurched into the compartment. It was Stodola, his eyes blank and sightless, a second red mouth opened across his throat. Someone shorter than him was behind the dead police officer, shoving his body forward as a meat-shield, with the Slovakian's weapon pointing out from beneath his armpit. The barrel of the dead man's .38 revolver twitched in Jakobs' direction and spat fire.

The Belgian threw himself aside, the motion exagger-ated by the rocking of the train as it rounded a turn in the hills, and he bounced off a support pillar. Jakobs returned fire, but the shot was wide, more to break the intruder's concentration than to hit him.

Stodola's body pitched forward and fell to the metal decking with a loud crash, revealing the train conduc-tor behind him, the young cop's pistol in his hand. The man that Jakobs questioned before they set off had seemed mousy and ineffectual, thoroughly invested in remaining ignorant of whatever the policemen on his train were doing. That had clearly been a ruse. The conductor's florid face was devoid of emotion, his eyes cold.

Jakobs had seen that expression in the mirror. It was a soldier-face, an assassin-face. The aspect of someone who had been trained to kill.

He put another shot in the conductor's direction, no longer giving him the benefit of the doubt, but a sec-ond shotgun blast filled the air with lead pellets and he flinched away.

"Fuck me!" Jakobs heard Verbeke shout out the curse. "Watch where you are fucking shooting!"

The shotgunner was the civilian, the smoker. He ratch-eted the slide on a pistol-grip pump-action weapon, swarming into the compartment on the heels of his comrade. Dropping into a crouch, Jakobs put two 9mm rounds from the Smith & Wesson into the man's chest and blew him off his feet.

The sound merged with the thunder of the .38 as the conductor used it to kill Briss with a head shot. The other Slovakian slid down the wall of the cargo wagon, his hand flapping at the pistol he had been too slow to pull.

Jakobs pivoted, bringing his gun to bear on the conductor, but then a blast of pain flared in the side of his head as Verbeke booted him in the skull. In the chaos of the gunfire, the Belgian had fallen back, close enough that his prisoner could strike out and hit him.

It was enough to rob the older man of vital seconds. Verbeke was up off the metal chair, spitting and straining at his chains like an angry dog at the end of its leash. He managed to hook one of the policeman's ankles and pull it. Jakobs went down, and immediately tried to bounce back up, but a blow from the butt of the revolver hit him in the same place Verbeke had kicked him, and he crumpled.

Someone pulled his pistol out of his hands and planted a boot in his belly. He blinked through the pain and saw the smoker rolling over, gingerly getting up. The bearded man swore violently in English, and pulled open his jacket to paw at a bulletproof vest beneath.

"Time?" shouted the conductor.

"Three minutes."

The smoker consulted his wristwatch before hanging his weapon on a strap over his shoulder. He produced a tiny skeleton key and jammed it into the cuffs to free the prisoner.

Jakobs lurched over on to his side, wheezing through the pain.

I never should have come, he told himself, his gaze finding Stodola's and Briss's bodies, knowing that Gatan was as dead as they were. *Should have sent someone younger and faster.*

He had leaned on the man who had prepared his last fitness report, "encouraging" the doctor to give him a clean bill of health so he could remain field-rated. If only to see this transfer to the end, if nothing else. Now he was going to pay the price for that hubris.

For my obsession.

Verbeke shrugged off the cuffs and the chain, and then, with deliberation, he walked over to Jakobs and kicked him three more times. They were sharp, vicious blows that landed in his belly and his crotch, burning the air out of his lungs in jolts of ragged pain.

"We have some fresh clothes," said the conductor, signaling to the smoker to bring in a sports bag.

Verbeke stepped away and emptied the bag's contents on to the chair, stripping off his prison attire. He grinned as he listened to every wheezing, agonized breath that Jakobs took.

"So who are you two?" he asked, glaring at his rescuers. "I do not know you."

"We were paid to get you out," said the conductor.

"All right."

Verbeke accepted that and flexed his arms as he bared his chest. Jakobs saw the full tapestry of the man's tattoos in the harsh illumination from the overhead fluorescent light. It was a chaotic mess of violent imagery. Runic symbols co-opted from Nordic myth, graphic depictions of screaming skulls and tortured demons, and fascist iconography of all kinds. Noah Verbeke's skin was his heraldry, his manifesto. It was the outward expression of the hate that drove him on.

Pride of place was given to the portrait of a male lion

captured in full-throated snarl, bigger than any other design upon him. Rendered across Verbeke's back and shoulders, the gold and black tattoo sat above a scroll bearing a single word in Gothic script: *Leeuwenbrul.*

The Lion's Roar—every police force in Europe knew the name of that particular far-right group. They knew about their campaigns of firebombings, their assassinations. The riots they started and the toxic climate of hatred they stirred up against anyone who didn't match the group's idealized model of racial supremacy.

Verbeke shrugged on a T-shirt and a military-style jacket over the top of it.

"That's better," he said to the air, before his gaze dropped back to Jakobs. And out came the grin again.

"One minute," said the smoker.

He moved to the loading door in the side of the cargo wagon and used the shotgun to blast off the lock holding it closed.

"We don't have time for you to play around," added the conductor, offering Stodola's revolver to Verbeke. "Hurry up."

Jakobs drew himself shakily to his knees, as a dreadful sense of the inevitable settled upon him.

Verbeke sniffed and his grin became a frown.

"I'll make the most of it," he said, and unloaded the last two rounds from the .38 into the Belgian police officer.

The white woman ushered Susan Lam, her husband, and his son into the lounge at the point of a gun. She made Susan sit on one of the sofas and Michael and Simon on the other, so that they were facing each other.

Three men, who also appeared to be Europeans, came in and secured the front door behind them. Without speaking to one another, the two more muscular of them broke off and conducted a search of the house. The third, who revealed a mop of curly hair and an acne-scarred face beneath his muslin mask, stood behind Susan's husband. He held his pistol at the ready a few inches from the back of her stepson's head. Michael still had the juice in his hand, and he chewed on the rim of the plastic glass.

"What do you people want?" said Simon, straightening in his chair, attempting to maintain some degree of authority in the situation. "Money? Valuables? Is that it?"

He seemed to assume that this was a robbery, and Susan wanted so much to believe that too.

"We'll take those," said the woman, and for a moment Susan dared to hope that maybe this *was* just about that. But the pale woman's next utterance killed that possibility dead. "It will give the police the wrong idea."

The woman moved and perched herself on the side of the sofa where Susan was sitting.

"Don't hurt them," Susan whispered. "*Please.*"

"How long have you been married?" The woman's tone was casual.

"Please—" repeated Susan, but she was waved to silence.

"I already know the answer," came the reply. "Five years. You met a few months after you came to work at MaxaBio. The genius biochemist who did not talk about her past, and the great lawyer-turned-professor with the sad story of his dead first wife."

Simon stiffened at the glib description of his personal tragedy, and he pulled closer to his son.

One of the men came back into the room and gave the woman a nod, no doubt to tell her that there was no one else on the lower floors. A moment later, the other returned from upstairs.

"Found a safe," he grunted.

"Empty it," said the woman. Then she looked at the acne-scarred man. "Get your kit."

"Okay."

He nodded and stepped away, gathering up a hard-shell plastic case that he had brought with him.

The woman's attention returned to Simon.

"Do you know how many lies your wife has told you in those five years? It has to be at least one a day. *At least*. Two thousand lies or more, I would estimate."

"What the hell are you talking about?" Simon's face hardened, and he took on the tone he used with students who disrupted his lectures. "Take what you want and go!"

"What is the biggest one?" The woman went on, asking herself the question. "Oh, I know. *Her name*. It isn't Susan. It never has been."

"Is that true?" Michael asked, eyes widening.

"Yes, yes, little man," said the woman, before Susan could answer. "You look like you are clever. You must wonder why it is your stepmother does not speak about where she grew up, or the family she had before you and your papa. Yes?"

Michael shot her a look that cut like a razor, full of unanswered questions and formless fears.

"Her real name is Ji-Yoo Park. She isn't from Busan in South Korea. But that isn't the worst thing she hid from you, no."

"I don't care what you are saying," Simon said firmly. "I won't hear it. I won't listen to you try to torment the woman I love." He stared at his wife imploringly. "Susan, look at me."

But she couldn't bring herself to do it, not when she knew what was going to come next.

"Ji-Yoo Park is a liar and a fake, and she is responsible for the deaths of dozens of innocent people." The pale woman relished the secret's revelation.

"That's not true!" shouted Michael, throwing his cup to the ground. "No! She is a good person!"

"Are you going to lie to them again?" Tears streamed down Susan's cheeks as the pale woman studied her. "Go on. *Lie*. One more atop the others won't make any difference."

"Susan?" said Simon, and that single word was enough to break her. Contained within it was the doubt from every single instance when she had deflected his questions about her past.

She tried to form a denial, but nothing came. Her chest ached with the wrenching churn of her emotions, trapped between the cold cruelty of the pale woman's words and the inescapable reality these intruders had brought into her home.

The acne-scarred man was indifferent to it, carefully removing a number of devices from his case—a video camera with a wide-angle lens, a laser scanner, and other equipment she didn't recognize. He set up the camera on a tripod and nodded to the woman.

"Ready to roll."

"Get up."

The pale woman pointed with her gun, and when Susan—*no, remember her birth name*—when Ji-Yoo didn't move fast enough, she grabbed her arm and dragged her up.

Simon bolted to his feet, coming to her defense, but one of the gunmen grabbed his shoulder and forcibly slammed him back into the sofa.

"You're coming with us," said the woman. "This must be familiar to you." She gestured with the gun again. "You're going to do what we tell you. If you disobey, these two will die. Just like old times."

A whimper of fear escaped her throat.

"I'll do it," she said. "You don't have to hurt them. They don't need to be involved."

"Ah, but they do," countered the woman. "You are such an experienced liar, Mademoiselle Park. We need to make sure you are telling us the truth."

As the pale woman guided her out of the room, she took a last look at her husband and her stepson. The man with scars was pressing a sheet of paper into their hands.

"Don't look at her, look at me," he snapped, aiming the camera at them. "You first, Daddy. Read the words out loud, if you don't want your little runt crippled in front of you."

Simon clutched at Michael's hand and reluctantly began to speak.

"*The beige hue on the waters of the loch impressed all, including the French queen . . .*" He glared at the man. "What is this? It's nonsense!"

"Say it. Don't mess it up. Then the kid goes next," said the scarred man.

"Move it," snapped the woman, prodding Ji-Yoo in the shoulder with the barrel of her gun.

"Twenty seconds."

The call was the signal for the man who had freed Verbeke to haul open the sliding hatch on the side of the train carriage, and he gave it a forceful shove. The hatch slipped back, as the endless wall of fir trees beyond retreated away to become a shallow bank of hillside, falling down toward a river a few hundred meters below. In the dark of the night, the river was a ribbon of black glass, snaking up alongside the railway.

The carriages rocked and began to decelerate as the train entered a shallow curve.

"Driver has to slow the train to make the turn," the man in the conductor's uniform explained to Verbeke. "This is where we get off."

He jerked his thumb at the open hatch, pausing to button up his jacket.

"Tuck and roll when you land," began the bearded man. "Then you—"

"I know what to do. Stop talking to me unless you have something useful to say."

Verbeke gave them both a sneering look, and stooped to help himself to the pistol that Briss had not fired.

"Whatever," said the man with the beard. "Time!"

Verbeke's military training had included numerous parachute jumps, both daylight and night-time drops, so he drew on the skills he had been taught to orient his body and make the fall from the moving train without breaking any bones.

He would have liked to do something more with the body of that shit-rag cop Jakobs. Maybe mutilate him so that he couldn't have an open casket funeral, just to leave his mark behind, but there wasn't the time for it. Verbeke leaped into the dark and the night air embraced him, whirling around.

Then there was the juddering impact against the damp grass and he rolled, pulling tight to protect himself, bleeding off the energy of the jump until he slowed to a halt. He was on his feet in a heartbeat, the stolen pistol drawn and ready.

The chatter of the train over the rails rattled on and

faded as it disappeared around the turn and into the treeline. Verbeke panned the gun around, finding the two men who had freed him as they stood up from where they had landed in the thick, wet grass. He took a deep breath and nodded to himself, enjoying the moment of liberation. *Of course he was free*. His enemies could not hold him.

Verbeke thought about killing his rescuers while they were still disoriented from the jump. In the darkness, they would never see it coming, and he could be away in moments. *Find a car, a telephone, reach out to his people . . .*

He hesitated. There were too many questions that only these men had the answers for. And then he was awash in bright light and it didn't matter anymore.

Pivoting instinctively toward the illumination, he saw the headlights of a 4×4 pickup as it bounced along the bank of the river. The vehicle turned around, orienting itself to speed them away, and Verbeke watched as a densely built man climbed out. The man's searching gaze found the three figures up in the grass and he beckoned to them.

"Move quickly," he called. "We need to be away from here."

Verbeke heard the accent—Japanese, it sounded like—and he sneered reflexively. He jogged down to the vehicle, still dangling the dead cop's revolver at the end of his arm.

"Who are you, eh?" he demanded. "My welcoming party?"

He had been right about the driver's ethnicity. *Another foreigner*. The man moved like he was a fighter, but he favored one side as if unconsciously protecting the site of an old injury.

"My name is Saito," said the Japanese, in clipped and

mechanical English. "You have my employers to thank for facilitating your escape."

Verbeke's knuckles whitened as they tensed around the revolver, a passing memory rising to the front of his thoughts.

"I know who you are," he said, thinking it through. "Oh, yes. The little soldier for the rich men." He brought up the gun and waved it around carelessly. "Did you forget that conversation we had? I told your masters to go fuck themselves." He turned his head and spat. "You want to get into bed with the blacks and the ragheads, that's up to you, but the Lions don't want any of your shit."

"You would prefer us to put you back on the train?" Saito said evenly.

"You can try." Verbeke punctuated his statement by cocking the revolver's hammer.

A couple of years ago, after they had started making an impact on the European scene, men with money and flashy cars had tracked down Noah Verbeke and offered him suitcases full of euros in exchange for doing them "a few favors." They had a list of targets they wanted to be hit, and for a generous cash payment, they wanted the Lion's Roar to do it for them.

It was coming back to him now. Toussaint, that arrogant crone who ran a dozen TV stations—she had been behind the meeting. This Jap had been there, lurking in the background like he thought he was some kind of ninja. His presence had immediately pissed Verbeke off, and in the end the Lions rejected the offer. They fought for white nations, for white men and white men's hegemony—and that didn't involve making pacts with a gang of trust-fund assholes who were willing to sell out anything and partner with anyone, as long as they stayed wealthy.

"The Combine," he said, sounding out the name, "can eat my shit."

That was what the group called themselves, a shadowy means-nothing designation that was designed to obscure fact and encourage disinformation. Verbeke knew enough of the truth about them, though—quaking old bastards and overripe bitches in their billion-dollar bubble, who traded power and influence between themselves like poker chips among card players. They had built their fortunes on having no cause of any kind other than making a profit, selling weapons to all sides and pouring fuel on the fire to keep everyone scared. His disdain for them was all jealousy and dismissal. These were weaklings who allied themselves with animals and traitors. They had no code.

He stepped back, getting enough distance to keep Saito and the other two men in sight. The one with the beard had his shotgun at the ready, while the second was changing out of the train conductor's jacket, seemingly oblivious to the tension in the cold night air.

"If I may?" Saito reached into a deep pocket of the coat he wore, making no sudden movements, and removed a satellite phone. He flipped up a tube-like antenna and hit a speed-dial button. "My employers are aware of your issues with them. But they are also aware of the problems that have plagued your confederates in recent months."

Verbeke's jaw hardened, annoyance flaring as Saito's words brought up a truth he had no business knowing. The fact was, the Lion's Roar was on the back foot. A concerted effort by Interpol, led by that asshole Jakobs, had seen them lose a dozen of their safe houses in as many weeks. Two of their high-profile backers had been arrested on trumped-up charges, and a handful of

Verbeke's best soldiers were trawled up in raids across Central Europe.

He was arrested in Slovakia because circumstances forced him to be there, for a meeting with representatives of a neo-Nazi collective that the Lions were looking to ally themselves with. They needed numbers and support, but no one was supposed to be aware of that. His scowl deepened. *Had somebody talked?* If so, he would lock them in a cage and burn them alive.

"You don't know a fucking thing," he spat.

"I know at this moment in time you have limited options."

Saito was infuriatingly calm about the whole thing. The sat-phone connected with a beep, and he offered it to Verbeke.

"What is this?"

He took the phone warily, eyeing the encrypted dialing code on the illuminated display.

"Speak to your comrade before you decide what to do next."

"Piss off!"

Verbeke's anger was building at the Japanese man's emotionless affect, and he thought about how much he would enjoy using the phone handset to beat him. Still, he raised it to his ear.

"Yes?"

"*Hello, Noah,*" said a familiar voice. "*How was the Bastille?*"

"Axelle . . ." Like her pale face, the French woman's words were cold and honey-sweet, but his annoyance prevented Verbeke from being distracted by them. "What took you so long? They had me for nearly two months!"

"*Are you grateful?*" She purred the question. "*You don't sound grateful.*"

"Don't play games with me," he retorted, and he heard her sharp intake of breath. She knew she had stepped over a line.

"*The police made you hard to find. I had to take steps.*" She paused, becoming contrite. "*You're angry.*"

He glared at Saito. "This was the best you could come up with?" When the Combine had first come to them, Axelle had been one of the few Lions who wanted to work with the group. It made sense that she would have turned to them for help—but he was furious she had done so. "You've made us weak by doing this."

"*Connard!*" she shot back. "*You would still be rotting in a prison cell if I hadn't done this. Don't be too arrogant to see the opportunity here!*"

Something in her words gave Verbeke pause. He would not admit it, but the woman was the smartest of his people, smarter than him and as loyal as she was sadistic.

"What opportunity?" he asked, at length.

"*I made a deal to get you out,*" Axelle told him, and a chill smile came into her words. "*Trust me when I tell you . . . you're going to like it.*"

Verbeke listened to her explain the high points of the arrangement, and gradually his annoyance faded, in turn replaced by a feral grin.

— TWO —

It was the second night they had been at sea. Somewhere during the first day, the fishing boat's engine began to stutter and belch black smoke, and the men who had been put in charge of sailing the little vessel told the rest of them that they would have to drift with the currents for a while. Oil leaked out behind them on the surface of the waves, as if the old boat was bleeding.

Fatima tried to pass the time by counting the clouds in the sky and the faces of the dozens of other people packed into the overloaded boat alongside her. Her elder brother Remi still had the fever from the days before they had paid their way to the smugglers, and he spent most of his time asleep. When he was awake, he didn't talk much. Sharing mouthfuls of tepid, metallic-tasting water from the bottles they had brought with them, they rationed each sip as much as they could.

The smugglers who put them to sea said that the boat would get them across the ocean to an island near a country called Italy, and once they were ashore there, they would be safe. There were good people in Italy, they said. There was no threat of constant attack, there was food and medicine and clean water. And for people who were willing to work hard, there could be a better future.

Remi believed that, but Fatima didn't. Remi had many beliefs that seemed foolish to his little sister, but she was smart enough not to call him out about them. She might have been younger but she was definitely the more adult of the two siblings, forced to grow up quickly after their parents had been killed in a bombing on the outskirts of Tripoli. If anything, Remi seemed to have stopped where he was, as if losing their mother and father had frozen his maturing.

Fatima took care of them both, but still she couldn't stop Remi when he told her he had decided they were going to escape to a better life. And truthfully, there was nothing for her in Libya anymore—no prospect for a safe future, no education, no job, no money. She was old enough to understand that her country was coming apart around them, and that one day another bomb might take her or Remi, erasing them from the world in a screaming blast of dust and smoke, as it had their parents.

So they went. They sold what little they owned, until sister and brother had only the clothes on their backs, trading one uncertain tomorrow for another. As the boat was pushed out on to the waves, Fatima looked back to see her homeland falling away. She wanted to stay. She wanted to live a good life there. But angry men, soldiers and fighters and politicians who cared nothing about her and Remi, had stolen away that possibility for . . . *what*? She wondered what reward the chaos could ever bring.

Across choppy waves under a burning sun, they sailed into the unknown. There was some shade under a corrugated steel awning at the stern of the boat, and at first people took it in shifts to get out of the heat. But gradually the shade was colonized by those who were sick or those who simply refused to give up their places. The vessel was an old tuna trawler, barely patched together and steadily leaking. It stank of rot and dead fish, of diesel fuel and human fear.

By the morning of the second day, there had already been two deaths from heatstroke, and those bodies were hefted over the shallow gunwale and into the ocean. As the day drew on, even the youngest of the children stopped crying as they learned that it made no difference, and that no matter how many tears they shed, the murderous heat and the sickening lurch of the boat would not ease.

Now the sun was long gone and the temperature had plummeted. The boat's passengers were packed into every square meter of available space, bodies lined up next to one another, keeping warm against the ocean chill beneath a cold and starry sky.

"I think we are going to die out here."

It took a moment before Fatima realized that she had said those words aloud. She licked her dry lips and tasted salt.

"No, little one. Have faith."

The woman lying next to her against the frame of the hull was called Aya, and she said she was from Nigeria. Her skin was darker than Fatima's, and it reminded the girl of the teak of an old chair her father had owned. Somehow, the association made her want to trust the woman. Aya spoke with a lilting accent and she was pretty, her face peering out at the girl from the folds of her dun-colored hijab. In the darkness, Aya's bright eyes glittered like jewels.

Fatima felt so tired and so empty of energy, she couldn't understand how Aya was able to keep her spirits up.

"I am afraid Remi will not make it," she whispered, glancing at her brother as he twitched in a fitful sleep. "Or I am afraid I will not, and he'll be lost without me."

"That won't happen," Aya insisted. "I promise you."

But there was a shadow over her expression, and the older woman couldn't hide her fear.

"Thank you," said Fatima, "but you can't promise that."

Her mother had said something similar, and never come home again.

Aya sighed and shifted, pulling up the sleeve of her dress to reveal a large watch around her wrist. It was bulky and it looked out of place, like something a rich lady would wear and not a fellow refugee. Fatima guessed it was worth a lot by the way Aya kept it concealed from everyone else. Her face was lit by a soft glow as she touched the watch's face and it briefly illuminated, then dimmed.

The woman stiffened, and the watch was hidden again.

"Listen to me," she told Fatima. "You and Remi need to keep your heads down. I mean it. Don't do anything silly, just concentrate on keeping each other alive."

There was a new urgency in Aya's words that Fatima didn't understand. The woman found her own water bottle and pressed it into the girl's hands.

"I can't take this," Fatima began, but Aya shook her head sternly.

A man at the bow, hanging half over the frame of the boat, suddenly burst into life, his motions jerky and panicked. He scrambled backward and stepped on his neighbors, in seconds creating a ripple of angry curses from all around him. He was a Berber, so it took Fatima a moment to think through his dialect and figure out what he was so animated about.

"A boat," she said automatically. "*A ship!* Out there."

People who understood the man were standing, turning to look in the direction he was pointing, and Fatima sprang up, her curiosity momentarily overwhelming her fatigue and her wariness.

She glimpsed a dark shape, angular straight lines like a giant shark's fin, a shadow against the night's blackness moving off beyond the fishing boat's prow. The wind changed direction and brought with it the low murmur of idling engines.

In the next second the pitiless glare of a spotlight flooded their vessel with a blinding white glow, and Fatima reflexively put up her hand to shield her eyes.

At her feet, Remi awoke and his jaw dropped open in shock.

"Is . . . Is that a rescue ship?"

People started waving and shouting, calling out for help in as many languages as they knew. A surge of hope stirred the refugees and they scrambled to get a better look at the approaching vessel.

Five times the size of the old fishing boat and much better suited to the waves than the old shallow-water trawler, the ship was painted a deep green, and Fatima thought she could make out people on deck moving back and forth. There was a symbol like an arrowhead on the hull and words in English written after it, but the girl had no idea what they meant.

She turned back to Aya, and the woman's expression had changed, so much that she seemed like a different person.

"What's wrong?" said Fatima.

"Stay behind me," Aya replied, as a metallic noise issued out over the sea. The rattle of guns being readied. Fatima knew that sound and wished that she did not.

* * *

"Look at them," Lazlow said with disgust, spitting over the rail and into the sea. "Packed in like stinking rats." He jutted his chin at the deck of the refugee boat and the snarl of bodies atop one another. "We should sink it and let them go to the bottom."

The big, sweaty deckhand kneaded the butt of his AK-47 and toyed with the idea of firing off a few rounds. He glanced at Maarten, who stood alongside him, but the new guy said nothing, holding on to his own gun with a glum, unreadable expression on his face.

"Eh?"

Lazlow gave him a prod, trying to elicit an agreement from the young Dutchman, but all he got was a weak nod.

He scowled and looked away. They were recruiting idiots these days, he told himself.

"That won't be enough," said DeVot, in answer to his declaration. "We need a deterrent. They're simple-minded. We have to teach them a lesson. They have to spread the word, and they can't do that from the bottom of the sea."

The sour-faced man was the closest thing the ship had to a captain, but he was paunchy and narrow-eyed, and none of the volunteer crew had a good word for him. He was marginally in charge because he had the money and the connections.

"Bodies washing up on the beach tell the tale well enough," insisted Lazlow. He was never one to let anybody have the last word. "Eh?" Again, he elbowed Maarten, trying to get him to agree. "Eh, Genius? That's right, yes?"

"Maybe," offered the Dutchman, as he watched the other crew lash the refugee boat to their ship and sling a cargo net across the rails. The men didn't offer to help the ragged immigrants make the transfer up on to the bigger ship, but they made it clear with menacing gestures that the refugees couldn't stay where they were.

"Maybe?" echoed Lazlow, and he spat again. "Are you sure you got the guts for this, Genius?"

Maarten didn't reply. Lazlow had coined the nickname for the wiry, blond-haired Dutchman soon after they left port in Naples, needling him with it at every opportunity after the new guy had made the mistake of talking shit about the symbol on their flag that recalled the shields of the ancient Spartans.

DeVot had given a talk that first night out, stirring up the men with the promise of getting a bit of blood and action out here, telling them that they were warriors just like those Greeks.

Their ship was a defender, a bulwark in the undeclared war that the gutless politicians and spineless lawmen were too afraid to admit was being waged. DeVot said there were hundreds, thousands of people who thought the same way they did, who were sick of the tide of immigrant parasites flooding in to Europe, looking for handouts, taking homes and jobs from the decent people who lived there. This ship, paid for by a group called the Bastion League, drew support from nationalists all over the continent and further still— and it also drew in men like Lazlow, who hadn't been able to make selection into the German army but still wanted to carry a gun and have a little swagger with it.

Lazlow firmly believed, if the government or the bleeding hearts found these animals in that shit-heap boat, they would have handed them a wad of cash and the keys to a new house.

The Bastion League had different plans. The sea was a big place, and the so-called navy "peacekeepers" sent by their New World Order masters couldn't be everywhere

at once. So, like the Spartans who had defended their
nation from the invading Persians—Lazlow had seen
that movie a bunch of times—the men on this ship
were turning back the tide of these foreigners, one refugee boat at a time.

But Genius over there said something about how the
real Spartans weren't all that history painted them. He
was even stupid enough to say that they'd been okay
with queers.

Where the fuck did you hear that? Lazlow had
shouted.

I read it in a book, replied the Dutchman, like he
thought that made him smarter than the rest of them,
like he was some kind of clever bastard.

Lazlow had made the man's life hell from that day
onward, and that stopped the little shit from talking out
of turn.

The refugees were all on board now, and one of the
crew who spoke French was telling them to obey or suffer the consequences. The foreigners easily outnum-
bered the men on the ship, but not one of them had
the guts to stand up and show some backbone. Anyone
who so much as eyeballed one of the crew was cowed
by the automatic rifles that could cut them down in seconds.

DeVot put his fingers in his mouth and blew a piercing whistle, sending a signal to a man on the flying
bridge. The ship immediately rocked into motion as
the props bit into the waves, and the bow swung back
in the direction of the Libyan coastline. At full steam
ahead, the decrepit fishing boat was dragged alongside,
seawater spilling into it as they made headway.

Lazlow heard some of the refugees jabbering to one
another. They knew what was going on. He waded
in and joined the other men with rifles as they went

through the next step, forcibly separating the males and the females. He looked forward to the moment when one of the men tried to stop them from pawing at the women, and he was soon rewarded.

Lazlow clubbed the man who dared to rise, hitting him across the face with his rifle and breaking his nose, slamming him down to the deck in a gush of blood. The deckhand laughed and scanned the terrified faces in front of him, hoping to find another one who wanted to be defiant. But they didn't oblige.

Too pathetic to defend themselves, he told himself, *they deserve everything they get.*

He aimed his rifle at the men and made gunshot noises, sniggering when they recoiled. DeVot shouted at him to stop, and at length he walked away, frustrated that he couldn't take out his bottomless wellspring of anger on someone. Lazlow was always annoyed about something. It was how he got through the day.

Anything the refugees had on them that might be valuable was taken and tossed in a plastic drum. Any cash made from selling it later would be divided up among the crew as beer money—not that these mongrels ever had much worth stealing. Tonight was a little different, though, as one of the other men came up with an electronic watch he had cut off the wrist of some Nigerian. Lazlow took it from him and eyed it, unsure of what it could do.

"It's a smartwatch," offered Maarten.

"Did I ask for your opinion?" Lazlow snarled back on reflex, and he tossed the watch into the drum with the rest of the meager pickings.

"Keep your guns on them," DeVot was saying, pointing at the men as he strutted up and down the deck between the two groups of refugees. "I'll look over the women and see what we can use."

Lazlow nodded. This was where they could make some serious money. DeVot had a connection with the Albanian mafia, and those creeps were always on the lookout for new merchandise to traffic. DeVot had already spotted a few good candidates, and he was weighing up his options. There would be a bonus if the women were in good condition, but then again Lazlow had his needs and it would be a while before they made port again.

His short attention span was broken by the sight of the Dutchman, looking around like he was up to something, instead of doing what he was told.

"Hey! I'm talking to you, Genius! What are you doing?"

"Nothing." Maarten looked morosely at the deck.

"You're such a pussy." Lazlow strode over to the Dutchman, getting in his face, leaning over him. "With your fucking hipster beard and your long hair."

He flicked a finger at Maarten's neck, where his shoulder-length hair was hanging unkempt and messy. The other man didn't react, meekly refusing to meet his gaze. Lazlow kept on goading him.

"Are you queer? Is that why you said that shit before? Because you're a fucking faggot?"

"No."

The Dutchman fingered the strap of the rifle hanging off his shoulder.

"So prove it." Lazlow jabbed a finger at the women. "Let's have a little show." He smirked at the idea of it, moving to grab one of the female refugees at random, a skinny little one not much more than a kid. "Go on. Get in there, Genius."

He shoved the terrified girl in Maarten's direction, then glanced at DeVot and saw that the other man was smirking as well. DeVot was an old pervert, and he wasn't going to stop this from happening or challenge Lazlow for his place as top dog among the crew.

"Do it!" shouted one of the other men, gathering in for the entertainment.

"I'm not touching her," said the Dutchman, and he shook his head.

"Told you he was a faggot!" Lazlow barked, getting a swell of callous laughter in return.

But then a sly smile that Lazlow had never seen before crossed Maarten's face and he pushed the young girl away, instead nodding toward another woman. The Nigerian.

"I like that one better."

That earned the Dutchman a round of raucous cheers as he walked up to the older refugee and pulled her out of the group, ignoring the pleas of the others around her. Lazlow blinked. He hadn't expected the little shit to show any mettle.

"What are you going to do?" said the Nigerian, as Maarten unbuttoned the camo jacket he was wearing.

"I've got something for you," said the Dutchman, and he reached into his waistband.

But Lazlow's amazed laughter died in his throat when Maarten's hand came back with a small-frame semi-automatic that he slapped into the woman's open palm. In the same motion, the Dutchman shrugged his AK-47 off his shoulder and into his hand, as the Nigerian brought up the pistol and fired at Lazlow.

A single .25 caliber round smacked into Lazlow's forearm and he screamed, dropping his Kalashnikov as blood flowed from the wound. The pain was intense and his knees turned to water. Collapsing to the deck, he saw Maarten sprint forward and grab DeVot by the back of the collar, pulling the captain to him as a human shield.

"Drop your weapons or I slot him," the Dutchman shouted at the other men, and suddenly his voice was different, with all the rough edges of a British accent.

"You heard the man," said the Nigerian, who went through a similar shift from African to American.

"Do it!" cried DeVot, folding immediately. "Guns down, guns down!"

The other men didn't obey, but through his fog of hurt Lazlow was barely aware of it. The bullet had splintered bone and torn nerves, and he could barely breathe for the agony of it. He lost control of his bladder and shuddered.

Another shot rang out from the little pistol, this time blowing off a chunk of someone's foot, and he heard the woman call out.

"Were you not listening?"

At length, the crew dropped their weapons to the deck and Lazlow saw men among the refugees spring up to grab them for themselves. Then he fainted, remembering vaguely as his world turned dark that his poor pain tolerance had been the reason why the German army had passed him over. That, and his hateful personality.

"Was that good for you?" she asked, and he had to crack a smile.

"Oh yeah."

He expected her to toss away the hijab now that their undercover identities were well and truly blown, but she didn't, instead slipping the little Beretta 950 pistol into the folds of her robe and gathering up the AK-47 that Lazlow had dropped. For his part, he was happy to stop being the meek "Maarten from Amersfoort" and go back to being Marc Dane, ex-MI6 field officer turned private security specialist.

With the professionalism Marc expected of her, Lucy Keyes checked over the Kalashnikov with a soldier's careful eye, and pursed her lips.

"This is okay."

Years back, long before Marc knew her, Lucy had been a recon-sniper specialist assigned to the US Army's 1st Special Forces Operational Detachment-Delta, more commonly known as "Delta Force," and she had lost none of the skills they had taught her. Most of the world believed that unit was crewed only by men, but inside the clandestine structure of the detachment there was a team-within-a-team, that used women on missions where a female operator was a tactical requirement for infiltration. Now, like Marc, Lucy worked in the private sector for the Rubicon Group.

He still didn't know the full story behind Lucy's recruitment into Rubicon's "Special Conditions Division"—just bits and pieces. A dishonorable discharge, an escape from a military prison. There were a lot of unanswered questions, but Marc respected her privacy and he didn't push to know more.

His own journey into working for Rubicon's enigmatic CEO Ekko Solomon wasn't exactly conventional either. Accused by his own agency of being complicit in the deaths of his former team—including a woman he cared deeply for—Marc had been a fugitive when he crossed Solomon's radar. Working together, he and the Rubicon team had exposed the real traitor in MI6 and gone on to avert more than one catastrophic terrorist attack in the months that followed. It wasn't an exaggeration to say that, cut off from everything that he had known, Rubicon had become Dane's lifeline.

Solomon had pledged to use his wealth and the reach it gave him to better the state of the world, and that intent expressed itself in covert actions like this one. Rubicon gave Marc a purpose when his future was at its bleakest, and he couldn't deny it felt good to know he could make a difference.

The two of them were an unlikely pair. Lucy—the dark-skinned New Yorker with an athletic build, a boyish face and a sleepy gaze—was proficient at blending in, making herself part of the background. An expert markswoman, she carried herself with a wry manner and a ferocity that could be intimidating to some. Marc—a working-class white guy born and bred on a London council estate, wiry and fast, with a wolfish cast to him—was a dyed-in-the-wool techie who had become a field agent the hard way, and he was still strung somewhere between those two points, surviving on his wits and his ability. Like all of Solomon's people, they were a couple of outsiders who had found a renewed purpose working for the African billionaire.

Marc watched as Lucy talked with the refugees in Arabic, calming the teenage girl that Lazlow had tried to force on him, and rallying the ones who had taken up the guns. Soon, they were turning things around on the Bastion League crew, forcing DeVot and his men to surrender all they had on them. They searched the ship and marched everyone they found up to the deck to join their comrades.

Marc didn't speak the language, but he could tell that the angry refugees, strung out and weary from their ordeal at sea, were furious enough to start shooting. Lucy talked them down, even though Marc had to admit he felt the same way. If even half the deeds they had bragged about doing were true, Lazlow and the others didn't deserve any restraint.

For months, Rubicon's digital hunter teams had been building up a virtual model of the Bastion League's network of influence, tracking their connections to other extremist groups and criminal organizations. This mission was the end result of an operation to interdict and dismantle a human trafficking ring that stretched from North Africa to Russia, a trail of misery and suffering that had ruined hundreds of innocent lives.

Tomorrow, offices of the Bastion League in four different countries would be raided by police armed with warrants to seize their computers. Forensic data sweeps would find a money trail tying the group directly to incidences of bribery, corruption and worse. At this moment somewhere in Eastern Europe, thanks to iron-clad intelligence given to them by Rubicon, an Interpol-backed strike force was moving on a compound run by the Albanian mob, where dozens of kidnap victims were being held.

The private contractor's Special Conditions Division had taken on the task of handling this end, inserting Marc into the activist group via a compromised contact in Amsterdam, and dropping Lucy in-country over the Libyan border to follow the line via the smugglers' route. Within a few days, this horrific scheme to prey on the weak and vulnerable would be in ruins. But first DeVot and his men would face summary justice.

"What do you think you are doing?" said the captain. "Are you going to arrest us? Who are you people?"

"That's a lot of questions," Lucy replied. "If I were you, I'd be thinking more about my immediate future."

"You gonna kill us, bitch?" Lazlow had come to

when another of his buddies had slapped him awake, and now he was cradling his ruined arm, swaddled in bandages from a first aid kit. "You can't!"

"I shot you one time already," she retorted. "You reckon I won't do it again? Don't you get it? We're here to mess with your program."

DeVot ignored her and put his attention on Marc.

"Are you going to let these . . . ?" He faltered over the word. "These *people* gun us down in cold blood?"

Marc's jaw stiffened. He'd had his fill of these racist dickheads within an hour of stepping on board this tub, and playing dumb for the last few days had taxed him to the limit.

"Get over there." He pointed at the refugee boat with his rifle. "All of you."

"What?" DeVot actually gave an indignant snort. "This is my ship, I'm not leaving it to you."

"We're not asking," said Lucy.

"No—" DeVot began again, and that was enough for Marc.

He levelled his AK-47 over the heads of DeVot and the others, and let off braying bursts of orange fire that lit up the darkness, spraying rounds left and right. The men immediately reacted, flinching back, ducking away. Some of them got the message and scrambled into the leaky fishing boat. Marc marched forward, ejecting the spent sickle-shaped magazine from his rifle and grabbing another from the pocket of his threadbare camo jacket.

"You hear that?" he snarled. "That's the wake-up call those *people* get every bloody day!"

DeVot saw the furious look in his eyes and decided to jump for the boat himself, stumbling aboard after Lazlow.

"Easy, tiger . . ." Lucy spoke quietly, so that only Marc heard her.

"You're not the one who had to share a boat with these bigots for the last week," he replied.

"No," she agreed, slinging her rifle so she could pull a corroded fire axe from its mount on a nearby hull frame. "I was just undercover in a war zone."

"Fair point," he agreed.

"What do you think is going to happen when we get back to port?" DeVot started speaking again, proving beyond any doubt that he didn't know when to shut up. "You can't hijack this ship, that's piracy!"

"Yo ho ho, asshole."

Without warning, Lucy brought the axe blade down on the lines tethering the refugee boat to the Bastion League ship, again and again until they were severed.

The choppy waves immediately took hold of the old fishing vessel and pulled it away. Marc stood with one foot on the rail and took aim at the aft, where the boat's fuel bladder was located. He fired off another burst, holing it in several places. Diesel sputtered out and washed across the waterlogged deck. Then he pointed southward, pitching his voice up to be heard.

"Get that engine going, and I reckon you'll have enough fuel to make it back to the Libyan coast before it pisses away." He scanned the fearful faces of DeVot and his men. "If you're quick, that is. You can walk home from there."

Lazlow started shouting something, but Marc didn't hear it. The bigger ship's motors revved and drowned him out as one of the refugees took the throttle, and they left the old trawler behind in the swell.

Lucy asked Fatima and Remi to help her organize the people from the boat, taking them below to find the cramped mess hall the Bastion League crew had been using, and dividing out food and water for those who needed it most. It took a while for her to explain it so that all the refugees understood, but eventually she won them round with the promise that help was a few hours away. They were going to be safe, and no one was going to try to hurt them.

She emptied the ship's medical locker for the ones suffering from sunstroke and dehydration, while Marc walked off to the flying bridge to make sure they were sailing in the right direction. Somehow, through a combination of sign language and pointing at maps, he was able to get the man on the wheel to put them on course for their rendezvous.

As the adrenaline from the hijacking faded, Lucy felt the fatigue of the last few days threatening to overwhelm her, but she beat it back with a mug of tarry, acidic coffee. Glancing through a porthole, she caught sight of the Brit standing at the rail on the open deck. He was staring out at the dark waves, lost in thought.

Her first instinct was to go and speak to him, but something pulled her back and she frowned. Suddenly Lucy felt awkward about it, dwelling on a sense of distance between the two of them.

It had been several months since they last worked together on an operation, but it felt like longer. Their last assignment—a fraught race against time to chase down a rogue hacker collective in possession of a deadly digital weapon—had ended in fire and recrimination on the streets of Seoul. Dane and Keyes had almost lost their lives stopping a plot to provoke open war between North and South Korea, but worse still had been facing up to a betrayal from one of their own. Kara Wei, the Special Conditions Division's cybersecurity expert, had put them in jeopardy to follow her own agenda, and Lucy had learned how little she really knew the woman she called her friend. And if that wasn't enough, she and Marc had come down on opposite sides when it came to finding forgiveness for their former teammate. It had pushed the two of them apart, and now Lucy wondered if they could bridge that gap. She didn't want to admit that she was fond of the reckless Brit.

Lucy grimaced, and not just at the horrible taste of the ship's coffee.

Act like a professional, she told herself.

Marc looked up as she walked across the wet deck toward him and a few emotions crossed his face—surprise, worry, concern—before he settled on a wan smile.

"Hey," he began. "How's it going?"

"It's going . . ." she replied, with a weary sigh.

Marc fell silent for a moment, looking back out over the water again.

"You think we did the right thing, shipwrecking De-Vot and his bully boys? They know our faces now."

"We made 'em an offer they couldn't refuse," she said, with a smirk. "I reckon a taste of their own medicine is the least they deserve. They've been preying on these refugees for months. Now they're gonna learn what it's like to *be* them."

"Let the punishment fit the crime," said Marc. "That's what Rubicon's about, right? *Justice*. That's the cornerstone of Solomon's crusade."

"It's why I'm here," said Lucy, and the reply felt like a kind of confession.

"Yeah," Marc said, drawing out the word. "You and me both."

"We did a little good today," she added. "Gave some desperate people a second chance. Took some bad ones off the board."

"It's almost like we make a good team, yeah?"

"Aw, you missed me. That's sweet."

Marc chuckled, and the tension between them dissolved.

"'Course I did. I mean, I reckon I need someone around to warn me when I'm doing something risky."

Lucy rolled her eyes and smoothed back her hijab, a smile crossing her face.

"Dane, where you're concerned? That's a full-time job."

They both heard wary footsteps behind them, turning to see Fatima hesitating a few meters away. Marc gave her a grin.

"Hello." He looked at Lucy. "Who's this?"

Lucy beckoned, her smile widening.

"Come on, I'll introduce you."

— THREE —

A constant rain fell from the clouds over the 6th Arrondissement, driving Parisians indoors and leaving café tables and chairs abandoned beneath dripping awnings. The buildings throughout Saint-Germain-des-Prés glistened in the downpour as it rattled off the blinds across their windows, and from the upper floor of a spacious apartment on the Rue Bonaparte, the weather seemed intent on drowning out the sounds from the streets below. The antique frontage of the building was deliberately discreet, unadorned in such a way as to make the passing eye slip over it. Recessed doors concealed state-of-the-art security systems, and a set of wrought-iron gates provided entry to a large courtyard within, where security-enhanced cars patiently awaited their passengers. Viewed from above, clumps of umbrellas moved along the pavement outside the apartments, undulating like clusters of cells in a bloodstream.

Pytor Glovkonin watched the motion from a window without registering it. He never really *saw* ordinary people, not as anything other than a resource or an impediment. Tall and stylish, with that indeterminate mid-fifties look that other men envied, the businessman showed the world a commanding, challenging manner and an easy charisma. But none of that was truly who he was. He hid himself down deep, bringing daylight to that only rarely. Alone at this moment, his focus was turned inward, his outward persona muted and sullen.

It was always difficult for him to step outside himself, especially when something was irritating him. The Russian nursed his annoyance as if it were a lit match cupped in his hand, protected from a stiff breeze. With each minute that passed, the little flame of it burned brighter.

The men he had come to see were making him wait. It was such an uncommon experience for him that at first he found it amusing, almost novel. But that had been thirty minutes ago, and Glovkonin had quickly crossed the threshold of his tolerance.

Men like him did not wait for anything. He couldn't remember the last time that a car had not been waiting for him, a meal had not been quickly served, or a want of his was not attended within moments.

It was a well-constructed insult, this delay. Glovkonin was an extremely wealthy man, lord of his domain atop the mountain of money earned by G-Kor, the energy conglomerate that he owned. There were few commodities that men as powerful as Glovkonin could not control, but *time* was one of them.

In order to show him that his power and his money mattered little to them, these men squandered his time, knowing that every lost second would remind him of who was in the superior position.

He turned away and his gaze ranged around the room, never settling. The place had the clinical quality of an exclusive art gallery, unwelcoming to those who were not in the know and archly inviting to the select. Glovkonin imagined that the room was laced with monitoring devices of all kinds, so he gave nothing away, knowing that he was being watched every second that he stood there.

From what he knew of this building, it had been in the possession of the Combine for generations, originally owned by the founders of the clandestine group. So the story went, their gathering had emerged a few decades after the end of the Franco-Prussian War, when a handful of moneyed industrialists had foreseen that another large-scale conflict between nation states was inevitable. Those first founders had opened lines of secret communication among their number, planting the seed of the global network that today's Combine had grown into. It found its basis in a single concept—if warfare was a fundamental part of the human condition, it could be made profitable.

At the beginning, the Combine were the quartermasters of conflict, selling guns and shells, fuel and materiel, even soldiers, to any side in any battle. By the latter half of the twentieth century the Combine were not just supplying conflicts, they were manipulating them. Prolonging them. Even creating them.

The war on terror provided the greatest opportunity in their history—an asymmetrical battleground where victory could not be quantified or declared, an ongoing skirmish fueled by fears they were happy to stoke.

Pytor Glovkonin was a man who looked at such an ideal and wanted a piece of it. *No, more than that*—he was the kind of man who wanted *all* of it. He had worked his way into the Combine's periphery, drawing close to their inner circle, but it was taking too long, wasting too much of his time. He decided to set his own pace, and through guile and bloodshed, it had brought him here, to the inner circle. To a face-to-face meeting with the committee who sat at the Combine's head.

His anticipation briefly overrode his annoyance.

I will be one of them, he told himself. *I will make that happen.*

A door opened and a severe-looking Asian woman in a featureless gray dress stood on the threshold.

"They will see you now."

She wore a wireless headset in one ear and she carried a digital tablet in the crook of her arm, tapping at it as he crossed the room to her. She matched the décor of the room, as if she was some sort of tailor-made appliance.

"I appreciate the opportunity," he replied, steely and cold.

The woman ignored his tone and opened the door wider.

The next room was dominated by an ornate antique table that seemed out of place compared to the rest of the apartment's modernist-minimalist ethic, in the Louis XV style, detailed with gold and intricate marquetry in patterns of suns and moons. There were only three chairs, and they were arranged at the far end. Only one was occupied, by a wizened older gentleman in a suit of royal blue who seemed lost in the data streaming down another tablet, similar to the one held by the woman. Two other men stood by the window, laughing as they shared a joke. Both of them were around Glovkonin's age, at a guess. One was a stocky fireplug of a man, balding and ruddy, with animated fingers that never sat still; the other was suave and rakish, wearing an impeccably tailored outfit and a manner that seemed so casual it was almost lazy.

"Gentlemen—Mr. Pytor Glovkonin," said the Asian woman, as if she was presenting a debutante at some high society function.

He gave a nod as they turned to study him. The

woman melted away and then it was just the four of them.

"I think I know you," Glovkonin began, deciding to set the tone.

When he had been summoned to the meeting, there had been no word of whom he was to see, but one could not move in the world of billionaires and oligarchs as he did, and not know the players in that arena.

The suave man was an Italian engineering magnate known for his investments in aerospace and motorsports; his balding friend, an agricultural and biomedical industrialist from North America. The older man was a mystery, though.

"No names," said the Italian, before Glovkonin could say more. "We have no need of them."

His stiff smile didn't reach his eyes, making it clear the new arrival had transgressed some unwritten rule.

"We're all friends here," said the American, with false joviality.

"All friends," echoed the old man, and Glovkonin detected a Swiss-German accent.

A banker, then, he surmised. That fit the profile.

"It's good you could find the time to see us," said the Italian. "We've been impressed with the work you've done, covering operations after the loss of our dear sister."

"Horrible business," added the Swiss, with a grave shake of the head. "But not unexpected. She moved in dangerous circles." He looked up at Glovkonin for the first time. "She frequently spoke about you."

He couldn't help but wonder what Celeste Toussaint had said on those occasions. The woman was icy and unapproachable, resistant to any charms the Russian had tried to deploy. She, like Glovkonin, stood on the lower tiers of the Combine's cellular power structure.

Toussaint was the conduit for his dealings with the group, an assertive and uncompromising media heiress, whose control over news networks in the European Union allowed the Combine to subtly advance their agenda. But she had also been an impediment to Glovkonin's ambitions. Combine "associates"—as the lower ranks were known—could only access the committee through a more highly placed senior member, and there was little opportunity for advancement.

And so Glovkonin had chosen the only logical path. He removed her using an associate of his own, the terrorist assassin Omar Khadir, a surviving member of the near-eradicated Islamist extremist group Al Sayf. Glovkonin had Khadir in his debt because he had kept him alive, and now the man was the Russian's personal knife in the dark.

"The likely identity of her killer has been determined," he said.

Never one to waste an opportunity, Glovkonin made certain that Khadir left behind evidence at the murder—evidence that implicated Marc Dane, a key operative working for the Rubicon Group. Ekko Solomon and his band of vigilante-mercenaries were a constant thorn in Glovkonin's side, and they had already made enemies of the Combine by interfering in the group's activities. Implicating one to induce the other to destroy them was simply sound strategy.

"I had my best people look into it," he added.

"So did we," said the American. "The circumstances aren't as clear-cut as you suggest."

Outwardly, Glovkonin's expression remained unchanged, but inwardly the oligarch's mind raced.

Is it possible the committee know the truth about Toussaint's murder? Did they summon me here to confront me with it?

He dismissed the possibility. He had been careful, and Khadir was too methodical, too thorough, to leave anything to chance.

"Rubicon . . ." The old man said the name with a shake of the head. "One of these days we will put the African in his place."

"But not today," added the Italian, cutting off Glovkonin before he could seize the opening. "We're aware of your personal issues with Ekko Solomon, but there are more significant matters at hand."

Glovkonin's lips thinned. He had not come here to be humbled like some supplicant, and have his plans denied.

"We have an opportunity to—"

The Italian spoke over him. "You need to understand . . . What is the phrase? *The bigger picture.*"

"It is imperative to remain focused on the Shadow project at this time," insisted the Swiss. "For now, all other matters are irrelevant."

"With respect," Glovkonin said, meaning nothing of the kind, "I do not agree."

"We know," said the American. "But the decision isn't yours to make. Rubicon is an impediment, yes. But they have utility."

"When the current project is successfully concluded, some of the blame will fall upon Solomon's organization . . ." added the Italian. "Call it . . . a beneficial side effect."

"They have technological assets we can exploit at a later date." The old man looked down at his tablet screen. "We will not waste what we can conserve."

"You're making a mistake."

Glovkonin stiffened. The energy and money he had sunk into getting him into this room was too great for it to end with little more than a pat on the head for a job well done. His ploy was in danger of unravelling in front of him.

"Rubicon should be eradicated. Give me the resources. Let me show you what I can do for the Combine."

"We are well aware of what you can do." The Italian winced at Glovkonin's mention of the group's name, and his indolent manner turned colder. "Your lack of patience is apparent."

"Our association has not existed for over a century by moving without care," said the old man, without looking up. "Had we been successful in our earlier bid to secure the Exile nuclear device, this operation would not have been required. But with all we do, there is always an alternative stratagem, a fallback. The Shadow project is in motion because of that . . . disappointment. This must now be our priority."

Glovkonin's lip curled. The poorly veiled comment was solely directed at the Russian. He had been the one tasked with pressuring a disgraced Rocket Corps officer into selling the Exile weapon to the Combine, and responsibility for the failure to procure it had fallen on his shoulders—despite the fact that Rubicon's operatives had been instrumental in preventing the acquisition. And before that, Marc Dane and Solomon's agents had stopped a terrorist attack in Washington, D.C., which would have disrupted U.S. financial markets. G-Kor—and by extension, the Combine—would have made millions in shorted stocks. He reminded them of those facts, but it made little difference.

"Let me spell it out for you," began the American. "So that there's no misunderstanding."

He walked away from the window and looked up at Glovkonin.

The Russian entertained the thought of what it might be like to snake his hands around the shorter man's pink, jowly throat and choke the life out of him. But he swallowed the urge and said nothing.

"Toussaint's loss created a vacuum. You filled it because you were there, not because it was decided upon. Taking her place doesn't grant you her privileges." The American paused. "That may come in time."

"But not today," the Italian repeated.

"Show us you can work toward the group's interests and not just your own," the other man went on, "and then your voice will carry further."

"You performed adequately facilitating the release of Verbeke," said the Swiss, still refusing to grace him with a glance. "Your resources will continue to function as a firebreak between us and the operation. Monitor, but do not deviate from the plan. Is that clear?"

In effect, the committee was telling Glovkonin that he was to retreat to the sidelines and have no further active involvement.

"Clear," he replied tightly.

It was a testament to Pytor Glovkonin's iron self-control that he retained his rigid and emotionless affect after leaving the conference room, walking down to his waiting limousine, and riding away from the curb.

The cracks in the façade only began to show as he poured a heavy measure of Stolichnaya Elit into a glass and drank it down, savoring the smooth burn. In his other hand, he gripped the bottle tightly, his knuckles whitening around it as the impulse he had denied in the room cut free.

He swore in gutter Russian and smashed the bottle

into the limo's minibar, over and over, shattering glass
and plastic, spilling vodka across the carpet and over
his hands.

Fire screamed through lacerations on his palm as
the alcohol stung them, and Glovkonin turned his hand
over to glare at the self-inflicted wounds, and the blood
seeping out of them. He let the pain center him.

*How dare those debased old fucks believe they can
dictate what I will and will not do?*

The limo slowed and the voice of his driver Misha
issued out of the intercom.

"Sir, are you all right? I heard—"

Glovkonin stabbed at the intercom's control, switching it off. After a moment, the limo picked up speed
again. His men knew his moods well enough not to
question them.

With care, he opened a panel on the wall and removed
a first aid kit. Recalling the drills he had been taught
during his conscription in the Soviet army, he cleaned
and bandaged the cuts as the limo knifed through the
traffic and turned on to Pont de la Concorde, heading
north toward the airport at Le Bourget. His private jet
would be waiting, ready to whisk him back to Moscow,
where the committee expected him to remain and do
nothing.

When he was finished, Glovkonin picked up the encrypted satellite telephone mounted on the bulkhead
behind him and spoke an auto-dial code. He heard the
ghostly, metallic whispers of encoding artifacts as the
call connected. On the third ring, the man he was calling picked up.

"Go ahead," said Saito.

Glovkonin resisted the temptation to ask him where
he was. It didn't matter.

"Status?"

"*Exfiltration occurred with no complications. Verbeke is now on his way to the mine.*"

Glovkonin scowled. "Why?"

"*He wanted to oversee the programming himself. He doesn't trust us.*"

"As if a thug like him would understand it. Of course he doesn't trust us." Glovkonin shook his head, dismissing the issue. "It's not important. I want you to proceed with the other matter."

There was a long pause, filled with the low buzz of static.

"*Are you certain, sir?*"

"Don't question my orders," snapped Glovkonin. "Toussaint is dead, so you report to me now." He took a tight breath. "A data package will be sent to you. Find the Egyptian and give it to him, set him loose. Within twenty-four hours he will have recovered the asset I require, or he'll be dead."

"*And if Khadir is successful?*"

"Bring the asset to me."

Glovkonin cut the call. With this act, he was committed. Having Toussaint murdered was only the first test of his resolve. Only he and Khadir knew the full truth of what had happened, but there could be no turning back.

Acknowledging that immediately brought him a renewal of his purpose. There were only enemies surrounding him now—the men of the Combine's committee, Solomon's Rubicon, and everyone else who stood in his way—only enemies to be destroyed or resources to be used. It made everything so much easier to understand.

Glovkonin smiled as he plucked tiny diamonds of broken glass from where they had caught on his jacket, lingering again on the purity of his pain.

* * *

It was midday by the time they sailed the Bastion League ship to the rendezvous coordinates off the southern coast of Calabria, in the Gulf of Squillace.

Waiting for them was the *Aphrodite*, a modern catamaran cruiser. She belonged to Emigrant Aid, a non-profit, non-governmental organization dedicated to assisting refugees braving the dangerous crossing from North Africa. The group also happened to list Ekko Solomon as one of their foremost charitable donors. There were a few raised eyebrows from the *Aphrodite*'s crew as they caught sight of the League-sponsored vessel approaching. Before today, the pro- and anti-refugee groups had crossed paths with each other, and not on good terms. The right-wing collective were accused of actively sabotaging the work of Emigrant Aid and other similarly inclined NGOs, and so no tears were shed when the men and women on the catamaran learned of the fate of the other ship's crew.

Lucy thought that the sailors' "code of the sea" might have overridden the *Aphrodite* crew's antipathy for the Bastion League—but as it turned out, not so much. The transfer of the refugees happened quickly, and she felt a weight lift off her as she stepped on to the other ship. She'd been carrying it since the moment she found herself on the beach at Derna on the Libyan coast, wading out into the shallows toward that wallowing fishing boat among dozens of terrified men, women and children. These people would get a chance to live, instead of having that denied to them like so many others.

Looking back to the other ship, she saw Marc there, supervising a couple of the men as they methodically dumped the League crew's guns overboard. Everything else that could be useful—paperwork, ship's books and

GPS logs, laptop computers—had been quietly gathered and carried over to the *Aphrodite* as well. In a few days, Interpol's human trafficking unit would receive a weighty package of actionable intelligence. The League ship itself would be left at anchor to be recovered at a later date.

"Hello," said Fatima.

The girl had a habit of sneaking up on her. Lucy knew black ops specialists who were less stealthy than the young girl, and she threw her a grin.

"You took off your hijab," Fatima added, touching her own.

"Yeah," admitted Lucy. "It's not really who I am."

"Aya isn't your real name. You're an American."

She nodded. "I'm sorry I lied to you."

"It's all right." Fatima considered the thought. "You and your friend had to pretend to be other people so you could help us. Like in the movies."

Lucy chuckled. "Yeah, like in the movies."

Fatima's expression clouded, and it looked wrong on the face of one so young.

"I am very scared," she admitted. "My brother is too, but boys always pretend to be tough, so he won't say it."

"They're dumb that way," Lucy noted. "Listen, you don't have to be frightened." She gestured around. "There are doctors on board here. People who will take care of you and find you a place to stay."

Fatima looked off toward the Calabrian coastline in the distance.

"In . . . Italy?" She sounded out the name like it was alien to her.

"The people who run this ship work with governments in lots of different places," Lucy explained. "Italy, Germany, Belgium, France . . . They've agreed to take in anyone seeking asylum. I gotta tell you, it won't be easy. A lot of folks don't understand the reasons why you fled your home, and some won't welcome you. But others will, and if you and Remi want the chance to start a new life somewhere else, you can have it."

"I can work hard and study," said Fatima, with a determined nod, "and so will Remi."

Lucy smiled and patted her on the shoulder.

"Then you'll be okay."

She caught sight of a familiar face as one of the *Aphrodite's* crew came jogging up along the deck toward her. A young Turkish man in his early twenties, he had wavy black hair and serious eyes that were undercut by his wide smile.

"Hey, let me introduce you to someone I trust," she told Fatima. "He'll look after you two."

"It's good to see you, miss," said the young man. "It's been a while!"

"You look well, Halil," she replied. "How are you doing?"

He unconsciously patted his belly, where Lucy knew he sported a wicked surgical scar.

"I am well. I like this job a lot."

"That's great," she said, and she meant every word.

Seeing Halil like this—strong and smiling, doing something positive with his life—made Lucy feel like the risk and the danger was worth it.

A few years ago, Lucy and Marc had found Halil in a highway diner outside of Boston, with a time bomb surgically implanted in his stomach cavity. Orphaned and forced to become a terrorist suicide weapon, he had come within seconds of dying in a destructive firestorm. Together they saved his life, and ultimately it had been a vital clue Halil gave up that stopped an even worse attack from unfolding in America's capital. Being part of something so shocking could easily have

broken a person with a weaker spirit, but Halil had rebuilt his life. With the help of Rubicon, he had found a
way to make a positive difference in the world.

Halil beamed at Fatima and offered his hand.

"Hello to you. Welcome aboard the *Aphrodite*. Do
you know that name?" Fatima shook her head and he
went on. "Oh, let me tell you about her. She was a god-
dess, you see . . ."

The young man led the girl away, talking animatedly
about Greek mythology, making shapes in the air with
his hands.

"Is that . . . ?" Marc appeared at Lucy's shoulder, and
she nodded. "Wow. He's doing all right for himself."

"Remember this moment, right here," she told him,
prodding the Brit in the shoulder with a long finger.
"Next time you ask yourself why we do what we do."

"Speaking of which . . ." He jerked his thumb at the
Aphrodite's upper deck. "I reckon we're needed."

"Are you kidding me . . . ?"

Lucy trailed off as she saw a light-skinned man leaning over the rail above them. He studied her from behind a pair of dark glasses and a blue watch cap, then
nodded wordlessly toward the upper cabin and vanished inside.

"Malte's here? That does not bode well."

"My thoughts exactly," said Marc, blowing out a
breath. "If he's here, it's trouble. I mean, you know
how much he hates coming out in the sun . . ."

"Five'll get you ten," she said, grabbing the nearest
ladder, "someone, somewhere has pushed the panic
button."

Malte Riis was waiting for them in a narrow cabin,
working at a ruggedized plastic transport case packed

with electronic gear and a collapsible satellite antenna. The taciturn Nordic was another member of Rubicon's Special Conditions Division, a former member of the Finnish security services before he was recruited as a vehicle specialist for the team.

Marc had known him since he first crossed paths with Rubicon—although saying he *knew* him was a bit of a reach. The Finn didn't talk much, saying what he needed to through a look or a gesture with as few words as possible. At the start, Marc had felt that the other man had little time for him, but now he understood that reticent manner was how Malte treated everybody. Having both gone in harm's way several times since then, there was a mutual respect between the two of them.

Maybe one day he'll get blind drunk and we won't be able to shut him up, he thought.

For now, though, Malte gave Marc and Lucy another terse nod, and reached into the case for something.

Marc saw comms gear in the box and what looked like the guts of a hi-spec image processing unit, before Malte tossed something to him: a pair of video glasses, stripped-down lightweight versions of the rig one might find in a commercial virtual reality gaming kit.

The Finn passed a second set to Lucy and she eyed them warily.

"What's this?"

"Encrypted video conference," said Malte, taking a third pair of the glasses for himself. "Sit. It can be disorienting."

"What's up?" she added.

"You'll see," said Malte.

The appeal of trying out some new tech was all Marc needed to slip the rig on, and he blinked as a digital overlay faded in across the *Aphrodite*'s cabin. Motion sensors mounted in the glasses communicated with the control module in the case, mapping the movement of Marc's head so that the projected images he saw moved seamlessly with his point of view.

The walls of the cabin vanished as first a wireframe model of a much larger room overwrote the virtual space, and then that mesh accreted layers of detail that grew quickly from blocks of basic color to something photorealistic. The words CONNECTION CONFIRMED and ENCRYPTION ACTIVE materialized in the air in front of his face and floated there for a moment, before dissolving away.

He decided to take Malte's advice and sit down, fumbling into a chair. Through the glasses, he saw a room he recognized, one of the secured conference spaces in Rubicon's Monaco headquarters. Glancing to the right, he saw two plain digital avatars seated nearby, basic geometric human-shapes like the symbols you might see on the doors of a public bathroom. Still images of Malte's and Lucy's faces floated in front of the avatars, pictures taken from their security passes.

To the left, the real-time video feed allowed Marc to look out of the solarized glass windows of the Rubicon tower on Avenue de Grande Bretagne, over the rooftops of the business district and down to the bay and Port Hercule.

"Cool," he noted.

"So glad you approve."

At the far end of the conference room's ash-colored table, Ekko Solomon's ubiquitous executive assistant Henri Delancort looked up from a display screen built into the wood surface. He peered in their direction with dismay, adjusting his rimless spectacles.

"Forgive me if I do not look you in the eye, but from

my end of this the three of you are represented by a set of spherical cameras. I am having a conversation with an abstract art installation."

The rail-thin French-Canadian's default setting was more arch and clipped than usual. Marc disliked the perfectly calculated, stiff and prickly attitude that Delancort displayed, and he tried to have as little to do with the man as possible. But Delancort's role as Solomon's right hand meant he seldom had the opportunity to avoid dealing with him.

"So?" said Lucy, putting all their questions into a single syllable.

Delancort launched into an explanation without pause.

"I'll begin by disappointing you. Your involvement in the current operation has been canceled, with immediate effect. Clean-up will be handled by local assets. There will be no stand-down as previously indicated. Malte has already been briefed on transit provisions. Once the *Aphrodite* docks, you will transfer to the closest airport and proceed under separate snap covers to your destination."

"Okay . . ." Marc took in the rapid-fire briefing with a blink. Through his feet he felt the rumble and pitch of the *Aphrodite* as the catamaran got under way, and the disconnect with the image in front of him made him slightly dizzy. "You know we're both worn out, right? Weeks of undercover does that to you."

"I am certain you will rise to the challenge," said the Québécois assistant, rolling smoothly over Marc's protest before it could gather momentum. "These are the details of a dilemma that has come to our attention. A highly valuable company asset, a scientist working in Singapore at a Rubicon subdivision called Maxa-

Bio, went missing from her home less than twenty-four hours ago. Her location is currently unknown, as is that of her husband and stepson."

Delancort tapped at the screen in front of him and images appeared in the virtual space, floating untethered before them. Marc saw a plain East Asian woman in her mid-forties in a lab coat, caught in another unflattering security pass photo that made her look pinched and unhappy. The name DOCTOR SUSAN LAM was displayed underneath.

Marc caught the sound of Lucy taking a sharp breath and instinctively turned in her direction, but all he saw was her blank virtual avatar.

More images slipped over the first one, like cards laid atop one another. Husband and son, in an altogether more human shot showing the pair of them having fun on a beach.

"We suspect all three were forcibly abducted," continued Delancort.

"Why?" said Malte.

"Evidence on site fits the profile," said Delancort, then added: "A complete picture is still forming."

Marc studied the pictures, committing them to memory. The shots changed to an image of a black and white colonial-style home surrounded by lush vegetation, then the steely exterior of the MaxaBio building in some modern industrial park.

"What does she do at that place, then?" he asked.

"They're trying to cure cancer." Delancort's reply was flat, as if the answer was obvious. "Developing programmable virus systems. Feel free to look it up on your way there."

"To Singapore," Marc noted. "That's . . . what? Sixteen hours and change?"

"You wanted time to rest," said Delancort. "Silber has already been sent out with Kader from cyber-ops to get a head start."

Ari Silber was the handsome ex-Israeli air force officer who served as the SCD's operational pilot. Where Malte handled anything with wheels, Ari dealt with the team's fixed-wing flying needs. Typically, his duties kept him close to Ekko Solomon, captaining the billionaire's private Airbus A350, so the fact he had been cut loose for this new situation only underlined its seriousness. As for Assim Kader, the British-educated Saudi's hacking skills were good, if not better, than Marc's.

"Assim is a smart lad, so why do you need us there?" Marc's irritation flared at Delancort's tone. "Look, I get this might be serious for Rubicon's shareholders if it goes public that some scientist dropped off the grid, and the company stocks tank—but this kind of thing isn't what we deal with. This sounds like a job for Rubicon's regular security bods to handle, yeah? I mean, we are the *Special Conditions Division*. What's so special about these conditions?"

"This is not as clear-cut as corporate espionage, or some errant wife running off for an affair," said the French-Canadian. "We suspect it is more than a criminal matter." He took a breath. "You are correct that this is a *security* issue, one of the highest urgency that must be kept compartmentalized."

Marc had the sense those words were being directed at someone other than him.

"So again," he said, becoming aware that the conference room's door was sliding open, "why send us? Doesn't Rubicon have assets out there already, closer to the problem?"

"We do," said Ekko Solomon, as he came into the

room, looking out of the simulation at them. "But I want the people I trust the most to deal with this."

Marc unconsciously straightened in his chair now that the boss was in the room, even if the room was hundreds of miles away. Solomon had that kind of effect on people; one of the world's richest men, the imposing African had a quiet sort of intensity, projecting a cool confidence that could effortlessly hold the attention of everyone around him. But his normally refined manner seemed rough around the edges today, as if forces were acting on him that Marc couldn't see.

He was uncharacteristically terse.

"Look into the situation, quietly. I know you are capable. Do not underestimate the seriousness of this."

"Yes, sir," said Lucy, as if the comment had been directed solely at her.

Solomon nodded, and Marc felt like the man was staring out of the virtual conference room and right into his eyes.

"Be careful," he said, and then the image faded, back into the wireframe, then nothing.

— FOUR —

Delancort watched the red lights on the front of the cameras wink out one after another, and he let out a low sigh.

"It never rains but it pours," he began, rising to his feet.

"My people know their jobs." Solomon stood in the doorway, his arms folded across his chest. "That is why I chose them."

A jibe about the suitability of certain members of the Special Conditions Division rose instantly in the French-Canadian's thoughts, but he silenced the urge to say it out loud. Still, Solomon knew his assistant well enough to intuit the unspoken words, silently waiting for his reply.

Delancort decided to take a different tack.

"Sir, the other matter, the meeting with the board of directors . . ." He nodded across the office, in the direction of one of the other conference rooms, where the glass walls of the space had been set to a frosted "privacy" mode. "Shall we proceed?"

Solomon frowned. "Their timing is inopportune. The situation developing in Singapore requires my full attention."

"With respect, sir, we have delayed them long

enough. They will not tolerate another deferral . . . and rightly so."

"Indeed," said Solomon. "As tempting as it would be to retreat to my private quarters and tell the board I am indisposed . . ." He shook his head, dismissing the notion. "No. I have never run from a fight in my life."

He was already walking away, and Delancort had to rush to catch up, grabbing his digital tablet, jogging after the other man's long-legged strides.

He followed Solomon across the open-plan floor to the main conference room and schooled his expression as the doors opened to admit them. The six people waiting inside—three other senior members of Rubicon Group's board of directors and their personal equivalents of Delancort—all stood as a gesture of respect to the company's chief executive officer.

"My apologies for keeping you waiting," began Solomon. "Thank you for coming."

He extended his hand to shake that of the closest man, starting with his sole ally on the board.

"Any excuse to visit Monte Carlo is a good one." Gerhard Keller smiled and pumped Solomon's hand with his own.

The barrel-chested financier was descended from German barony, and Delancort had always sensed something medieval in the man. In his late fifties, Keller was a genius mathematician, but he would have looked at home in some forest-bound Schloss, gnawing on a chicken leg and swigging from a flagon of mead. When he wasn't keeping a hawk-like eye on Rubicon's bottom line, the German liked to use his skills in number theory to gamble, and win more often than the casinos liked.

"Speak for yourself, Ger," said the woman standing at his side. "Too damn warm for me."

Esther McFarlane's native Edinburgh accent grew more noticeable when she was irritated, and Delancort marked it now. The Scot's tone was like a barometer of her mood and what he read there he seldom liked. A few years younger than Keller, McFarlane was the daughter of oilmen and engineers, and she was fond of saying that for all the expensive education her parents had given her, she still had crude oil running through her veins. Brisk and uncompromising, she was totally lacking in artifice. Solomon respected that about the woman, but Delancort found her uncouth, at times vulgar. She gave the African a perfunctory handshake and drifted back to her chair.

"Let's get down to it, shall we?"

"Of course."

The final member of the board was Victor Cruz, a Chilean industrialist with a thoughtful demeanor whose own corporation—a mining and technology concern called El Solar—had been bought out by Rubicon in the early 2000s. Cruz had an unerring knack of absorbing everything said around him and elegantly parsing it. His skill in making connections that other people did not see was what had made El Solar the success it was, enough that Solomon had brought him on to Rubicon's board after the takeover, so it could benefit the group still further.

"It's good to see you, Ekko. I wish it could be under better circumstances."

"That sounds ominous."

Solomon took his seat and then the rest of them sat.

Delancort saw that his opposite numbers—Cruz's, McFarlane's and Keller's own executive assistants—

were poised over their individual data tablets, and he
skimmed over his own.

I know where this is going, he thought. *I warned
Solomon that we have been pushing at the limit for
a while now. It was only a matter of time before the
board decided to push back.*

"Let's talk about some of the choices you've been
making over the last year or so, Ekko," said McFarlane.
"Discretionary purchases and operational decisions
that we haven't been read in on. Funding diverted from
some divisions into parts of Rubicon that we don't have
oversight for."

"I've done what I considered necessary," said Solomon.

"Was it necessary to contract a Swedish shipyard to
build us a submarine?" she shot back, gesturing to her
assistant. The woman at her side sent a graphic to the
shared screen on the far wall, an image of the Saab A26
stealth submersible that Rubicon had yet to take delivery
of. "I didn't see this item on our oceanographic program
or the coral reclaim operation."

"We have projects that will utilize that unit when it
comes on stream," came the reply.

"What about the acquisition of the Horizon Integral Corporation?" said Keller, turning serious. "Before you say it, of course we see the value in such a
procurement—their market share in digital infrastructure is substantial. But you went ahead without con-
sulting the rest of the board."

Solomon gave a slow nod. "I have that power. I chose
to exercise it."

"The timing, though, that's fishy." McFarlane leaned
forward, glancing toward Cruz, then back again. "Horizon Integral suffered a major security incident several

months ago, while you were actually present in their
building. Along with members of the Special Conditions
Division. Then within days, HI's chief executive officer
brings you an acquisition package so good it's impossible to turn down." She took a breath. "Ekko, if I look
closely at this, am I not going to like what I find?"

The "security incident" McFarlane referred to was
far more than that. Horizon Integral's main product—
advanced software that managed major infrastructure
systems, from traffic control to power grids, self-driving
cars to automated factories—had been compromised by
a black-hat hacker cadre. Those hackers had sought
to create chaos and ultimately destabilize nations, and
their plan would have worked if Rubicon's operatives
had not stopped them. In the aftermath, the agreement
between the two corporations had helped keep that
truth from the wider world, in order to prevent a panic.

On the surface, it seemed like a cold, mercenary act.
Perhaps it was, mused Delancort, but in the end, a
worse fate had been averted.

"If you have no need to pull on that thread," Solomon said, "I would suggest you do not."

"Ekko . . ." Cruz gave a sigh. "No one in this room
doubts the good work that you have done with the Rubicon Group. You've made this corporation an exem-
plar of ethical capitalism. We're proud to be a part of
that. But there are facts we cannot overlook. While
Rubicon's private military and security contracting divisions do their work in the light of day, your special
conditions people do not. There are unconfirmed reports of Rubicon assets being deployed against active
terrorist groups and criminal conspiracies, even talk
about nuclear weapons, for God's sake! What are we
supposed to think?"

"Aye," agreed McFarlane. "And then there's the work

of data gathering going on. I mean, monitoring our rivals and the stock exchanges for an edge in the markets is one thing. But running a private intelligence database, this so-called"—she she looked down at her notes—"Gray Record? We're not a nation state. Activity like that draws the wrong kind of attention."

Delancort shot Solomon a sideways look. The Gray Record was the informal designation for an SCD data server, where every piece of intel they gathered was stored and cross-referenced, ready to be utilized. Its existence was not a widely known fact.

"Those of us with long memories recall your former partner," said Keller, and Solomon's expression turned stony. "And how that turned out. No one wants to see a repetition of those events."

Delancort watched Solomon frame his reply with care.

"I have never made my intentions secret from any of you," he began. "Rubicon's aegis encompasses aviation, mining, biotechnology and many more interests. Our security arm is only one part of that great machine, but within it is an entity that can do as much good as our medical research, our clean energy initiatives . . . The Special Conditions Division operates under my personal direction, and yes, it may exist on the edge of legality. But it works to even the balance in the dark places where the strong prey upon the weak." His gaze briefly turned inward. "You all know . . . I came from such a place." Solomon reached up and touched the silver necklace at his throat. An abstract piece of metal—the trigger from the rifle he had once carried as a child soldier—hung from it. "As long as I have the wealth and the ability, I will do what I can to bring justice there."

"Very admirable," said Cruz. "But there must be limits to this . . . *adventurism*, Ekko. You must see that?"

"Is that what you believe, Victor? This is some sort of game?"

"We can't make a profit if money is being diverted to bribes, buyouts and a private crusade." McFarlane's tone was damning. "We share some of the blame. For too long, we didn't look too closely at what you were doing off the books. But the board is losing patience, Ekko. There have to be limits, even for a man like you."

"I forged Rubicon with blood and sweat and sacrifice. Be careful when you tell me what I should do with it."

Delancort had rarely seen Solomon roused to anger, but he saw it now, the African's dark eyes turning steely, his jaw set hard.

He saw his opportunity to intervene.

"Sir, perhaps there is a middle ground we can seek here? Maintain the integrity of the SCD's work and keep Rubicon protected as well?"

"I'm glad to see where your loyalty lies, Mr. Delancort," said McFarlane. "I was afraid I'd have to remind you that you're in the employ of the Rubicon Group, not Ekko Solomon."

"That is not what I meant . . ." he began, but Keller and Cruz were already nodding along to the woman's words.

"We feel it is best to limit the operations of the Special Conditions Division for the time being," said Cruz.

"While we undertake a review," added Keller.

"We have an operation under way at the moment," Delancort noted.

"Close it down," said McFarlane.

"That would be ill-advised." Delancort shook his head.

"Then *limit* it," said the woman, with finality.

Solomon broke his silence, folding away the moment of annoyance he had shown as if it had never been there.

"I believe you had already decided on your course of action before I arrived, yes?" He didn't wait for the others to reply. "It seems I have no alternative but to agree."

He stood and turned to the door, and Delancort rose with him, but the African put out a hand and held it to his assistant's chest, halting him in place with firm pressure.

Delancort hesitated, suddenly unsure of where he was supposed to be.

"Sir?"

"Give the board whatever they require," said Solomon, and there was a distance in his tone Delancort had never heard before.

He walked away, leaving Delancort with a growing sense of unease.

The first leg of Marc's journey had him out of Naples toward Germany. It felt odd going through the outskirts of that city again. The last time he had been there, it was the end of a pursuit across the globe chasing a stolen portable nuclear device, and the tension of those desperate hours came back over him like a cold shadow.

He tried to push it away, but in the end Marc let a restless sleep take him under. The next thing he knew, a flight attendant was nudging him awake and they were at the arrival gate in Munich.

He drifted around the airport's huge enclosed atrium, unable to settle. Malte and Lucy were on separate flight plans—the Finn going via his native Helsinki and then

Bangkok, the American through Istanbul—to meet at
Singapore Changi within a few hours of one another.
He wondered why Delancort had insisted on routing
them differently, and only one possibility seemed to
fit. The situation with Doctor Lam was more sensitive
than Rubicon were letting on.

On the next leg of the flight, which at least was com-
fortably in first class, Marc logged on to the airliner's
in-flight wifi and did a little pre-mission prep of his
own. He pulled up the hood of his dark SeV fleece and
leaned over his ruggedized computer tablet. It was his
own personal piece of kit, not the one that Rubicon's
techs had issued him. It wasn't that he didn't trust Solomon's people, but there were times when it felt smarter
to maintain his own degree of operational security.

As they flew east and the evening drew in, Marc's fellow passengers slipped off their expensive shoes and
tailored jackets, drank their cocktails and ate their meals,
while he lost himself in the web. Using custom search
tools and back channel protocols, Marc dredged the
internet for whatever he could find about Susan Lam.

There was plenty about MaxaBio, the research lab
where she worked. Set on an elegantly manicured
campus in Singapore's tech-industry quarter, the Rubicon subdivision was right at the bleeding edge of
oncological medicine. Their stated goal was to find the
vital key to unlocking a cure for cancer within the next
decade, and if the papers and seminars their scientists
presented were accurate, they were well on their way
to achieving it. Biomedicine wasn't exactly in Marc's
wheelhouse, but he had the soul of a tech-geek and
he'd read enough issues of *New Scientist* to get the basics. MaxaBio were developing an artificial biological
agent that mimicked the action of a virus, but instead
of infecting and destroying the host's tissues, their cure

would target only the deadly cancer cells and eliminate them, leaving the patient's body to recover naturally.

Marc balked at the mention of the word "virus," his blood chilling.

Would Rubicon ever be involved in something as dangerous as biological weapons?

He couldn't believe that Ekko Solomon would countenance something like that. The African had been born in the chaos of destructive brushfire wars, and he had seen famine and disease first-hand. He knew better than any of them the misery they left behind them.

Marc read on. A typical virus found in nature, so the MaxaBio brochure said, was in many ways the genetic equivalent of an empty container. A "shell" element did the work of getting the disease into a living host, but it was the genetic material within it that did the unpleasant things. Their plan was to use such a shell to deliver a genetically tailored payload to kill off malignant cells, and Doctor Susan Lam was at the head of the team leading that initiative.

"And of course, this kind of thing could *never* be misused," muttered Marc.

"I beg your pardon?"

He looked up at the flight attendant standing in the aisle next to his seat. Marc managed a weak smile and became aware that some of the other, well-heeled passengers were looking questioningly in his direction. In his jeans and hoodie, with the taint of two weeks of shipboard life barely off him after a cursory shower, Marc suddenly realized how out of place he looked.

"I'm fine," he said, and the attendant took the hint, moving on.

Stifling a yawn, Marc rubbed his eyes and continued, changing tack, looking into Lam herself. There wasn't much to grasp, beyond a terse bio on the company website and a few contributing bylines on articles in journals of note like *Nature* and *The Lancet*. Lam seemed respected but not lauded, the kind of diligent researcher who was toiling away toward an essential goal, uninterested in the limelight.

Or maybe not. Maybe that was what people were supposed to believe. In his time at MI6, before he had become field-rated, one of Marc's duties had been pattern analysis. He had a sixth sense for it, something that his recruiter-instructor John Farrier had once called his "ear for music." It came from the same tech-nerd data-hungry compulsion that made him good with computer code, able to reel off the specs of military hardware at the drop of a hat, or quote the entirety of the original *Star Wars* trilogy from memory. Marc saw the shape of data as a whole, analyzing the entirety of the "take," not just the individual pieces of it. He knew a manufactured identity when he saw one.

Susan Lam's life was just on the wrong side of artificial. It wasn't ragged enough to be real; it didn't have the loose ends that normal people had. Her social media comprised a lonely photo-sharing page that didn't contain a single shot of Lam's face, and some oblique comments on a gardening newsgroup. By contrast, her husband Simon was active across a dozen different platforms, the lecturer engaging with his law students on many subjects, and posting family pictures of his son week in and week out. Susan was in some of those shots, but never fully, always as if she had been turning out of frame when he took them.

Just shy? Self-conscious about her looks? Marc wondered. *Or is there another reason?*

Tracking back through the years, he came across images of the boy's birth mother, after a sad oasis of shots where dad and son were clearly trying to carry on as

usual without her. That gave him a time frame, and he
matched it with Susan Lam's sparse digital footprint.

The scientist had been working at MaxaBio for a
few years, marrying Simon six months after being announced as part of the oncology project. But before
that, she had barely existed at all. Every reference he
found that pre-dated the MaxaBio gig had the same
whiff of the artificial to it. It was a decent cover, Marc
allowed, but it wasn't designed to be bulletproof.

*Whoever put this together didn't expect anyone to
give it any serious scrutiny*, thought Marc, studying the
photo of Susan Lam.

All of which raised a single pertinent question: who
was this woman?

Twelve hours later, most of which Marc had passed in a
deep, dreamless sleep after surrendering to his fatigue,
he sat in the back seat of a black Maserati Levante.
Lucy lounged across from him like a dozing cat, her
face half-hidden under a tan baseball cap. Up front,
Malte drove the big SUV westward through the traffic
on Singapore's Pan Island Expressway, keeping on the
button of the speed limit as a heavy rain squall passed
over them.

"I checked in with Assim," she said, directing the
comment at no one in particular. "He's still at the lab,
sifting security footage."

"Oh yeah?"

Lucy nodded. "Seems Delancort was wrong about
Lam vanishing completely. She made a stop at Maxa-
Bio before she ghosted."

Marc's skin prickled.

"Making a deposit or a withdrawal?" He knew the
answer before she gave it.

"Take-out. Local cops are on it, which means we need to work fast. They've already entered her house and searched it."

Marc was going to ask another question, but then Malte took them off the highway and on to an upmarket residential street.

"This is it," said the Finn, pulling to a halt on the driveway of a two-story colonial house.

Leaving Malte outside, Marc and Lucy dashed through the rain to the house. The upper floor of the building was larger than the lower one, supported by square pillars that matched the black-and-white exterior décor, forming a veranda around the front door. Behind streamers of crime scene tape, a modern electronic lock secured it, but Marc had the necessary kit in his pack to run a bypass, simulating the wireless electronic key fob needed to open it.

He peered at a data panel on the screen.

"The lock's memory shows another hack took place here," he said, without looking up. "Someone used the same kind of gear I have to get in without setting off the alarms."

The lock clicked open and Lucy slipped a slimline Glock 43 pistol from a hidden pocket in the back of her jacket, before nudging the front door wider with the tip of her boot.

"The place should be empty, but don't make assumptions. You know the deal, touch nothing."

Marc waggled his fingers in front of her. Like Lucy, he was wearing a pair of thin tactical gloves.

"Copy that."

They stepped under the tape barriers and moved inside, securing the door behind them. Room by room, they swept the ground floor, starting in the lounge and heading back toward the open-plan kitchen-dining area. Discolored spots here and there showed where the police had dusted for fingerprints, and there were markers on the floor where boot prints marked the deep pile carpet.

Marc was instinctively drawn to the bookshelves, glancing over the titles. Mostly it was biographies and law texts, but then suddenly it shifted sharply to a collection of classic fiction.

"Austen, Brontë, Defoe and Dumas . . ." he said aloud. "All the romantic and escapist works."

"Seen the movies," said Lucy. He turned to find her standing in the doorway between the two halves of the house. "For a crime scene, this place looks pretty damn neat."

Marc gave a nod and ran his gaze over the rest of the room, looking at the location of objects, ornaments, lamps and the like. Nothing seemed out of place.

"Their taste in home furnishings is a bit bland," he admitted, "but yeah, I see your point."

Lucy spotted something in the next room and pointed it out.

"Security hub's in here."

He stepped after her, bringing up the tablet again. Marc aimed an antenna wand at an electronic control panel tucked discreetly in a small alcove and ran an icebreaker program.

"It's encoded," he began, "so—"

"One two one zero one six," Lucy cut in. "That's the override."

Marc raised an eyebrow and tapped in the code. It did as promised, releasing full control of the house's security system to him.

"And how did you know that? What is it, the little lad's birthday?"

He pressed a tab on his hand-held screen to start a download of the data from the outdoor security cameras.

"No, that's the back door Rubicon had loaded, in case we ever needed to get in here discreetly."

He eyed her. "You could have told me that outside."

"Wanted to be sure our bad guys hacked the door."

Marc paused, processing that.

"So I've learned something, then." He ticked them off on his fingers. "One: someone cracked the digital lock to silently gain entry to the house. Two: you're not telling me the whole story."

"Both true." He glared at her, and at length she gave a sigh. "Okay. Sure. I know her. Lam, or whatever."

"Or whatever?" echoed Marc. He thought back to that moment in the VR conference room when Lucy had reacted to the picture of the woman. "I took a fishing trip on the plane over here, I knew right away Susan Lam was an alias." He glanced down at the tablet, seeing the download was complete. "I do not appreciate being kept in the dark, Lucy. I thought you and me were past that."

"It's . . . complicated," she allowed.

Marc scowled as he swept through a playback of the last few days of security footage. There was nothing but static.

"Someone zapped the solid-state memory in the cameras, blanked it. It's worthless." He looked up at her. "Right, I'm done being on the back foot about this. Explain it to me."

Along the wall of the dining room area, there was a mantel displaying the only family photos Lucy had seen in the entire house. Most of them were of the kid, Michael, a particularly poignant one showing him as a baby in the arms of his late mother. But pride of place was a shot of the Lams on their wedding day. Simon beaming in a linen suit, his son in a cute ring-bearer outfit, and Susan in an elegant cheongsam dress. Husband and wife were showing off identical rings, white gold bands with writing on them that Lucy couldn't read. They looked so happy, but there was a particular kind of melancholy in there too. The snapshot had captured three people in the instant that life was giving them a do-over, a second chance at something good.

"Okay," she said, taking a deep breath, "Doctor Susan Lam was a new identity cooked up by Rubicon, for a woman whose real name was Ji-Yoo Park."

"Korean?"

"*North* Korean," Lucy corrected.

"Oh great." Marc made a face. "Them again? As if we didn't piss them off enough after that thing in Seoul."

"This was way before that, before you and I even knew each other."

Lucy put her pistol back in its concealed holster, hesitating as she wondered exactly how much to reveal to him. She trusted Marc with her life—he'd put himself on the line for her a dozen times—but still she was reticent to break a confidence. In the end, she erred on the side of conviction.

"Park was a defector from the North. A bioscientist, originally working in medicine for their military. She was forcibly conscripted into their WMD program, lost her only sister to the work camps when she tried to refuse. Rubicon offered her an escape hatch. A better life."

"You're the one who got her out."

The Brit was always quick to put details together, sometimes annoyingly so.

"Wasn't easy. She was at a facility outside of Pyongyang, and we . . ." Lucy drifted off, then shook her head. "The details don't matter. I saved Park's life. We set her up here, where she could put that big brain of hers to some good use."

"When were you going to tell me this?"

"About now?"

"Funny," he grunted. "Okay, so if we're assuming that someone kidnapped Lam—"

"Park," said Lucy.

"Yeah, the next question is *who* and *why*? Is it her people come looking? I mean, the DPRK has a storied history of illegal renditions and covert actions in other countries. And they hold grudges for a long time." He considered that. "Assassination is their standard operating procedure. So the fact that we didn't find a bunch of deaders here means they want her alive for something—for what she knows."

"That's a lot," agreed Lucy. "Even if it isn't the North Koreans, anyone dialed in enough to run a snatch job like this has to know that Park is more valuable alive than dead."

Marc studied the wedding photo.

"Before she was a cancer doctor . . . Do I even want to ask what Park was working on?"

Lucy gave a shrug. "Let's call it *end-of-the-world shit* and leave it there."

She heard the door open and Malte entered the house, shaking off rainwater from his jacket. He was holding a brick of camo-colored plastic with a plastic dome at one end, and inside it a ring of tiny camera lenses was clearly visible. It looked a lot like the remote camera units nature photographers deployed in the wild, to spy on animals in their natural habitats.

Marc took the device and turned it over in his hands. He knew exactly what it was.

"Where was this?"

"Tree in the garden," said the Finn. "Emergency backup monitor."

"Your actual black ops nanny-cam," added Lucy.

"It's a stand-alone unit," Marc went on. "Not connected to the house cameras. Which means the erase command that wiped them won't have affected this."

"Can you read what's on it?" she said.

"It has a 360-degree camera eye," he told her. "I can do better than read it . . ."

Marc shrugged off his ubiquitous backpack and dug inside it, returning with a pair of video glasses. They were the same model as the ones Lucy had used on board the *Aphrodite* for the virtual conference with Solomon and Delancort. Marc slipped them on and ran cables from the glasses to his tablet, and from there to the camera unit.

"This'll provide a full surround image."

Marc heard Lucy send Malte off to finish checking the rest of the Lam house as he found himself a seat and booted up the spy camera. Sure enough, the memory card in the device was still intact, and while he couldn't remove it, he could scan the contents. He took a seat at the dining table and set up his gear.

"The lock software on the front door said it was opened from the outside at 8:17 a.m., three days ago," he said to the air, "so I'll spool back to just before that."

The virtual image flickered in the glasses and Marc

put them on. He moved his head experimentally, letting the sensors in the rig map the motions.

When the clock read 8:10 a.m., the footage began to play. Through the lenses, it appeared to Marc as if he was sitting atop a vantage point out on the grass in front of the Lam household. Moving his head left and right allowed him to pan around, seeing down to the end of the driveway, or toward the house's picture window that looked into the lounge. A time code floated at the corner of his vision, ticking off the seconds.

"What do you see?" Lucy's disconnected voice came from somewhere close at hand.

"Nothing yet . . ."

He hesitated. Right on time, he spotted a couple of dark shapes at the long wall marking the western edge of the house's property line. Two figures slipped over the barrier, one moving fast and low toward the gates at the end of the drive, the other in the direction of the house. He described them to Lucy.

"Both in similar clothes, black outfits. They have hoods on . . . Guessing from the bearing, I think the one coming to the house is a woman."

He flicked a look at the figure by the gate, and saw the man opening them. Out on the road, two identical blue vans were coming up the street.

"The cops reported the front gate was open when they arrived," noted Lucy.

Marc turned back to look at the woman and he shifted in his chair, unconsciously wanting to move his point of view inside the footage's virtual bubble but unable to. This wasn't like a VR game where he could shift position in a simulated environment; the replay was coming from a simultaneous video capture gathered by the camera's 360-degree imaging head. He was stuck in his fixed location, only able to see what the immobile camera had seen.

"Wait one."

He paused the playback, glimpsing a shadow moving inside the house. Someone had passed through the lounge, but they had not spotted the intruder. The woman in the black outfit was half-turned, not quite looking in the direction of the hidden camera. And her face . . .

"They've got masks on," noted Marc. "Not like rigid plastic ones, though. It's more like . . . black muslin maybe?"

The hooded face had an eerie, inhuman appearance to it. The hollows where the eyes should be were deep pits of darkness, and there was no visible mouth.

"That is fucking sinister," said Lucy, as he described it.

"Clever," he added. "Not only are they disturbing as hell, they'll fox any facial recognition software."

He hit the control tab and the replay resumed.

The woman approached the house and Marc saw the door open dutifully for her as she waved a hand-held device at it. She moved inside as the two vans rolled slowly up the driveway, doubtless holding the speed down to keep noise at a minimum so the residents wouldn't be alerted. He kept up his running commentary, as more masked figures in black carrying handguns climbed out of the vehicles. The point of view became cluttered, the vans positioned near the front door so Marc could only catch glimpses of what was going on through the gap between them.

"I see a guy with a hard-shell case," he noted. "Same type I use for transporting delicate electronics. He's taking it inside."

"The hacker?" offered Lucy. "Maybe with the kit they used to zero the house's security cameras."

"You don't need a case that big for gear to do that. A smartphone jacked into the hub would be enough."

For long minutes, nothing changed. Marc tensed. He was waiting for the worst, to see a flash of muzzle flare in one of the windows, and then someone coming out with a body bag over their shoulder. But that never happened. Instead, he saw the black-suited woman again, her shroud-mask in place, leaving the house with another person walking stiffly beside her. Doctor Susan Lam, aka Ji-Yoo Park, moved with a haunted, broken pace.

Park and the hooded woman exchanged a few words, and then the scientist disappeared into the back of the first van. She looked fearful, but there were no restraints visible, no handcuffs or zip-ties. No one was aiming a weapon at her.

"She went without resisting," said Lucy.

"But not willingly." Marc rocked the recording back to the moment where the two women spoke, trying to intuit what had been said. "Park is saying . . . *Please*. Asking for something?"

"Please don't execute my husband and my stepson," Lucy offered. "That's why she isn't putting up a fight. The lady I knew wasn't the type to give up easy. They have to be coercing her."

"Likely," agreed Marc. "That's what this is about. Snatch the family, pressure the wife."

The windowless van carrying Park drove away, and he tracked it until it vanished out of sight, giving Lucy details to follow up, reading off the license plate.

"Those'll be fake," she said.

"Still need to check, though."

One of the armed men stood in the shadows, out of sight of anyone passing down on the main road, while the others remained inside with the husband and the stepson. Once or twice, Marc saw a shadow moving around past the upstairs windows, but never defined enough to get a good read on it. He turned up the time index, zipping forward through the footage.

Then finally, nearly thirty minutes after Park had been taken, Simon Lam and his boy were marched out of the house by two masked figures. Marc's hands clenched as he got a good look at the kid; his face was a picture of desolate terror, cheeks streaked with tears, eyes wide with panic. His dad held him close, and if anything, the parent's dread was deeper than the child's.

What had to be going through that poor sod's mind, right there? Marc studied his face. *This has to be any father's worst nightmare.*

The two hostages passed out of sight behind the second blue van and the vehicle rocked as they were put inside. The masked men followed them, all except the one carrying the heavy gear case. He had something else in his other hand—not a gun, but an odd, bulky camera unit. Marc watched as he panned it around, and the light of the morning sun glittered off a quartet cluster of video lenses. The "cameraman" moved as if he was making sure to get footage of all of the outside of the black and white house.

"He's using a quadrascopic camera," explained Marc.

"Like the ones we use for snooping under doors?"

"You're thinking of *endoscopic*," he snapped. "Different thing. This is expensive gear. Records multiple overlapping images to render video in 3D."

"Why the hell would anyone want pictures like that of this house?" Marc lifted up the video glasses on to his forehead. Lucy stood close at hand, peering around at the walls. "You think maybe they documented the whole snatch-and-grab?"

He thought on that for a second. In the modern arena

of covert ops, helmet- or gun-camera footage from state-sanctioned missions was streamed live to a tactical operations center, so that commanders in another location could watch events unfold in real time. Part of Marc's duties back when he had been a field technician in the British security services had been to safeguard those digital feeds from his OpTeam, making sure they were transmitted safely back to Vauxhall Cross for the viewing pleasure of the armchair generals in the room.

But that didn't seem right. The set-up, the gear the unknowns were using and the way they were using it, didn't fit the hypothesis.

"There's more going on here than we know," said Marc, after a moment.

Lucy grimaced, the expression marring her face.

"Same as it ever was. This whole deal is gonna be us playing catch-up, believe it."

Marc could only nod in agreement.

— FIVE —

When they pulled up outside the main entrance of the MaxaBio campus, the first thing Marc noticed was the row of windowless blue vans parked off to one side, in the lab's service area. He shot Lucy a look and she nodded back at him.

"Yeah, I'm thinking the same," she replied, before he could voice his thoughts. "It's not a coincidence. Hide in plain sight."

"Police are here," added Malte from the driver's seat, pointing with the fingers of his hand atop the steering wheel. There was a white Hyundai patrol cruiser with red and blue stripes on the hood on the other side of the car park, next to another sedan that was obviously a plain-clothes unit.

"We'll tread carefully, then."

Marc threw Lucy a nod and grabbed his pack, sliding out into the rain.

The two of them jogged across the wet asphalt to the modernist glass awning that fronted the lab's reception area, but even across the short distance, the downpour soaked them both. Shaking it off as best they could, the pair passed inside and Marc took in the place. The reception was all clean lines of white and silver, with scattered planters of cacti and a two-story sculpture in the shape of a DNA strand.

"Décor by the Apple Store," Marc said, out of the side of his mouth. "Hi-tech and flavorless."

"I'd bet that's deliberate," Lucy replied, catching sight of a large MaxaBio logo on the far wall. "Camouflage. They don't want rivals figuring out what they have going on here."

Beneath the company logo was a smaller panel that read A SUBSIDIARY OF THE RUBICON GROUP.

"Corporate espionage?" Marc sounded out the words. "That's as good a motive as any. Maybe we need to look closer to home for who's behind this, instead of at the Hermit Kingdom . . ."

He trailed off as a tall young man in cargo shorts and a polo shirt came across the reception toward them, intercepting Marc and Lucy before they went too far.

"Hello, hello." Assim Kader smiled and gave Marc's hand a perfunctory shake, but the faux-eager grin didn't reach his eyes. "Keep walking, come with me, and don't look back over there."

The young Saudi technician cradled a tablet computer in the crook of his arm, and he blinked at them from behind his thick-rimmed glasses.

"Back where?"

Despite himself, Marc couldn't stop from taking a peek. He saw a couple of uniformed Singaporean cops and a severe man in a black suit. They appeared to be grilling a member of the MaxaBio staff, the man in the suit punctuating his questions with sharp jabbing motions.

"Don't draw their attention," insisted Assim.

His enunciation was cut-glass Received Pronunciation English, the legacy of a childhood in the best British boarding schools that money could buy, and it was the polar opposite of Marc's rough-edged South London accent. Assim Kader was the Special Conditions

Division's cybersecurity expert, or as he liked to joke, their "hacker without portfolio."

Thin and animated by a constant nervous energy, Assim had been pushed into the front rank a year ago when the SCD's previous digital warfare specialist Kara Wei had gone rogue in pursuit of her own agenda. Months later, Marc still couldn't bring himself to call what Kara had done a "betrayal," something that Lucy was more than happy to do. Kara and Lucy had been friends, after a fashion, and the other operative had not taken it well.

For his part, Assim was still struggling to find his rhythm in the team. He was smart and sharp, and his skills behind a keyboard were the equal of Marc's—or better on his best day—but he still didn't have the confidence he needed to be in the field. That was plain right now, as he hustled Marc and Lucy toward a side door, the unease coming off him in waves.

"Here, take these."

Assim handed them a couple of smartcard passes on lanyards, and they followed him through the door and back out to a covered walkway. The fat, heavy drops of subtropical rain clattered off the metal roofing over their heads.

"We didn't expect the locals to be back here again," he explained, his words coming thick and fast. "Not so soon, anyway. Someone at police headquarters downtown has got it into their head that this is a giant insurance scam of some kind, and I suppose they have good cause to—"

"Slow down, mate," said Marc. "Take a breath and bring us up to speed."

"Right. Of course." Assim made a show of breathing in and out. "Okay. Sorry. I've been at this since last night, haven't even gone back to base . . ." He beckoned them again and they started walking toward another building in the campus. "So the police scene-of-crime team swept the Lam house first and told us about the blank security logs."

"Yeah, we went there, we saw," said Lucy.

"We have the same thing in this place." Assim pointed at a monitor camera on the walkway as they passed it. "On the morning the Lams were abducted, a robbery took place right here. Someone spliced into the main hard line, right to the core security server, flushed the lot of it."

"A robbery?" echoed Marc.

He nodded. "They drove straight on to the campus using Doctor Lam's pass. She was with them."

"In a blue van with no windows." Marc jerked a thumb at one of the parked vehicles.

"The same as MaxaBio uses." Assim's eyes widened. "How did you know that?"

Pausing, checking to make sure they were not being observed, Marc handed over the 360-degree camera module to the other man.

"Failsafe from the house. Our scumbags didn't know it was there."

"Huh." Assim took the camera and turned it over in his long-fingered hands. "Well, I'll be buggered. This is the best thing I've seen since I arrived. And the footage is intact?"

Marc nodded. "Don't get your hopes up, there's not much to work from. Two vehicles took the family, there's visuals on the number plates, images of the kid-nappers—"

"They wore masks, right?" Assim passed a hand over his face. "There were a couple of eyewitnesses here when the robbery started."

They reached another door and he opened it to let them through.

"So what happened?" said Lucy.

"I've built up a rough timeline," Assim explained.

Marc nodded, listening with half an ear as he looked around. This building was as bright and steely as the other one, but it was clearly a working facility. Compartmentalized lab chambers sat like giant plastic cubes inside the echoing, warehouse-like space of the facility, interconnected by sealed walkways and safety airlocks. The fat silver snakes of air purification and circulation systems dangled down from catwalks along the ceiling, keeping the internal environments of the lab modules within a strict set of limits. There was only a skeleton staff on duty, he noted, half a dozen people in lab coats or anti-contaminant suits working at centrifuges and microscopes.

This was just one of the lab clusters that MaxaBio—and by extension, the Rubicon Group—were using to crack the genetic code of cancer, in the hope of one day eradicating the disease forever. Marc had lost his mother to it, ultimately, when complications due to kidney failure took her down a road there was no coming back from. He chewed on that bleak memory for a moment, then shuttered the thought away.

Not the time to dwell on that, he told himself, and tuned back in to Assim's explanation.

"We've kept this quiet for now, but it looks certain that Doctor Lam was helping the masked men. Our witnesses fled, but they saw enough to confirm. She brought them on site, and her pass code and identity badge were used to access this building and the main storage area around this corner—"

They turned as the corridor branched into a junction and Assim stopped dead. Marc and Lucy both caught the odor of old blood; she reacted by tensing, unconsciously ready for conflict, he by dropping back a step. There was a set of temporary folding panels made from translucent plastic standing up against one wall, arranged to cordon off a section of the corridor. The same yellow crime scene tape that had been around the Lam house, with its *Do Not Cross* warnings in English, Malay, Tamil and Mandarin looped around the panels. Marc's eye was unerringly drawn to what might be hidden behind them. He thought he could make out a dark, discolored patch on the wall.

"They killed a man here. One of the security guards," Assim said quietly. "Shotgun, at close range. He . . . uh . . . He had two children."

"We know why?" Lucy said, her tone hard.

"As far as I can determine, he was just . . . in their way."

"Did the police find a spent cartridge?" It was an effort for Marc to look away. Assim shook his head, and he considered the silent reply. "So these pricks either picked up after themselves or they used shell traps on their weapons. That shows forethought."

"Another tick in the column for an experienced crew," noted Lucy. "The masks, the cameras, no casings . . . They're trying to leave as little evidence of who they are as possible."

"But killing a man who couldn't see their faces, that's unnecessary. It's vicious." Marc shook his head.

"This isn't what I wanted to show you." Assim was becoming animated again, eager to be away from the area. "As far as I can determine, the robbery took place up here."

They passed through another set of coded locks and emerged in the storage section. All around, refrigerated containers held chemical compounds and there were tanks for liquid storage, as well as pallets of scientific hardware in plastic shrink-wrap and large equipment cases. The storage area was easily the size of a small warehouse, extending back to the full length of the building.

Marc surveyed the racks as they walked between them.

"What did they take?"

"I don't know yet." Assim walked to one of the racks and tapped on a barcode sticker indicating its location and contents. "Everything in here, from test tubes to fractionators, is logged and recorded in a central materials database." He indicated a drum of reactant fluid, which had a similar barcode tag attached to it. "These tags contain a radio frequency ID circuit, like you have in a credit card or a travel pass. Active sensors in the building talk to the campus database, which automatically logs items out as they get used, replacements are automatically ordered, that sort of thing."

"So if something is missing, the system will know it," said Lucy. "I wanna say *problem solved*, but you're giving me the wrong vibe."

He nodded. "The hack that tanked the security monitors also shut down the RFID monitoring array, allowing whoever kidnapped Lam to take whatever they wanted and leave no trace. I haven't been able to get it back up and running."

Marc leaped straight to the next logical step.

"Someone has to do a manual inventory and find out what's missing, yeah?"

Assim's shoulders drooped. "I already have people on it, but we're looking at a day, maybe two, to check it all."

"These creeps *already* have a seventy-two hour head start on us," said Lucy. "We gotta do better than that."

"I know . . . I know," Assim said wearily, a note of self-reproach entering his voice. "I'm sorry. I'm doing the best I can here. I know Kara would have had a better handle on this—"

"That's bollocks," Marc cut in. "You're here because

you're the best we've got, mate. Work your end of the problem, we'll try the other angles."

"The footage from the back-up camera at the house," said Lucy, "Rubicon has their image analysis geeks in Palo Alto, they love a challenge. Send it to them, they can rip it apart frame by frame, maybe find something we missed."

Assim gave her a look. "No can do. While you were in transit, Delancort sent out a new directive. You didn't see it?"

"I don't like the sound of that." Marc shook his head. "We went straight to it, to the house. We didn't check in with the crisis center in Monaco yet."

"Ah." Assim nodded again. "All right. Well, I don't know the full details, but the long and the short of it is, the Rubicon Group's board of directors are reviewing the operations of the Special Conditions Division. Apparently there have been some . . . concerns."

Marc remembered Solomon's manner when they had been talking in the virtual conference room. *Terse, even distracted.* Now he understood why.

"*Reviewing,*" echoed Lucy. "Which rhymes with *dicking around with.*"

"Quite," agreed Assim. "As such, the option of deploying any additional Rubicon Group assets is on hold. For now."

"It's Solomon's company, isn't it?" said Marc. "Why can't he do what he likes with it?"

"Sometimes, even a billionaire has to answer to someone," noted Assim. "I mean, if we are being honest, the SCD does skirt the edge of legality." He paused. "Often. It was only a matter of time before someone noticed."

"Solomon is Rubicon, but Rubicon is not Solomon." As usual, Lucy cut straight to the heart of it.

"Okay, I suppose we're on our own, then."

Marc wanted to add something more, but then he heard the security door opening and through the lines of the racks, he glimpsed the man in the black suit—a detective, he guessed—stride in with the pair of uniformed cops at his side.

"You should go," said Assim, looking the same way. "That brisk gentleman has already put me through the wringer, demanding to know why Rubicon sent in an external technician to deal with this. He thinks we're covering something up."

"He's not wrong," said Lucy.

Assim shook his head. "The point is, he gets hold of you two, he'll put you in a locked room for hours and ask you the same questions over and over."

"And that's not time we have to waste," concluded Marc. "Look, Assim. Throw the bloke a bone, yeah? Tell him about the vans we saw, give him the numbers to run. That'll keep him sweet." He beckoned to Lucy. "Come on, we'll sneak out the other way."

"I'll be in touch," Assim called after them, as they slipped away.

The stench of the slums was unlike anything Saito had encountered, and he had visited many places where hardship and poverty wound together in a lethal, inescapable spiral of decay.

Dharavi had the dubious honor of being known as the largest slum in Asia. It dwarfed the favelas he had seen in Brazil and the trash-laden landscape of Ciudad Neza in Mexico City. It was a rancid network of hovels built from recycled plastic sheeting, cinder blocks and repurposed wood. Boiling up from the hide of Mumbai, the veins of the shantytown were open sewers thick with stagnant water fouled by human effluent. What had once been a mangrove swamp was now a chaotic sprawl thick with activity.

Buildings crowded in on one another, in some places so close they created narrow alleyways barely wide enough for a person to pass through. Saito was reminded of the backstreets of his native Tokyo, where small homes were similarly tightly packed and byways were constricted. But it was a world apart from the clean, moderated city of his youth. Dharavi was a wild explosion of human community, messy and foul. It had the character of something that had bloomed like a fungal growth, rooting into Mumbai so deeply it could never be dislodged.

Above his head, webs of cable snaked between makeshift poles, supporting lines for power hijacked from the city grid or stolen telecoms. The ever-present stink of stale excrement was overpowering, and as he traveled further into the slum, Saito expected to become habituated to it—but that moment never came.

The oppressive heat made it worse. It made everything an effort, exacerbated by the aches from Saito's healed injuries, clustering around the sites of bullet hits and stab wounds. It aggravated the fragments of a 7.62 rifle round that the Combine's doctors hadn't been able to dig out of him. Years after he had earned that mark on a rusting gas platform off the Somalian coastline, the pain still gnawed at him like a parasite burrowing into his back. He dry-swallowed a mild analgesic before moving on. Saito would not risk taking anything stronger, for fear it might slow his reflexes.

Poring over aerial shots from drones and documents that approximated maps, he had committed his destination to memory. Dharavi's structure was not easy to navigate without a guide, but Saito was an accomplished city-stalker and the rules he applied in Tokyo, London, Moscow or Rio de Janeiro worked equally well in the Indian metropolis. Fixing the location of a nearby mosque through the reeking, dusty haze across the early morning sun, he picked his way down a shallow incline and crossed a patch of barren, exposed earth. A cluster of schoolchildren passed him going the other way, incongruous in their neat uniforms amid the squalor, and he cut through an open shed where old men were shredding discarded plastic bottles into strips with wicked knives.

Despite the grinding poverty, the dirt and the smell, Dharavi was alive with activity. It teemed with people and a clever kind of industry that fed off the refuse dumped upon it. An entire society operating freely under its own rules, far removed from the rest of the world.

Which made it an ideal place for one of the most wanted men on Earth to go to ground. Saito's quarry was here. A lion hidden amid these sheep, biding his time.

Eventually Saito emerged into a kind of courtyard, where four buildings formed the walls around a sunken section of old roadway. He waited under a sheet-metal awning, watching a pair of old men engaged in an energetic argument over something. They didn't notice him.

This was the place. It matched the images from the drone, the most likely location for the target to be concealing himself. Saito looked up and scanned the upper floors of the two-story shanty-buildings, finding one that had the best lines of sight. He was about to step out of the shade and make for the door when another thought occurred to him, and he froze.

It is *a good position*, he thought. *Too good, in fact.*

His quarry was a shrewd, calculating man, and not the sort to pick the obvious choice. His target had set up that location as a lure, to draw anyone coming after him into a dead end.

And to be sure, the target would need to be close. He would need to be able to see anyone entering or leaving.

There.

The building to the south, its upper walls corrugated iron and undulating sheets of blue plastic moving in the breeze. A staircase made of scrap wood climbed the exterior to a door made from a repurposed advertising billboard.

The steps creaked loudly with each footfall, and he made no attempt to quiet his ascent. This was not a man to sneak up on, Glovkonin had warned him, but in truth, Saito was not as nimble as he once was.

The makeshift door had no lock, and he eased it open, entering the hot enclosed space beyond. The room was basic: a sleeping pallet and a low table at the far end, a cooking plate next to a solar cell at the foot of the bed. A pile of dog-eared paperbacks sat beside a folding lawn chair. Tubular metal bars had been erected to the other side, making a crude exercise frame. It looked like a soldier's quarters, bereft of anything that had no tactical value.

Saito stepped inside, opening his hands to show he wasn't armed. The air was close and heavy with humidity.

"I am not here to kill you," he said, in English.

"So says the assassin."

The voice came from a corner of the room drenched in daylight, and a figure moved out of it toward him. Saito blinked and there was a muscular man with a silenced pistol in his hand in the room with him. Naked from the waist up, his flesh was a deep bronze and filmed with perspiration. He had dark, furious eyes in a patrician face, framed by black hair that was graying at the temples.

The man was panting; Saito assumed he had caught his quarry in the middle of exercising on the frame. He imagined the Egyptian had little else to do while marking time and waiting.

"You know who sent me," he offered.

"The Russian."

Saito nodded. "He has work for you. If I may?" He indicated the bag hanging over his shoulder, and on the other man's wary nod, he slipped it off. "The details are here." He showed him the files inside. "You should destroy this when you have assimilated the information."

The pistol dropped away.

"I have done this before." He paused. "You know who I am, yes?"

"Anyone who pays attention to the war on terror knows who Omar Khadir is," Saito said levelly. "Former officer in the Egyptian Army. Senior cell commander of the Al Sayf Islamist extremist group. Wanted fugitive."

"The *war on terror*," Khadir repeated, with a sneer. "As if there could ever be such a thing." He took the bag and moved to the low table, emptying the contents on to it. "Terror is not a foe that can be defeated. It washes in and out like the tides, but the ocean it comes from remains."

Saito resisted the urge to engage with the man, but the reality was that the tide had gone out a long way for Khadir. Al Sayf was virtually nonexistent, all but a few of its cells hunted into extinction by the American military, after Khadir's plan to kill the president had been thwarted. The CIA and the Secret Service took credit for stopping the attack, but the reality was more complex. It had been agents of Rubicon who had disrupted the plot.

Al Sayf's bold strike only progressed as far as it did thanks to the funding of the Combine, one part of their complex plans to enrich the group of power brokers and maintain a profitable level of discord in the nation states of the West. But in the ashes of his failure, Khadir—the amoral nihilist, the killer and schemer—had lost everything that had defined him.

Never one to waste a useful asset, as Saito knew only too well, Pytor Glovkonin had secretly protected Khadir, given him somewhere to hide—and a purpose as well.

I wonder what he has promised this man, thought Saito. *The chance to take his vengeance on those who wronged him? But only after Glovkonin's own agenda is served, of course.*

"Who are you to him?" said Khadir, as he pawed though the files. "A messenger? That seems a poor task for a soldier."

"I do my duty." Saito stood there, watching.

"You do what he tells you to," Khadir snapped. "I watched you, climbing the stairs. Stiff. Out of step. You were hurt serving the Russian's needs, yes? But still you march on. Proud and stoic." Now he looked up and met his gaze. "A Japanese. Like the Samurai of your ancient history." He nodded to himself. "I've read Nitobe's *Bushido* and Tsunetomo's *Hagakure*. I understand the loyalty of the faithful retainer to his lord. The matter of honor, even if the man who commands you is himself faithless."

"Tsunetomo was only a clerk," noted Saito. "He never carried a weapon."

"But you parry words as if you have a sword," countered Khadir. He walked away from the table, working the joint of his shoulder. "Yes. I think I know you."

The man's penetrating gaze made Saito's jaw stiffen. He was close to a truth that Saito did not want to study too closely.

"What does the Russian have over you, Samurai? It cannot just be duty and nothing more. Someone you care for, perhaps? Something you fear will be revealed?"

The simmering, steady anger underlying everything about the Egyptian rose, becoming visible.

"You will never know," Saito said, at length, and he was immediately irritated at himself. Even those meager words were an admission of sorts.

Khadir stepped back, smiling thinly at the little victory he had gained.

"I am going to kill him. When the moment is right." He paused, considering his own statement. "If you stand in my way, you'll fall with him."

"You believe you have nothing to lose. But there is always something. The . . . Russian is adept at finding what is meant to stay hidden."

"Like this?" Khadir tapped a finger on the files. "I see a man here. A person who has been erased from the world by his own masters, and yet not granted the dignity of a good death. *Any* death, in fact." He plucked out a blurry, blown-up photo of a Chinese man, malnourished, dejected and bleak of gaze, offering it to Saito. "Lau." He toyed with the name attached to the image. "This man is like us. You see it, don't you? In his eyes?"

Saito said nothing.

The other man shrugged and returned to the papers.

"Where did this data come from?" He looked at the maps and reference documents. "It's extensive, indeed, but how old is it?"

"Approximately eight months," Saito told him. "It

was gathered by a team of hackers . . . Their services have unfortunately been terminated. We have had their data corroborated as closely as possible."

"Eight months is forever," Khadir snapped. "Every factor here could be invalid."

"That is true. But you are capable of adapting to a fluid scenario. Mr. Glovkonin is confident you will be successful in locating the captive."

Khadir looked at the photo again.

"Who is this man? Why is he so significant?"

"Lau is a means to an end."

"What end?"

"The destruction of Ekko Solomon and the Rubicon Group."

Saito had been given permission to reveal that fact, although he knew little of how Lau might bring that about.

It had the desired effect, however. Khadir's dark eyes flashed at the mention the name.

"You should have led with that," he replied. "So. This man, is he to die?"

"This is a recovery, not an assassination. You are to secure Lau and get him out alive."

Khadir grunted. "I will need equipment. Transport. Papers. Weapons."

Saito produced an encrypted sat-phone and handed it over.

"Already taken care of. A vehicle is on station, waiting to take you from . . ." He gestured at the walls, letting his disgust show. "All this."

Khadir pocketed the phone.

"You don't like this place? The filth and the stink, you are disgusted by it." He showed his teeth. "You don't understand. This slum, this place is *true*. It is the world, Samurai. Humans living ankle-deep in their own shit. But the difference here is, they are free of the lies that try to hide it. Here, you can see the whole truth at once." The Egyptian pointed at him. "You could use some of that perspective."

"I see clearly enough," said Saito, and it almost sounded as if it were true.

Allowing her to go outside was the first remotely human thing her captors had done since the moment the woman in the mask stepped into her home.

They gave her a heavy coat and allowed her to see the sky for the first time in what had to be days, to breathe in the open air and take a moment to reflect on her changed fortunes.

They didn't send a guard after her, and she wondered why until the door opened and the icy chill hit the bare flesh of her face. She was confronted by a stark, alien landscape that vanished toward a cloudless blue horizon in the near distance. Black volcanic earth extended away in all directions, broken only by the shapes of steel geodesic domes and concrete bunkers, interconnected by metal pipes. Low chimney stacks vented massive plumes of brilliant white vapor into the air, the hard and constant wind pulling the trails over until they were parallel with the ground.

There was no fence, no guard towers with sharpshooters as she expected. There was no need for them. The obvious remoteness of this place, the desolation of it—those were the walls to stop her from running. To flee would be to risk exposure and death.

The hard cold was familiar; it reminded her of a time at a research base in the Taebaek Mountain range where she had worked in the first years of her enforced military service. But the dryness of it, that was very different.

The French woman ignored every question she had put to her, and no one explained where she had been brought. At each stage, she hoped that she was at the end of the nightmare, but with every new revelation, she was only falling deeper and deeper into the abyss.

At the lab, she had given them what they wanted, accessing the storage facility and the MaxaBio research database. She watched them load their van, the echo of the shot that had killed the security guard still ringing in her ears.

His name had been Ko. She had never really spoken to him, only nodded vaguely as they passed in the corridors. Now he was dead because of her. Another life taken, and added to her burden. The line of ghosts trailing her was already so long, she was afraid to look behind her in case it became visible. Afraid that Simon and Michael might have joined it.

Thinking of them made her next breath turn into a shudder, an almost-sob that she stifled by putting her gloved hands over her mouth. Still, it escaped through her fingers in a thin white mist, dragged away by the chilling breeze. She thought of the two of them, of the disbelief in their eyes slowly turning to betrayal. Susan had lied to them about so much—about who she was, about the woman she had been before knowing a life with them.

Susan Lam was the fabrication she had fooled herself into thinking was real; scratch the surface and beneath was Ji-Yoo Park, the defector who had fled her home carrying a lifetime of guilt and a deadly secret.

The sickening fear and the remorse were heavy like lead, and she held herself tightly, trying hard to hold back the need to cry. She had already wept, long and mournful, as she rode out the journey that had brought her to this place. After the house, after the lab, the French woman had forced her into a cargo container, the kind they carried in the belly of an aircraft. They gave her this coat and gloves, some food and water, a bucket, and then locked her in.

She sat in the corner and waited for the end. She cried until fatigue dragged her into a dreamless sleep, waking now and then to hear the vibration of jet engines coming up through the ice-cold decking. She lost track of time, convinced that they were taking her home, back to the North she had abandoned. Later, she awoke to juddering motion and the thudding of rotor blades. She called out for help, but someone outside smashed a fist into the metal and that silenced her. It was torture, being trapped in that steel box with only the worst of her terrors to keep her company.

But when the hatch was opened and she staggered out into the light, there was no firing squad awaiting her, no men in uniform ready to judge her for traitorous acts against the Dear Leader.

The French woman and the others brought her to another laboratory, appointed with banks of the most advanced digital biomodeling systems she had ever seen.

"This is where you are going to work," said the woman. "Make yourself comfortable."

And then she saw what they wanted her to do.

The gasp-sob came again, and this time she couldn't hold it in. Her eyes misted with tears and she took a half step away, the urge dying before it was fully formed.

If only I had the courage to kill myself, she thought. *Then they would have nothing.*

But the French woman had been quite clear on that matter. Any act of rebellion, large or small, would be taken in kind by punishing Simon and Michael.

Her hands shook. For the first time in years, she desperately wanted a cigarette, but, like her old life, that vice was something she had left behind in the North.

Behind her, boots crunched on the frost-rimed earth.

"I know that look," said a voice in Korean. "Here, take one."

She turned around and saw a ghost.

"Kyun?"

He wore the same winter jacket she did, his oval, pockmarked face peering at her. He was offering a packet, a single cigarette extended from it like a gift.

"Yes." He waved them at her. "Go on, take it."

She gave in and snatched the cigarette up, shakily putting it to her lips. Kyun produced a butane lighter, lit hers, and then took one for himself.

She pulled on a long inhale, and at first her lungs rebelled. But the taste was embedded in her memory, and in a moment it settled.

"Are these . . . ?"

He showed her the distinctive red packet with its gold lettering.

"Lake Samilpo," said Kyun, referring to the make. "I tried often but I couldn't stop," he added, with a chuckle.

In a rush, the incongruity of it caught up to her and she shook her head violently.

"No. *No!* What is happening?"

She stared at the cigarette in her hand. A North Korean brand? And who better to give them to her than a man she had left behind there when she fled?

"How are you here? Where *is* here? What is going on?"

"Calm yourself," said Kyun, with that sly little smile of his she had always loathed. He reached out and patted her on the arm, oozing insincerity. "That isn't important. What matters is that you do what you are told." He flashed what he thought was a friendly grin, but to her it seemed like a sneer. "Dear Ji-Yoo. This doesn't have to be an ordeal!"

His mendacious tone pushed her over the edge and she exploded.

"An ordeal? Do you know what I have gone through? I was abducted, my husband and stepson stolen from me, my life ruined—"

"Your fake life?" Kyun snapped, and his expression shifted in an instant, becoming hard and unsympathetic. "Do not shout at me! I am your superior!"

She couldn't count how many times he had said that to her, before. But even if he outranked her, Kyun was half the scientist that she was, and he knew it.

"No longer!"

"Wrong!" he spat back. "You always thought you were better than the rest of us, didn't you, Park?" His face reddened and he waved the lit cigarette in her face. "Do you know what they did to us when you ran away? Ch'oe and Khoo were executed in front of the laboratory when they didn't denounce you swiftly enough! The rest of us were suspects just because we worked alongside you!"

"Khoo?" She shook her head. "No, I told him . . ."

Words failed her as she imagined the technician's smiling face.

More deaths added to my bill.

"I was beaten every day for a week!" snarled Kyun. "To make sure I was not your co-conspirator!" He took a shaky breath, forcibly calming himself. "Eventually they relented. But the wreckage you left behind, Park. Did you ever stop to think about what your selfish act did to the rest of us, when you were living your bourgeois new life in the West?"

"Every day," she admitted, her burst of rage faltering. "So this is my penance, then? My past catching up with me?"

Kyun gave a callous snort. "The Homeland is a long way behind us both," he said, regaining his unctuous manner. "I left too . . . When these people made our leaders a better offer, they traded me. Like a player of football." He laughed at his own joke.

"What people?"

"They call themselves the Combine. They have a . . . singular vision for order that I must admit is quite attractive." He took a long draw on his cigarette. "You don't need to know the details. It's enough to say they recruited me because of our experience with the *Geulimja* program."

"Those machines . . . You've been rebuilding it here . . ."

She felt the blood drain from her face at the horror of that idea. Then another connection came together in her thoughts.

"I am here because of *you*." She let her cigarette drop and backed away from the grinning man. "You could never put it together, that's why *Geulimja* was a failure. You never had the insight!"

"But *you* did," said Kyun. "I see now that my past discrimination toward you because of your gender was in error . . . Back home, I should have been more observant! You knew all along how to make the design work correctly, you just hid that knowledge from the rest of us. Because you were weak! And by the time I realized that, you had already defected." He spread his hands and chuckled again. "But now we have a second chance to finish what we started."

She saw it now. Kyun had always disrespected her, even in the early days, after she had deflected both his advances and his attempts to claim the credit for her lab work. That enmity had hardened into something vicious and spiteful, after her defection had destroyed his plans to rise high in the DPRK's scientific community. His hatred and jealousy for her would have made it easy for him to have her new life obliterated in kind.

And he was revelling in it.

"You are reaping what you have sown, dear Ji-Yoo. I told the Combine how to find you, what to look for. I knew you were arrogant enough that you could not live a quiet life in the West. I knew you would have to indulge your foolish ideals somewhere. And they unmasked you, *Susan Lam*, even when our own nation could not." He laughed again. "You could have vanished and become a no one and this would not have happened! But you had to seek the path of glory, didn't you? The cure for cancer—as if being a part of that would wash away the blood on your hands."

"No." She shook her head. "I never wanted anyone to suffer!"

Kyun made a mock-serious face.

"All those unfortunates who perished in the experimental phases—the prisoners, the dissidents, traitors and foreigners, the ones there were no use for. Your flaw was your inability to see them for what they were. An expendable resource." He shook his head. "Not that it matters. We are almost done. Almost." Kyun held up his hand, the thumb and forefinger a short span apart. "This close. But that last assemblage phase was always where we failed. I know you know how to complete it."

I will not help you.

The words formed in her thoughts, but they were trapped there, unable to escape her. If she uttered them, she would destroy her husband and stepson.

The door leading back to the lab banged open and the French woman stepped out, looking around.

"Here they are," she said to a man who followed her out.

The man was broad-shouldered and shaven-headed, and he had a pitiless gaze that locked on to Kyun like a searchlight. Kyun flinched as the woman strode over to him, his fear of her writ large across his face. The man followed, his gait lazy and menacing.

"We are . . . uh . . . We . . ."

Kyun switched to English, stumbling over the words. He was trying to find something to say to mollify the French woman, and failing dismally.

"This is her." The man pointed in Susan's direction. "Park. The one you need?"

Kyun nodded. "Yes. Yes. We'll be able to finish now." He was absolutely terrified of the two black-clad Westerners. "It won't take long."

"Forty-eight hours," said the woman. "We need to stay on track."

The man was still pointing at Susan, but glaring at Kyun as if he was a distasteful insect to be crushed beneath his boot.

"Does she know what she has to do? Did you explain it to her?"

"I . . . I did, I did," managed Kyun, with a weak smile. "Park will comply, I promise."

"Then get to it," snapped the man, dropping his arm and turning away.

She started after him.

"Who are you?" She shouted the words at his back.

He halted, and then shot Susan a savage smirk.

"I am the one holding your leash. So be a good little bitch and obey your master."

— SIX —

It was late afternoon by the time they returned to the temporary base of operations set up for the Special Conditions Division. Marc expected Malte to drive them into Singapore's business district, where the Rubicon Group had a slick branch office in the giant Capital Tower building, but instead they sped by the off-ramp and past the dense tropical greensward of Telok Blangah Hill Park, heading into an upmarket condominium complex.

Singapore was a city bristling with unusual and challenging architecture, and this place was no exception. Craning his head to get a better look from the SUV's passenger seat, what Marc saw resembled a strange hexagonal construction of apartment blocks, white six-story chunks piled one atop another at oblique angles that connected in unexpected ways.

"Looks like someone crossed a skyscraper with a Rubik's cube," he noted.

"*The Interlace,*" said Lucy, reading the name off a sign near the entrance. "Huh. Very cyberpunk."

He had to admit it was. A lot of Singapore had that sci-fi *Blade Runner* vibe that appealed to the city kid in Marc, but there was also something artificial about it. The whole place seemed a little too engineered for his tastes.

They drove into an underground car park and Malte handed them keys.

"Suites for all of us," he noted. "Connecting room in the middle, for ops."

Marc nodded approvingly at the shape of the mechanical, non-digital key. Smartcards were too easy to hack, a fact he had often exploited himself. He grabbed his bag and stifled an unexpected yawn, glancing at the scruffy, weather-beaten Cabot dive watch on his wrist. He hadn't set it to the local time, and jet lag from the journey was still messing about with his body clock.

"Why are we set up here instead of the local office?"

"You heard what Assim said." Lucy took her gear from the back of the SUV and followed him toward the elevators as Malte parked the vehicle. "Maybe Solomon is trying to keep this on the down-low. Off the books."

Marc eyed her. "I thought he owned the books."

She shrugged off the reply, but he could tell she was wondering the same thing.

They rode an elevator to one of the uppermost blocks, the floor numbers pinging off the indicator as they rose. Marc caught himself studying the tension in the muscles of Lucy's spare, athletic back through her skin-tight workout top and told himself it was purely out of concern for his teammate.

"What?" she said suddenly, without turning around. "I can almost hear you keeping your mouth shut. I know something's been bothering you since the house. Spit it out."

His first impulse was to deflect the comment, but she was right. Something was on his mind.

"Tell me about Park."

"I already told you," she replied. "She defected. I got her out. Rubicon set her up a new identity here."

"I was hoping for a little more than the high points."

"What else do you wanna know?" Lucy said it like she really meant *shut the hell up*.

The elevator slowed and deposited them on the top floor. Marc followed her out into the deserted corridor, automatically scanning around for points of egress and shady corners. He wasn't going to let the other thing drop, though.

"So how did Rubicon know what Park was doing inside North Korea? How did they know she was working on weapons of mass destruction?"

"Solomon has a lot of contacts, you know that."

Lucy unlocked the door and entered the central suite. A large open room branched off toward bedrooms, bathrooms and a basic but well-stocked kitchen. Some equipment had already been laid out, with computers and communications gear powered up but set in sleep mode.

"Why do you care?"

Her tone was becoming defensive, but Marc pressed on, unwilling to let it drop.

"The boss plays his cards close to his chest. I've been inside the SCD for a couple of years now, but every so often, I trip over something that tells me there's a dozen other secrets for each one I can see."

"That's about right."

"Yeah, well . . ." He dropped his pack on the sofa and sat heavily, while Lucy stalked around the room. "It's not like when I was at Six, when I could get read in on a higher STRAP clearance if I needed it. I'm either trusted or I'm not." Marc fixed her with a steady look. "Which is it?"

Lucy's eyes narrowed. "Listen, if you'd seen what I saw, the human trials they were doing . . . It was a weaponized virus, Dane, a project called *Geulimja*. Korean for *Shadow*. AKA, a fucked-up cocktail of some seriously nasty shit. You heard of Marburg, right?"

He nodded slowly. "Viral hemorrhagic fever. Basically, the Ebola bug with the dial turned up to 11."

"Yeah," she said coldly. "You get infected with it and your guts slowly turn into slurry, you puke out your insides. It's goddamn *horrific*, is what it is. That was what they were basing Shadow on. They were trying to make it *worse*."

He took that in. Part of Marc's analyst work at MI6 had been threat studies before he moved into field support, and he recalled the grisly facts of hazard files that had crossed his desk, each dealing with the potential casualties of a virus-based attack on a British city.

In the bad old days of the Cold War, the Soviet Union ran a program called "Vektor" that worked toward developing the Marburg virus into something suitable for battlefield deployment—but they hadn't been able to tame the lethal bug, and some rumors alleged that it had broken containment in one of their labs, killing dozens of their top researchers.

All at once, a missing piece of the story snapped into place. Marc was always good at seeing the connections between fragments of data, and he saw them now.

"Solomon didn't send you in there to get Park out. He sent you to neutralize her."

"I really hate it when you do that," Lucy grated. "Yeah. Right. Because that's what the SCD does, that's Solomon's crusade. Small actions leading to big consequences, right? And terminating the key researcher developing a catastrophic bioweapon for a rogue state would fit the bill." She leaned up against the wall, fading into a pool of shadow cast by the room's half-drawn blinds, unconsciously concealing herself before she went on. "But it got complicated, like it always does."

Lucy gave him the story in snapshots, skipping from one to another, never dwelling long on one element.

A dissident group in North Korea that Rubicon had contact with got Lucy over the border and close to the military hospital where Park was working. Under a stormy sky, she tracked her down, in the frame, ready to commit. It was going to be a close-quarters assassination, choking her out. Lucy had already prepared to send Park and her car to the bottom of a local ravine, make it look like an accident.

If that sounded cold, she had good reason. Infiltrating the hospital took Lucy past furnaces where the bodies of test subjects were being burned, in rooms right next to the dirty, iron-walled cells where those still alive were dying in agony. The enemies of the nation, be they petty criminals, the disloyal or just the unlucky, were used as live fodder for the Shadow program. Lucy's tone hardened as she told Marc of the stink of stale blood, of how the place reeked of death. What she saw there hardened Lucy's determination to complete her mission.

"Didn't work out that way," she noted. "Turned out Ji-Yoo Park wasn't a willing player."

The woman was weeping when Lucy finally found her, up on a derelict floor of the crumbling hospital. She learned later that Park had been informed that morning of her sister's death at a labor camp. Her sister was there, not because of anything she had done wrong, but because the scientist's superiors needed something to motivate her.

"She had a pistol. Stole it from the locker of some junior officer. I watched her psyching herself up to put the barrel in her mouth and pull the trigger. If I'd let her do it, the operation would have completed itself." Lucy shook her head. "That's when I knew this had to play out differently."

All along, she admitted, Lucy had hoped that she could find a better solution than one more notch on her kill list.

"After everything I saw in there, I needed to do something *good*. Balance out the world a little. So I had to improvise, make shit up on the fly . . . Not as good at that as you, but . . . I brought her out."

Marc let Lucy find her way back from the desolate memory before pressing on.

"That still doesn't answer my question. Rubicon is a corporation, a private military and security contractor. It's not a government power. Sure, Solomon's money and his contacts open a lot of doors, but they're not MI6, they're not the CIA. How did they know about Park in the first place?"

Lucy shot a look at the door. Malte would be coming up soon, and if she was going to confide something to Marc, she would only do it while they were alone.

"There's this thing called the Gray Record . . ."

Despite himself, Marc snorted at the name.

"What, like 'the White Album'?"

She ignored the flippant comment.

"It's a secure database. Rubicon maintains files on persons of interest. Not just corporate intelligence for their business, but data for the Special Conditions Division. How else do you think Solomon picks the targets we go after in our operations? He's constantly watching, looking for troublemakers before they start to make it. Remember back in Somalia, that whole thing with the phones?"

Marc nodded. During their pursuit of the Exile nuclear device, the Rubicon team had tracked the weapon to East Africa, and a vital clue that enabled them to trace the men holding it had come from data covertly harvested from local cellular phones. That data had been sifted illegally by a telecom subsidiary of Rubicon, essentially trawling hundreds of thousands of innocent people's phone conversations. Despite their denials, government organizations like America's National Security Agency or the British GCHQ routinely flouted privacy laws by doing similar warrantless wiretaps, but for a private group like Rubicon to do the same thing . . . That was different.

At the time, the criminality of the phone taps ran a distant second to the issue of stopping a nuke from blowing a hole in the Horn of Africa, but that revelation had planted a seed of concern in Marc's mind. If Ekko Solomon—if Rubicon—had the capacity to secretly gather that kind of data, and more, where did such an action sit on Marc Dane's moral compass? If the SCD used it for the right reasons, did that make it fair? And who was the arbiter of what *the right reasons* were?

He thought about Lucy and Park. Rubicon's data had sent her to terminate that woman in order to forestall a greater horror. If someone else had been there to make that call, someone without the compassion of Lucy Keyes, an innocent woman would be dead—but then this situation would not have taken place.

Marc trusted Ekko Solomon with his life. The African was responsible for pulling him back from the brink, when his own country had declared him a traitor to the Crown and the sharks had been circling. But there was darkness in that man.

He's got a lot of secrets trailing after him.

Marc remembered a rainy afternoon in a London graveyard, and his old friend John Farrier warning him that Solomon was more dangerous than he knew.

He couldn't help but wonder what might happen if one day Rubicon went down a darker path. The thought chilled him.

"The question I keep asking myself," said Lucy, breaking his reverie, "is how the hell those black masks knew where to find Park?" She shook her head. "Did I leave something behind, a lead that took them this long to figure out? *Shit!* Is this my fault?"

Marc tried to find a reply, but before he could the door opened and Malte entered. The Finn was holding his smartphone in his hand.

"Assim has new information," said the driver.

Marc glanced back at Lucy, but the brief moment of vulnerability she had shown him was gone. She was all tactical now, straight up and tensed for action.

"Let's hear it."

Malte snapped the phone into a data cradle next to one of the computers, and a built-in video projector stuttered into life as it connected, throwing an image of the young Saudi up on one of the suite's white-painted walls.

He was in a car, the feed captured from a camera on the dashboard. Like Malte, Assim was using one of the Rubicon-issue "spyPhones," a custom-made satellite-enabled smart device that packed in the capabilities of a regular smartphone along with a bunch of other tech that was strictly black book.

"*Okay, so I am on the way back to the apartment,*" he said, the words spilling out of him in an anxious rush. "*I don't think the police are following me, but they were asking a lot of questions, I thought it best to make myself scarce—*"

"Malte says you have something?" Marc broke in. He knew from experience that Assim had a tendency to go off-piste if he wasn't kept on task.

"*Yes!*" He paused as he steered the car around a turn. "*Nanoscale bioprinters! Two of them are missing from the MaxaBio inventory. It was pure chance I checked that section of the storage before the rest . . ."*

"Bioprinters." Lucy looked at Marc, and made a winding motion with her hand. "Come on, Dane, you know how this goes, make with the nerd explanation for those of us without a subscription to *Wired*."

"It's not that hard to follow," he shot back. "You've seen 3D printers that make objects out of plastic, yeah? Same deal, but with biomaterials. You can use them to construct a cellular matrix, artificial tissues, that kind of thing."

"Replacement organs," offered Malte.

"Yeah, that too," agreed Marc. "But nanoscale units work on the really tiny stuff, building . . ." He trailed off as his train of thought caught up to what he was saying. "*Ah.*"

"I do not like that look," said Lucy. "So let's assume the black masks have Park, all the shit they need and two of those things. Worst-case scenario, what can they make?"

"The short answer?" Marc said grimly. "Anything they want. It's like dial-a-bioweapon."

"And these machines were just . . . what—lying around in a warehouse?" Lucy shook her head.

"*The bioprinter is the fabrication system,*" insisted Assim. "*The difficult part is getting a viable cell matrix design and the biomaterials to build it with.*"

She glared at the image on the wall.

"Do these fuckers seem like the kind of people who *won't* have thought of that already?"

"*No,*" admitted Assim. "*Not really.*" Then he became animated again. "*I know it sounds like I have discovered something that has made this ten times worse, and I suppose I have, but there is an upside!*"

He explained that the machines, which were worth more than a mid-range sports car, were carried in secure cases protected with a cellular tracking device.

"The printers are lo-jacked?" Lucy nodded to herself. "Okay, now we're cookin'. Where are they at?"

"*They are still in Singapore, or close by,*" said Assim. "*I need to run the signal through the processor in my gear in the apartment.*"

"I can do that." Marc dropped into the seat in front of the laptop screen. "Forward me the data."

"*Okay . . .*" Assim pulled into a lay-by and the image spun around as he grabbed the phone and tapped across its screen. "*Sending it.*"

Malte hovered at Marc's shoulder, and asked the question that was preying on everyone's mind.

"Still here, after four days?"

He didn't need to add how unlikely it was that the black masks were sitting on the tech they had stolen, but a lead was a lead. The only one they had, in point of fact.

Marc ran the cellular tracker data through the triangulating software and set a scanner subroutine running. The cell towers in Singapore were not easy to spoof, but he had an icebreaker program that could grant a brief window of access before automatic network security locked him out. It was a gamble that was worth taking. If the bioprinters were within the city limits, it would only take a few seconds to find them. He held his breath.

A low double-ping sounded from the laptop and two red dots—right on top of each other—winked into existence on a map overlay. Marc's jaw dropped open and he had to recheck the data to be sure.

"I have a hit . . . It's close! I mean, like a fifteen minute drive away!" He zoomed out on the map so Malte and Lucy could see it. "Just over a kilometer from here, as the crow flies."

"*Where?*" asked Assim.

"The dockside," said Lucy. "Cargo terminals."

"Good cover," noted Malte.

"Did we just catch a break?" she went on.

Marc gave her a severe look.

"Don't jinx it."

Axelle began to gasp as she approached orgasm, and from behind Verbeke snaked one hand around her bare arm, the other clutching her throat. He started to tighten his grip on her neck and she bucked against him, struggling to push away. He held on firmly, aggressively slamming himself into her over and over, and the woman's pale buttocks slapped hard against his muscular belly. She cried out, but that was part of their little game. Axelle knew her cry would excite him, lure him to make their rough, jagged intercourse even more forceful.

She gasped, but it became a strangled choke as he cut off her breath. The woman's sweat-smeared face turned back to look at him, but he held her tight, stopping her from twisting her neck.

Verbeke didn't want to look her in the eye. He wanted to relish the moment, the ferocity and the power of it. Each time they had sex, each time they reached this point, he played with the idea of constricting his grip until he heard the cartilage in her throat crack. He liked the control that gave him over her. It was as strong a thrill as the act itself, potent and heady. Verbeke brought her right to the edge, but his sole concern was his own pleasure, and with a grunting shout he reached his climax. He immediately disengaged and shoved Axelle

away, letting her fall gasping on to the bed while he rose
to clean himself off.

He stalked across the room to where his clothes
lay in a pile on a chair, and picked through them. The
air was cold on his bare skin. These quarters were a
converted office space, and not fit for purpose, but he
had lived in worse places. He pulled on his underwear
and a pair of trousers. His gaze drifted to the window
in the far wall. Outside, a heavy rain was pelting the
glass, turning the view of the black rock landscape beyond into a blurry, ill-defined mess.

"Did you enjoy that?" said Axelle from across the
room. Her voice was coarse and husky from the exertion, and she rolled over, reaching for a towel. "I think
you missed me in prison . . ."

Her tone ignited an instant anger in Verbeke.

"Be quiet, slut," he spat. Any suggestion that there
might be something approaching affection between
them infuriated him. His hand formed into a fist and
he wondered if it would be necessary for him to make
her understand that wasn't so. "Your *chatte* isn't that
impressive."

"*Connard!*" she shot back, with enough force to
show some spirit, but not enough to truly rile him.
Axelle knew Verbeke's moods well, and that too aggravated him. It meant she thought she could manipulate
him, like women always did.

Shrugging on a shirt, he poured himself coffee from
a flask on the table and considered her over the rim of
the mug as she started to dress. There were few females
he had allowed into the ranks of the Lion's Roar. He'd
learned early in his life to distrust them and be wary of
their faults, but the French woman was one of the rare
exceptions. She was useful for those tasks when a man

might raise suspicions, and he reluctantly allowed that her innately callous, calculating manner was a good balance to his more aggressive impulses. The sex was a bonus.

In that way, she was a good example of what the Lion's Roar needed in their females—loyalty and obedience, and the unquestioning resolve to do whatever was needed for the cause.

Most of the time, Axelle stayed on the right side of that measure. But he decided it wouldn't do for her to become comfortable there, to think that he might be soft on her. Not that he ever would. Verbeke had seen strong, potent men enfeebled by the toxic influence of sly women, and he had vowed never to fall victim to such a thing.

They are necessary, he reminded himself, *even pleasurable. But in the end, just tools. Without a man's hand upon them, they can do little for us.*

Verbeke remembered where he had first heard those words. He had been standing in a corridor, in that cramped old apartment on Avenue Clemenceau. No more than a child, the sounds of shouting and violence had drawn him to the door of the room where his mother slept with his stepfather. When the man came out, still holding the strap of his leather belt in one hand, little Noah had seen a glimpse of her, bruised and cowering in the corner, before the door shut again. He knew that belt; the sting of it was familiar to him from the days when he whined about something, or showed what the big man called "weaknesses."

His stepfather crouched down, so that they were looking each other in the eye, and he told Noah what women were worth as his mother wept quietly in the next room.

Only men know how to be strong, he had said, putting a paternal hand on the boy's shoulder. *Men like us. We are the lions, not the sheep.*

It was the first time in his life Noah Verbeke had not felt like a child, like someone lost and subject to the whims of an uncaring world. It was the first time an adult had trusted him with something—this truth. It was the boy's epiphany. He could become strong, be a man, if he was willing to follow the path.

The path his stepfather showed him was easy to grasp. It was made of hate. Not just his animosity for the pathetic, venal ways of womenfolk, but for anyone who was not *a man like us*—and there were so many of them. The apartment was in Kuregem, one of the poorest districts in Brussels, and with that poverty came resentment. Every day, more and more foreigners flowed into the country grasping for handouts, and an idiotic bleeding heart government gave them everything they wanted, edging out the whites who deserved to be there.

Belgium is for Belgians, his stepfather would say, *for lions not sheep*, repeating the refrain until it became embedded in Noah's mind. When his mother finally fled the abuse she was suffering at both their hands, he barely noticed.

His stepfather was so proud when young Noah told him the stories of the windows he broke in immigrant homes, of the epithets spray-painted on walls, the shops set alight. He told him it was permissible to steal from these mongrel foreigners, torment them and make their lives a misery, because they were the enemy.

On some level, Verbeke knew he was being raised in a churning cauldron of hate, but the fury of it gave him life. It freed him, knowing for certain that every hurdle in his life, every refusal he suffered, was the fault of the weak and the different. They had no right to be here, to take what was supposed to be his, and he had every right to detest them for it. He had an enemy for all his ills, and a limitless rage to direct at them.

There was, of course, a second lesson his stepfather taught him. That came later, when he was much older, a man in his own right with his own cadre of thugs and a growing territory of hatred. It was a revelation, learning that even the strongest could be corrupted. If anything, that lesson was more valuable than the first.

One night, Verbeke left a man dead in a filthy alley behind a backstreet bar, after he had dared to suggest that Noah's stepfather liked to put his cock in black whores. Through the red haze of his rage, as he kicked the man's skull in, he refused to believe it. His stepfather had shown him the path. He had made a boy into a man capable of becoming a lion.

But then he found the old fool screwing an immigrant prostitute and he realized that the weakness could take anyone. The anger which came upon him in that moment was far worse than that he had inflicted on the man in the bar. It was the totality of every other rage he had ever experienced and more.

Lost in the memory, Verbeke's hand gripped the coffee mug, knuckles whitening around it.

He remembered killing the woman, crushing her neck until it broke, but memory blurred around the facts of what he did to his stepfather. All that mattered was that the old man died of his stab wounds on the way to the hospital.

His men and the others who hated, they lauded him for what he had done, and while some of the police were on their side, enough were not. Verbeke had to vanish, and a friend helped him enroll in the Belgian armed forces, covering up the parts of his criminal record that otherwise would have halted him.

As a soldier, he learned much more, channeling his impulses and aptitude for violence to the work of the state that he loathed so deeply. He sought out and nurtured contacts with the like-minded few he found within the military. For a time he rose high, and he might have gone further—if it hadn't been for cowards like that rat Jakobs.

He grinned, thinking of the other man, wondering how long it had taken him to bleed out in that train carriage with two bullets in his gut. It was a pity he had not been able to relish that murder a little more, after the trouble that self-righteous bastard had given him.

Jakobs had been the one who forced Verbeke out of the army, after it came to light that he had been abusing prisoners of war and non-combatants. But that had been a boon, in its own way. Returning to civilian life put him back in the place he had come from, and reawakened the old hate. The city he had grown up in, the country he called home, was infested with more foreigners than ever before. Verbeke saw that and his rage rose high. His thuggish charisma found him a ready audience of other angry men who felt the same way he did.

He picked up where he had left off, but this time his cadre, his *Lion's Roar*, would be something more than a gang of directionless hooligans, striking out at random. They would become soldiers, as he had, fighters in a war between cultures to preserve their way of life. He knew the cause was right, he felt it in his blood and bone. How could he be wrong, when so many in the nation felt the same way? And not just in mainland Europe, but in Britain, Scandinavia, Russia and even

America? He had more allies, and more enemies too—
but that made him bare his teeth in a hunter's snarl.

*The more of these mongrels there are, the easier it is
to destroy them.*

Axelle saw him staring in her direction and she ran
an inviting hand over her bare breasts, mistaking his
savage smile for renewed carnal interest.

"You want to go around again?"

He sneered at the offer, snatching up some of her
clothes and throwing them at her.

"I'll tell you when."

The faint shade of coyness faded from her expression.

"You're angry with me." She swore under her breath.
"You're always angry about something."

"I should be happy?" He growled out the words and
took a threatening step toward her. "You climbed into
bed with the Combine and you want me to be pleased
about it."

"Fuck you!" she retorted. "I made a choice. The Lion's
Roar needed you on the outside, not rotting in a cell!"
Axelle jerked her thumb in the direction of the other
rooms. "The men follow you, Noah. They need their
leader! How long do you think the group could operate without you?" The woman snorted. "That poseur
Van de Greif can't control the men, they laugh at him.
And Duz or Brewn? They're vicious but they're not as
smart as—"

"They also don't pay any attention to *you*," he interrupted.

"True. That's why they're only fit to be followers, not
leaders. They don't see the way it really is."

"And you do?" He advanced on her.

She nodded warily. Still half-dressed, Axelle held the
bundle of her clothes to her chest as if it would project
her.

"The Combine have been observing us for a long time, you know that. Our interests align with theirs."

He made a show of glancing around.

"They're certainly generous with their resources. Giving us these toys. But I have to wonder what the price is?"

"It is simple," said Axelle, with an arch sniff. "They're fearful. Oh, they want to thin the herd like we do, but they are afraid to get their hands dirty. No different from Van de Greif—just with more money."

"And better weapons." He looked back at the window, picking out the metallic domes against the dark hillside. "I do like that."

"I knew you would," she went on. "They need people like us. People with vision, purpose, and *will*."

After his arrival, Axelle had shown Verbeke the elements of the opportunity the Combine had laid out for them, and it made his pulse race. It was one thing to spill mongrel blood and throw firebombs, but this scheme was an order of magnitude beyond those acts of violence. It made such deeds seem petty.

Executed correctly, it would change the map of Europe and bring thousands to their banner.

There was a sharp rap on the door and he went to it, wrenching it open.

"What the fuck do you want?"

Verbeke glared at Duz, who stood with another of the men and the foreign woman, Park, at his side.

Duz nodded at the woman. "She needs to talk to you."

He was the same height as Verbeke, but he always seemed to be slumping, hunched forward as if he expected to be rushed at any second. He fingered the poorly groomed anchor beard that did little to distract from his ruddy complexion and close-set eyes.

"So—"

"I repeat," said Verbeke, turning his attention on Park, "what the fuck do you want?"

He wandered away from the door, while Park nervously followed him inside. Duz hesitated on the threshold, leering when he saw Axelle still half-undressed.

"I won't do any more for you," said Park, with the forced firmness of someone who was afraid and trying hard not to show it. "I want to know my family are safe and well before I will proceed."

"Do you?" Verbeke's hand shot out and he grabbed her wrist, twisting it hard so she cried out. "I don't see why."

Axelle pulled on her blouse and came toward him.

"She needs her hands to work."

"Didn't I already say to you, *Shut up, slut*?"

He glared at the French woman. Still, he let go of Park and wiped his hand down his trousers. The Korean's eyes were brimming with unshed tears and he felt his gut twist with disgust at the sight of her. She was everything that he loathed—a gutless refugee who had fled her own nation, a traitor to her people, and the worst kind of female, the kind who thought they were cleverer than everyone else.

Would she be able to out-think me choking the life from her? The idea amused him.

At length, he relented, making a dismissive gesture.

"Fine. Show her."

Axelle picked up a tablet computer from the desk and swiped across the screen, finding a still image.

"Here. This was taken this morning."

She handed the tablet to Park, who stared at it, shaking her head.

The image was of two more of her kind, a man and a boy, standing in front of a black and white house. They looked terrified, which satisfied Verbeke, and the man was holding up a newspaper. Park pawed at the screen, enlarging the picture to get a better look at the paper's masthead. The copy of *The Straits Times* bore today's date.

"N-no," she stuttered, after a moment. "This isn't enough. I want to speak to them."

Verbeke snatched the tablet from her and shoved it into Axelle's hands.

"Who do you think you are, making demands?" He prodded Park hard in the chest. "Perhaps I'll call up and have them shoot the boy in the head while you watch?"

Park gave a pained moan as he spoke, and her hands flew to her mouth. She shook her head, the tears streaking down her face.

"No. No. If you kill them I won't help you. I won't. They're all I have."

Verbeke stayed silent for a long moment, letting her dwell on that horrible image in her mind's eye, and then he snapped his fingers at Axelle.

"Fine. Show her."

Axelle carried the tablet to a docking station on the desk and locked it in place. With a few keystrokes, she opened up an encrypted video window and connected to the staging post back in Singapore, from where the team had coordinated the initial abduction.

Ticker's face appeared on the screen.

"*I'm here,*" he began, slightly out of sync with the movement of his mouth on the video. "*Prepping to go. Problem?*"

"Show us the hostages," Axelle told him.

"*Right now?*"

"Right now," she repeated. "The wife is here. She wants to see them."

"*Yeah, sure,*" Ticker drawled, catching on quickly. "*Gimme a second.*"

The visual turned blank for a few moments, and when it returned, it was coming through a grainy digital camera feed.

The picture showed Simon Lam and his son seated at a folding camping table, in what resembled a nondescript industrial space, a basement or a warehouse. The two of them looked up, as if someone out of sight had entered the room.

Park took unsteady steps toward the tablet, her hands bunching.

"*Talk,*" said Ticker's voice, from off-screen. "*Your wife's watching.*"

"*Susan? Susan, are you there?*" The husband leaned forward, then back, his motions stiff. "*Susan?*"

"*Mommy?*" The boy blinked, as if he was holding back tears.

Verbeke watched Park silently come to pieces in front of him. She shuddered and wiped at her eyes with the heel of her trembling hands, drawing in a tremulous breath.

"I'm here," she called out, "Did they hurt you?"

"*What?*" said the husband, before he answered. "*We're okay. Okay.*"

"*Please help us,*" added the boy. "*Come and get us.*"

"I will, as soon as I can," insisted Park. "I promise."

She straightened, making an attempt to find her courage, but Verbeke easily saw through her false bravado.

"That's enough," he snapped, and made a throat-cutting gesture.

Axelle cut the video and Park gave that pitiful moan again.

"This is the end of me being generous with you," he growled. "Your friend Kyun told me you could give us what we need in a day, so get in there and do it." He pointed in the direction of the lab. "If I have to look at you again before that, someone is going to get cut."

"You will kill us anyway!" Park screamed abruptly.

"You're going to stay alive until we see a success," Axelle countered. "Who dies between now and then is up to you."

Duz saw his cue and grabbed Park by the arm, dragging her away before she could protest any more.

When they were alone again, Verbeke snorted.

"We need to watch her. She's going to be trouble."

Axelle nodded at the tablet screen.

"Not as long as we have that. What did you think?"

He reached for his discarded jacket, giving her a mocking nod.

"I think it was worth every cent of the Combine's money."

— SEVEN —

It was after nightfall before they were ready to deploy. Lucy had been the one to make the call, as the senior operative in their cell, deciding that a couple of hours delaying and preparing was worth the risk that their targets might have moved on in the interim. Every instinct in Marc wanted to get in there and search for the abductees, but he knew as well as she did that the right prep before a mission could make the difference between life and death when an agent was in the field.

Malte secured another vehicle for them—a fancy euphemism for "hot-wiring"—and now they were close, threading through traffic on the four-lane highway in a black sedan with darkened windows.

Marc ran the briefing on the move, keeping everyone on comms as he looked through the slim intel package he had assembled on the location where the lo-jack trackers were pinging. Dredging the web for whatever he could find about the target, Marc left Assim to work at finding a way into local traffic cameras soon after he arrived back at the apartment.

"It's not a warehouse," Marc explained. "At least, not anymore."

On the screen of his weather-beaten laptop, he showed her a shaky YouTube video of a rave party in full swing.

Hundreds of sweaty Singaporeans and drunken Westerners were bounding around under strobing lights and laser displays, while a DJ in a face mask made of glowing LEDs nodded along to a thudding bass beat rippling with electronica.

"Apparently, pop-up nightclubs are this season's new in thing," he went on. "Reclaimed industrial spaces are where the hip kids are getting their jollies."

"Did you just use the word 'hip' unironically?"

Lucy paused in the middle of applying a cherry red lipstick and gave him a withering look from across the sedan's back seat.

Marc shrugged. "What do I know? I'm more of the rock-metal type." He made a devil-horns sign with one hand to underline the point. "These dancey tunes aren't really my jam."

"Whatever." Lucy leaned in and examined some stills of the building's exterior. "So where are we at?"

"*Target location is on the far side of the West Coast Highway,*" Assim volunteered, "*sandwiched between the Pasir Panjang cargo terminal, and Labrador Park.*"

"It has that whole fake-dangerous, edgy-urban feel to it," Marc went on. "I found a few pearl-clutching news items in the mainstream press talking about the club, usual screeds crying over moral turpitude and the fear of drugs and violence. Not that the police have had much actual evidence of that."

"Gotta be there, though," said Lucy. "Even if they're keeping it on the down-low, clubs always have mob connections, no matter what city you're in. Which syncs up with the Lam abduction. Whoever the black masks are, they'd need some local contacts for logistics."

She pulled on a shiny, wet-effect PVC jacket, adjusting her look in the reflection from the windows.

"It's a good base to operate from." Marc tapped a map on the screen. "Decent transport links. Close to the water and the highway. Straight run in either direction, east to the airport or west across the bridge into Malaysia."

Lucy nodded. "And the club makes good cover for out-of-towners coming and going."

"*I'm in the cameras at the intersection across the street,*" said Assim. "*Big queue outside. It's a popular place.*"

"What about the building itself?"

Marc looked up as they turned a corner.

"*Is it unusual for a rave-club warehouse to have a stand-alone security system with no external hard lines?*" Assim asked the question and then answered it. "*It bloody is. And add to that, the fact that the building's architectural plans are missing from the city record, along with those of several others owned by the same private concern.*"

"Triad front," said Lucy, with a firm nod. "Called it. The Singapore cops might say they pushed the gangs out of the city, but where there's money, there's vice. They just hide it better these days."

"*There's definitely a lower level to the warehouse,*" said the Saudi. "*There are loading ramps leading down to secured doors. Given the attenuation of the tracker signals, I think that's where the bioprinters are being kept. But I can't give you any lead on how to get in there or what you might find.*"

The car began to slow, and Marc folded his laptop shut.

"Assim raises a good point. There could be anything waiting for us."

"That's what we're here to find out," Lucy replied,

as Malte brought the sedan to a halt at the curbside. "We locate the printers, figure out our next move from there."

"Metal detector at the entrance," noted the Finn.

"So no weapons." Lucy shot Marc a look. "We'll have to—"

"Improvise," he finished, and opened the car door.

She stalked past him, the ice-white high heels she wore click-clacking over the pavement, swinging her shoulders with catwalk confidence. Marc pulled his jacket tight and fell in behind, trying to project an air of casual indifference.

Assim had been right about the queue. The rain had stopped, but despite the heavy clouds overhead threatening more of the same, a line of people had come out in force in the hopes of getting in. The queue extended along the front of the converted warehouse, everyone in it cast in blue and pink thrown from a neon sign fixed to the exterior. The club's name was *SKORE*, rendered in a faux-80s style font, and to Marc's eyes the place looked like the backdrop for a glossy Cantopop music video.

Lucy ignored the faces gathered behind the velvet rope and passed right by the two thickset bouncers in their black bomber jackets and earpiece radios, without slowing her pace. They eyed her as she entered the dark, pulsing pit of the doorway, but neither raised a hand to halt her.

Not so with Marc, though. One of the men pivoted into his path and he had to stop dead.

"Get in line," said the bouncer.

"I'm with her," Marc replied, but the words sounded lame coming out of his mouth. Lucy had already vanished inside and he was still out here in the chill evening air.

"I have to repeat?" The bouncer pointed at the queue with a thick-fingered hand.

Marc pondered pushing the point, but he wasn't ready to start trouble thirty seconds into the operation.

"No," he said at length, then scowled and wandered away. He pulled a Bluetooth micro-bead from his pocket and inserted it in his ear. "You're going to have to teach me how you do that."

The tiny bone-induction radio carried his words to the rest of the team.

"*Do what?*" He could barely pick out Lucy's voice from the rumble of the music. "*Shit, this is . . .*" He lost the rest of her words in the noise.

"*Loud,*" offered Assim helpfully. "*I think she said* loud."

"Yeah, thanks," Marc sniffed, going to his spyPhone. From the corner of his eye, he saw Malte guiding the black sedan into a parking spot, putting the car into a position from which they could make a fast exit, if they needed to. "If audio isn't working, let's try smoke signals . . ." He tapped out a quick message and sent it.

Sound no good. Text only?

A moment later he received a reply—a crying sad-face icon and then a thumbs-up symbol.

"I am not going to talk to you in emojis," Marc said to himself, with a sigh. He sent another message.

Find lower level entrance.

The next icon that appeared was a hand making the sign of the horns.

Lucy bought a colorful, overpriced drink and wandered in a way that would have seemed aimless to the untrained eye, snaking around the edge of the dance floor as the driving beat made the air hum. She kept one hand near her pocket, ready for the buzz of her smartphone when a new message came in, and scanned the crowd.

It was easy to pick out the obvious class structure at play in the club. The regular fun-lovers were thronging the floor, getting their kicks grinding and bouncing off one another. A ring of wide booths at ground level was where the cool kids sat, the ones too nonchalant to actually dance. She saw locals and not-so-locals with bottles of liquor or champagne, engaged in their own little dramas and show-offs. They weren't who she wanted.

Built into what had once been the warehouse's service walkways and elevated platforms was the territory of the VIPs. Hemispheres of plastic ringed by plush sofas, each connected by a gantry to a central axis, allowed those with the money and the influence to sit up there above the gyrating crowd and pretend they were the gods. Someone had sensibly rigged a near-invisible mesh net beneath the upper level to catch any dropped bottles or drunk idiots that might slip over.

From down below, Lucy could see a few rich kids, but mostly it was hatchet-faced men in bulky suits up there, all of them attended by a parade of hot girls and younger guys with the hungry look of wannabe thugs.

"Could you be any more Triad?" she said aloud, her words absorbed by the music.

Those were the men in charge, there was no doubt about it, but the SCD were not here to mess with them. Lucy's target was elsewhere.

She swung away, fending off the enthusiastic advances of a local whose pinprick pupils told her he was high as a kite. Lucy reached down and found a nerve point in his thigh that made his leg instantly go dead. She was gone before he collapsed on to a bar stool, waving mournfully after her as if he was bereft at her departure.

Lucy made her way through a set of heavy swing doors into a corridor that led to the restrooms and service areas. Back here, the music was still loud, but not so much that you couldn't hear yourself think over it. Further on, the corridor branched with the restrooms to the right, and she hesitated at the intersection, where a sign in three languages warned ONLY EMPLOYEES PAST THIS POINT on the left-hand side.

Pretending to stop at a mirror on the wall to check her make-up, she observed another suited guy standing guard next to a door protected by a secure keypad. He glanced her way once, but he seemed more interested in chatting up a leggy Malaysian girl with bleached-blonde tresses that reached to her butt. She looked for a security camera, but didn't see one. Clearly, the club's owners thought that the guard on the door was enough.

Lucy slipped out her phone and snapped a few captures of the door, sending them to Marc and the others.

That's it, he texted back. *Next move?*

W8-1 was what she sent back: *wait one*.

Lucy hung around for longer than she dared, and in the mirror she could see the guy on the door becoming more interested in her as the seconds ticked by. Then a light on the secure keypad flashed green and the door opened.

Exactly the man she wanted stepped through, exchanging a few words with the guard. In his forties, she estimated, with the kind of rough-hewn look sported by ex-boxers or cops who were too long in the tooth, he was most likely a mid-level enforcer, what in the old days the Triads would have called a "Red Pole." The East Asian gangs were more lax than they used to be when the Triads were at the height of their powers, but some of the old ways endured. Ranks and positions were based on the numerology of the *I Ching*, and the Red Poles carried the number 426 to signify their seniority.

The man was stone-cold sober, which meant he was here tonight for work and not play. As he made his way past her, Lucy saw him fiddle with a packet of cigarettes and then put them away again. No one smoked indoors in this town, not even the criminals. The man started pecking obstinately at a smartphone with one finger and she smiled. This was getting better by the second.

Angling her phone, she used the mirror to catch a couple of shots of the older guy. A moment later, the phone vibrated in her hand and she saw the next message from Marc.

Anything yet?

The guard looked up at her as the Red Pole vanished into the crowd, and she melted away after the other man.

"Oh yeah," she said to herself, formulating a quick response.

"Guy in a tuxedo, a cigarette, a key." Marc looked at the icons and sighed. "Is she deliberately trying to make this hard or what?"

"*She doesn't have time to write you a sonnet,*" said Assim.

Marc's retort was cut off as his phone buzzed again. This time Lucy had sent him a snapshot of a man in a suit, caught in the low light of the nightclub's interior.

"Who's this guy?"

He had barely uttered the question when the same man exited the club, nodded to the bouncers and wandered over to the outdoor smoking area. Marc watched him light up and start to fiddle with his phone.

"*He's got a key?*" said Assim, seeing the same data mirrored to his screen.

"Actually, he's going to *be* our key."

Marc smiled and tapped out two icons in reply.

Lucy bought another drink at the bar—a club soda this time—and sipped at it as the Red Pole walked back past her, a whiff of fresh tobacco trailing behind him as he made his way toward the corridor to the rear. He was still tapping at his phone.

Marc picked his way through the crowd to her and she gave him a nod. He leaned close, raising his voice to shout into her ear.

"Good eye, there." He waggled his spyPhone in his hand. "Should do the trick."

She turned her face to reply to him.

"Did you sneak in through the ladies' room?"

He shook his head. "Got in the old-fashioned way. Bribed the bouncer with a fifty."

Lucy nodded. "So what the hell does this mean?" She showed him her own phone screen, and his earlier reply—two icons, a cellular phone and a dolphin. "Is this like a weird come-on, or something?"

"Watch and learn," he replied, and beckoned her to follow him.

She trailed Marc into the back corridor, careful to put the Brit between her and the guard, who was still engaged with the leggy blonde. He nodded at the other woman.

"Can you run some interference for me?"

"No problem."

Lucy pitched into a purposeful swagger that took her straight toward the blonde, while Marc slipped around to the secure door. The guard saw her coming and reacted, standing up from where he was slouched at the wall.

"Bitch, what you think you doin'?" snarled Lucy, channeling her best faux-Ghetto accent.

The blonde woman spun around in time to get a face full of soda. The drink spilled down the front of her low-cut dress and she squealed, stamping on the spot like an angry toddler.

"Get the hell away from my boy!" added Lucy, and the blonde bolted for the ladies' room.

"You *siao*, hah? You are insane woman!" cried the guard, his hand clutching at a touch-taser in his belt. "I don't know you! Step off!"

The man saw movement from the corner of his eye as Marc came up behind him and he tried to twist around, but the Brit was too quick for him, putting a knee-kick into his back.

He crumpled. Marc got an arm around his throat and pulled tight. The guard tried to struggle, but Lucy was there to grab his arms. In a few seconds the man was gasping as Marc put his other hand up and forced his head forward, cutting off the flow of blood to his brain. On a five-count, the guard's eyelids fluttered and the strength dropped out of him as he lost consciousness. He fell back, almost slamming Marc into the wall, and the Brit let him go.

"I guess you were paying attention with that Krav Maga," said Lucy.

"I'm out of practice," Marc admitted, pulling out his

phone. "One second. Be ready to peg it if this doesn't work."

"Still waiting for the dolphins," she noted.

He worked a series of apps on the glassy black face of the spyPhone and held it to the electronic lock. It gave a series of quick beeps, the same kind that a touch-tone keypad would emit, and the lock light flashed green.

"Thank you, Flipper," he muttered, and nudged open the door.

The thin slice of the space beyond revealed a shabby concrete corridor ending in a set of metal steps that descended to the lower level. Marc grabbed the unconscious guard, hauling him over the threshold as Lucy followed. She secured the door behind them. No one had seen them, and the doused blonde was still in the toilet.

"Storeroom here."

Marc nodded toward a wide janitorial closet a few steps away. Together, they manhandled the guard inside and Lucy found a role of duct tape to serve as bindings and a gag.

As they secured the man, she shot Marc a look.

"Okay, so how'd you do it? You clone that other guy's phone or something?"

"I used a Dolphin Attack," he explained. "You know how they communicate, yeah? Ultra-high-frequency clicks and whistles."

"I watch *Animal Planet*," she said, with a nod.

"Most smartphones have voice recognition software built in, same as those talking home assistants. You say it, they do it. *Call Mum. Open web browser. Play music.* That kind of thing."

"Always thought it was a shade creepy myself . . ."

"Good instinct, because they're also very insecure.

See, what most people don't know is that the microphones that pick up your voice commands are not just sensitive to the sound of speech, but frequencies way higher than that. Right up into the UHF, beyond the range of human hearing."

"So what? You're telling me Flipper could order a ton of shrimp on my cell and I wouldn't know it?"

He nodded. "Hence the name. Outside, while that other bloke was having a smoke, I sent an inaudible UHF command to his phone that told it to connect straight back to Assim in the apartment. He injected some hijacker malware, and turned the phone into a short-range monitoring device . . ." Marc showed her his spyPhone. "When that guy entered the code for the door, his phone heard the tones—"

"And so did you. That's real clever, Cousteau."

He shrugged. "It got us through the door. We still have to find those bioprinters."

Lucy grabbed the guard's touch-taser and tossed it to Marc.

"No heroics down there, Dane," she said firmly. "I mean it. If it goes south, we get out. Cut and run."

"Okay," he said, without weight.

"Assim, Malte. You read me?" She tapped the comms bead in her ear.

"*Yes,*" said the Finn. "*Barely.*"

"*You're patchy,*" said the hacker. "*Breaking up.*"

"We'll stay radio-silent unless the shit hits the fan," Lucy went on, and took a deep breath, pausing to snap the quick-release fittings in her high heels that turned them back into flat shoes. "If we're not out in twenty minutes, call it scrubbed and exfil without us." She glanced at Marc. "You and me'll split up, we can cover more ground that way. Copy?"

"Green for go."

Marc nodded and reached for the door handle.

At the bottom of the steel staircase, the basement of the warehouse extended away under the full footprint of the building. The space was broken up by thick concrete columns and elevated storage racks that went to the ceiling. Industrial bulbs enclosed in wire cage hoods cast a grimy light in narrow pools, conveniently providing zones of deep shadow that Marc and Lucy could exploit. Further down, parts of the space appeared to be closed off behind prefabricated walls.

Lucy threw him a thumbs-up and vanished away to the right. Marc waited a beat and then moved left. The air in the basement was dense and humid in his lungs, and it vibrated with the heavy rhythm of the music seeping down from the club. Focusing past the sound, he heard the voices of men, their lazy chatter in the hodge-podge local creole called Singlish. The tone of the voices was relaxed, which meant that no one was alerted to the SCD's intrusion.

Marc kept low, using stacks of wooden crates for cover. Assim had shown them what to look for with regard to the bioprinters, and he scanned around for any sign of the gray plastic hard-cases the devices were carried in. But the machines were not what he was searching for—not really. In Marc's mind, the abductees were of greater importance, even if Lucy had insisted they were a secondary priority to losing control of the bioprinters.

She was a soldier, and that meant she could make ice-water flow in her veins when the time came to give the hard call. But he wasn't wired that way. Despite everything that had changed in Marc Dane since he started working for Rubicon, despite everything that had impacted on him, he didn't find it as easy to go to that darker, colder place in himself.

He knew objectively that in the wrong hands, the bioprinters had the capability to fabricate creations that were truly appalling, things that could threaten countless lives. But that was theoretical, and he could only see the actual in his mind's eye, recalling the abject terror on the faces of Simon Lam and his young son as they were hustled into the van outside their home.

Moving forward, planting each step to make it as silent as he could, Marc took a long path around, avoiding the group of men. They were cut from the same cloth as the guy upstairs, but most of them went around without jackets on and he saw a couple with the telltale shapes of shoulder holsters tucked in their armpits. One of them told a joke and it set the rest of them roaring. He used the distraction to slip across an open area to another stack of crates.

Some of these were still open and Marc stole a look inside. Packed within the closest one was a set of vintage Chinese chairs in dark, ornately carved hardwood with disc-shaped marble inserts. Another held a collection of ancient Imperial porcelain, brightly colored bowls and vases wrapped up in thick foam sheets, and in a third he found a loading sheet in Mandarin and English that listed dozens of items as "Han Dynasty Jade Figural Pieces." Marc didn't know much about historical relics, but these items definitely *looked* valuable, and there didn't seem to be anything in the way of official certification with the crates. Destination stencils on the outside marked them as bound for cities in America and the Netherlands, Belgium and Switzerland, Canada and the UK, but the logos suggested the contents were machine parts, not antiquities.

A smuggling operation, then.

Marc snapped images of the items in the crates and the paperwork, in case there was some useful scrap of data to be gleaned from them.

That dovetails with the black masks using the Triads on this. Smugglers would have a pipeline in place to get cargo in and out of Singapore on the quiet.

Moving on, he edged up to a pillar and spotted an open doorway leading into one of the prefab sections. On the far side, he could see the back end of one of the blue vans from the camera footage, parked in front of a roller door leading up and out to the waterfront. But what drew his attention were two plastic crates in battleship gray, sitting unguarded on a shipping pallet.

He slipped the taser prod into the sleeve of his jacket and started moving, weaving from shadow to shadow, closing in on the open door.

Lucy pressed herself up against a low wall and used the camera in her spyPhone as a makeshift periscope, peeking over and through a dirt-smeared window into one of the "office" areas. There was no sign of the printer cases or the abductees. Instead, three men, all of them white guys, were engaged in packing their gear into heavy matte black duffel bags. They wore the same type of nondescript semi-tactical clothes that she always associated with hired guns—MA-1 jackets, and cargo trousers that weren't properly bloused into off-the-shelf tactical boots. Just from their body language she could tell that none of them had ever served, but it was clear they wanted people to think that they had.

Months ago, she and Malte had run across a gang of troublemakers much the same as these guys, in another basement on the other side of the Pacific. Those men had been planning to detonate a truck-bomb in the middle of downtown San Francisco, and she remembered the hard zeal in their eyes as they made ready to commit mass murder. These men had that look as well, casual and predatory, as if they believed that nothing was going to get in their way.

Beg to differ, she said to herself.

The one who appeared to be in charge was an American with a mop of unkempt curly black hair and a tendency to wave his hands around.

"Get this out to the boat," he was saying.

She pegged his accent straight away, recognizing a Long Island native when she heard one. Born and raised in Queens, Lucy picked out the subtle differences and filed that bit of data away for later consideration.

One of the other men was at the Germanic end of the spectrum, and he grunted out a reply.

"What about that?"

He jutted his chin, indicating something in the corner of the room.

Lucy angled the phone's camera to get a look at what he was talking about. She saw a patch of rust-red on the concrete floor, and a spatter pattern low on the far wall.

"What do I care? We're paying these assholes to clean up our mess," said Long Island. "We're outta here."

"Should have put down some plastic," said the third man, in a low grumble.

Lucy crouched back down as the men left the room, the image fixed in her mind's eye of what could only be bloodstains.

* * *

Marc waited until the joker on the far side of the basement cracked another funny, and when the men laughed, he bolted through the open doorway and pushed it shut behind him.

There was a pungent chemical odor lingering in the walled-off area, but he ignored it and went straight to the gray plastic cases, giving them a quick once-over. The MaxaBio logo was prominently displayed on the lids, along with a metal data plate attached to the exterior that corresponded with the serial numbers of the two stolen bioprinters. He bent down and fumbled for the latches holding the lids shut, but the metal fasteners were missing. Bare steel showed where someone had used bolt-croppers to cut them off, and Marc's heart sank. He lifted the lid.

Empty.

The case was about the size of a small dining table and contained nothing but balled-up sheets of packing foam and the broken ends of the latches. He flipped open the second one and it was the same story. The black masks had taken the bioprinters away and left the cases here, with their lo-jacks still chirping mindlessly away regardless of the fact that their contents were gone.

Marc dug around inside the cases, finding the hidden panels that unclipped to reveal the battery-powered locators built into them. With a sigh, he flicked them on and off a couple of times, then closed everything up. Back at their base of operations in the Interlace complex, Assim would see the two tracking icons wink in and out, and hopefully put two and two together.

Leaning back against the cases, Marc cast around the room, his irritation building at the possibility that they had arrived too late after all. His gaze fell on the blue van. The back doors were hanging open.

Checking to make sure he was still undetected, Marc warily approached the vehicle. The thudding noise from the nightclub was loudest here, and he guessed they had to be right beneath the DJ's massive speaker stacks on the ground floor.

The bitter chemical smell was strong in the back of the van. Refuse sacks filled with empty polymer jugs sat in one corner, but the cargo space was dominated by a forty-gallon drum made of green plastic. Marc knocked on the side of it and it rang dully, oily matter sloshing around inside.

A sudden sense of foreboding settled on him as he reached for the drum. It had a circular lid held in place by spring-loaded clips, their metal surface smeared with acid burns.

Acid.

He stopped and pulled open a refuse bag, peering at one of the jugs inside, taking care not to touch it with his bare hands. Every single one of them bore a bright orange warning strip with a skull and crossbones. The text on the bottles was in Chinese, but there were two English letters that stood out a mile: HF. The chemical designation for *hydrofluoric acid*.

Numbly, Marc moved back to the forty-gallon drum and released the lid, sliding it open a few degrees. A foul reek like sour bile hit him in the face and he gagged, biting down on the compulsion to vomit. The drum was filled to the brim with a dirty, mud-brown fluid that shimmered with oily deposits beneath the basement's lights. Something black and fibrous sat close to the surface of the stinking liquid, and in a heart-stopping moment Marc realized it was human hair. Vanishing into the acidic broth was the hazy shape of what had to be a body, curled up in a fetal ball—and it didn't appear to be the only one in there. He slammed the lid back into place and secured it, staggering out of the van, gasping as the full import of what he had found hammered home.

There was a repulsive method that the notorious La Noche cartel and their rivals in the South American drug empire used to get rid of human evidence, when a corpse might be too inconvenient to have around. The nickname for this technique was *pozole*, after a traditional Mexican stew made from pork, maize and peppers. It involved either solutions of boiling sodium hydroxide—commonly known as lye—or gallons of hydrofluoric acid. Poured into a sealed drum with a body, and given enough time, human remains could be turned into a liquid slurry, a "stew" thin enough to be dumped down a municipal drain, or straight into the ocean if one was close enough to the waterfront. The technique had clearly been adopted by the Triads as well.

Marc caught the sound of voices approaching the room. Shaking off the sickening churn in his gut, he scrambled down into the only place where he could conceal himself, beneath the wheels of the parked van.

Lying face down on the concrete, he saw the door open and a pair of army boots stride in.

"We had a deal, right?" said a rough-edged American. The boots turned as a couple of pairs of smart shoes followed him in. "Why is this shit still here?"

"Takes time," said another voice, in a drawling East Asian accent. "No problem."

"It is a fucking problem!" insisted the American. He walked over to the gray cases and kicked them. "I told you to dump them in the sea last night, they're still here. We not paying you enough to do what you're told, you stupid dink?"

One of the others said something insulting that made his buddy laugh, but the American only grew more incensed.

"If I had my way, we'd never have used you fucking chumps. Can't you do one thing right?"

"Sure, sure," said the first voice. "We get done, all good."

"This goddamn country . . ." muttered the American, and he shoved his way back out of the room, past the two men.

Marc felt the van move over his head as the other men grabbed the gray cases and tossed both of them into the back of the vehicle. He held his breath for a moment, ready for them to climb in and start up the van, but instead they turned away and wandered off. Clearly, the Triads had no intention of jumping when the black masks told them to.

The presence of an American confirmed something else. Susan Lam's kidnappers were looking more and more likely to be independent actors, not operatives backed by a nation state.

When he was sure he was alone again, Marc slid out from his hiding place and made for the door. Across the way, another series of cube-like offices sat in a row, each one walled off from the others by prefab panels that stopped short of the ceiling. Marc glimpsed the familiar digital glow of a video screen reflecting off a half-open door and decided to investigate. But more than that, he wanted to put some distance between himself and the van, the horrible cargo it carried and the grim possibility of exactly who lay in that drum, slowly dissolving into nothing.

*　*　*

Rubicon's Special Conditions Division had no legal jurisdiction in their operations, no mandate beyond their agreed moral code. On the occasions when a government hired Rubicon's private military contractors, there was a precedent in law set in place, but the SCD's missions were rarely connected to that.

What we do is justified not by law but by ethics. Ekko Solomon had told Lucy that when she questioned him. *I am a wealthy man, a powerful man. And so I am morally obligated to use that power to better the world. We act when others are afraid to do so, when they cannot or when they refuse.* But within that mission statement was another unswerving truth: *Those that we target are enemies of the world. We do what we do for a greater good.*

And that meant obtaining proof. That moral authority had to be backed up with hard evidence. Every covert action the SCD had ever engaged in, every operation—from the smallest data interdiction to the prevention of a terrorist atrocity—was documented in the secret files of the Gray Record. If the day did come when they were to be judged for taking part in Solomon's crusade, there would be no doubt as to their intentions.

Lucy held on to that thought as she entered the room and logged everything she could with her phone camera, taking high-definition shots of the blood spatter and the area around it. A cold sense of familiarity came over her, bleak and uninvited. She had seen this kind of thing too many times, and it left a mark on her.

She turned away, opening up one of the duffel bags that the men had yet to move. Inside she found a black muslin hood, and photographed it. Beneath, there was a hard case that contained a 1911-style semi-automatic pistol and three magazines of .45 caliber ammunition.

"I'll take that," she said aloud, pausing to sniff the barrel before checking and loading the gun. The weapon had been fired recently. She tucked it in her belt loop and did not look back at the corner of the room.

The rest of the gear in the duffel was men's clothing, except for a resealable plastic bag containing a few personal effects. Among them was a wristwatch, a big expensive thing larger than the Cabot that Marc habitually wore, along with a fountain pen and a silver ring.

Lucy picked out the ring and held it up to the light. She recognized the design of it. She had seen it that morning, visible on the groom's finger in Simon and Susan's wedding day photo.

Then a thought occurred to her and she rechecked the bag, to be sure she hadn't missed anything. There was only one ring; the bride's was not there.

— EIGHT —

What Marc *didn't* expect to find in the nightclub basement was a half-dismantled set of video processing equipment, and a portable rig that any indie film-maker would have given their right arm for.

He saw the camera that the black masks had used outside the Lam house, and weighed it in his hand. The thing had a quartet of high-acuity digital lenses and a built-in laser ranger for pinpoint accurate focus. He knew a guy in the games industry who used similar kit to this for motion capture, where they filmed some actor in a suit covered in glowing ping-pong balls, and used that as the skeleton for computer graphic space aliens mapped over their body movements.

"What the hell are these dickheads doing with this?"

He put the camera back where he found it and looked around the large open area, finding a workbench stacked with more gear cases. There was an open laptop sitting next to a disconnected satellite communications node, and he instinctively homed in on it, mentally measuring up the machine with a tech-geek's eye for hardware specs. It was a modular device, a military grade Kontron NotePAC variant set up for field use.

Marc gave the keypad an experimental press and the standby screen flicked away. The computer's desktop was a mess of icons for various kinds of image processing and audio editing software. Once again he thought of some amateur movie-maker salivating over the thing.

Most of the device's internal hard drive was heavily partitioned with redundant firewalls that Marc couldn't bypass, not without a few hours of working at it, but the owner's layout suggested someone who was sloppy with the details. The "recent programs" tab showed that the last person to use it had been rendering a big file in real time, but Marc couldn't locate the actual data. What he did find was a set of raw audio source files, and leaning in close, Marc dialed down the volume and listened close as he hit play.

"*Read the words out loud, if you don't want your little runt crippled in front of you,*" said a voice, and he recognized it as belonging to the American with the army boots.

Another man spoke, hesitant at first. "*The beige hue on the waters of the loch impressed all, including the French queen . . .*" He became irritated. "*What is this? It's nonsense!*"

"*Say it. Don't mess it up. Then the kid goes next,*" said the American. "*Do it again, from the top.*"

"*The beige hue on the waters of the loch impressed all, including the French queen, before she heard that symphony again, just as young Arthur wanted.*"

"I know this." The odd words and the strangely poetic combination of their order rang a distant bell in Marc's thoughts, but he couldn't place it. "Think, man, think . . ."

A door slammed in the next office along and Marc jumped, the peculiar sentence momentarily forgotten. He hit the sleep key on the laptop and shrank back, eyes darting toward the door he had come in through. Another entrance led to the next room in

the cubicle row, and someone was in there now, pacing around.

A string of high-pitched beeps sounded out and Marc
flattened himself against the dividing wall, letting his
stolen stun prod slip out of his sleeve and into his grip.
In the other office, he heard the tinny *buzz-buzz* of a
ringtone and then a woman's voice, muffled by distance
and encryption.

"*What is it?*"

"Was he happy?" It was the American on the other
side of the wall. The agitation Marc had heard in his
voice minutes before was now subsumed into a needy
almost-whine. "I mean, I dunno, he cut me off and—"

"*Is he ever happy?*" The words were thick with static,
but Marc could pick out a polished French accent. "*Do
not shit yourself, Ticker. The video was perfect.*"

"It wasn't easy with this short turn-around."

"*You'll need to be faster with the next one.*" Marc
heard the American—Ticker, she called him—walking
in circles. "*You have four more days to iron out any
problems. Make the most of it.*"

Four days. The deadline could mean anything, but
Marc guessed it wouldn't be good.

"I'll be in the air for half of that," Ticker complained.
"I hate flying."

"*Just get moving. You've been there too long, and Rubicon has people in Singapore now, sniffing around.
You need to be gone before they get a clue.*"

Marc stiffened as he heard the woman say the name.
What do they know about us?

It wasn't much of a stretch to figure that the black
masks had their local talent keeping an eye on Maxa-
Bio, and that they had observed the SCD team's arrival.
There was even the possibility of an insider working
for the Singapore police force to consider. But Malte

and everyone on the team had been well trained in the art of losing tails, so Marc didn't think that they were blown, not yet.

This conversation would be going a whole different way if she knew we were already *here.*

"I'm working on it," said Ticker. "What about our pickup?"

"*They are on station. But they won't stick around forever, so don't keep them waiting. Take what you need, leave the rest . . .*" Marc heard a cruel smirk in the woman's voice. "*And don't forget to wrap up warm.*"

"Yeah, right."

The pitch of the man's voice changed suddenly as the phone beeped off, unexpectedly coming closer. Before Marc could react, the door to the other office swung open and Ticker came striding in, jamming the phone in his pocket and muttering angrily to himself.

He was three steps into the room before he realized he wasn't alone, but Marc was already swinging up the prod to a ready position, aiming the metal tines at the other man's chest.

Ticker spun, saw the flicker of bright blue electricity at the end of the stun baton and held up his hands.

"Easy there, pallie. Don't do nothing stupid."

The man's faux-tough-guy manner made Marc's lip twist in annoyance.

"You're going to talk to me or you get lit up," he snarled.

"Sure, man, sure . . ." Ticker tried to back away, but Marc moved with him, close enough that he could jam the prod into the man's torso in an instant. "You're Rubicon, right?"

He ignored the question and countered with one of his own.

"Where are the Lams?"

Ticker's face betrayed his intention to drop a reflex denial, but he must have caught the look in Marc's eyes, because he thought better of it. Instead, he tried on a callous sneer.

"You take a look in the van yet?" Marc's expression told him the answer, and he snorted. "Then I guess you know already."

Marc closed the distance, thumbing the prod's trigger stud, and the arc across the tines crackled loudly.

"Where is Ji-Yoo Park?" he demanded. "Where are the bioprinters?"

A slow, oily smile spread across Ticker's face.

"You don't know jack, do you? *Ha!*" He leaned back. "Oh, we sent the gear where it's gonna do the most good, count on that. You'll see it on the news, just wait a little."

Ticker's shit-eating grin and his hateful disregard for the Lams made Marc want to jam the baton into the guy's belly, make him scream and piss himself. But he reeled that fury back in and nodded toward the workbench.

"No problem. I'll peel it out of your laptop. Won't be hard. I mean, what kind of pillock leaves his machine unlocked, eh?"

The grin on Ticker's face faltered.

"You're welcome to try. My shit's tighter than Fort Knox! Touch the wrong thing and everything burns."

Marc gave him a level look. If this guy wanted to engage in some hacker dick-swinging, he was happy to oblige.

"Let me guess, you're using 2–5–6 symmetric encryption, yeah? 'Cos you don't look like the imaginative type."

"Fuck you, limey," Ticker said hotly. "Custom quad block cipher," he added, with a *beat that* sneer.

Marc gave an exaggerated shrug.

"Oh. That's nice. It'll give me time to put a brew on while I crack it like an egg."

"Kiss my—"

Ticker never finished the sentence, as Marc saw his eyes dart to the right, clocking something in the open doorway to the other office.

Marc made a rapid pivot to meet another man who had crept up silently behind him, brandishing a Taurus semi-automatic in one hand. The gunman drew up fast and his pistol rose in a blur of motion, but Marc was already reacting and struck out wildly, jabbing the tip of the stun baton into the closest target—the gunman's shoulder joint.

The prod discharged with a sizzling snarl and the gunman cried out. Some misfiring nerve in his arm jerked and he pulled the trigger, firing a round into the concrete floor that screamed away in a ricochet. Even with the ceaseless thud-thud-thud of the nightclub's music from over their heads, the shot echoed loudly across the basement.

"Get this prick!" Ticker shouted at the top of his lungs, sprinting for the other door, snatching up the offending laptop as he ran. "In here! Shoot him, *shoot him*!"

Marc clubbed the gunman across the face with the length of the baton and knocked him back, before hitting him again in the chest for another full-on discharge. The man thrashed and howled as the voltage crashed through him, losing his gun and collapsing against a desk into a twitchy heap. Marc left his would-be assailant gasping and retching, stooping to snatch up the Taurus that had skittered across the floor.

The action saved his life. The grimy windows and prefab walls of the office space erupted into a storm of glass and fiberboard, as the Triad goons out in the basement proper took Ticker's orders literally and opened up on the room.

The dazed gunman lost the top of his head to a stray round that killed him instantly. Marc threw himself flat on the floor as a spray of bullets turned the stale air into a storm of cordite and lead. Swearing a blue streak, swarming forward on his forearms and knees, he made for the far door as quickly as he could move.

Lucy heard the first shot and dropped down low, aiming in the direction of the discharge through the gaps in the metal storage racks. On the far side of the basement, she saw the Triad goons reacting, scrambling up from the folding chairs where they had been sitting, in their rush knocking over a makeshift table piled with beer bottles and mah-jong tiles.

The guns came out, the men pulling their weapons as they advanced in the direction of the office cubicles. Lucy flicked off the 1911's thumb safety and pulled it in close to her chest, but in the next second she heard a man yelling and then saw the dark-haired guy from the kill room sprinting toward a fire exit, hauling a laptop computer under his arm.

The goons didn't hesitate, firing wildly into the office space that he had just left. If Marc was in there, he was about to get chewed to bits.

Lucy aimed down the pistol's iron sights and made a split-second tactical evaluation. The Triad shooters were oblivious to her presence and she had a good angle on one of them; she could take him out of play with a hit to his center mass. A second man was a less definite target, a 70–30 hit or miss, and then there were half a dozen more. She needed to mess with all of them at once, not just one or two.

Hanging from an iron support pillar was the fat crimson cylinder of a pressurized fire extinguisher. Not exactly a grenade, but close enough in a pinch. Lucy turned her aim toward the body of the canister and let off a single round.

The bullet over-penetrated and the extinguisher leaped off the pillar, spewing great white plumes from the holes punched through it. Clouds of chemical vapor doused the Triad goons, sending them back in disarray.

Lucy was already running for the wrecked office cubicle as the choking retardant gas seared her throat, and she almost collided with Marc as he dashed out into the open.

"Which way?" he shouted.

The Brit had to be talking about the American.

"There!"

She pointed with her gun and he set off in that direction, barely breaking stride to yank at the red T-bar switch of a fire alarm as he passed by it.

A clattering old bell-ringer spun up, and the alarm began to sound in earnest. Upstairs in the nightclub, the drinkers and the dancers would have their revels cut short as the warning circuit shut off the music rig. Creating some disorder was the best chance of them getting out alive.

Hell, by now I should know, she thought, *it's a Marc Dane signature move*.

They crashed through the half-open fire door together and out on to a wide loading ramp that led straight to the water. Lucy saw the dark-haired guy vault off a nearby jetty into the back of a half-cabin motorboat stacked with gear cases, and cast off.

"Printers are gone!" Marc yelled. "Need his laptop!"

"Copy."

Lucy skidded to a halt and leaned into a modified Weaver stance, firing off another round toward the stern of the vessel. It cracked off the hull, close enough to make the target dive into the gunwale, but not enough to stop the boat from leaving.

With the growl of a hard-pressed engine, the motorboat bucked against the low swell and zoomed away, curving out from the dock and into the midnight blue of the starlit bay.

"There's a RIB here," called the Brit, pointing to another moored-up craft. "Fire it up!"

He ran to the cleats on the jetty and pulled away the ropes.

Lucy put her stolen .45 in the back of her jacket and leaped aboard the rigid inflatable boat. A standing podium in the middle of the orange-hued RIB held the controls and luck was on their side; the starter key was dangling from the steering wheel on a fluorescent tether. The motor turned over at the first try and as Marc scrambled aboard, she rammed the throttle bar as far forward as it would go.

The RIB gave her a little bronco and then shot forward like a stone skimming over the surface of a pond. Fans of salt spray came up over the boat's bullet nose, and she leaned into it, carving a zigzag course out into open water.

"Where's he at?" she called.

"Looking . . ."

Marc sat low toward the RIB's bow, resting in the curve of the hull, scanning the dark bay opening up in front of them.

In the middle distance across the water, the vast industrial complex of Bukom Island and its little sister Sebarok lit up the western horizon, the glow of hundreds of spotlights illuminating a cityscape of massive bulk petroleum tanks. To the southeast, toward the Straits of Singapore, Lucy could make out the vast shadows of a flotilla of container ships. This was one of the most heavily trafficked waterways on Earth, and if they lost their target here without an eye-in-the-sky to back them up, the black masks would be gone for good.

But then the Brit pointed and yelled.

"Right there! He's going around the island!"

Lucy hauled the RIB around and aimed it to run parallel with the long edge of Sentosa resort island, south of Singapore proper. She caught sight of the fleeing motorboat up ahead and eased back a little on the throttle. The other vessel had a bigger engine, but it was larger and loaded with heavy gear, while the low-slung RIB traded mass for speed. Lucy had trained for deployment from military versions of this craft in her army days, so she knew how to handle one. Now she had the target in sight she was sure they could catch him. The only question was what they would do when they got there.

Can't exactly flash my lights and get the prick to pull over.

Belatedly, the comms bead in her ear gave a low buzz.

"*Marc? Lucy? Does anyone copy, over?*" Assim sounded nervous. "*Is something on fire?*"

"Not yet, but the night is young," said Marc, pitching his voice up over the roar of the RIB's outboard motor.

Malte cut in. "*Where are you?*"

"We're feet wet," Lucy replied. "In pursuit of a HVT. Didn't have time to loop you in."

"*Copy, tracking high-value target,*" said the Finn. "*Can we assist with intercept?*"

"Negative, we're in this on our own. Stay on comms, we may need an exit strategy."

"*Understood.*"

Directly ahead, Sentosa's golden sands were lit up against the evening with the overspill glow from cartoonish hotel complexes and loud beach clubs. Music drifted out over the water from open-air festivities and dance boats riding in the shallows. For a moment, it looked like the motorboat was slowing to make for the shoreline, and then suddenly the water behind the craft frothed white and it veered away, cutting toward lines of party barges and anchored yachts.

"He saw us!" called Marc.

"Yeah." Lucy pushed the throttle back to maximum. "Hang on to something."

Marc slipped his arm around the grab-rope ringing the hull as she gunned the outboard and cut across the motorboat's seething wake, racing to steal a march on them. Lucy had a glimpse of the dark-haired American behind the boat's cabin, and saw light flash off a pistol in his hand. He had to know that if they started shooting in close proximity to so many civilians, the Police Coast Guard would be on them in minutes.

Or maybe he doesn't give a damn.

The motorboat slalomed around a floating restaurant and side-slipped to port, veering away from the RIB. Lucy was going too fast to make a turn after them, so she pressed on, passing between a party cruiser festooned with trains of blinking bulbs and a single-mast sailing boat riding high in the swell. The shocked faces of astonished tourists flashed past so close, she could have reached out and stolen a piña colada off their tables.

They shot through the gap between the two craft and bounced over a whitecap, but where the motorboat should have been there was nothing but empty water.

"Where . . . ?"

The rest of Lucy's question was drowned out when the other boat roared out from the shadows and slammed into the side of the RIB, striking the smaller inflatable with enough force to lift it clean out of the sea and into the air.

The RIB rolled hard toward starboard, reaching a ninety-degree angle and threatening to pitch them into the drink, as the motorboat droned by and shot away. Marc and Lucy both threw their weight to port, leaning hard against the impact, and the RIB seemed to hover for a moment before it slapped back into the surf, righting itself with a bone-jarring jerk.

The outboard coughed, spluttered and then finally roared as the propeller bit into the water, and they were off and moving again, but the collision had given the motorboat a lead that they would have to work to narrow. Lucy wrenched the wheel around, sending a high tail of spray up over a gaggle of well-dressed partiers watching from the sundeck of a luxury yacht. Their angry yells faded astern as the RIB sliced through wave crests, heading away from the shore and out into the main channel at speed.

"Still got him?" she yelled.

"Right there," began Marc, as a blink of yellow light flashed on the motorboat and low thunder cracked over the water.

A split second later, a bullet whirred past Lucy's head and she ducked reflexively. It seemed that their target's patience had reached its limit.

Marc dropped semi-prone over the curve of the RIB's flank with his stolen pistol in both hands, aiming it in the motorboat's direction. He cracked off a couple of shots in return, but they went wide.

As they closed the gap, the shooter on the boat fired again, missed again. Sudden frustration burned in Lucy. Maybe it was the jet lag, maybe it was the blood she'd seen on the floor and that asshole's callous attitude, but in that moment she wanted nothing more than to put a bullet in him.

"For cryin' out loud, hit that fucker!"

"Trying!" Marc retorted.

"I swear, you hacker nerds can't shoot for shit."

"Pardon me if my range training didn't take place on a bloody speedboat in a two-foot swell!" He pointed at the fleeing craft. "Just get us closer. He's running for cover in the big ships out there, see?"

She couldn't miss them. A silent, unmoving fleet of massive supertankers, container haulers and bulk carriers lay at anchor near the Singapore coast, their running lights shimmering off the low cloud overhead. Most of the huge vessels were riding tall in the water, the rust-red of their lower hulls beneath the Plimsoll line showing that they carried little or no cargo. Their owners victims of global economic instability, some even left abandoned after corporate bankruptcy, the ships were moored here in a ghost flotilla, manned by skeleton crews serving as caretakers until the day the cash started flowing again.

From down on the waves, the scale of the vessels was monolithic. The ships were the size of skyscrapers lying on their sides, sheer walls of steel rising up from the water.

"He gets in among this lot, and we've lost him," called Marc.

As if they had heard the Brit's words, the running lights on the motorboat winked out.

* * *

Ticker's boat turned into a shadowy blob that lost itself
in the mass of a Panamax freighter across their path. The
burning sodium lights of the bigger ship destroyed Marc's
night vision, making it almost impossible to see where
the smaller vessel was going, down in the darkness.

He heard more than he saw the motorboat, catching
the rumble of its engine on the breeze as the craft raced
toward the freighter's stern. There was no spotlight
among the RIB's gear to use for illumination, and even if
they had one, Marc would have been reluctant to use it
for fear that Ticker would see them before they saw him.

He strained to listen over the slapping of the waves
against the hull of the RIB and the low rattle of the outboard. Back in his Royal Navy service with the Fleet Air
Arm, Marc remembered nights like this on the deck of
HMS *Ocean*, listening to the strange quality of sound
as it carried over the sea. It could be misleading if you
weren't used to the way acoustics shifted out here.

There.

The drone of the motorboat's engine lingered briefly
and he pointed Lucy in the right direction. He looked,
shading his eyes from the floodlights in a vain attempt
to claw back some dark adaptation, and spotted a
black-on-black shape cutting through the water.

"Go, Lucy!" he called. "Get in there, give him a kick
in the arse!"

She pushed them back to top speed, racing over the
waves at a high rate of knots.

"What the hell are you doing, Dane?"

The motorboat rose up in front of them, and they
were coming at the aft quarter of it too fast to avoid
hitting it. Marc gripped his pistol and braced himself
for another impact.

"Going over with a cutlass in my teeth, aren't I?"

The two boats struck each other and the collision was worse than before. The lighter RIB reared up and skidded noisily over the square stern of the motorboat, knocking the heavier vessel off course and into a hard list before it slipped back into the sea.

Marc jumped as they connected, and after a sickening lurch he landed badly on the other boat, going shoulder-first into a pile of gear crates lashed to the aft deck. A juddering surge of pain exploded across his left arm and he hit hard enough that he lost his grip on his gun. Hissing with effort, he rolled over in time to see Ticker coming up the deck toward him. The other man spotted the Taurus pistol where it had fallen, and he gave it a showy kick that sent it over the side and into the water.

"Dumbass move," sneered Ticker, pulling his own gun from his belt.

Marc bellowed wordlessly and leaped forward, bull-rushing Ticker before he could get the weapon clear.

He slammed into the other man and knocked the wind from him, shoving Ticker up against a stack of crates secured to the deck with a cargo net. Ticker brought down the butt of the pistol in his hand in a hard falling strike that missed the mark, failing to hit his opponent in the temple and instead scraping across his cheekbone, tearing a gash.

Marc felt blood flowing over his face, but he was focused totally on the metallic shape of the pistol dancing in front of his eyes. He grabbed the wrist of Ticker's gun hand and forced it up and away, struggling to stay balanced as the deck of the motorboat yawed. He smashed Ticker's hand against the crates over and over, and the gun went off, shots blasting up into the night sky, muzzle flares briefly strobing.

Finally, Marc's repeated attacks had the desired

effect and Ticker lost his grip on the pistol, but before he could do anything about it, the other man brought up his kneecap and planted it with full effect in Marc's crotch. A surge of pain shocked through him and he disengaged. Ticker took advantage and followed through with a clumsy roundhouse punch, which again did not quite connect, but did enough to send Marc reeling into a pile of equipment and black duffel bags lined up along the port side of the deck.

The motorboat rolled as it cut around the stern of the freighter, hitting choppy water stirred by the waves lapping against the giant ship. Marc was distantly aware of Lucy and the RIB somewhere off to the side, still keeping pace with the other boat. He stumbled, ignoring the sting of seawater spray over his face, trying to pull himself up as Ticker scrambled after the fallen weapon.

Marc's fingers closed on the first thing that came to hand—the grip of a small carry-case—and he yanked it free as Ticker pivoted back in his direction.

Ticker wasn't weapons-savvy. If he had been, the man would have held his .45 pistol closer to his chest. Instead, he brandished it at arm's length, all drama and no forethought.

Marc had already started the carry-case on a fast arc at the end of his own arm, leaning into it, letting the mass of the object chart the course. The narrow side of it connected with the side of Ticker's chin and there was a sickly crack as his jaw dislocated, mingling into a stifled moan of agony. The man floundered against the pitching deck.

It was only then that Marc realized what he was *actually* holding on to—not a carry-case at all, but the ruggedized Kontron NotePAC laptop Ticker had been so desperate to protect. He drew it near, eyes darting around for a way out.

Ticker was swearing violently, but his busted jaw turned his pain-laced words into incomprehensible mush. Without hesitating, he aimed the pistol in Marc's direction and emptied the rest of the clip.

Most of the rounds were wild, but one shot was right on target. A single .45 caliber bullet punctured the center of the laptop's armored lid and spent its force within, turning the machine's circuitry into splinters and shrapnel.

For Marc, the impact was like being hit in the chest by a bowling ball covered in razor blades. The shock blew him off his feet.

Gravity took hold and he tumbled over the side of the motorboat, into the black water. The air in his lungs blasted out in a gush of bubbles and he twisted into the undertow.

Lucy heard the shots and saw Marc go overboard, clutching the laptop. She had her gun in her hand and she started firing back at the motorboat, trying to land a hit on anything moving over there, but the other craft was already veering off, trying once again to extend their lead and escape pursuit.

"*Shit!*"

There was a split-second decision point where she could cut the engines and try to fish the Brit out of the water, or press on and risk letting him drown. Lucy was under absolutely no illusions that these black mask assholes were into something big, something serious, and if it revolved around Ji-Yoo Park and what she knew, one guy lost at sea wouldn't even measure on the scales against the deaths that could result.

But for all the lives she had taken in cold blood during her service, at a distance through the scope of a sniper rifle or striking unseen from the shadows, she couldn't bring herself to let Marc drown out here, wounded and alone. She *owed* him; and for all the hard-earned armor over her soldier's heart, she could not let herself be responsible for the death of a friend.

Lucy pulled the throttle back to idle and the RIB slowed to a rolling halt. Snatching her spyPhone from a pocket, she used the device's flashlight to sweep the dark waters off the bow. With the vertical wall of the freighter's hull looming over her head, it was like looking into an abyss. In the near distance, she heard the fading mutter of the motorboat as it raced further away with each passing second.

Then she caught sight of a tan-colored mass a dozen meters away. It was Dane, floating face down with his arms pulled close to his torso. Lucy called his name but he didn't respond.

She feathered the RIB's outboard and sent it in the right direction, and as it passed Marc's drifting form she leaned out over the bow as far as she could and grabbed handfuls of his jacket. Hauling him back and up was an effort, and as he came into the bobbing boat, she saw he was still clinging on to something like grim death—the smashed-up laptop computer.

Peeling the handle of the busted device from his fingers, Lucy let it drop and turned Marc over. The cotton shirt he wore was plastered to his chest and it was pink with his blood. The material was shredded and torn, and the skin beneath it lacerated. Fearing the worst, she felt around for a bullet wound but came up with nothing. Marc was on the edge of consciousness, and she rolled his head aside, letting brackish water trickle out of his mouth. His pulse was thready but he wasn't breathing. There had to be water in his lungs, and every second she didn't do something about it, he edged closer to slipping away.

"Okay," she told herself, tilting back his head and lifting his chin. "Pucker up, handsome."

Filling her lungs with air, she pinched shut his nose and pressed her lips to his, exhaling hard into his throat. His chest rose, but it wasn't enough. She tried again, this time with compression against his breastbone. The dozens of oozing wounds on Marc's chest turned her hands red and slippery, and a sudden fear gripped Lucy that she could be making it worse.

If he has a busted rib in there, a puncture in his lung . . . I could lose him.

She rejected the bleak thought and stamped down on the ember of nascent panic before it could catch.

"Don't you do this to me," she growled, and started the resuscitation cycle again.

On the second time around, muscles in Marc's arm jerked and he twitched against the RIB's deck. Suddenly he rolled over and retched, bringing up salt water with a noise that was half a choke, half a howl.

Lucy pulled back to give him room and Marc sagged against the side of the inflatable boat, shaking with near-shock.

"What . . ." he began, then lost the words and had to start over. "Oh bollocks. Not again."

Marc ran a trembling hand over his bloody face.

"Welcome back," said Lucy, with a weak gulp. The rescue had taken it out of her as well, and she felt the twitchy backwash of an adrenaline comedown in the tips of her fingers. "I thought you'd be . . ." She gasped. "Better kisser."

Marc gave a laugh, a slightly drunken, *amazed-to-be-alive* laugh that tailed off.

"Not without . . . dinner and a movie first."

Then his gaze settled on the blasted laptop and he suddenly became animated, scrabbling to grab the wrecked machine. He hissed in pain as he snatched it back up.

Lucy hunted around for the RIB's first aid kit, finding a tiny travel-size one under the steering wheel.

"Easy, tiger. You're bleeding pretty bad."

"Later," he muttered. "Need to . . ."

His ragged breathing came in fits and starts as he wrenched at the broken frame of the waterlogged computer.

Lucy could see where the device had taken a round at point-blank range, the innards of it a mess of shattered circuit boards and busted components. Marc pawed doggedly at the laptop, pulling modular sections out of it one by one and discarding them, until he seized on what he was looking for.

"This," he said, waving a battered solid-state hard drive in her direction, tearing wires from its connecting ports. "I think I pulled it out before any . . . any autoerase." Marc gave that faintly wasted chuckle again. "Yeah, good," he panted, and nodded weakly toward the darkness of the distant sea.

She sat down heavily next to him.

"Yeah, we're okay, I guess."

"Thanks for . . . stuff." He was nodding woodenly, trying to smile. "I just need to . . . uh . . . you know . . . pass out now."

The nodding stopped and Marc fell silent, his head lolling forward.

— NINE —

When the lightning hit, the sound shocked through the cockpit of the Lynx with a noise like the hammer of the gods. White light, hard and searing, momentarily blinded Marc through the night-vision goggles he had been wearing, and on reflex he had flipped them up, clutching at his eyes even as he felt the world dropping away beneath him.

Helicopters and thunderstorms are a bad mix, an instructor had once told him. *Spinning rotor blades create a negative charge in the air around your bird. And lightning loves that. Comes looking for it. Out of the sky like . . .*

Like the hammer of the gods, yeah.

And as something went catastrophically wrong, and the power in the aircraft turned dead, there was this moment as the crash truly began, when Marc looked out of his window and saw the deepest darkness he had ever known.

Then they were falling, spiraling out of the sky, down toward the gray churn of the South China Sea, and he had thought to himself *I didn't join the Navy to die out here, not like this, not on a bloody training exercise*—

That was then, but this time the stricken Lynx didn't crash into the waves, and this time there was no ocean, only a depthless, unending void.

And Marc was trapped inside the dying helicopter, falling, falling into an ink-dark abyss that carried on forever. His chest was on fire, and his heart was hammering.

But he wasn't alone. His gaze drew inexorably around to find the face of a woman slumped in the seat across the cockpit. She was clad in burned-black tactical gear, at once seared raw from fire and soaked through like a drowning victim. Dark, lank hair caged an ashen face and searching eyes. Her mouth opened but no sound emerged. She was trying to tell him something. *Sam*. Sam was trying to tell him—

Marc awoke.

It took long seconds for the dream-reality to slip off him and fade. His skin was filmed with sweat and at first it was hard to breathe. He wasn't in any rush to close his eyes again, so he stared fixedly at the mottled ceiling above the bed, letting his heartbeat normalize, stopping himself from taking panic-breaths.

He could almost taste the metallic seawater in his mouth, and that sense-memory threatened to trigger off a whole raft of unpleasant recollections. The exercise, the crash and the aftermath of it were a long way gone, but the moment was embedded in the center of Marc Dane, lodged in his brain like a splinter of shrapnel. The death of Samantha Green had come much later, but the shock of that moment was just as intense, as immediate as it had been on a Dunkirk dockside three years ago.

In the helicopter crash, Marc had gone to the brink of death and somehow survived. When Sam and the rest of his MI6 OpTeam had perished in fire and betrayal, he had been the only one to survive it. When he least wanted it, the dark recall of these moments would come up and smack him around, like an old and spiteful enemy he could never escape.

Rubicon employed a specialist in their medical team, a counselor named Benjamin, an expert in post-traumatic stress disorders. Marc had taken sessions with the man. Every active operative in the SCD did so annually, as a condition of their contracts with the company. He'd sat across from this big, burly Frenchman with a manicured mustache like an old-time circus strongman, and lied to him about how he was dealing with it. Marc suspected Benjamin knew he was covering—the guy was former *Légion étrangère*, and he had likely seen enough combat trauma to fill several lifetimes. But he never once called him out over the deceit.

The searing salt taste faded but the steady burning over his chest remained. Marc winced as he sat up. He'd been stripped down to his boxers, bandaged up and left to sleep it off. He scratched at an itchy spot on the crook of his arm where a tiny scab showed someone had given him an injection. By the fuzzy sensation in his head, he guessed it was a mild sedative and something to stall any infection. Swinging his bare feet over and on to the floor, he took in the room.

He was back at the Interlace, in one of the apartments the team had secured for their base of operations. The room was large and practically empty, except for the folding camp bed he sat on and a pile of gear arranged against a nearby wall. Cream-colored pile carpet extended away to a floor-to-ceiling window that looked out across the top of the apartment complex toward the heart of Singapore. A line of pinkish radiance on the horizon signaled that dawn was not far away, and he stood up to take a closer look.

At the window, Marc probed the surgical tape over

the cut on his cheek and the bandages taped across his chest, hissing in pain as he touched the raw areas. When Ticker had shot at him through the toughened laptop, the shock of the hit had stunned him. A jet of searing hot fragments of plastic and metal showered his torso, and then he was in the drink, struggling to stay upright. Failing, now that he thought about it.

Lucy dragged me out of the water. I pulled the drive . . .

Those moments seemed less real, blurry and untethered like the helicopter nightmare.

Did that actually happen?

Blinking away dizziness, he pulled on trousers and a T-shirt from his gear bag, then padded barefoot back through the connecting apartments. He followed the soft mutter of a keyboard and a whiff of tobacco smoke into the open-plan kitchen–dining room that was their temporary command center.

Assim looked up as Marc approached, and guiltily plucked a cigarette from his mouth and looked at it.

"I un-quit again," he said sheepishly. "Are you all right? I mean, you're up, so I suppose that means yes."

"How long have I been out of it?"

Marc dropped into a folding chair next to the younger man, casting an eye over the dense wall of text on the screen in front of him.

"Eight, ten hours, I think?"

"You been awake all that time?"

"I don't need much sleep," Assim replied, with a shrug.

Marc saw the solid-state hard drive he had rescued on the table, wired up to a buffer module that in turn was connected to Assim's computer.

So I didn't dream that bit, then.

"What'd I miss?"

Assim's brow furrowed in concern.

"Marc, you don't have to get straight back into this . . ." He was going to say more, but Marc waved the comment away. "Okay. All right then." He pivoted the laptop screen so they could both see it. "Bloody awful housekeeping, if you ask me. Whoever this belonged to, they left their drive contents looking like a rubbish tip."

"Yeah, I got that sense from the bloke." Marc studied the display. The hacker was running a cluster analysis. "So you pulled—what? Communications metadata off this?"

"Money transfers," Assim confirmed. "Lots of them."

Down the corridor, a toilet flushed and the bathroom door opened. Lucy, now dressed in a baggy gray sweatshirt and matching tracksuit trousers, wandered into the room and gave him a sustained frown.

"How are you feeling?"

"Like crap," Marc admitted, and he tried to laugh it off, but the action made his chest sting and he winced. "Where's Malte?"

She jerked her thumb at one of the other rooms.

"Sleeping like a big, bearded baby." Lucy picked up a wadded ball of paper towels and bandage offcuts lying on a nearby table. "Here, some souvenirs I pulled out of you."

She dropped it in his hand and Marc peeled back the bloodstained material, finding dozens of little shards, each one a tiny piece of Ticker's ruined computer.

"You're lucky that guy went for the toughened option," she continued. "I found the bullet lodged in the power pack."

He waited for the expected lecture about taking unnecessary risks, but she didn't follow through with one.

"Thanks for having my back out there," he said, after a moment.

She nodded. "We lost Ticker and his buddy out in the ghost fleet. I'm guessing they had a pickup waiting further out to sea, either took the motorboat on board a bigger ship or scuttled it."

"Indonesia is only a few hours' sailing from there," noted Assim. "It's a good bet they made port in Jakarta and boarded a plane or another ship to their next destination."

"Plane," Marc said absently.

He remembered something the French woman said to Ticker over the phone. *Wrap up warm.* Marc put the debris from his injury aside and leaned forward in his chair.

"All right. Let's string together what we know."

"The bioprinters were gone before we reached the club," began Lucy, sitting heavily in a folding chair. "The gang running the place . . ." She threw a look at Assim.

"The Ang Soon Tong," he replied.

"Those Chow Yun Fat wannabes, they're part of a smuggling network that goes to the US, the Middle East, Russia, Europe. Their speciality is trafficking in black market antiquities. Rubicon's security division has a file on them an inch thick."

Assim nodded. "Over the last few years there's been this spate of robberies in Europe, targeted thefts of ancient Chinese antiquities that are supposedly being 'repatriated' by the government in Beijing." He made air quotes with his fingers. "Allegedly, the Ang Soon Tong have been helping with that, upping their game globally. They have contacts everywhere."

Marc scowled. "Which makes them the ideal middlemen to send those bioprinters to wherever the hell the black masks want."

"Speaking of them, we have a couple of faces now," said Lucy, motioning at her head. "Your buddy the hacker and some of his playmates were caught on camera outside the club."

Assim opened up a data panel on his screen, presenting grainy image captures from the traffic monitor.

"The equipment I have on site here is a bit lacking," he said apologetically, "so a full-on deep dive data sweep wasn't possible—but it turns out we didn't need it. Facial recognition pinged this chap to an open FBI warrant."

"Let me guess," said Marc. "Cybercrime?"

"And a lot of it, too. As you already know, he runs under the *nom de guerre* Ticker, along with a dozen other aliases." Assim flicked up a virtual panel showing the *be-on-the-lookout* bulletin bearing the man's details. "Add to that aggravated assault, conspiracy against the American government, incitement to violence . . . All of it with a strong race-hatred element."

"I read his jacket. This prick is your classic angry white boy," said Lucy, folding her arms across her chest. "Grew up cussing people out on Xbox, straight into credit card fraud and right-wing conspiracy theory country, next stop white hoods and cross burning."

"What's he doing helping to kidnap a bioscientist in Singapore, then?" Marc eyed the man's photo. "The bloke looks like the true believer type."

Assim was silent for a long moment, before he went on with the next piece of data.

"I've been monitoring the local police force. Singapore CID's specialized crime unit has been called in to go over the incident at the warehouse club. They haven't connected anything up to the MaxaBio theft and the Lam abduction, but it's only been a few hours."

"They will," Marc said grimly.

Lucy and Assim fell silent as he described to them the horror he had found in the plastic drum down in the basement, and the comments that Ticker had made after the fact.

"He told you that?" Lucy asked quietly. Marc nodded and she swore under her breath. "Son of a bitch."

"The bodies in the drum . . . That was the boy and his dad." Assim had to voice it out loud to grasp the awfulness of it. "That's what we're saying?" His hand rose to his mouth. "*Ya Allah . . .*"

"Why kidnap them just to kill them?" said Lucy, her cold anger seething beneath the words.

"I have an idea about that."

Assim worked the keyboard and brought up a fragmented file menu gleaned from the recovered hard drive. He explained that he had been concentrating on the data pertaining to the money transfers, but that the drive also contained partially deleted video and audio files.

"The footage is shots of Simon Lam and his son, and their house. At first, I couldn't understand what the purpose of it was, but now . . ." He trailed off.

Marc nodded. "There was camera gear and an audiovisual editing kit in the basement." He looked at Assim. "Are you thinking . . . ?"

Assim returned his nod. "I believe it could be raw material for a deepfake."

"By the look on your faces," said Lucy, "I know I am going to regret asking you to explain what that is."

"Basically . . . It's a piece of software that will make sure you never trust anything you see on a screen, ever again."

Marc gave her the high points, watching as her expression shifted from incredulity, to concern, and finally to outright disgust.

A deepfake, he explained, was video and audio foot-age compiled from real sources and blended seam-lessly together using an artificially intelligent heuristic program. The program could take disparate recordings and patch one over the other, learning how to better manipulate images and sound to create something that looked seamless to the human eye.

"The first ones were bogus sex tapes, slapping the faces of movie stars on top of pornography. Then poli-ticians swearing or giving speeches they never had. And that's the amateur work. Think about what a non-state actor with an axe to grind and some funding could do." Marc let that sink in. "It's the same tech that gives you movies about dinosaur theme parks and superheroes beating each other up. Only you don't need a Holly-wood special effects studio to do it."

"*Shit!*" Lucy shook her head. "Okay. I'm officially freaked out by that."

"Ticker and his mates were assembling deepfakes of the husband and the kid." Marc voiced the thought aloud as it occurred to him. "There was an audio file I heard . . . It was Simon Lam talking, reading out a bunch of nonsense sentences." He nodded to himself. "I knew I'd heard something like that before. It was es-tablishing a baseline for his voice."

"You're describing a phonetic pangram." Assim swal-lowed hard. "A string of words that contain all the phonetic sounds of a given language. We have a few on file ourselves in the SCD's secure server."

"We have?" Lucy gave him a sharp look.

Assim nodded again. "Remember last year, when you two broke into the Horizon Integral tower in Sydney? How do you think we were able to simulate the voice of the CEO to open those digital locks?"

"Yeah?" Her eyes flashed. "If I find out you have

video of me humping a hockey team, I will straight up cut your balls off." She shuddered. "Just hearing about this shit makes me want to take a shower."

"Okay, before we go any further, I reckon we need to call this in." Marc looked to Lucy. She was mission leader, so the decision would be hers.

She didn't hesitate. "Agreed." She glanced at Assim. "Contact the Monaco office, give them a sitrep."

"Okay. I've been mirroring the data recovered from the hard drive as I decrypted it," he replied. "Delancort won't be happy about our results."

"My heart bleeds."

The words came out in a snarl, and Marc winced as the bandages across his chest went tight.

The pain in the prisoner's foot had worsened, after one of his tormentors smacked him too many times on the base of his callused sole. There had been a lot of blood and a desultory attempt to bandage the injury, but like so many of the ways in which the prisoner was treated, it was done in a careless and indifferent manner.

He limped toward the waiting truck, its engine idling in the overcast morning, flanked by a pair of guards who were young enough to be his sons. One carried a rifle, forever tugging on the strap, while the other smoked a cigarette in clear violation of standing orders. Neither made a move to aid him in any way, but that was to be expected. Some distance ahead of the truck, a black car was parked near the camp's main gate, and he sensed that it too was waiting for him.

The prisoner flexed his wrists in the handcuffs holding them together, and chanced a closer look at the guards. Like the men who fed him in the camp's sparse mess hall, the ones who patrolled outside his isolated cell, or those who came to administer his regular "correctional" beatings, they were ignorant of who he was and why he was a convict. They followed their orders to keep him alive and uncomfortable, but he imagined they did not dare to ask *why* they did so.

How many years had it been? After the first decade he stopped counting the days. The prisoner's existence flattened into endless bleak nights on hard bunks and dull daylight hours of stultifying routine and back-breaking work. Sometimes they allowed him to read books or join the other prisoners to watch films in the common area, but these were always insipid entertainments designed to reinforce the rightness of the State. These respites were only granted so they could be taken away, and after a few years he had learned to see the patterns in the mechanical cruelty of it.

Last night it had rained, and the chill remained in the damp air. He navigated around puddles in the pock-marked road, aware that he was being watched by several convicts from the exercise yard. They hung on the wire of the inner fence, indolently observing him making his way, wondering what made him so special. To them, he must have seemed like a phantom. A thing glimpsed from the corner of the eye, a rumor more than a man.

This was an old and familiar parade for the prisoner, of course. At random intervals chosen by those who judged him, guards would come to his cell and lead him out. There would be a vehicle waiting for him, a truck or a car, on the rarest of occasions a helicopter, and he would be placed aboard and taken elsewhere. This particular camp, which he guessed to be somewhere toward the northwestern border, was what had once been known as a *laogai*. It was one of a myriad of penal labor sites scattered throughout the wilderness of the

People's Republic of China, where those who broke the law or opposed the Party would be brought to engage what the State called "reform through labor." Such camps might be tanning works or asbestos mines, tea plantations or wheat farms, where the inmates worked their sentence for the good of the country. Other times, the prisoner found himself in military-style stockades or windowless bunkers where the most reviled enemies were entombed. The only constant was the inconstancy, as if the government that he had wronged could not bear to keep the prisoner in one place for too long.

He sometimes wondered if the men who had condemned him were still alive. Did they too observe him from a distance, content that they had done their jobs well? Or were the reasons for the prisoner's incarceration lost and no longer remembered?

He was a forgotten man, of that there could be no doubt. All trace of him erased, his previous honorable service to the State wiped out after his crime. This was his lot.

The smoker became irritated at his slow pace, but the prisoner made no attempt to move faster. He did not want to chance reopening the wound on his foot. It was an old scar, from many prisons ago, and he didn't heal as well as he once had. Poor subsistence-level food kept him weak, and the years of confinement had aged him prematurely. The prisoner was somewhere in his mid-fifties, he estimated, but the face that he occasionally studied in the mirror resembled that of his grandfather.

The thought of the time stolen from him hardened his resolve. It was the core around which his resistance was built, the last thing he held on to after everything else had been stripped from him.

His punishment for daring to believe he could out-think the State and pursue his own agenda was a prison sentence with no end, a penance that did not officially exist in any records. He was that transient phenomenon the other convicts saw, the ghost trapped inside an engine of contempt, with no hope of escape.

At the back of the vehicle, another guard, with the cow-eyed look of a country yokel, dropped the cargo gate and beckoned him up. The Jiefang truck was a heavy three-axle affair, a brutish diesel machine in drab military camouflage with a mottled fabric canopy suspended over the flatbed. The prisoner knew from experience that the ride would be uncomfortable.

He climbed aboard, taking his time, careful not to snag the dark blue material of his too-thin jacket on the protruding spars of the truck's frame. As he settled in, a senior guard appeared around the side of the vehicle, and the smoker jerked in shock, caught in the act. He threw his cigarette into a puddle but it was too late. The senior man berated him for a few moments before ordering him to follow the prisoner into the truck. The guard with the rifle on his shoulder came next, shoving up next to the yokel. Inside the close confines of the covered flatbed, he could smell the rifleman's breath, like sour milk.

The senior man banged hard on the side of the truck. As the vehicle lurched away, the prisoner saw him speaking into a handheld radio.

When he looked back, the smoker was glaring at him, as if it was his fault that he had been reprimanded. The prisoner automatically let his gaze drop to the floor, showing passivity, but it was too late.

"What are you looking at?" spat the smoker. He prodded the prisoner in the chest.

The prisoner said nothing, his face a mask of dumb penitence. But that was not enough.

The smoker took his silence as an insult and slapped him about the head, spending his anger in a few quick blows. When he was done, he leaned back and glowered.

The pain in the prisoner's foot was now a throbbing twinge, and he had the beginnings of a headache from the slaps. He hunched forward and stared at the wooden floorboards and the chink of visible road in the gaps between them, losing himself in the nothingness of the action. This was how he survived—by disconnecting from the world around him. Only when he was truly alone would the prisoner allow himself to reach down for old memories, for the warm recall of the good days and the steady burn of resentment for everything left unresolved.

They drove for several hours along dirt roads and desolate highways. He guessed they were heading south. From what the prisoner could see out of the back of the truck, they were moving into craggy lowland territory, where the roads cut through the hills with arrow-straight efficiency. The yokel dozed off and the rifleman traded stories with the smoker. Once in a while, the driver up front would beg a cigarette.

The daylight changed as they entered a snaking canyon. The prisoner heard the grind of gears as the driver nursed the elderly Jiefang's engine. And then suddenly the brakes bit hard with a low squeal.

Everyone in the back of the truck lurched forward, and the yokel was thrown out of his sleep with enough shock that he called out a woman's name in surprise, slurring like a drunkard. The rifleman laughed at him.

The smoker lifted a flap in the cover and peered through it at the empty road behind them.

"What is this?" he demanded.

"Hey!" the rifleman called to the driver. "Why did you stop?"

The prisoner heard the sound of breaking glass and the driver slumped forward against the steering wheel. Blood smeared the sliding window that looked into the truck's cab.

The yokel recoiled, then grabbed for his weapon where it lay on the floor. Beside him, the rifleman was turning toward the rear of the vehicle, his aspect hardening. The dark tarpaulin over the flatbed crackled as something punched through it. An ugly blossom of red burst on the rifleman's chest and he rolled on to the floor. The prisoner heard the bullet that struck him drone past, passing out through the other side of the vehicle. The rifleman gasped and a horrible wheezing, sucking sound came out of the wound as it began to end him.

The smoker vaulted over the dying man, scrambling out of the back of the truck, fumbling with his own weapon. The yokel dashed after him, leaving the prisoner and his wounded comrade.

Out on the road, the smoker had his gun up and he was panning it around, trying to aim in the direction of the incoming shots. The prisoner watched him take two rounds, one in the chest and one in the belly, before collapsing on the highway.

The prisoner slipped off the bench mounted inside the flatbed and made himself as small as he could, pressing himself against the steel frame of the truck. The silent shots might penetrate the metal, or they might not. He wasn't going to take the chance.

The yokel started firing, sending bursts upward at the crags, but if he had a target he was missing it. The man started to retreat back toward the truck when a shot passed through his kneecap and he fell down in a screaming heap.

The prisoner watched this through a hole in the metal

frame, as detached as he ever was. The yokel cried out for help, and for the moment the shooting stopped.

From behind the prisoner, the rifleman continued to die slowly and noisily. He turned to look at the young man.

The rifleman's face was bloodless with shock as he clutched weakly at the grotesque wound in his chest.

It was easy to pull the rifle from his hands. The gun was a modern bullpup-fashion assault weapon, familiar to the prisoner but not something he had ever trained with. Still, a rifle was a rifle. He turned it over in his hands, considering it. Then he shot the young man through the head rather than prolong his agony.

The act of mercy surprised him. He did not owe these men anything, after all. They were cogs in the same machine that had made his life a misery. He put the weapon across his lap and searched the dead man, finding the keys to his handcuffs.

The yokel cried out in alarm, and when the prisoner looked up, a new figure was standing at the edge of the dusty road. Tall and imposing, his head was wrapped in a scarf so only his eyes were visible, and he had a camouflage cloak that was the same hue as the rocky hillside. The figure held a rifle, a gun that the prisoner was much more accustomed to. It was a Type 56, the PRC's copy of Russia's workhorse AKM assault weapon. It was clear the user knew exactly how to wield it to best effect.

One hand came up to pull down the scarf and the prisoner saw a foreigner's copper-shaded, leonine features. The man walked over to the smoker, kicked his rifle aside and put a shot through his skull. Then he closed in on the yokel, ignoring the guard's entreaties, and finished him too.

The prisoner held his stolen rifle close, ready to defend himself if the need arose. Instead, the foreigner walked to the front of the truck to make sure he had killed the driver. His thoroughness was remarkable.

The prisoner rose slowly and kicked open the drop gate, before dismounting. The yokel's sightless eyes stared up at him where he lay slumped against the Jiefang's bloodstained rear wheels. The prisoner looked away, and for the first time he saw why the truck had stopped. Up ahead, slewed sideways and blocking the road, was the black car he had seen near the gate of the labor camp. From this distance, the crimson smeared over the windscreen and the holes in the glass made it clear that everyone inside was dead.

Presently, the foreigner came back around the far side of the truck, his rifle shouldered. Unhurried, he pulled a photograph from his pocket, comparing the image to the man in front of him, then nodded toward the crags.

"I have food and water, clean clothes," he said, in accented English. "Also medicine, if you require it."

He moved to a gulley at the side of the road and pulled away another camouflage covering, to reveal a long, heavy bag that he dragged back toward the truck.

"Who . . . are you?"

The words sounded strange coming out of the prisoner's mouth. He had not spoken the other language in a long time.

"Does it matter?"

The foreigner unzipped the bag and there was a corpse inside. A man around the prisoner's age, dressed in a threadbare *laogai* laborer's uniform identical to his. The foreigner reached past the body and pulled out a pair of magnesium road flares. They would burn all remains and leave nothing recognizable.

"I want to know the name of . . . the man who liber-
ated me," said the prisoner.

The foreigner shrugged. "I am Khadir. And I am not
the liberator I once was."

"Khadir," repeated the prisoner. "I remember, it
means *one who is powerful*."

"For now, less than I would wish," admitted the other
man. "But I am patient."

"I know a lot about patience." The prisoner nodded
as an understanding came to him, as he saw the reason
for all of this. "I think I have become useful to someone. Yes?"

Khadir nodded. "I'll take you to him."

It was after midnight in Monaco, and Delancort cradled a cup of potent espresso, breathing in the aroma.
He stared out through the conference room window,
out at the black expanse of sea. Beneath the Rubicon
tower, the city extended in either direction along the
coastline in a glowing belt of light, glittering and moving like streams of molten gold. Delancort was oblivious to it, lost in the distant dark. He blinked and
adjusted his rimless spectacles, catching sight of his reflection in the bronzed glass.

Outwardly he was, as always, carefully managed in
his appearance and poise, lacking nothing. Inwardly, the
situation could not have been more different. A day ago,
Ekko Solomon had retreated to his yacht, the *Themis*,
down there on the black water. Solomon had made it
clear that Henri's services were not required and he was
not to be contacted unless the matter was of the utmost
urgency.

This wasn't an uncommon occurrence. Solomon's executive assistant didn't live in his boss's back pocket,

despite what other Rubicon personnel might have thought, but years of working for the African billionaire meant Delancort had a clear sense of what the man meant when he *didn't* speak as much as when he *did*.

The echo of the conversation with the board members still hung in the air, like the scent of the rich coffee turning sour as it cooled. There was an unpleasant inference in it that Delancort was unable to shake off. First and foremost, he was an employee of the Rubicon Group, and his loyalty was to the corporation, but Ekko Solomon was his superior, and the plain truth of it was that Henri would not be alive now without the man's intervention. Solomon liked to say that Rubicon in general and the Special Conditions Division in particular were places that gave people a second chance. That was an undeniable truth for Delancort. But for all he had done and his laudable intentions, Solomon was just one man. Rubicon was his life's work, yes, but it had a life of its own. Then a soft chime sounded through the room and he was spared any further introspection.

Delancort straightened in his chair as a rectangular shape drew itself into being on the window glass, transforming into a video screen. A thin layer of transparent electrosensitive polymer coating the inside of the window allowed it to become a display like any desktop monitor, and he preferred that to the peculiarly disconnected conversations that took place through the VR rigs in the room. Speaking to someone on a screen gave Delancort a sense of control over the discussion that the other method did not. The VR system lacked the theater of being able to hang up on someone if the moment demanded it, for example.

An encryption chyron marched across the top of the screen, promising that the video link was scrambled

and secure, and presently a dim image of an ill-lit room
appeared on it. Dane and Kader were framed in the
foreground, peering into the eye of a digital camera,
and he could make out Keyes perched on the edge of a
chair behind them.

"*Still awake, Henri?*" said the woman, with a cat-
eyed glance.

"You know me well enough to understand what a
foolish question that is." His reply was instinctively
sharp. "I have been monitoring your uploads of the intelligence taken from this hard drive—"

The Englishman opened his mouth to speak, but
Delancort did not give him the opportunity. The reckless recovery of the device had Dane's fingerprints all
over it, with his usual disregard for his safety and that
of the larger operation. Delancort wasn't about to allow him the chance to make excuses.

"That material, along with the connections it sug-
gests, are disturbing," he concluded. "The involvement
of a Triad group, the thefts of our equipment . . . But
first, I need more context on these 'black masks' you
encountered."

"*The men we could identify belong to a far-right activist group called the Lion's Roar,*" said Kader. "*Once
they were small-scale, largely confined to Belgium and
the Netherlands, but in recent years the shift in the political landscape has allowed them to expand. Now
they're active all the way out to Russia, and there's evidence they have alliances with white power groups in
America, and violent identitarian factions elsewhere in
Europe.*"

"*These creeps aren't sign-wavers and social media
tough guys,*" added Keyes. "*They're the real deal. An
active terrorist organization.*"

"And they have abducted Dr. Park, and you suspect, murdered her new family."

"*I don't* suspect *any bloody thing about that,*" said Dane, with grim-faced certainty.

Delancort swore under his breath, quietly enough that the room's microphones didn't pick it up. His first instinct was to advise they cut their losses and disengage from this mess while they were still able. It could be done, quickly and discreetly, turning over what data they had to Interpol and the local authorities in Singapore. But on the other hand, doing that would open up Rubicon to a whole raft of liabilities, and force them to answer unpleasant questions about Ji-Yoo Park's defection from North Korea and the falsehood of her new life as Susan Lam. There were some situations that not even Rubicon could buy its way out of.

"Is there anything you can tell me that won't fill me with dread," he went on, "or is that too much to ask?"

"*Assim's rebuilding some fragmented data trails from the recovered drive,*" said Dane. "*You know what Bitcoin is, right?*"

"I am not completely ignorant about digital technology," Delancort replied.

Granted, he was not steeped in esoteric hacker lore like the Englishman, but he knew how the so-called cryptocurrency operated.

As he understood it, Bitcoin was a form of virtual money that could be instantaneously traded around the world, allowing parties at both ends of the transaction to remain essentially anonymous. Difficult to trace, it was perfect for dealings that were less than legal. Certain black book operations undertaken by the SCD needed just such an invisible finance stream in order to remain viable. But it wasn't infallible, and in Delancort's

eyes it was no substitute for a bag of untraceable diamonds or a suitcase full of used bills.

"*I've been running a cluster analysis remotely, via
the main server in Monaco, trying to backtrack a series
of Bitcoin transactions that terminated here in Singapore,*" Kader said quickly. Delancort raised an eyebrow.
He had not authorized that. "*And it's likely that payments to the Ang Soon Tong fronts came from the same
real-world location that has been sending money to
other places as well. Transfers have gone out to India,
Syria, Russia, Croatia, and a few other nodes I haven't
been able to identify as yet.*"

"*It's gotta be the bankroll for this entire op,*" added
Keyes.

"What is the location?"

"*Unclear.*" The young Saudi's hands knitted together.
"*There's a number of possibilities.*" He paused to study
a list on a tablet screen. "*One in Cyprus, one in Sen-
egal, another in Iceland, and a fourth in Mauritius.*"

Delancort leaned back in his chair, assimilating this
new information.

"How long will it take you to be certain?"

"*Too long,*" insisted Dane, reaching over to take the
tablet from Kader, to look more closely at it. "*I heard
these creeps talking about a deadline. Four days until
who-knows-what. It won't be something pleasant.*"

"*I could run this faster if I have access to a mainframe,*" said Kader. "*Can you clear me to use the system at Rubicon's local office over here?*"

Delancort didn't hesitate over his answer.

"No. I am afraid for now, you will need to work with
what you have to hand."

It would be better for Kader's work to be confined
to a system other than a company server, one a long

way out of sight of the visiting board members and their staff.

"*Wrap up warm . . .*" Dane was staring at Kader's tablet, lost in the lines of data there. He sounded like he was talking to himself. "*Huh. Iceland is the one. Yeah, it tracks. The Bitcoin connection is dead on.*"

"How are you so sure of that?" said Delancort, but now Dane was ignoring him as he continued to think out loud.

"*Bitcoin from Iceland, though, that's like saying someone sent chocolate from Switzerland.*" He made a vague gesture with his hand and Delancort felt his patience eroding. "*Iceland has cheap geothermal power and a cold environment, which is ideal for big server farms to mine Bitcoin by the virtual truckload.*"

Now Delancort really was at the limit of his knowledge, and it irritated him to admit it.

"Explain," he snapped, and nodded at the little cup in front of him. "But if you continue to veer into the realm of technobabble, I'm afraid not even this espresso will keep me awake."

Dane gave him a withering look back through the screen.

"*For the noob, then. Bitcoin isn't just digital cash you trade, yeah? You can create it as well, out of mathematical code. Run the right algorithm through a high-powered computer, you're in with a chance of getting free money. But the algorithms are extremely complex and you need some heavy iron to do the computing. That takes a lot of electricity and generates a lot of heat.*"

"*Which is why Iceland is a prime location for such activity,*" added Kader. "*Hotter countries, not so much.*"

Dane continued, returning to the conversation he had overheard where one of the Lion's Roar suspects spoke

of the four-day deadline. There had also been mention of
moving to another location.

"*She told him to wrap up warm,*" he concluded, and
held up a hand. "*The only cold place on our list is Iceland. And I know, I know, before you say it. It's a slim
lead.*"

"*Slim?*" From behind him, Keyes gave a derisive
snort. "*Hell, it's so thin I can see through it.*"

"We don't have the option of dispatching operatives
to each one of these places," Delancort said firmly.
"Not with the limits currently in place." He fell silent
for a moment.

The standing orders in this active operation were to
follow Susan Lam's trail wherever it led. But if the Englishman's lead proved useless, the blowback would
be considerable. He frowned. This was the core of his
dislike for Marc Dane—the man's reckless tendency
to trust his instincts over more measured and calculated actions. It didn't help that he was often right, but
Delancort was convinced his luck would run out one
day.

"Lucy," he said, at length, "what is your evaluation?"

Her expression shifted, hardening into something taciturn and calculating.

"*We know what the stakes are. Park is in the wind,
and so is tech that can pump out the worst kind of bioweapons imaginable. Both are Rubicon's responsibility.*" She glanced at Dane. "*I don't like going out on a
hunch, but what else we got?*"

And with that, the choice was made for him. Delancort gave a nod.

"After the incident at the warehouse club, the Singapore authorities will be looking for you, so removing
you from the country has its merits. Malte and Assim
can remain in the city and continue to investigate from

there." He looked at Dane. "If you intend to insert into Iceland undetected, you will need to do so under your cover identities, via civilian routes."

"*That'll be tricky,*" said the Englishman. "*They know our faces. They know Rubicon is tracking them.*"

"It was your idea, Mr. Dane," he replied. "So make it work. Quickly."

— TEN —

The painkillers Marc had downed distorted the flight into a dreamless gray nothing, but they were not powerful enough to stop him from being bounced back to wakefulness as the narrow-body Airbus jet began a hard descent toward the Icelandic coast, and into Keflavík Airport. His drug-assisted doze broke apart as the airliner side-slipped through a dense wall of storm cloud, a heavy vibration shuddering up through the deck beneath his half-laced hiking boots.

Straightening in his aisle seat, feeling unpleasantly dehydrated, Marc wiped a hand up over his face and through his hair. He chanced a look across the other passengers in his row and out of the window. A man wearing a rumpled suit was in the middle seat, his eyes screwed tightly shut and his knuckles white around the end of the armrests. The window seat was vacant except for a discarded copy of the *Kleine Zeitung*, and Marc watched the folded newspaper shuffle its way across the shuddering cushion before making a break for the floor and vanishing into the footwell.

Through the oval window, Marc could see the Airbus's port wing tip as it oscillated alarmingly against the wind and the lashing rain. The airliner fell through a stomach-turning drop and several of the passengers let out cries of alarm. Marc's row-mate muttered something under his breath in anxious German. The plane dropped again, and a few rows back a baby wailed.

The FASTEN SEATBELTS light on the bulkhead above him flashed a reminder and Marc straightened, looking ahead through the gaps in the headrests. Anyone releasing the latch during this kind of chop was asking to be thrown out of their seat.

He made out a sliver of Lucy's face, there about six rows ahead in the business class section. She was running under a snap cover like he was. Her passport made her appear to be a wildlife photographer from Guyana coming to Iceland to shoot stills of the indigenous horse population. Marc's legend played to his strengths, casting him as a Canadian blogger arriving to write an article about the country's fastest-growing video games studio.

From the moment they left the Interlace in Singapore, Marc and Lucy had been studiously ignoring each other's existence, inhabiting their covers with as little fanfare as possible. He had modified his look by cleaning up his shabby beard, affecting a pair of thick-rimmed glasses and some visible fake tattoos. Lucy had changed her hair, pulling it into a topknot and doing something clever with skin toner to make the shape of her cheekbones change. She was a lot better at this than he was, Marc reflected. The American seemed to have a flawless, almost casual ability to slip into a disguise like she was putting on a new jacket. For Marc, it was a constant effort to be someone he wasn't.

Both of their false identities would be good enough to pass muster with Icelandic border control—but the point would be moot if they never made it to the ground in one piece. The aircraft gave a low, tortured moan as the fuselage fought the wind on the way down.

Flat, craggy and beautifully desolate, Iceland sat in

the North Atlantic like a defiant fist raised against the
weather gods, and that was a challenge they frequently
accepted. Squalls and gale force blizzards were regular
visitors to the country's glaciated shores and black volcanic beaches. Today was going to mark another such
arrival. The Airbus powered in toward the runway,
racing to stay beyond the leading edge of the monster
storm front that was chasing it.

There was a sudden blink of weak daylight as the jet
broke through the base of the cloud, and Marc's gaze
was pulled back to the window. Vicious gusts buffeted
the aircraft and he took a deep breath, seeing a snow-
mottled plate of white and brown landscape rising up
to meet them. Off in the near distance, the low, hard-
sided shapes of military hangars from the old NATO
airbase were visible, and the gray orb of a radar dome
stuck up from the airport perimeter, stark against the
distant hills.

He held his breath and counted off the distance until, with a juddering crash, the Airbus's undercarriage
hit the tarmac hard and it skidded into a crosswind. Engines howled as the flight crew compensated and Marc
felt the lurch as they started to slow. A scattered round
of uneasy applause rose up from some of the passengers, and the businessman at Marc's side let go of the
armrests with a jolt. He opened his eyes, blinking and
pale, glancing around.

"Welcome to Reykjavík," said Marc, with a wan
smile.

The man gave a weak nod and pulled a tiny bottle
of vodka from the seat pocket in front of him, twisting
off the cap and downing the entire contents in a single,
shaky pull.

Everyone was eager to disembark swiftly, and Marc
trailed the businessman on to the jet bridge, pausing

as he adjusted the bag on his shoulder. Through the elevated walkway's windows, the light had a strange quality to it, as if the sun was being attenuated through a gray filter. Marc turned and saw the reason why. The storm front was still bearing down, a wall of slate-colored cloud advancing even as he watched. Specks of windblown ice were already flickering off the glass. Behind him a young guy in a ground crew hi-vis vest gave a chuckle and said something wry in Icelandic.

"Pardon me?" Marc glanced back at him.

The guy in the vest pointed at the storm, and grinned with the kind of gallows-humor relish that only a local could have.

"It's going to be a big one!" Then he added another thought. "You should buy a hat. You'll need it."

By Lucy's reckoning, the local time was around mid-morning, but everything about the Icelandic sky and the angle of the sun was telling her different. She knew that this far north the length of daylight hours were a little weird, but it was still unsettling. The heat and humidity of Singapore was quite literally a world away, and the biting cold was finding its way through the heavy, purple ski jacket she wore.

Hauling her gear bag and a steel camera case, she left the airport terminal building and found the minibus that would take her into Reykjavík. The icy wind tugged at her faux-fur lined hood as she trudged across the snow-patterned asphalt.

Going through passport control, she stood behind a queasy-looking American couple animatedly discussing the weather they had barely escaped. It was shaping up to be one of the worst storms Iceland had experienced all year, a fact confirmed when Lucy looked up at the arrivals boards in passing, and saw that the flights following theirs had been delayed or diverted. Reading the board had also given her the opportunity to surreptitiously check the faces in the airport lounge for anyone who looked like an obvious watcher.

She came up empty. Lucy hoped that was a good sign. It was either that, or the watchers were so accomplished she didn't see them. In the end, it made no difference. This was an undercover infiltration, and that meant operating as if she was in enemy territory at all times.

Moscow Rules, she thought, going back to the old Cold War espionage rubrics. *Go with the flow. Vary your pattern. Maintain cover.*

The bus was half-empty, and as she boarded the vehicle started up. The driver, like the new arrivals, was eager to get back to the city before the storm hit. Lucy dragged her luggage to the back of the vehicle and made it look like a random choice when she sat down in the seats behind Marc. As they set off along the highway, he was feigning disinterest, staring blankly out of the window from beneath a dark blue winter cap.

She followed his line of sight, out over the bleak wilderness of brown-black earth and scrub.

"I like the hat," she said quietly. "It's a cute look for you."

"Cheers," he said, keeping his voice low so it wouldn't carry. "Bought it in the gift shop. Don't ask how much it was, I nearly died of fright."

"I didn't make anyone in the terminal," she went on. "You?"

"Nope. If the Lion's Roar have someone watching the incoming flights, it'll probably be a digital interdict, scanning the passport logs."

"Our pal Ticker?"

"Yeah."

She was silent for a moment.

"I was thinking on the flight . . . about what doesn't add up."

Marc nodded. "Same here."

"The Lion's Roar, they have muscle and good reach, I'll give them that. But I've dealt with these kinds of assholes before, and they seldom come this well organized."

He nodded again. "We've heard this song, haven't we? A mid-league bunch of scrotes with a manifesto and an axe to grind, getting ideas above their station." Marc tapped the window with a finger. "Who's funding them? Where's the unseen hand?"

She considered that as the bus rumbled over the road.

"You wanna say it, or shall I?"

"The Combine aren't behind all the bad that happens in the world." Hearing the name of the shadowy group of power brokers always made Lucy tense up. "Even if they would like to be."

"No," she admitted, "but you can't deny this *is* their usual MO. Co-opt an active terror cell, use them in a bigger action for their own gains."

"It would explain how Ticker's contact knew about Rubicon," Marc allowed. "In Singapore, they knew who we were. And everything that happened there was about targeting Rubicon's assets."

Lucy lost herself staring into the distant storm cell.

"I want to know who gave up Park to them." Her eyes narrowed. "I made that woman a promise. I told her she would be safe. Some motherfucker out there has made me a liar, and that will not stand."

She remembered Ji-Yoo's eyes as she had said those words, the two of them hiding on a cold rooftop as a cadre of soldiers were hunting them through the streets below. Park had escaped that life and made a new one, a better one. The other woman didn't deserve to be dragged back into this game.

"A bunch of thugs couldn't get that kind of intel," Lucy concluded, "but someone rich and well-connected could." At length, she let out a low sigh, and glanced at Marc's reflection on the inside of the window. "So, coming out here was your call. I'm guessing that means you have a move in mind?"

"I know a guy," said Marc, fishing his smartphone from an inner pocket of his padded jacket. He worked the tiny screen, typing out a message on the encrypted email app that would ghost its way into the web and seek out a recipient before erasing all trace of itself. "A native. If the Lion's Roar have people operating out of Iceland, he's going to know about it."

Twists of blown snow were coiling off the roadway around the bus, the ice crystals ticking across the window as the storm picked them up. Overhead, the strangely frozen half-daylight was fading as the dark clouds swallowed what little there was of the sun. The barren landscape outside turned gloomy, becoming threatening and alien.

Lucy gave an involuntary shiver and pulled her ski jacket tighter.

As the day drew on, the sky turned into a cauldron of ominous black that lashed Reykjavík with intermittent blasts of icy, driving rain. The locals shrugged it off, though, and Marc tried to follow their example as he made his way toward the harbor. Keeping their covers intact, he and Lucy were staying in two different hotels along the Laugavegur, the main drag through the middle of the town. She would have set off first to scout the meeting point they had chosen, while Marc followed protocol by thoroughly "washing" his route—taking a circuitous, almost aimless path to make sure that no one was following him. He deliberately followed a track up the hill to the Hallgrímskirkja, the great cathedral that dominated most views of the town, pausing in the rain-mist to gaze up at the stratified shape of the building and its high tower. Nestled in the haze and the cold, the church resembled something out of myth and legend—*a doorway to Asgard*, he thought, with a smirk.

Out in front of the cathedral, it was easy to sift the people braving the rain for some cool holiday photos from those who might have had other business there. Marc glimpsed a stocky man in a dark coat near the statue of the great Nordic explorer Leifur Eiríksson, and he seemed to be paying a bit too much attention to where Marc was going.

Reykjavík was a grid of criss-crossing roads, and that had its uses. Marc had committed as much of the layout to memory as he could. He took random turns into the residential backstreets, and seemed to lose the man within a few minutes. Glancing at his battered dive watch, Marc saw that the clock was running against him, and took the direct path the rest of the way to the meet site. If he was late, he didn't expect his contact to wait around. The man he was to see was a precise type, he recalled, not given to wasting time.

Marc would never have admitted it to Lucy or the others, but it was a 50–50 gamble that his contact would even respond to the cryptic email he had sent. The fact that the meet was happening confirmed to Marc that for now at least, his good fortune was holding.

He emerged on the shoreline and followed the line

of the town's edge until his path led him toward a gigantic glass box.

Nestled between two concrete jetties extending out into the water, the Harpa was a concert hall and conference center, an impressive piece of modernist design that resembled a mathematical construct forged into physical reality.

It reminded Marc of a crystal lattice glimpsed through an electron microscope. The building was made up of hundreds of rectangular glass cells, each one illuminated from within, and waves of color shimmered across the exterior as he entered, joining a crowd who were on their way to see an early afternoon performance of Ravel's Piano Trio. Marc blended into the concertgoers as they moved deeper into the building, and looked around, taking it in.

Inside, the Harpa was wide open from its basement level below to the walkways four stories above, each floor accessed by lifts or long sloping stairways. The ceiling was patterned with mirrored hexagonal tiles, and with the inner structure of the building so exposed, there were few places someone could hide. Marc had picked it as a rendezvous point for this reason, and as his gaze crossed over one of the upper galleries, he spotted Lucy leaning casually on a glass barrier. She pretended to be taking in the view, but her position was perfect for observing the larger part of the Harpa's interior.

The concertgoers went their way and Marc disconnected from the group. A short distance away, he saw the man he was looking for, sitting alone at a table in front of the ground-floor coffee bar. The café's trade was sparse, just the contact and a couple of tourists a few meters away engaged in quiet discussion over a guide book. Marc used the mirrors and the reflective glass to check around him, and there was the man in the dark coat again, off near the gift shop. He tensed.

If I see one guy, then there have to be others that I don't.

The contact was toying with an app on his phone and he had yet to look up. Aborting the meet would have been easy. All Marc had to do was keep walking, out through the other exit, but there was too much at stake. If he ghosted now, he would lose this opportunity.

Marc bought a coffee and approached the table. His contact looked up and something like mild surprise flickered briefly in his eyes.

Andri Larsson was short for an Icelander, a fact he didn't help with his taste in bulky raincoats. The sand-colored mackintosh hung off his slight shoulders and pooled around him like it was a cloak, making him look even smaller than he was. He had close-cropped hair and a matching beard in the same metallic-flaxen hue. Hard, unblinking eyes fixed Marc with a severe stare. He had always found Larsson to be bit too intense for his liking, always blunt and painfully direct. In Marc's experience, shorter guys always had that aggressive streak.

"It actually *is* you," said Larsson. "I wasn't entirely certain until now." He sighed. "I am marginally disappointed. I thought it might be someone using your identity to covertly make contact with me."

"Sorry." Marc's lip curled and he took the seat that afforded him the best view of their surroundings. "Lovely to see you too, Andri. How's your pooch?"

"She's had another litter." Larsson gestured with the phone. "Would you like to see some pictures?"

Marc recalled that the man shared his home with a pedigree fårehund, a kind of Icelandic sheepdog that was the closest thing Larsson had to family.

"Maybe later."

Larsson nodded sagely. "You're more of a cat person, I remember." He took a breath. "Why are you not in prison?"

It was less a question and more a demand.

"Should I be?"

Marc removed his hat, using the action to glance toward the gift shop. The man in the dark coat was coming their way.

"The last thing I heard about Marc Dane was an Interpol alert with your face on it. I recall something about you being suspended from duty, something to do with undertaking an unsanctioned investigation? When the alert was lifted, I assumed they had arrested you."

Larsson sipped the dark tea in front of him, waiting for an explanation.

Marc gave a heavy sigh. "Yeah. It's a bit more complicated than that."

"I don't doubt it."

Larsson took another sip, still waiting patiently for the full story.

The stocky man in the dark coat was almost on them now, making no attempt to conceal the fact he was heading in their direction. Marc saw a flicker of purple from the corner of his eye. Lucy was vectoring in as well, having made the man's approach from her high vantage point, and she was a few steps behind him.

Marc put his hand around the bottom of his coffee cup and angled his wrist. If it came to it, he could flick it up and douse the man with searing hot fluid, give

Lucy the all-important seconds she would need to neutralize him before he could draw a weapon.

Larsson looked directly at the man in the dark coat and made a vague, dismissive gesture. The man's body language changed like a switch had been flipped, going from purposeful to neutral, and he threw Larsson an obedient nod before wandering off to find a table of his own.

"What?" Larsson turned back to Marc. "You didn't think I would have someone tracking you? The moment that message came in, I had people deployed. You were not difficult to find." He turned to the tourists with the guidebook. "*Thú mátt fara.*"

They both nodded, rose and left.

"Oh." Marc felt a little deflated. "Right."

Having left her post, Lucy committed to the moment and took the other seat at the table. Larsson gave Marc a questioning look.

"And this is?"

"His glamorous assistant," she replied, with a winning smile.

"Andri Larsson, meet Lucy Keyes." Marc inclined his head. "She's part of the reason I'm not in prison."

"Charmed, I'm sure," Lucy added. "Marc says you two worked together when he was doing that analyst gig with the United Nations."

"That is so." Larsson gave a nod. "At the time, he was with NSNS, the office of nuclear security. Their parent agency were collaborating with the Icelandic government to follow the money trail of a criminal cartel."

"Bunch of thugs trafficking toxic waste from the Middle East," explained Marc. "Caesium slurry, laundering the cash through a shell company here in Reykjavík. Andri was instrumental in getting that nasty little enterprise shut down. This was a couple of months after I started with NSNS, though. Way before that crap with Serbians and the suitcase nuke."

Larsson's eyes widened. "I beg your pardon?"

"The Interpol warrant," said Marc, waving it off as if it hadn't been a big deal. "Long story short, I stumbled on an ex-Soviet weapon of mass destruction and it got me into a lot of trouble. All sorted out now, though."

"I am pleased to hear it." Larsson took that in with another nod.

"Andri works for the Financial Intelligence Unit," Marc told Lucy, grasping for a good analogy. "Tax law is serious business here. Think of the Internal Revenue Service crossed with the Central Intelligence Agency."

"That's a genuinely terrifying thought," she replied, looking at Larsson. "So you're an accountant with a badge?"

He removed an identity card from his pocket and showed it to her.

"You can call us the SR. But please don't ask me to explain what it stands for in Icelandic, you will only make yourself look foolish trying to pronounce it."

Lucy shrugged. "No argument there, pal. Every word I see in this country looks like someone knocked over a Scrabble board."

Larsson tapped his phone with a stubby finger.

"Catching up with former work colleagues is pleasant," he said, in a flat tone that suggested otherwise, "but perhaps you would like to tell me why you are actually here. And why we are not having this conversation in my office."

"We're tracking the victim of an abduction," said Marc. "We suspect the woman's family have already been killed by the people who took her, and that she'll be next once they have what they want from her."

For the moment, he skated over the high points of the situation, wary of pulling Larsson in too deep. Marc believed the man was trustworthy, but the degree of need to know was very much on his mind. Larsson's first loyalty would always be to his agency and his country, and everything else came a distant second.

"So I need a favor."

He produced a tiny SD card, the same type as a memory chip for any conventional digital camera, and slid it across the table to the other man.

"That contains data on a Bitcoin cluster here in Iceland. I need to know the real-world location, and I need it right now."

"In forty-eight hours it'll be too late," Lucy added.

"Track down a cryptocurrency farm?" Larsson gave a humorless chuckle. "These days, it seems like that sort of thing is all my job is." He examined the SD card, then slotted it into his phone, paging through the data on it as he went on. "You understand what you're asking for? This kind of dark net financial malfeasance has become an epidemic here. We have more cases than we can deal with. Illegal transactions, tax evasion, wholesale theft of computers, not to mention the breaches of environmental law. The amount of electricity those server farms demand is huge and their carbon footprint is atrocious." He shot Marc a look. "Who is the abductee and what is she to you?"

"We're employed by the same corporation," said Lucy.

"I asked him, not you." Larsson didn't take his eyes off Marc.

Marc knew this conversation would end if he didn't give the other man something more.

He's asking me to trust him, Marc thought. *To bring him in to the circle.*

He didn't need to look at Lucy to know that she wouldn't like that idea. In the end, he stayed with a half-truth.

"She's a bioscientist, a cancer researcher. We think the people who took her are coercing her into working on something . . ." He struggled to find the right phrasing. "Something much worse than caesium slurry."

A light came on in Larsson's eyes and he looked away, back at the data. But Marc had caught the moment, and he could see what it meant.

He knows something.

Ever observant, Lucy saw it too.

"That ring a bell for you?"

She watched the man moderate his expression. Lucy had seen enough faces down her sniper scope, going through the same kind of mental process, to know what Larsson was thinking. He was weighing his options, considering the choice between going to ground and clamming up completely, or reacting in a way that wouldn't turn out well for her and the Brit.

The Icelander had to know they had entered his country illegally under false identities, and if he was as sharp as Marc said he was, the man knew he could shut down their entire mission in a heartbeat, just by calling the cops. If he wanted to burn them, there was not much they could do to stop him. But she could sense that there was something else going on here, some piece of the puzzle that neither she nor Marc had the shape of.

Whatever happened in the next thirty seconds was going to determine how it would go from here. Her hand slipped around the small spray can secreted in the pocket of her ski jacket, flicking off a safety catch over the nozzle. The aerosol's label said it was a ladies' deodorant, but that was cover for a capsicum spray powerful enough to cause agony and temporary blindness in anyone unlucky enough to take a dose.

Larsson met her gaze and he saw the intention there.

"This conversation puts us in a delicate situation," he began. "A legal gray area, as it were."

Marc nodded at the menacing, slate-colored sky outside the Harpa.

"Gray is right . . ."

"There are certain persons within the government who are paying undue attention to the SR's investigations regarding cryptocurrency." Larsson picked his words with care, giving his colleague in the dark coat a glance to be sure he wouldn't be overheard. "One might suspect that they have something *invested* in ensuring that my agency give priority to certain cases."

Marc made a motion with his hand.

"And let others slip to the bottom of the pile?"

"Not that anything could be proven, you understand? SR is thinly spread. We only have so much in the way of resources." Larsson removed the data card and handed it back to the Brit, before bringing up a map on his device. "One of these lower-priority cases involves the Frigga facility, a medical research laboratory near the edge of the Northwestern Region. They were flagged because they have their own geothermal power plant and their data transactions have been atypical."

He showed them a location that quite literally appeared to be in the middle of nowhere.

Lucy exchanged a loaded look with Marc. If the Lion's Roar were going to make use of Ji-Yoo Park and the stolen bioprinters, an isolated medical lab in the Icelandic wilderness was the perfect spot.

"If there are no illegally active servers on site," Larsson continued, "we would only need to send our computer forensics team in for a few hours to give it the all-clear. And yet, my department has been unable to secure a warrant for search. Insufficient grounds for suspicion, I am told."

"You don't agree," said Lucy.

"I don't have any choice," he replied. "If only I had more men, more influence . . ."

Marc stared at the table, thinking it through.

"Hypothetically speaking, if an anonymous source was able to provide SR with actionable intelligence that financial crimes were taking place in there . . ."

"I would be duty-bound to make it an immediate priority," concluded Larsson. "Of course, that anonymous source would quickly find themselves under a great deal of scrutiny."

"The trade-off is worth it," said Marc.

"*If* that's the right place," countered Lucy.

"You have a better idea?"

She frowned. "You know I don't."

Larsson pocketed his phone and drained the last of his tea.

"I don't wish to be melodramatic, but I think it is best for now to proceed as if this conversation never took place. The less I know about your intentions from this point onward, the better for all of us." He stood up, adjusting his jacket, and his colleague in the dark coat rose with him. "I will give you some advice. Get a good vehicle and go prepared. It's a long drive."

"Understood," said Lucy, but Larsson shook his head.

"That's not the advice; this is." He put a hand on

Marc's shoulder. "Be careful out there. Iceland embraces courage, but she does not forgive the reckless or the unready."

"That sounds more like a warning," said Marc.

Larsson gave a wan shrug and walked away.

Reykjavík vanished swiftly in the rearview mirror as Lucy took them out past the halo of suburban clusters surrounding the town, and soon they were powering along a lonely two-lane highway.

In the end, the drive took around three hours, with Marc and Lucy sharing the work in ninety-minute shifts. She rented a jet black three-door Toyota Land Cruiser and they set off into the teeth of the storm. Marc hacked the Toyota's on-board lo-jack, spoofing the GPS system to make it look like they were driving west toward the tourist route known as "the Golden Circle." The fake route took them past the usual sights—the giant waterfall at Gullfoss, the Strokkur geyser and around the Thingvellir National Park—while in reality the 4×4 was speeding northward to a barely existent spot on the map in the highlands near Kjalvegur, east of the Langjökull glacier.

The storm ebbed and flowed around them, at times retreating enough that they could see for miles over the bleak landscape, toward white ice fields in the far distance.

For Marc, much of the countryside brought to mind Yorkshire and the Pennines, but flattened out and going off into a long, level forever.

Lucy had never seen anything like it outside of a science fiction movie.

"Now I know what driving a moon rover feels like," she said dryly.

"Little further out than that," he noted. "NASA uses Iceland to simulate the surface of Mars."

"Huh. I can believe it."

At other times, the storm came in to toy with them like a bored cat with a mouse, throwing blasts of freezing sleet across the road and buffeting them whenever they crested one of the hills. Smoky curtains of gritty white powder marched over the landscape in waves, and despite himself Marc gave a shiver as they pushed through it.

They were around a kilometer away from the location Larsson had given them when the storm let go again, folding away into a black sky, retreating toward the distant hillside. With Marc currently handling the second driving shift, Lucy had slipped into the back seat. She was busy with the steel case holding the kit to sell her wildlife photographer cover story, but she stopped to look out at the sudden wall of darkness arching up over them.

She cocked her head to get a better angle.

"It looks like the dead of night out there."

"Better this than the other way around," noted Marc. "If we were here in the summer, it'd be daylight all . . . day."

The highway beneath the Land Cruiser's wheels had grown steadily rougher as they ventured closer to the core of the island, and loose scree skittered out as they pulled off the road and into the hollow of a low rise. Killing the engine dropped them into a lightless void and the constant wind moaned around the vehicle as the metal ticked and cooled.

"We walk from here," said Marc.

* * *

Finding the Frigga facility turned out to be easier than he expected, but then the area was so lifeless that even the smallest of human constructions would have stood out a mile.

They stayed low, keeping close to the rocky, frost-marked landscape, moving to a ridge line that over-looked a shallow valley. In the center, around the four hundred meter mark, a cluster of metallic domes and square blockhouses were connected by lines of dark-colored pipes. North of that was a helipad with a black Bell Jet Ranger sitting on it. Weather blankets covered the helicopter's nose and rotor blades, and a dozen ca-bles had it tied down to steel eyebolts against the wind. To the west, a set of steel chimneys rose above the roof-tops, venting a stream of white haze into the air. It was run-off from the facility's power plant, where water was pumped down into the thermally active layer be-low the ground and turned into superheated steam to power turbines. The constant wind was pulling the rib-bon of vapor across the valley, in the direction of Marc and Lucy's vantage point.

"Upwind is good," Lucy said quietly, settling into a prone position.

She pulled a high-powered sniper scope from her pocket and used it to sweep the buildings. Marc did the same with a pair of compact Steiner binoculars.

"Should have brought a thermographic rig," she noted.

Marc shrugged. "Maybe. There's a lot of radiant heat bloom from the ground around here, that's why the snow won't settle. It would mess with the goggles." He paused. "The earth here is warmer than you'd think. There are places in Iceland where you can't bury the dead. The vol-canic heat from underground slow-cooks them."

"That's an unpleasant image," Lucy replied. "Thanks for sharing."

"I don't see any fence line down there," Marc noted. There was a vacant security hut where the sole entrance road approached the main buildings but little else. "No patrols."

"Who in their right mind would wanna be out in this chill?" Lucy's words were slightly muffled by the fur around her all-enclosing hood. "Gotta be electronic security instead."

"No doubt. I'll need to run a wifi sweep to be sure."

Lucy was quiet for a moment.

"Did it occur to you that your pal Larsson might be dirty?"

He put down the binoculars and shot her a look.

"For a minute, yeah. But if he wanted to mess about with us, he could have done that at the Harpa."

"Just checking." She continued to peer down her scope. "We're going a long way on your hunch, Dane. If this doesn't pan out—"

"Nobody knows that better than I do," he broke in.

Lucy stiffened. "Door's opening, blockhouse to the south by the smaller dome. I see someone coming out."

Marc put the binoculars to his face and swept around, finding the target.

"Got them. One person. Big coat." He zoomed in and his brow furrowed. "Oh shit. Is that . . . ?"

"It's Park." Lucy's reply was unequivocal. "Looks like . . . she's taking a smoke break."

They watched her in silence. Through the long-range optics, Marc watched the scientist shakily light a cigarette. He couldn't see her face clearly, but it appeared to be the same woman from the video, pacing dejectedly in a circle.

"This means we're in the right place."

"Yeah, how about that?" Lucy scowled behind her scope. "Real convenient, how it's all lining up."

"It's lining up because we followed the right leads," he insisted.

"I don't like coincidences. Makes me feel like I'm getting played."

He shifted his weight, moving down the ridge.

"You're senior operative here. If this smells wrong to you, if you want to pull the plug and drive back to Reykjavík, then say it."

Down in the valley, Park's diminutive figure began a march back toward the blockhouse. Lucy tracked her movements every step of the way until she vanished inside again.

"Back to the car," she said, after a long moment. "We're calling this in."

— ELEVEN —

The 4 × 4 rose out of the darkness as they approached, a black megalith, shiny and foreign against the rocky landscape where they had left it.

Once inside, Marc pulled the sat-com rig from his backpack and worked by the crimson light of the display while Lucy went to the camera case. Methodically, she removed the false panels in the steel container, to reveal the hidden storage areas underneath. She removed and strapped a sheathed ceramic combat knife to the inside of her forearm, before detaching her jacket's removable hood. If there was going to be some action, she would rather risk the cold than lose her peripheral vision.

Pieces of camera gear, sections of tripod, optics and other mechanisms came apart in her hands and went back together in new configurations. Bit by bit, she assembled a skeletal, compressed-air rifle, completing the puzzle of it by snapping the telescopic sight she'd used earlier to a mount over the barrel.

"Connection," said Marc.

It would be late evening at Rubicon's crisis center in Monaco and predawn back in Singapore, which explained the unsettled timbre in Lucy's bones. She was still on Far East time.

In the military, she had learned the knack of snatching fragments of sleep wherever she could, but even so, resting up on the flight to Iceland was no substitute for a full night on a comfortable rack. Lucy was operating at the same level of activity she'd been on during the mission in the Med—and Marc was probably doing the same.

Need to watch that, she told herself. *Fatigue kills as easily as bullets.*

Marc put the tablet computer on the Toyota's dash. He'd set it to operate in red-spectrum mode to preserve their night vision, so everything inside the vehicle had a dark, bloody cast to it. On the tablet's split screen, one side showed Henri Delancort's pinched and wary expression, the other Assim Kader, looking pale and sweaty.

"*Report?*" said Delancort.

Lucy launched into a rapid summary of the last few hours. She ignored the look on his face when she told him that the Icelandic SR were now effectively collaborators in the operation and pressed on, getting to the core of the matter.

"We have a positive ID on Susan Lam, aka Ji-Yoo Park. They're holding her here."

Delancort gave a curt nod. "*All right. You need to formulate a strategy for recovery.*" He glanced to one side, looking at a split screen of his own. "*Kader. How soon can you and Riis close down your operations in Singapore and be on a flight to Iceland?*"

"What?" said Marc, holding up a hand, but the conversation continued over him.

"*Uh, well, before we address that, you should know we've had some developments here too.*" The Saudi took a deep breath. "*I've been sweeping law enforcement databases for anything relevant connected to the Lion's Roar, and I found something that we should be concerned about.*"

He tapped a keypad and the tablet screen mirrored something from the hacker's computer. Lucy recognized the format of an Interpol Red Notice, the agency's equivalent of a BOLO bulletin circulated to police forces across the globe when a suspect of note was sought for arrest and extradition. A grimacing, hard-eyed white man looked back out at her from the screen, the red illumination making him deathly pale.

"*This is Noah Verbeke. He's single-handedly responsible for making the Lion's Roar into the international menace that they are today.*"

The Red Notice explained that Verbeke had escaped confinement during a prison transfer a few days earlier, killed a number of police officers, and then dropped off the grid. All that had taken place within hours of Park's abduction.

"That can't be by chance," said Marc. "Their top dog gets out of his cage and they start putting together a major terrorist hit? The Lion's Roar must have been planning this for a while. They're still two steps ahead of us."

"Them—or whoever is really running this," Lucy added. "Assim, what else?"

"*I tried a different approach to locate the bioprinters,*" he went on. "*They don't just fabricate materials out of thin air, you see, they need seed stock. A package called a biokit. I'm running a search protocol, looking for thefts or purchases of any regulated biokits with the correct profile over the last few weeks. There's a promising lead in Manila, but nothing firm yet, so I will—*"

"Wait," Marc said firmly, cutting off the other man in mid-sentence. "Back up a bit. Are we seriously saying that Lucy and I are going to sit on our arses for another ten or twenty hours while Malte and Assim fly over here on the company jet?"

"*You can conduct surveillance on the target site,*" said Delancort.

"Oh, great idea," Marc snapped, his tone rising. "Then we'll know exactly when they put a bullet in Park's head and dump her in a shallow grave." He leaned in before Lucy could speak up. "We lost them in Singapore because we were running behind. Park was already gone by the time we arrived, and we're only here now because their bloke Ticker is sloppy and we caught a lucky break. We have to move on this now. *Tonight!*"

"*The two of you,*" Delancort said, in a dour tone. "*Entering a location you have little intelligence on, facing threats you know even less about. Without backup. Do I have it right, Mr. Dane, or have I missed any of the reasons why this is a bad idea?*"

"Four days," Marc retorted, sounding out the words. "The woman on the phone said four days until they go live on whatever the hell they are planning—and that was two days ago. So you tell me how wasting more of that dwindling time is a *good* idea."

"We have limited gear," said Lucy, indicating the steel case. "Non-lethal loadout only, just tranks."

Marc turned on her, a dark intensity glittering in his eyes.

"We can work with that. Look, Lucy, I know it isn't protocol, but we can do this on the fly. You *know* we can." She shook her head, but he pressed on. "I infiltrated an MI6 station on my own with a couple of smoke bombs and some rich bloke's suit. I broke a convicted terrorist out of a CIA black site using a laptop and a cell phone. With your help, I can do this."

"Okay."

Lucy heard herself saying the words, even as a silent voice inside her was railing against following the least considered of their options.

But she couldn't shake that image of Ji-Yoo Park, shivering out there in the cold, her life ticking away on a clock held by her captors. There was a lot that Lucy Keyes had done in her life that she wasn't proud of, and precious few good deeds that worked to balance the scales against the bad. Liberating Park had been one of the first acts she had ever felt right about doing, and Lucy could not let that go. She could not allow that rescue to be undone.

"It's not a good idea," she went on, "but it's all we have right now."

"*Lucy,*" said Delancort, with all the steel he could muster. "*I remind you, even if you are the senior team member on site, you are contractually obliged to do as I say. I have the authority to order you to stand down.*"

"That's true," she agreed, leaning forward to pick up the tablet. "Let me know how it goes."

She tapped the connection tab and the screen displayed the words NO SIGNAL. Marc's face split in a lopsided grin, but it quickly faded when he saw the steely look in her eyes.

"Don't give me that," she snarled. "You better make this work! Or else you, me, and a lot of people are going to end up screwed."

"Copy that," he replied.

By the time they were back at the ridge, the storm had rolled back around and it caught the two of them as they reached the top. The icy blasts of wind snatched at the steam gushing from the vent chimneys and shredded it. Eddies of loose gravel and frost were swept up off the valley floor, rattling over the material of their cold-weather jackets—but as harsh as it was, it made good cover. Moving slow and low, Marc and Lucy advanced down into the valley proper, toward the misty lights of the Frigga facility.

Lucy led the way, keeping her dart rifle slung. Marc had a pistol-sized version of the same weapon, assembled from other pieces of the fake camera kit. It had a five-shot carousel of hollow, needle-sharp darts, each one fitted with a reservoir of fast-acting phenobarbital-based sedative. One shot was supposed to be enough to take down an average person, but anything involving chemical doses was always finicky, and Marc was looking on it as a weapon of last resort. Not that the weapons would have been any use outside. The gusting winds would make it virtually impossible for the slow compressed-air guns to hit what they were aimed at.

The dart thrower was not the only piece of kit Marc had taken from the steel case, however. He dropped into cover behind a broken boulder a few meters from the guardhouse and pulled out his tablet. The red-glow screen blinked on.

Lucy crowded in next to him.

"So?" She spoke into his ear.

He showed her the screen. Larsson had emailed him a layout diagram of the Frigga compound taken from official records, but it had no internal floor plan, which meant they were going to have to sweep the place until they found Park and the bioprinters. Logically, both targets would probably be in the main blockhouse across from the helipad, but right now Marc wasn't willing to take anything for granted.

The tablet's built-in wireless scanner was pinging the area around them, and as he had suspected, the lack of visible security did not mean a lack of actual security. There were cameras over the outer doors, and hidden among the rough black rocks was a ring of motion sensors. The sensors used near-field technology to communicate with each other and network their data, so anyone watching the ring would be able to instantly home in on where a breach was taking place.

"This is going to take spot-on timing," he told her, drawing the other bit of gear he was carrying from his backpack. "When I tell you to run, I need you to get to that vent stack as fast as humanly possible."

Lucy saw the boxy stand of metallic chimneys and nodded, eyeing up the distance.

"A hundred yards? Sure, okay. How long we got?"

"Honestly? I have no idea. Faster would be better."

She looked at the device in his hands. It resembled a bulky hairdryer, with a dish-shaped diffuser on the front.

"Is that . . . ?"

"HERF gun, version 2.0."

The unit was essentially a portable microwave generator, capable of putting out an invisible blast of high-energy radio frequencies. The experimental tech was still a bit too fragile for most conventional military operations, but under the right circumstances it could fry electronics and make a human feel like their skin was on fire.

"You brought that goddamn ray gun with you." Lucy was not impressed. "Didn't you learn your lesson last time?"

"Last time I used one, I shot down a drone and saved our lives," he retorted.

She made a face. "All I remember is a building collapsing underneath us."

"Everyone's a critic." He aimed the HERF gun over the top of the boulder, toward the approximate spot where the closest sensor was located. "I had Tech-Ops modify it after last time. It's new and improved."

"Still not convinced."

He took a breath and squeezed the trigger plate.

"Get ready."

The HERF gun hummed unpleasantly, the resonance making Marc's flesh crawl and the bones in his hand tremble. If this didn't work, he had little in the way of backup plans.

But then the tablet made a pinging noise, and at once three of the motion sensors blinked offline, their detection circuits momentarily overwhelmed by a flood of raw microwave radiation.

"Go go go!"

Marc snatched up the tablet and launched into a sprint, rocking off a heartbeat after Lucy. She flew through the haze like a rocket and he had to give it all he had just to keep up. It was hard work running over the broken, rock-strewn ground, and once or twice he misstepped and almost tumbled over. Then the steel chimneys rose up out of the windblown mist and he skidded to a halt in the shadows behind them.

They were inside the perimeter now, and the nearest door to the blockhouse interior was around twenty meters distant. A light above it shone down on a concrete apron, and Marc could see the boxy shape of a weatherproof security camera looking down at the doorway. The door didn't have a conventional mechanical latch on the outside, only a thick metal pad for a key-card lock.

"What next?" Lucy panted.

The tablet pinged again as the sensors started to come back online.

"Wait for it . . ."

Marc activated another program. It was clumsy work in the thick gloves he wore, and the cold was really starting to bite. The scanner software reconfigured and he worked to ease the racing breaths he was taking. The icy air seared his chest with each intake.

"Wait for it," he repeated.

The magnetic lock on the blockhouse door thudded open and a big guy in a dark heavy-weather parka trudged out. He glowered at the storm clouds overhead with a thunderous expression that told Marc he had drawn the short straw, and then advanced. The man brought up a shotgun with a tactical flashlight beneath the barrel and flicked it on, moving out toward the sensor line. The beam swept through the air, catching the wind-driven dust and gritty snow.

Marc and Lucy became still, watching him make his patrol. The way the big man moved sent the wrong signals. He didn't act like a security guard, like somebody trained for this kind of thing, like someone who did it day in and day out. If anything, his body language spoke of thuggish disdain for the job, and he showed his eagerness to get it done quickly by only giving the area the most cursory of sweeps before heading back in. As he did, the man cocked the shotgun up on his shoulder and snatched at a radio handset clipped to his collar.

"There's fuck all out here," Marc heard him say, in what was definitely an angry Irish accent. "If you pricks made me do this for shits and giggles, I'll fucking crucify you."

The big guy didn't pay any attention to the garbled reply over the radio, pawing his pockets for the keycard to get back into the warmth of the blockhouse. Lucy shifted, ready to slip up behind the man and take him out, but Marc put a hand on her wrist and shook his head.

Now, thought Marc.

His gloved finger tapped the "commit" tab on the screen in his hand, and the tablet's wireless scanner listened in to the silent communication between the lock mechanism and the RFID chip in the key-card, cloning the signal in a fraction of a second.

The door opened and the big Irishman vanished inside. The last thing Marc saw was a glimpse of the man's face, illuminated by the glow from within. He had the design of a flame-wreathed Celtic cross tattooed over the side of his throat.

"I'm going to go out on a limb and say that bloke isn't Icelandic," Marc said quietly.

"Who owns this place?" said Lucy.

"Larsson didn't say," Marc noted. "Shell company, most likely."

She jutted her chin at the tablet computer, fighting off a shiver.

"You get what you need?"

The compiler program's progress bar filled and he nodded.

"Here, take this." He pressed the HERF gun into her hand. "Shoot the camera."

"Pew pew," she said dryly, and did as he asked.

He would have to be near to make it work. The tablet could simulate the RFID's card's call-and-response signal to the lock mechanism, but only at close range. If the camera was active and he was spotted at the door . . .

Don't think about that, Marc told himself. *It's simple. Breaking into a secure building in the middle of an ice storm in sub-zero temperatures—easy.*

He rushed the door and slapped the tablet against the lock pad. The red light beneath the camera was out, but the HERF gun's discharge would only throw it into a reset cycle, not disrupt it permanently. He had no way of knowing how long he had.

Then the door unlocked with a thud and Marc almost

dropped the tablet in surprise. He opened it enough to slip through and Lucy was at his side in a fraction of a second. The wind pulled at the door as another gust rolled in, but together they eased it closed and the lock re-engaged.

Both of them held their breath for a long moment.

"Did that work?" said Lucy, dropping her trank rifle off its strap and into her hands. "No alarms?"

Marc slipped the tablet and the HERF gun back into his pack.

"We'll know soon enough."

The corridor they were in resembled that same kind of drab and unimaginative architecture that characterized military bases, hospitals and schools. A sparse hallway of blank walls and vinyl floors lit by fluorescent lights ranged off in either direction, and every few feet there were signs in dense industrial text that neither of them could read. Off to the right, a set of heavy double doors led deeper into the blockhouse.

"A map would be real useful right now," Lucy muttered.

"Why make it easy?"

Marc checked his dart pistol and put it in his pocket, moving off.

In the next area they came across a series of isolated laboratory modules that branched off the main corridor on both sides. The resemblance to the MaxaBio facility in Singapore was undeniable. Each one had a plastic glass door with an airtight seal mechanism around the edges, suggesting that the work done inside was sensitive to environmental change—but when Marc pressed his face up to peer inside, he saw nothing but unused workstations and empty cabinets.

"Where is everybody?" said Lucy. "This place looks untouched."

"Andri's hunch about it being a front is looking more certain every second," added Marc. He moved to a second lab module, and then another. "No sign of the bioprinters in here." He paused, thinking it through. "No sign of *any* biotech hardware, in fact. Not even a test tube."

"Could be they keep the cool toys deeper inside. Along with the cloned dinosaurs."

Lucy walked to a connecting door at the end of the section.

Marc made a face. "I see a velociraptor and you can color me *gone*," he deadpanned.

She pushed open the door a few degrees.

"Junction up ahead, corridor branches left and right. We'll split up, meet back at the intersection in ten mikes."

"Got it."

"Don't do anything stupid without me."

Lucy threw the words over her shoulder as she padded away from him.

"As if."

He watched her disappear around a turning, then set off himself.

At the end of the other branch of the corridor, the hallway switched sharply into a blind corner. Marc pressed himself flat against the wall and eased his head around the turn to see what lay out of sight.

The corridor mirrored the earlier one, with a set of workrooms branching off the hallway, and at the far end there was another set of windowed double doors looking into what seemed to be an active workspace.

But Marc didn't have much opportunity to consider that. Less than a meter away, the big Irishman with the neck tattoo was standing in front of a coffee machine, a half-full plastic cup in his hand and a look of shocked surprise on his face.

The two of them stared at one another, their reactions both frozen by the unexpected sight. Then a word slipped out of Marc's mouth—"*Shit!*"—and the bubble of inaction burst.

The big man burst into motion, throwing his coffee aside and storming toward Marc, bull-charging him. Marc snatched at his dart gun, but the weapon's long frame made it awkward to draw it, and the barrel caught on the lip of his pocket.

Twice Marc's size, the Irishman must have been a rugby player at one point in his life, because he moved like a center, all power and impact channeling straight into Marc's chest as they collided.

Too slow to get out of the big man's path in the narrow corridor, Marc came off his feet and the momentum of the hit carried them both into the wall across the way. The dart gun fell from his pocket and he lost sight of it.

All the air blew out of his lungs in a ragged choke, and the kit in Marc's backpack gave an unpleasant crack was it was sandwiched between a breeze block wall and his body weight. He lolled forward and the Irishman slammed him against the wall again, holding on to Marc with handfuls of his jacket and the straps of his pack.

His hands were still free, though, but he knew striking the big man in the torso would do little good. Instead, Marc brought up his palms and clapped them together as hard as he could over the Irishman's ears.

"Bastard!"

That had the desired reaction and the man let him

drop. Marc's gut reaction was to disengage and get away, but that would see the operation killed stone dead right here. Instead, he chose the act the bigger man least expected, and leaned into him, grabbing his shoulders as purchase for a downward head-butt. It was a crude and badly conceived counterblow, but the Krav Maga instructor who had done his best to embed some moves in Marc's brain had once told him: *whatever works, works.*

The blow mashed the Irishman's already unlovely, previously broken nose and set a dizzy shock of pain burning around Marc's skull. Blood gushed from the big man's nostrils and he swore again, swatting at Marc with his open hand. Again, he connected, slapping his opponent away with enough force that Marc lost his balance and went down to the vinyl floor.

One hand clamping his nose, the Irishman grabbed at his radio handset where it dangled at the end of a coiled cord.

Can't let him call it in.

Marc kicked out along the line of the floor and hit the man hard in the ankle. The Irishman slipped on the puddle of spilled coffee and fell down on one knee, his big hands slapping at the floor to arrest his fall.

Marc was already rolling to his fallen dart gun as the other guy growled and hauled himself back up. He aimed for a torso shot, but the pistol was lighter than he expected and it rose high as he squeezed the trigger. It let out a cough of gas and the Irishman jerked back against the wall, giving a low wail of pain.

The dart had embedded itself in the man's right eye. He pulled it out, now emitting a stream of curses, and staggered forward, his face twisting in a murderous snarl.

This time, Marc braced the dart gun with both hands and fired another shot into the Irishman's chest—and that did the trick. The big man's breathing slowed and he sank into a heap in the middle of the floor.

He weighed a ton, or so it seemed. Marc took a wrist and an ankle, and dragged the unconscious Irishman into the nearest vacant workroom, stowing him as best he could out of sight from anyone passing in the corridor. The job took forever, and Marc's head was constantly on a swivel, aware that it would all be over if someone caught him in the act.

Stopping to catch his breath, Marc rifled through the man's pockets for his RFID pass and anything else that might be useful. The Irishman had nothing of note beyond a nightstick and a disposable plastic wallet with a few Icelandic króna notes and what had to be a fake EU driver's license. Of the shotgun he had been carrying outside, there was no sign. Marc used his smartphone to take stills of the license card and the man's face before leaving him trussed up with a pair of plastic flex cuffs.

He glanced at his Cabot dive watch. Lucy's ten minutes were up. He glared at the unconscious man.

"You're messing up my day, mate."

The fact that Marc wasn't at the intersection when she returned started Lucy's warning bells ringing. In fact, scratch that—it was more honest to say that she already had an orchestra of alarms going off in her head about every damn aspect of this infiltration.

Following the corridor she had taken after they split up took Lucy into a section of the blockhouse that was cordoned off into more sub-areas, each one containing a computer server module on a vibration-resistant plinth. Ducts channeling in the wintry air from outside through massive dehumidifiers gave the space a dry, oppressive chill, and there was little sound in there except for the humming of the fans and the soft chitter of electronics. The Brit would have been able to give her chapter and verse on the capabilities of the computer rigs, but even Lucy's limited understanding of the tech made it clear to her that this was a *lot* of computing power. She kept out of the server rooms themselves, spotting cameras watching the machines from shadowed corners, and after taking snapshots of the layout, she retreated back the way she had come.

The quiet and the lack of any opposition were preying on her mind. Was the Lion's Roar really complacent enough to rely on the facility's remoteness alone to protect it? So far, what she had seen of the group didn't give her a coherent picture. Their tactics were strong and well thought out, but their operational security was lacking.

Dangerous, she concluded, *but not professional.*

The Lion's Roar was not a hard-core terrorist group in the mold of top-tier threats like Al Sayf, more along the lines of a criminal gang or a rogue militia. That didn't make them less of a threat, however—if anything, it made them unpredictable, and an enemy you couldn't predict was the worst of all foes.

Marc appeared around the corner up ahead and beckoned her to him. He looked worse for wear, and when she came closer she knew something was up. There was a puddle of coffee on the floor and nearby, a few spots of blood. She looked around and saw where paint had been chipped off the far wall.

"I miss something?"

"Nothing to worry about." Marc showed her the side of Irish beef sleeping off a double-dose of tranks.

"I checked his ink," he went on, indicating his neck. "More of the same faction tattoos—lions, lightning bolts, crooked crosses, the whole lot."

"You upload them?"

He nodded. "What did you get?"

She told him about the computer stacks, showing him the images she had taken of the servers.

"I guess this confirms SR's suspicions."

Marc nodded again, scrutinizing the pictures.

"Yeah, that's some serious heavy iron there. Way more than an industrial biolab would need."

"Let's keep up the momentum."

Lucy pocketed her smartphone and set off again. Marc kept pace with her, and together they pushed open the doors into the next sector of the blockhouse.

There were more labs here, but this time they were bigger and in active use. Through windows alternating strips of frosted and clear glass, Lucy saw two figures in white coats moving around inside a compartment off to the right. She spotted a too-big cold-weather jacket hanging on a coat hook, and heard a woman's voice.

Marc shot her a questioning look and she returned a nod.

"In here," she whispered. "On three."

Lucy counted up with her fingers, and on the mark, she shouldered open the door and surged inside, with Marc a step behind her.

Two East Asians in lab coats, a man and a woman, were standing around a computer workstation, and Lucy saw she had interrupted them in the middle of a disagreement.

She raised her tranquilizer rifle.

"Step back from the keyboard, hands where I can see them."

Behind her, she heard a crunch of plastic as Marc

smashed in a security camera watching the compartment from over the doorway.

"What is going on?" The male scientist demanded an
answer, blinking furiously at their intrusion. "This is a
restricted area!"

Lucy only half-heard the man. Her attention was on
the woman, whose face became a complex mix of am-
bivalent emotions as recognition dawned in her eyes.

"Katelyn?" said the woman. "Is that you?"

Marc shot her a questioning look, and it look Lucy a
second to remember that "Katelyn" had been the cover
name she'd operated under during the Pyongyang mission.

"Hello, Ji-Yoo."

"You know her?" The man almost shouted the question at Park, but she didn't hear him.

"Are you the reason they abducted me?" Park's expression hardened and she took a step toward Lucy. "Is
this because of what we did? You told me they would
never find me!" She spat the last words at her, fearful
and venomous.

"Ji-Yoo, move away from these people!"

The man in the lab coat grabbed at her arm, but Park
angrily shook off his grip.

"Don't touch me, Kyun!" she snapped. "You're the
worst of them!"

"How dare you!" The man recoiled at the accusation,
and began to rant. "I am only trying to help, you foolish sow! Can't you understand that? I am your one
chance to get through this alive!"

"Do we need this bloke?" said Marc, out of the side
of his mouth. "He's starting to piss me off."

Lucy gave a terse shake of the head, and the Brit put
a dart in him.

"Wha—?" The man called Kyun staggered backward,

looking down at the barb that had suddenly appeared in his chest. "Oh . . ." he managed, before slumping against the workstation and folding to the floor.

The guy's name rang a vague bell in Lucy's thoughts, recalling something from the Pyongyang mission briefing.

There was a man named Kyun on Park's team, back in the North. What are the odds this is the same person?

Park didn't seem that upset that Marc had tranked him. She was still set on Lucy, her fear and despair warring with the need to trust someone.

"I don't know what is happening to me."

Tears rolled down her cheeks.

"We're here for you," Lucy told her. "Just like before. I told you then, I would get you out, and I did." She extended her hand. "Come with me. It'll be okay."

"I can't go." Park shook her head, as Marc slipped past her to run his eye over the workstation. "I can't go with you. Not this time. I have too much to lose."

Lucy and Marc exchanged a loaded glance. On the drive out from Reykjavík, they had talked over what their approach would be if they had to get Park on their side. The easy way would be to put her out with another dart and carry her to safety, but there were too many variables, too many unknowns in play.

"Ji-Yoo, we know what is going on here," said Lucy, reframing her approach. "We know these people are pressuring you into helping them. If we get you out of here, we can stop them."

"No." She kept shaking her head. "You don't know, Katelyn. You really don't."

Marc turned back toward her.

"This is like the other rooms," he said. "There's no

lab gear, nothing for culturing, no microscopes and centrifuges, no Petri dishes. Just a computer running a molecular simulator program."

"What are you working on in here?" said Lucy. At length, she let her rifle drop on its sling, closing the gap between her and the scientist. "Tell me."

Park looked at the floor, wiping the tears from her face.

"They made me . . . improve the virtual genetic model." She gestured at the workstation. "We enhanced a synthetic infective agent. It's a crossbreed, it's the weapon we were making, back then before everything changed." She let out a sob. "It's *Geulimja*."

"*Shadow,*" said Marc.

A crawling chill marched up Lucy's spine, and she took Park's hand. She could see the other woman was trapped by her panic, and she had to snap her out of it.

"We'll just go, all right? And once you're someplace safe, we'll get this place and everyone in it wiped off the map."

"It's too late," insisted Park. "It's already done. They were almost finished. They needed me to take it to completion. The French woman, Axelle . . . She said they're going to hold us until they have proof it works as expected."

"We're talking about a bioweapon," said Marc, in a dead voice. "In the hands of a bunch of ultra-right-wing extremists. That's going to end badly." He turned to Park. "Look, you must help us stop this. We still have time! There's another day before—"

"*No!*" Park screamed the word and snatched back her hand from Lucy, as if she had been scalded. "I don't care what happens to me, but if I cross them, my family is dead, don't you see?" Her shoulders shook with emotion. "They're all I have. The only good thing that has come out of my life."

She pulled a small digital tablet from the pocket of her lab coat, tapping shakily at the screen. It displayed a series of video files. The videos appeared to show Simon Lam and his son Michael, in a space that looked a lot like the basement of the warehouse in Singapore.

Lucy gave Marc a look and he came close, gently taking the device so he could examine the footage.

"These are time-stamped," he said. "Uplinked every twelve hours. The last one came in forty-five minutes ago." He took a moment to frame his next words. "Have you . . . spoken to them?"

Park nodded. "They don't let us say much." She pointed at the screen. "Last time, Michael was sleeping. Simon said he was being brave."

Marc met Lucy's gaze and the weight of the terrible truth they both knew hung there between them. It was as if the room shifted around her, a dreadful certainty coming into sharp and unforgiving focus as Lucy saw the stark choice that lay in front of her.

"Ji-Yoo, tell us where the bioprinters are," said Marc. "Tell us what we're dealing with here. If we don't stop these people, hundreds, thousands of families like yours could be in danger."

"I won't, I can't! I don't care about that." Park's voice became plaintive. "I only care about them."

On some level, Lucy had known this moment was coming ever since she had stood in that room in the warehouse basement, seeing the dried blood on the floor, the looted watch and the silver ring. The crushing inevitability was inescapable, and every way around it was a false hope, built on deceit after deceit. If she didn't tell Park the truth, if she didn't shock her out of this lie that was imprisoning her, they would fail.

Lucy reached into an inner pocket of her jacket, removing the burden she had been carrying since Singapore, and did something terrible. She took Park's hand and placed Simon Lam's bloodstained wedding ring in her open palm.

The woman's eyes widened.

"This . . . This isn't mine. They wouldn't let me wear my ring, it's safe in a locker in the other building with the rest of . . ." She faltered and the color drained from her face.

"Your husband and your son are dead," Lucy told her. "They were killed a few hours after you were abducted." She took a deep breath. "We found them."

"These videos are fakes." Marc held up the digital pad. "I think you know that, don't you? You knew something wasn't right about them. But you didn't want to think about it."

Ji-Yoo Park looked up and met Lucy's gaze.

"No," she managed.

"Yes," said Lucy, her voice thick with emotion.

Her heart broke as the other woman saw the truth in her eyes, and Park collapsed against her, falling into racking, shuddering sobs.

— TWELVE —

Marc watched the Korean woman's world imploding and he felt an aching stab of empathy. He knew first-hand what it was like to lose someone you cared about in a moment of senseless violence.

Now he and Lucy had taken away everything that mattered to Ji-Yoo Park in the space of a few breaths, as surely as if they had killed her family themselves. He reminded himself that it was Verbeke's men, the Lion's Roar, who had done this to Park, but it didn't make the revelation feel any less hurtful. He hated himself for being a part of it.

"I'm sorry," Lucy was saying. "You had to know the truth. These people are using you, and when they're done with you, you'll be killed too."

"I know," managed Park. Breath by breath, the woman dragged herself back from her racking, sobbing sorrow. "I have accepted that. It's punishment. For what we made, back in the North." She took a shuddering breath. "I wouldn't have tried to stop them . . . As long as my family . . ." She choked as she tried to say the words.

Marc knew they had to keep her focused.

"Tell us about Shadow."

"It was . . . It was the codename for the military's attempt to create a tactical bioweapon for battlefield use." Park shot a look at Kyun's unconscious form. "We were never able to assemble the complete viral matrix. I defected before the terminal phase was perfected. Without me they couldn't do it."

"The modified Marburg strain?" Marc prompted.

Park pointed at the computer workstation.

"A hemorrhagic fever with a programmable duration was the goal. To make a disease that could infect a target city, eradicate the populace and then burn itself out before the army moved in to take over. Marburg was chosen as the core for the weapon not only because is it extremely lethal, but also because the effects are so terrible, the mere threat of it would cause enemy forces to surrender."

"That's pretty fucked up," he muttered.

"Why do you think I defected?" she replied.

"Where is it?" Lucy squinted through the gaps in the lab's frosted glass window, checking the corridor. "Where are they keeping the materials?"

Park took another shaky breath.

"Not in here," she began. "They haven't allowed me anywhere near the actual cultures." She nodded toward the door. "The fabrication lab is in the next section, that's where Kyun works."

Marc knelt and took the unconscious man's RFID card from his pocket, before offering it to Park.

"Show us."

"Follow me."

Park took a moment to compose herself, then set off.

Lucy readied her weapon and Marc did the same. He'd been caught off guard once and had no desire to take another beating. The pain from the still-healing wounds inflicted in Singapore was a steady burn across his chest.

"You okay?"

He put the question to Lucy, quietly so that Park wouldn't hear. The stricken look Lucy wore when she told the other woman of the deaths of her family had faded, replaced by the operative's usual stoic professionalism.

Lucy didn't look at him.

"She had to know."

"You had no choice."

He wanted to say more, but now wasn't the time. In the end, he just gave a nod.

They fell in line behind Park as she used Kyun's keycard to tap them through the next set of doors and into an airlock antechamber. The secure doors opened out into the largest space yet, a work area stocked with industrial lab gear. Most of the systems were automated machines inside clean boxes, locked into environmentally secure mini-chambers to keep out any potential contaminants. Robotic armatures moved back and forth in jerky, repetitive dances as they dosed sample trays with liquid-filled pipettes or agitated the contents of conical flasks. Some of the compartments were big enough for a person to enter, the entrances festooned with columns of garish caution labels warning against toxins, biohazards and other dangers.

"Nobody home," noted Lucy. "*Again.*"

"Yeah." The ghost town nature of the Frigga facility was preying on Marc's mind. "Is it usually this quiet?"

"There should be others in here," Park said warily. "I have seen a few technicians. Security staff, as well as Axelle and the others." She found what she was looking for and led them to it. "Here. This is the secure storage unit."

The unit resembled a decompression chamber, with a bank of controls on the outside for setting and monitoring the internal temperature. Marc looked it over, checking for any alarm systems or countermeasures.

"Open it," said Lucy.

She covered Marc with her weapon as he stepped up and grasped the twin twist-handle latches to open the heavy, pressurized door.

He hesitated.

"This is safe, yeah?"

"Anything within will be sealed," Park said glumly. "That is the only place in this lab where any kind of active culture could be held securely."

Despite himself, Marc still held his breath when he turned the latches, and the secure unit's heavy door opened with a *pop-hiss* sound. White vapor gusted out from inside and he eased it open.

Inside there were racks upon racks of metal shelves, and every last one of them was bare. Gingerly, Marc examined the interior, making sure there was no hidden compartment, no unseen container he missed on the first glance.

"What the hell is this?" Lucy turned on Park. "Why is it empty?"

Park's hands rose to her mouth.

"That's not . . . That doesn't make any sense." She shook her head. "This is the seed store. Any assembled viral stock would be held in there!"

The chill wafting out from the unit made Marc's skin prickle, as the beginnings of an unpleasant possibility occurred to him.

"Ji-Yoo, did you actually see it? The stock, I mean. Since they brought you here, did you actually *see* any physical materials?"

"I . . ." Park's gaze turned inward. "No. Not any live samples. I was told they were limiting exposure. Kyun told me it was for security and safety. He told me other people were working on the culturing and fabrication, in here."

"He was lying to you." Marc slammed the door shut.

"You were working on a molecular model where we found you, right?" Park gave a nod and he continued. "That's a virtual version of the Shadow virus vector. Like you don't have the architect laying bricks on a building site, do you? They work on the plans, some-one else does the heavy lifting."

"You're losing me," said Lucy, with a frown.

"We're in the wrong bloody place!" Marc snapped, the explanation falling out of him in a sudden rush. "There never was any of the actual bioweapon here, just an in-complete digital model of it—which they forced Park to finish up for them." He began to pace, thinking aloud. "It's no different from one of those guns made in a plastic milling machine . . . The thing is just a program, ones and zeros until you turn the data into a physical object."

"The bioprinters," said Park, with a sudden jerk. "They took two portable bioprinting machines from MaxaBio! They used my clearance to get them."

"We know," said Marc. "We assumed they brought them here."

"No. After they took me from Singapore, I never saw those machines again." Park looked at the floor. "I don't even know where *here* is."

"You're in Iceland," Marc told her, and the woman's eyes widened in shock. "Sorry. Should have . . . uh . . . mentioned that."

"Is it really that simple?" Lucy raised an eyebrow. "Load up a virtual model and press *print killer virus*?"

Park nodded. "There is more to it than that, but as long as they have the right seed stock, biokits and base materials, it can be done. It's the reason why high-acuity bioprinters are heavily regulated by the United Nations."

"It's a lot easier and safer to move around a bunch of inert chemicals and lab equipment, than it is to ship a live bioweapon." Marc looked back at the empty storage unit. "Much simpler to send the program rather than the virus."

"The Lion's Roar could have moved those bioprinters to anywhere in the world," Lucy went on. "If they can assemble a viral weapon on site, we are looking at the potential for a catastrophic terror attack we won't know about until it's too fucking late."

"I know where they sent them," said Park, in a small voice. Marc's head whipped around to stare at her. "I have the information in a safe place, I thought I could warn someone." She continued, her tone dropping to a hushed whisper. "On the plane, when Axelle was with me. She thought I was asleep, but I overheard her on the phone." Park gave a brittle smile. "*Elle ne savait pas que je parle français.*"

"Tell me where," Marc began, but at the corner of his vision he saw Lucy suddenly bringing up her trank gun.

"Heads up!" she called.

Marc drew his dart pistol and pivoted on his heel, in time to see figures moving behind the doors leading into the lab. The door opened a few degrees and the shapes of two mottled black cylinders came tumbling in through the gap.

Flashbangs.

An inner voice screamed out the warning and Marc lurched into a twisting motion, shoving Park to the floor behind a workbench. She fell into cover but he was too slow to save himself from the full effect of the ripple-blast from the stun grenades.

The air in the room turned into a caged thunderclap and a blinding luminosity seared his eyes. Marc staggered forward, groping sightlessly for the edge of the bench. A shrieking whistle echoed in his skull and he felt himself listing, the sonic blast so loud that it had affected his inner ear and disrupted his balance. Blinking furiously, trying to clear the raw purple after-image on his retinas, he collided with a chair and sprawled over it, almost going down in a heap.

Fuzzy blobs of color moved through his sight, dark dancing shapes full of menace coming closer. He picked out the ghost-image of Lucy's face turn his way, then retreat. Another form emerged out of the fog of bright color, a gaunt white woman as pale as death with the heavy rod of a shotgun in her hands.

The French woman from the phone, the one Park had called Axelle.

Marc cried out as she fired a close-range shot into Lucy, as the other operative tried to scramble away. He felt the tremor in the air from the blast more than he heard it, and then to his horror Axelle shot her again. Lucy crumpled behind a storage container and Marc lost sight of her.

He shouted, frantic and enraged, and fired the dart pistol in Axelle's direction. But what he was aiming at was the woman's blurry after-image, the space where she had been. Lurching up, his head swam and waves of nausea washed over him.

Another ghost-image took form in front of him, this one solidifying into a man with lupine features and a cruel grin. Noah Verbeke, as large as life and twice as vicious, came into being like he had been summoned by a curse. The bigger man swatted Marc with a haymaker that came out of nowhere, and in his half-stunned state there wasn't anything he could do about it. He lost the pistol again, and this time he had no idea where it had gone.

Next time use a bloody lanyard, he told himself.

"Be calm," said Verbeke, his voice muffled and faraway.

The bigger man landed another punch in Marc's solar plexus and this time his legs gave way. Marc collapsed against the workbench, eyes streaming, ears ringing.

He waited for the next blow, but Verbeke retreated. Second by agonizing second, Marc's vision cleared, and he saw two more men in the same black tactical gear as the Irishman moving to where Lucy fell. They hoisted her off the ground and shoved her up against a cabinet. She had the first blush of a wicked bruise forming across her right cheek, but she was alive and breathing.

Relief flooded through him as he caught sight of spent shotgun shells and a couple of small, tattered polymer pads scattered across the floor. Axelle had used flexible baton cartridges, tagging Lucy with the so-called "bean bag" rounds to put her down but not end her.

He was still trying to process what that meant when Verbeke hove back into view and made a broad *give-me* gesture.

"I'll need your weapons and equipment."

Marc feigned dizziness, which wasn't a hard act to pull off, and tried to get a read on the situation, his eyes darting around looking for something to turn the tables. In the back of his head, another thought was pressing at him.

Has Verbeke been here all along?

The other man pulled Park roughly to her feet and she spat in his face. Verbeke calmly wiped the spittle from his cheek, and then broke one of the woman's fingers in retribution. She screamed and he shoved her away, toward Axelle.

"I became bored with watching you stumble around like idiots," Verbeke told Marc, as if he was intuiting his thoughts.

He pointed at the ceiling and Marc looked in that direction. His vision was still hazy, but he suspected there was another security camera hidden up there.

"She wanted to kill you both before you entered the building," continued Verbeke, jerking a thumb at the pale woman. "But I said no, I wanted to see how far you could get before you figured out how fucked you are." His grin widened. "Which reminds me." He held out a hand to Axelle, and with a weary expression the woman handed him a fifty euro note. "You made her lose a bet," he said, leaning in to Marc and smirking, as if he was confiding a secret. "That's going to upset her."

"You . . ." Lucy said thickly, sucking in a breath. "You have about ten minutes before the whole of the Icelandic police force comes down on this place. You hear that, asshole?"

"Is it talking?" Verbeke faked a confused expression, looking at Marc but gesturing toward Lucy. "All that mongrel chattering. I don't listen."

"You should," said Marc, finally recovering his balance.

"Don't play games." Verbeke gave him a mocking pat on the cheek and a pitying look. "You're on your own here. You have no backup. And the SR are a bunch of gutless fools." He pulled Marc to his feet. "Your weapons and equipment. I won't ask a third time."

On that cue, Axelle lifted her shotgun and rested the barrel on Park's shoulder, the muzzle pressing against the side of the scientist's head. At point-blank range, even a non-lethal baton round would fatally fracture her skull.

Lucy reluctantly rose to her feet and followed the command. The thugs at her back already had her trank rifle and smartphone, and she removed her spare ammo clips, letting them drop. Next was a backup dart pistol, a couple of loads for that, and then the ceramic knife sheathed to the inside of her wrist. One of the thugs shoved her in the small of the back. She scowled, before producing a second blade hidden in her boot.

Marc gave a shrug and dropped the backpack containing his smashed tablet and the busted HERF projector, then removed his phone, smartwatch, the emergency flash drive containing his preferred suite of offensive software programs, and lastly a flexible microcircuit.

Verbeke gave him a long and disappointed look when he didn't produce any weapons, as if Marc was the most derisible excuse for a man he had ever encountered.

"How it is that soft little things like you are allowed to exist I will never understand," he told him. "Do you even know how to use the tools you are given?"

Marc returned a level look.

"I know a tool when I see one."

Verbeke grinned again, but it didn't reach his eyes. He gave Marc another pat on the face, but this time it was more of a slap.

"You recognize you are a failure here, yes?" He gestured around at the lab. "I let you get this far." He patted Marc to emphasize each word. "I. Let. You."

"You keep touching me." Marc leaned in and gave a stage whisper. "I mean, I don't have anything against it, and I am kind of flattered, but you should know I don't swing that way."

Verbeke's hand dropped and his smile turned rigid.

"We knew you were here. Didn't you think the people who run this place would monitor the approaches?"

"Given how sloppy your people work," Lucy chimed in, "we figured you'd have your thumbs up your asses."

"I sent out the woman to entice you." Verbeke continued to ignore Lucy, giving Park a careless kick as he fixated on Marc. "And in you came. Who was the idiot who thought that was a good idea? The mongrel, or you?"

Marc tried and failed to hide a grimace. He felt his

confidence crumble. All the velocity, the energy, that had been driving him forward on this mission leaked away. The reality of it was inescapable. This was on Marc, and his overconfidence had blown the operation. His luck had run out.

"Your friend Larsson," said Verbeke. "He's not smart. He keeps pissing off the wrong people. He should mind his own business." He paused, letting that lie for a moment. "So should you. Who else have you been talking to? I am told Rubicon have a nasty habit of sticking their nose in where it doesn't belong."

"Ruby who?" said Marc, making a face. "Never heard of her."

"English always think they are so clever," sneered Axelle, breaking her haughty silence. "But you're only good for the muscle we can use or the money to milk."

"Yeah," Marc admitted. "Sad fact is, there are a lot of assholes who think like you back home. But lucky for the rest of us, they're thick as shit." He fixed Verbeke with a steady gaze, changing tack. "Why don't we cut to the chase, yeah? Because you're talking to me like you're the one in charge but we know that's not true. You're a dog on a lead, aren't you? Someone else is pulling your chain."

He tried to close off the hollow feeling inside him and concentrate on the moment.

The momentum of this operation was in danger of unravelling and Marc knew he had to find some kind of leverage, some way to stay in the fight until an opportunity presented itself. And the only way he could see was to stick the knife in Verbeke's sense of self, to undercut this braggart's hard-man attitude.

"Did they make you say please and thank you when you were busted out in Slovakia? Sit, stay, roll over?" Marc faked a grin and directed it at Lucy. "Look at this

shower of shits. They're not smart enough to put this
together on their own, are they?"

"I am used to being underestimated." Verbeke's flinty
tone told Marc he had struck a nerve. "The bleeding
hearts always think their compassion makes them cleverer than the rest of us. But you're the biggest fools
of them all. You look down your noses at us. Blind
and ignorant, hiding it behind a veil of righteous arrogance. So busy signaling your virtues and preening,
you don't see the corrosion everywhere."

"We know you," insisted Axelle. "We know your
master and his self-centered crusade. There are a lot of
people who want you dead." She eyed Lucy. "Take you.
The Soldier-Saints in America have a bounty for your
pretty black head."

"Those pencil-dicks?" Lucy snorted. "Is it a lot? I'll
be insulted if it's not."

"Oh, I would hurt you for free," Axelle replied, and
her gun dropped off Park's shoulder, coming around to
aim at the other woman.

Marc saw the sudden change in the Korean's expression, the abrupt flash of rage in her eyes as she saw her
moment to act. She snatched at a metal retort stand on
the nearby workbench, and gave a wordless cry of fury
as she smashed it into the back of Verbeke's head with
all the force she could muster. As she was reeling back
for another blow, the man rounded on her, and he tore
the stand from her grip. His face turned crimson and a
punch came next, the blow landing hard in her stomach. Park crumpled to her knees and coughed out a
spatter of thin bile.

"You bastard!"

Marc rocked off his heels, his fists bunching, but
Axelle was suddenly aiming her shotgun at him and he
faltered as the muzzle rose.

Verbeke paid no attention to him, tossing away the stand. He put a heavy military boot on Park's ankle and pressed down hard, drawing a thin scream from the woman.

"I let you live," he growled. "Know your place!"

Through her tears, Park cursed him in her native language before finally sobbing brokenly.

"You lied to me! You murdered my family!"

He gave a sigh and removed his boot.

"Is it worth keeping up the pretense?" Verbeke asked the question and then answered it himself. "I suppose not. The test served its purpose."

"We need her . . ." began Axelle, but Verbeke shook his head.

"No, we don't. She's done all we required, we are close enough." He glared at the trembling woman, rubbing at the back of his head. His hand came away marked with streaks of crimson. "And she drew blood. That has to be paid in kind."

Verbeke grabbed Park by the hair and she howled again. He dragged her across the lab, and Marc took a step after her. Axelle jabbed him in the chest with the barrel of the shotgun and hard lines of pain rippled across his chest.

There was a cube with walls of thick plastic built into another workbench, the clear box maybe a meter and a half square along all sides, lined inside with more metal racks. Yellow hazard warning triangles adorned it and condensation hung on the frame in wet patches. There were silver pipes entering from the top, and a drain grid on the bottom. Verbeke wrenched it open, tore out the racks, and then forcibly shoved the Korean woman inside. Her small frame was too big to fully fit, but he slammed the panel down on her legs any-

way, confining her inside as best he could. Park fought
weakly, pushing back.

"What the hell are you doing?" Marc demanded.

"Industrial accidents happen more often that you
might think."

Verbeke reached down for a control valve on the side
of the cube. He gave it a savage twist and jets of hot
steam gushed into the box from the vents at the top.
Trapped inside, Park cried out as the scalding vapor
touched her bare skin.

"No!"

Marc surged forward, and this time Axelle hit him
in the chest with the butt of the shotgun, hard enough
that the burst of agony made him stagger against the
bench. Lucy moved and the gun swung in her direction.

Verbeke shut the valve.

"Run-off from the geothermal plant," he explained,
delighted by his own cruelty. "They use the heated
steam to boil away any dangerous germs."

"You fucking animal!" spat Lucy.

He quickly twisted the valve open and closed, blasting Park once again.

"*You* are the fucking animals!" Verbeke roared back
at her, his anger exploding into full display from out of
nowhere. "You stinking mongrels from your shithole
countries, all your filth and degeneracy pouring into
our world! You are nothing, bitch! You and your kind
need to be culled!" He shot a venomous glare at Marc.
"And every race traitor collaborator along with you!"
All the seething hatred Verbeke had been keeping in
check burst its banks, and he thundered at them, spitting bile. "Tell me how you tracked us here! Do it now
or I'll kill her!"

He cranked the valve again, slow and methodical, and

Park began to moan in agony as the vapor streamed in. Verbeke kept one hand on the latch, holding it shut. Marc could not tear his gaze away from the terrified woman banging helplessly on the inside of the thick plastic, her legs kicking in wretched panic.

"He's going to do it anyway," said Lucy, in a dead voice.

Verbeke turned the valve past the next increment and Park's screaming turned ragged.

"The money!" Marc shouted the words at him, unable to stay silent any longer. "Stop! *Stop!* We followed the money, you heartless bastard!"

"I thought so," said Verbeke.

And then with a flourish, he opened the valve as far as it would go, flooding the plastic chamber with a torrent of superheated steam. Park's agonized cries were drowned out in the hissing gush, and clouds of the boiling vapor spewed out around the half-closed panel. The woman stopped thrashing and Verbeke finally cut the feed, allowing the steam to dissipate. He let go of the door and Park's ruined, heat-bloated corpse tumbled out, crashing to the floor in a puddle of bloody fluids.

The appalling, sick horror of the brutal murder shocked Marc rigid, but Verbeke looked on at the dead woman with what appeared to be idle curiosity.

"Such a tragedy," he allowed.

A second ago, he had been caught in a towering rage, but now Verbeke was calm. It was as if a switch had been tripped, swinging him instantly from one mood's extreme to another. With revulsion, Marc realized that the man was quite pleased by what he had done.

"The money," Verbeke repeated, turning his back on his victim. "That's always a weak link. We will have to take steps."

"You . . . You didn't need to do that."

Marc met Verbeke's gaze and in that moment he was filled with such raw hate for the man that all he wanted was to throw himself at him, grab him by the throat, rip and tear until one of them was dead. The emotion was powerful, primal, and he wanted to give in to it.

Verbeke saw that in his eyes and smiled. He pointed at Marc's face.

"You feel it? That's what strength is, English. *Hate.* It's just another word for the same thing."

"Let's finish this," said Axelle, bringing up the shotgun. "If they knew where to find us, others will too. We need to get out of here."

"True." Verbeke gave a nod. "But first we need to dispose of our guests here, and that does present a problem." He wandered past Lucy, looking her over. "One industrial accident is plausible, that can be covered up. But three?" He shook his head, and reached out to finger her ski jacket. "Too many dead foreigners draws too much attention. This wretched little island, they have so few murders here." Then he smiled coldly. "Few killings. But a lot of unexplained disappearances. You two came here pretending to be tourists. I understand a lot of visitors arrive with a poor grasp of Iceland's climate. That can be deadly."

Marc faltered as Axelle shoved him forward, out through the doors and into the cold, biting winds. Lucy was a few steps behind, being marched at gunpoint by another of the Lion's Roar thugs, and he glanced back, trying to catch her eye.

"Move," snarled the French woman.

Ahead of them, the black Jet Ranger Marc had

spotted earlier that evening was lit up and the rotors were spinning lazily. In the pilot's seat, a skinny bean-pole of a man was nervously running through a pre-flight checklist, and Marc couldn't blame him.

"You actually think we can fly in this?" he said, over his shoulder. "Wind shear will smash us into the ground as soon as we get above the valley!"

That wasn't strictly true. Marc had flown helicopters in weather worse than this, although not by choice, and *weather worse than this* had almost killed him when he had, but the dark skies out here were change-able and that meant dangerous. Any pilot with half a brain would stay grounded on a night like this, and that meant that Verbeke's man clearly feared the mur-derous thug's wrath more than the power of a glacier storm.

Axelle shoved Marc into the Jet Ranger's rear com-partment, where all but one of the seats had been re-moved, and then climbed in up front, next to the pilot. He saw her conversing animatedly with him. The pilot nodded a few times as he snapped a set of night-vision goggles into place over his eyes. The inference was clear: *No problem.*

"Yeah, we'll see," muttered Marc, as Lucy was forced into the back with him.

The heavyset thug marching her up had a sawn-off shotgun that he brandished like a pistol, and he took the only seat in the back, before holstering the weapon in his belt.

Instinctively, Marc extended his hand to Lucy and she took it. The two of them huddled together on the floor of the helicopter, partly for stability, and partly for warmth. Before they were marched from the lab, Ver-beke's men went to town stripping off their outerwear, shredding their insulating coats. Gloves and hats were gone too, so now all Marc and Lucy had was little more than their underwear and base layers. Everything windproof and weatherproof was lying in a pile back in the blockhouse along with their kit. The only thing Verbeke had let them keep were wallets and passports.

Enough to identify our corpses, Marc thought.

"They're gonna take us out to the middle of nowhere and leave us for dead," said Lucy, leaning close to be heard over the thrumming of the rotors.

"Yeah." Marc gave a grim nod.

The helicopter pitched alarmingly and left the ground, skidding through the air and away from the Frigga facility. The lights in the cabin died as the pilot activated his NVGs. They powered up and away, leaving the compound behind, heading out over the barren landscape at high speed. The Jet Ranger labored against the winds, buffeted by every gust that flowed across the icy wilderness, rattling the passengers and prisoners against the inside of the fuselage.

They flew on in silence for long minutes before Lucy spoke again.

"You don't have a plan for this, do you?"

It didn't sound like an accusation, but it might as well have been one.

"Looks like I didn't have a plan for anything, despite what I thought," he said, grimacing. "Should have listened to Delancort."

"Park was dead no matter what we did." Lucy's reply was firm. "Just like her husband and the kid. Fates sealed the moment they were taken." She stared out into the darkness. "I let her down. I let them all down."

The Jet Ranger fell through a series of stomach-turning drops and the rotors slapped at the wet air as the storm gave them a passing nudge. Through the windows, Marc could only see a fathomless black void, and the memory of his dream in Singapore came crashing back down on him. It took a near-physical effort for him to push the bleak sensation away and concentrate on the moment.

"We only are going to get one shot at this." He whispered the words into Lucy's ear. "They'll have to put down to kick us out. Just before that happens . . ."

"Got it," she replied. "You'll have to deal with Axelle and the pilot."

Marc was going to say something more, but he heard the change in the helicopter's engine note and saw the pilot's hands moving on the controls. They were slowing and descending. The buffeting became worse the nearer they came to the ground, and the thug with the double-barrelled sawn-off snatched at a grab bar to hold himself steady.

Axelle shouted a command at him and jabbed her finger at the rear compartment's door. The helicopter's running lights were off, so it was almost impossible to see anything outside, but Marc caught a flash of weak moonlight off acres of frosty wilderness. They were coming down on an ice field at the edge of a glacier.

When they were less than a meter off the ground, the gun thug kicked open the door and a blast of freezing cold air filled the helicopter's cabin. He reached out and grabbed a fist of Lucy's undershirt, hauling her forward with a savage jerk. She let him do it, let the momentum carry her to him.

She was going to go for the gun. Marc twisted toward the gap between the front seats. He would make a grab for the collective lever at the side of the pilot's chair, intending to force it down to put off the pitch of the rotor blades.

But that plan, like the others, broke apart in an instant. Axelle had a stun baton in her hand and she jabbed it in Marc's direction, the metal tines at the tip spitting bright blue sparks. He flinched back before it could make contact, in time to see the gun thug produce one of his own and use it on Lucy.

She let out a strangled cry and her body jerked. The helicopter rocked in another heavy gust and the thug hauled her the rest of the way. She went out of the open door and into the blackness.

Immediately, the Jet Ranger sank into a shallow roll away from the ice field, and Marc knew what they were doing. Axelle had ordered the pilot to dump Lucy here, *wherever the hell that was*, and they were going to put Marc out somewhere else. Separating the pair immediately halved any chance either of them might have to survive the night.

Marc reacted before the helicopter could gain any more height, and threw himself at the thug, putting all of his body mass behind the motion. The man wasn't ready for it and he wasn't strapped in, two mistakes that proved fatal. He tried to hit Marc with his baton, but it was too little too late. The weight distribution inside the Jet Ranger shifted off base and Marc fell through the still-open door, into the black night, locked in a violent embrace with the gun thug.

The drop was almost ten meters, or so it seemed, dizzyingly long and terrifyingly short all at once. The man took the full force of the impact against the packed snow, his back giving a juddering crack as he hit. The shock resonated up through Marc's body and threw him off. He rolled away across jagged vanes of ice that cut at him like blunt knives, coming to a halt on his back in a cauldron of pain.

Overhead, the black helicopter was barely visible against the menacing sky, the phantom shape of some massive predatory hornet dithering over its prey. Marc lay there, every joint in his body on fire, waiting for Axelle to lean out and start shooting. But the wind clawed over him with icy needles and the aircraft reeled. The blades flickered in the darkness and the Jet Ranger left them behind. The noise of the rotors was quickly swallowed by the howling breeze.

With effort, Marc rolled on to his side and pitched up into a sitting position.

"Lucy!" He shouted her name into the dark, tasting blood in his mouth.

"Don't shout," she called back, emerging out of the gloom. "Right here."

She was limping, favoring her left leg, and her shoulders were already twitching with the cold.

"Y'okay?" He slurred the words and pushed himself to his feet. "Ow."

"Did you f-fall out?"

"Jumped out," he insisted. "Falling makes it sound like it was accidental."

He trudged over to the body of the dead gun thug.

Lucy stared off after the Jet Ranger.

"That did not go how I wanted." She hugged herself. "Think I threw up a little."

"Help me with this pillock," said Marc, crouching near the thug. He pressed a shaking finger against the man's neck to be sure, but there was no pulse and the expanding patch of dark, steaming liquid beneath the guy's head confirmed it.

Lucy bent down with him.

"How cold do you think it gets out here?"

"This far north? Like minus twenty with the wind chill, or worse."

"Swell," she managed. "Half an hour to frostbite, if we're lucky. Dead before sunrise, that's a given."

"That's the spirit, think positive." Marc's teeth chattered as he retorted.

"We need shelter," she insisted, casting around in the darkness.

In the direction the helicopter had taken, a gray field of ice extended away until it vanished in the blackness. The surface of the glacier was scarred and broken, dirty with black volcanic ash, a lethal terrain filled with bottomless crevasses that would have been dangerous to navigate in broad daylight.

"Not that way," Lucy concluded.

The other direction, off the ice and on to the tundra, was only marginally less threatening. The stark and treeless plain promised no cover, no respite from the elements, and no signs of civilization.

Marc dug through the dead man's pockets, searching for anything they could use. He still had the sawn-off shotgun, with two shells in the pipe and six more in his pockets. The stun baton was fully charged, but good for nothing out here. When he found a radio in the thug's back pocket, Marc's heart briefly leaped—but the device was broken open and inert, and with no available light he couldn't even think about trying to fix it.

"Help me strip him," he told Lucy.

The thug had only a fleece and a few more underlayers that they could share out between them, and at these temperatures anything that kept the cold a bay a little longer was a good idea. Marc took the fleece, Lucy got the layer beneath and the windproof trousers. Socks were repurposed as gloves for her, and when the dead man's cheap thermal leggings ripped, Marc wound strips of them into bindings to project his own hands.

It was a surreal moment, leaving a barely clothed

corpse on a glacier ridge, but they needed the gear more than the dead man. Marc gave the thug the finger.

"Thanks, mate," he added, and turned away.

Lucy huddled in with him and the pair of them started walking, each supporting the other.

"You were in the special forces," he said to her. "You trained for this, right?"

"You were Royal Navy," she shot back. "Didn't you?"

"Our survival drill was mostly to do with ditching in the drink," he told her. "This sort of thing not so . . . Not so much."

Each breath he took was rough and heavy in his lungs. He could feel the temporary sutures Lucy had put across the lacerations on his chest had split and he was bleeding there again.

"Did teach us about hypothermia, though," he remembered, pulling up the memory. "Starts with shivering. Then you don't think straight. Blood pressure and heart rate drops."

She glared at him. "I swear to you. If I f-fucking die out here, I will haunt you. Full r-rattling chains and spook-house shit, I mean it."

"What makes you think you'll freeze to death before I do?"

The question was so ridiculous he almost laughed out loud.

"Fair point," she allowed. "Your skinny ass will ice up faster than mine."

"Cold, Lucy," he admonished. "That's cold."

"Look around." She waved at the frost-covered landscape. "Isn't everything?"

— THIRTEEN —

A chill was coming in off the Gulf of Sidra, kicking up loose sand that flickered around the street lights along the highway leading out of Benghazi, and along the Libyan coast. Overhead, the cloudless veil of night stole the warmth of the day, and what few people were outside stood close to doorways or around portable heaters.

The bearded man paid a couple of kids to watch his weather-beaten Volvo, before slipping inside the shuttered garage and locking the door behind him. Although he had been born thousands of miles from this shell-shocked city on the edge of the desert, his serviceable Arabic and his resemblance to the locals meant he could pass for a native.

The cover he was using was thin, but it wasn't meant to be airtight. Part of the plan was that his fake identity would be discovered by the authorities. It was imperative to make sure that they left enough clues to lay the false trail and make it convincing.

He fingered his oily facial hair and glanced around, removing papers and a broken cellular phone from his bag, then placing them in a wastebasket. He arranged them to give the impression they had been disposed of in a hurry, then made his way toward the back of the garage.

The front half of the building had been left untouched, the elevator jacks, tool chests and storage cupboards still sitting where they had been when his partner had taken over the place from the previous owner. The old man who ran the garage lay where he had left him, wrapped in a dust cloth, the corpse half-hidden behind a pile of balding tires. Stale blood from where the fool's throat was slit had soaked through the cloth in a dark brown patch, and a colony of flies had made it their home.

The rear half of the garage was much changed, however. Double layers of thick polypropylene had been erected on a frame of scaffold bars, forming a box-shaped tent nested within the building's interior. A makeshift inflatable airlock was the only way inside, and right before the entrance was an industrial shower hanging from another of the jacks, the metal head dripping water on the stained concrete.

The bearded man's taller partner saw him through the clear plastic and made a sharp beckoning motion. He nodded and quickly changed out of his street clothes, stepping into a waiting hazmat suit. The all-encompassing bright yellow oversuit zipped closed and he took a quick self-check before venturing inside. Any rips or tears in the suit would have deadly consequences.

"Where have you been?" The taller man demanded an answer as soon as he came through the airlock's inner door. "I'm almost done. This needs two pairs of hands."

His florid, pinkish face looked odd framed in the bug-like shape of the suit.

"I thought it would take longer," said the bearded man.

"No," his partner replied. "Once the model uploaded,

it was actually quite quick. They told me how to prepare the base elements."

"Well, fine. I had to wait a while to get the tickets. But we're ready to go. First plane off the ground after morning prayers." He jerked a thumb at his bag outside, the movement exaggerated by the bulky hazmat gear. "Rome for you, I have Milan."

"Help me with this."

The tall man moved to the far corner of the tent, where the bio-printer had been set up next to a stack of car batteries. Inside the glass cube at the core of the machine, a moving tray beneath a set of delicate nozzles was in the process of retracting, mechanical armatures shifting into place to present a clear vial. The machine offered it up, waiting for them to take it.

He hesitated. "You are sure it is safe?"

"Of course it isn't safe, that's why we are wearing these." The other man plucked at his suit's baggy yellow sleeve. "But once we get the payload inside the dispersal unit, there will be no more risk of exposure."

The bearded man gave a reluctant nod, reminding himself that his employers valued his skill set too greatly to let him perish. Already, there was a generous fee sitting in his account from their successful operation on the train in Slovakia, and that would double once this assignment was complete. On the flight to Milan he would decide how best to spend it.

The taller man opened the glass cube with a hiss of escaping air and gingerly accepted the vial. He held it up to the light. Inside was a pinkish gel that seemed like nothing at all, but the deadly potential swirling in it was great enough to wipe out thousands.

Now the vial was out of the machine, the bearded man was suddenly sweating. What if he had missed a tiny pinhole in the hazmat suit? Would that be enough to kill him? He scowled and shook off the moment.

"You wanted to get this done. Stop admiring it."

He stooped and gathered up the delivery device, unscrewing the cap. Outwardly, it resembled a chrome thermal flask, the kind of vacuum-insulated container that could keep tea warm for hours. The innards had been stripped out and repurposed with a remote-activated aerosol dispersion mechanism, and beneath the cap there was a slot for the vial to fit into. He held it steady as the taller man slowly brought the vial over, fitting the payload into place. Finally, the cap went back on. The device was now live.

They abandoned the tent, passing through the airlock and showering off. One at a time, they secured their used hazmat gear and bagged it. Normally, the next phase in an operation like this would be an aggressive clean-up, a floor-to-ceiling burn to leave nothing behind—but not this time.

He put the flask inside a nondescript nylon daypack he had picked up from the morning market the day before, while scouting the target area. The taller man changed into street clothes, using a *shemagh* and a baseball cap to hide his Western features, then gathered up the gear that would detract from the narrative they wanted to leave in place.

Most of the equipment he left untouched, but the laptop computer and portable sat-com dish was too new, too high-tech to be left behind. If the police found them the wrong questions would be asked, so they would bury the gear in the desert, in some lonely spot off the highway. The sweep was thorough, and when it was done they moved back out to the car.

The street kids had gone but the Volvo was still intact.

"Let's go." The taller man climbed into the driver's

seat. "I want to get to the airport before dawn, and it's a long drive."

The bearded man nodded and walked down to the next building along, where their neighbor, an enterprising youth called Azeem, stored the wares he sold at the market.

He made a space in the back of Azeem's battered Toyota pickup, among bales of recycled clothing, and placed the nylon daypack there, set so the tip of the flask inside was exposed to the air.

He paused and checked a second cellular phone in his bag. It was an old model, an elderly Nokia out of date a decade ago, but it still worked. It was still capable of sending a trigger signal.

The tall man leaned on the Volvo's horn and it gave a strangled hoot.

Time to leave, thought the other man, and jogged back to the car.

There had been a moment, back when Marc Dane had been on his first tour at sea, when he found himself up on the aft deck of a ship in the middle of a force eight gale, and for the briefest of instants it had felt like the storm circling the vessel was *seeing* him, as a wolf would see its prey. It stalked him, swirling about, waiting for the moment to strike.

That moment had never come, but now out here in the black cold, on the barren, near-lifeless Icelandic tundra, that ominous threat had come back to finish the job. Grit and ice particles came at him in pitiless bursts, sweeping across the landscape with enough force to make him stumble. He and Lucy hung on to each other, marching robotically through the darkness. He estimated they had been walking for hours, but it was impossible to be certain. Frost formed on his ragged beard and patches of white rime collected on the front of his thighs and shoulders.

In the distance, stark black against the storm clouds, there was a line of hills and they used that as their landmark, navigating toward what Marc hoped would be the lowlands. Down there, they would find a road, maybe even a remote house or even a village. He kept telling himself that. With no stars to navigate by, even dead reckoning wasn't going to help them.

"I don't know where it is," Lucy said abruptly, slurring as she spoke. "Stop askin' me."

She pushed against him, half-heartedly trying to shove him away.

"What did you say?" He had to force out the words.

"I . . . I don't get it," she went on, detaching herself from him. "Really don't." Lucy was holding one half of a conversation, responding to what she thought he was saying. In the dimness he could see her windburned face was slack, her gaze vague and distant. "S'cold. But why . . . ? Why am I so damn hot?" Lucy staggered backward and pulled at the socks she wore as makeshift gloves. "Get these off."

"No."

Marc grabbed her hands and pulled her close. A sick dread churned in his gut.

This was how hypothermia gets you, he remembered. *It messes with your head. You become disoriented, confused.*

"Quit it!" she snarled, shaking him off, giving him an angry shove.

"Aggressive," he concluded.

"What?"

"Lucy, listen to me," Marc said, calling out over the moaning winds. "You just think you're warm. It's your muscles tiring out, the blood vessels relaxing. It makes you feel like you're heating up, but you're not. You hear me?"

"That sounds like something . . ." She marched away into the darkness. "You're making that up, Johnny."

John is her brother's name. Marc frowned. *If she's mistaking me for him, she must be losing it.*

He set off after her.

"Lucy, it's me, Marc. Hold on!"

"I know," she shot back, her voice trailing out of the night. And then in the next moment she cried out in alarm. "Holy shit!"

Marc heard the near-panic in her tone, heard the sound of rock shifting, and he broke into a full-tilt run. She rose out of the dark in front of him and they almost collided.

Lucy shoved him back and he was afraid she was going to attack him, but she seemed lucid again.

"Watch it, there's a goddamn hole here the size of New Jersey!"

He gathered himself and let his eyes adjust. She was right. Black against the blackness, directly in the path they had been taking, a yawning void lay ahead of them. It was a wide, jagged-edged sinkhole, opening into a shallow cave maybe ten meters below.

"It's a lava cave," Marc said, his heart hammering in his chest as he realized how close they had come to stumbling blindly into this gaping pit. Lucy flinched back and he shook his head. "I mean, not like *lava* lava, not molten or anything . . . But it's shelter!"

"Yeah." Lucy gave a weak nod. "Sure, why not. Let's hide out in a volcano."

* * *

It was hard work picking their way down the slope of rough, broken stone spilling into the cave space, and the frosty patina on the rocks made them slip and stumble several times. But once in the chamber, the difference was immediately apparent. It was still bloody cold down there, but the wind chill was cut to a fraction of its former ferocity.

"So d-dark here," Lucy managed. "Have I gone blind?"

Marc sat on the floor of the cave and fumbled in his pockets, removing the items he had on him, placing them so he could find them by feel alone. Lucy's speech was still slurred, and he knew that if he didn't get her warmed up soon, the hypothermia would bed in and loss of consciousness would be next.

He had to keep her alert, keep her focused on something else. He said the first thing that came into his head.

"Why'd you join the army? You've never told me the reason. I've always wondered."

He heard her sit heavily, close by.

"Oh," she began, after a low intake of breath. "That's a story."

"Can I hear it?" he prompted.

Marc found one of the unused shotgun shells he had taken from Verbeke's man and made a pit among the cracked rocks on the cave floor.

"There was . . . this dude who lived, few blocks from us. In Queens."

As Lucy picked out the words, Marc twisted and pulled at the shell's brass base, gradually cracking it open. He poured the cartridge's propellant powder into the pit and then repeated the action with a second shell.

"Rich guy," she went on. "Bought this old movie theater. Everyone thought . . . he's crazy." She sighed. "Mom. And my Aunt Dani. Said Johnny and me needed to learn some responsibility. Found us after-school jobs with this guy. Fillin' the popcorn machine. Wipin' windows." She shivered. "Big old projector there. Old movies. Kung fu flicks. Horror films and monsters. Musicals."

"Huh." Despite the severity of their circumstances, Marc smiled in the darkness as he dismantled the next shell. "That explains a lot."

More than once, Marc heard Lucy refer to films made years before she was born, and he had assumed that she was quietly a movie buff. But this made sense. He imagined a teenage Lucy Keyes in some unconventional indie cinema, toiling away under a flickering screen showing aging prints of old cult classics.

"Got a favorite?"

"*Fantasia*." She slurred the name. "You?"

"*Raiders of the Lost Ark*."

"Figures," said Lucy.

Marc pulled a handful of loose threads from the material strips wound around his wrists, then bunched them in the pit between the rocks, tamping them down.

"Okay. Moment of truth," he told her. He grabbed the stun baton from where it lay and pressed the tines into the mound of propellant powder. "Cover your eyes!"

Blue light flashed and crackled, and there was a flat chug of ignition. Marc recoiled as the contents of his makeshift fire pit caught and combusted. A smoky ball of orange flame grew into being and he gave a whoop of success.

Drawn by the light, Lucy crowded close and dropped to the ground, curling up around the fire. Marc stripped more cloth and tore pages from his snap cover passport, feeding them in to keep the meager flames burning.

"So, what then?" he asked.

"Aunt Dani," Lucy repeated, and a note of sadness

entered her voice. "Miss her. Was really her idea. She knew the guy. Knew Mom. Everyone."

The story had yet to connect up to Lucy's military career, but he wasn't about to push her. Even after all they had been through together, Lucy was never forthcoming about her past. Now something hidden was trickling out, something he had never heard before.

He lay down next to her and pulled closer, until they were side by side. She didn't object. Lucy knew as well as he did that the fire wouldn't be enough to stave off the cold, even out of the wind. They would have to conserve what body heat they could as well.

"Don't get handsy," she told him. "Break your fingers."

He fought back a shiver.

"Believe me, copping a sneaky feel is not on my list of priorities."

"First time I ever hit a guy for touching me, Dani arrested us both."

"She was police?"

"She was the *most* police," Lucy said, with real warmth. "MP in the army. NYPD when she got out."

"So you joined up because of her."

Lucy was silent, and when she spoke again, it was with the clarity and distance of someone with long-faded regrets.

"I lost my dad when I was ten. Shooting in the bodega on the corner. Robbery. He was just in their way."

"I'm sorry."

The face of Marc's own father flickered in his thoughts, then sank into the gloom again.

"Me too. Dani was the cop who came to tell us. And she stuck around. Looked out for us, me and my brother." Lucy's voice began to shift back to its more usual timbre, her breathing evening out. "Her and my mom made me what I am."

"They must be proud of you."

She gave a soft, sad grunt. "Mom thinks I'm a criminal. Dani . . ." Lucy paused once more, and Marc felt her stiffen. "I enlisted the year after 9/11. Johnny never forgave me."

All at once, Marc saw the tragic, unspoken thread running through the middle of Lucy's story, and he felt a stab of sorrow for her.

"Was Dani there? At the World Trade Center?"

"You always put it together real quick, don't you?" Lucy nodded. "Dani went into the North Tower and she never came out. She always told me I needed to have a purpose in my life. That's the day I figured out what it was."

Marc's own memory of the fateful day when Al Qaeda terrorists attacked New York and Washington, D.C., was blurred by time and distance. His unit had been on a military exercise along with hundreds of other British army and naval forces when the news broke. At first he had thought it was a random twist thrown into the operation's narrative, until his commanders called *endex*. They suspended the fake conflict as the first shots in a new and very real war were still echoing around the world.

A man his sister Kate once dated, a city dealer type who was in finance, had been in the South Tower and evacuated before the second plane hit. In a surreal moment, the bloke's face had popped up on the BBC, as one of the first British eyewitnesses they'd been able to get hold of. Marc remembered that clearest of all: the weird dislocation of watching a man he knew from thousands of miles away, shell-shocked and dazed, talking about streets full of gray ash and lost co-workers.

To have been there on that day, to have seen it and lost someone you cared about . . .

All of a sudden, a lot of what he knew of Lucy Keyes made sense. He gently put his hand on her shoulder.

"I'm sorry about your friend."

"Your turn," she replied. "If I have to overshare, so do you."

"I don't have anything to give you don't already know," he told her, and that was more or less true. "I joined the navy because I thought it would be cool." Marc paused, annoyed with himself for the reflex denial. "Nah, that's all. I joined because I wanted to get away from life on a council estate with zero prospects. I grew up trapped between being bored out of my mind or afraid I'd get eaten alive by the troublemakers and the crime. The navy was a way out."

And for a while, he'd found a place for himself there. But then came the crash that nearly saw him drowned in the South China Sea, and suddenly it wasn't so easy to be fearless anymore. After he got out, the security services had come calling, seeing the skills he had, and he took that path more from inertia than anything else.

For a while Marc Dane was okay with being the bloke in the van, running backup, acting as technician on field ops while it fell to other people to kick in the doors and pull the triggers. But that too was torn away from him. His unit was ambushed and the blame fell upon his shoulders.

Feels like forever ago, he thought.

"You know why I hooked in with Rubicon," he told her. "It's because I had no other option, not really. My

mum passed, my sister and me don't speak, haven't seen
my father since I was a kid. After Six turned on me, I
had nowhere to go."

"You talk like you didn't have a choice," Lucy said
quietly. "But you did, like I did. You could have sat
back and done nothing, but you didn't. *You wanted
in*. We're both here because we needed some payback,
Dane. And the fact is, what drives us is what put us
into this mess." She gave a humorless chuckle. "Shit,
we're both victims of our worst impulses, ain't we?"

He shook his head. "The blame for this is on me. I
pushed. I convinced you to go in when we should have
held back. And now Park is dead and we're one bad
night away from joining her."

"I've never done anything . . . I didn't want to," Lucy
said, fighting off a shiver as her fatigue drew her down
toward sleep. "You're not the white knight, man. Stop
thinking that you are. Because that's what'll get you
killed."

Marc lost himself in the flicker of the feeble firelight,
her words echoing in his mind long after she had spoken them.

Azeem's stall was in a prime place, across from the
school on the corner of the Keesh Square, a spot he jealously guarded from the others who came to sell their
wares at the street market. He had the old trestle table
in place across the drop-down tailgate of his pickup, angling the thin sunshade so that buyers could stop and
pore over his wares without having to squint as the day
carried on.

Right now, the sun was low in the sky, peering hazily
through low cloud over the old zoo. It hit Azeem's stall

at just the right angle to show off his stock. Second-hand clothes harvested from the castoffs of Europeans, lots of them flashy T-shirts with printed logos, out-of-date football team strips, sneakers and more. He had a cousin down at the waterfront, who also sold him the occasional box of pirated DVDs. Those were always popular. He imagined the new discs he had to sell to-day would be gone by noon, before the muezzin made the call for Zuhr.

This was the best spot in the Western Dawud, he told himself, perhaps even the best spot in all of Benghazi for a man like him. People would wander up from the cafés or across from the park all day, and the steady foot traffic made it the most lucrative of any pitch.

"*Salam, Khou-ya!*" called a rough voice, and Azeem's fellow stall-holder Gamal came waddling up, smiling widely.

Gamal had a bad leg, a reminder from the civil war, and it made him rock from side to side whenever he walked. He greeted Azeem with a two-fisted handshake, enveloping the younger man's fingers in his meaty paws.

"How are you this day?"

"Hoping for good customers," Azeem replied.

"As are we all, *inshallah,*" Gamal made a praying mo-tion. His gaze fell on the box of DVDs. "What do we have here?"

Immediately, the older man began fingering through the contents. He had three daughters who loved Amer-ican romantic comedies, and he bought them to bribe his way into their good graces. His big hands gave him the impression of someone clumsy, ham-fisted, but Ga-mal moved with great delicacy as he plucked one disc after another from the box.

Azeem left him to it and continued to unload his Toy-ota.

"I heard a story last night, from Badis at the café. He was telling me about Fatima and Remi."

Gamal made a negative noise. "Badis should mind his own business."

"He has no family of his own so he gossips about everyone else's." The boy Remi and his sibling were the only children of Gamal's second cousin, an unlucky woman who had died the previous year during the last violent spasms of the war. "Badis said they paid smugglers for passage out of the country. Is that true?"

"A lot is true," Gamal said testily. "A lot are lies. I can't say."

Azeem hesitated, afraid that he had inadvertently touched a raw nerve with his old friend.

"I'm sorry, I didn't mean to pry."

Gamal's shoulders sank. "No, it's all right. Yes, Badis is correct. They escaped on a boat. I didn't want them to go. Too dangerous. But Fatima called me two nights ago. They are well." The big man shuddered. "So many days without word. I was convinced they were dead, lost to the sea. But God kept them safe." He shot Azeem a look. "Speaking of divine intervention . . . Did you hear about the men who were washed up down the coast, near Bin Jawad? Europeans! From one of their 'protection boats'! Someone shipwrecked them!"

Azeem snorted. "I hope they were given a fitting welcome . . ."

He trailed off as he came across something he didn't recognize. A black nylon daypack, the flap hanging open so that a silver cylinder inside was visible.

"What is in there?" said Gamal. "Your breakfast?"

"I'm not sure." Azeem concentrated, trying to remember if this was something he had bought from the wholesaler. He had no memory of it. "Perhaps someone left it behind, and it was put in with my stock."

Still, something about the metal flask made Azeem uncomfortable. He remembered his father's stern warnings to him from when he was a boy, about the dangers of touching unexploded shells left over after the countless attacks that had bombarded Libya over the decades.

Azeem picked up the flask and turned it over in his hands.

"I think I should get rid of it."

He touched the cap, and without warning jets of cold fluid spat out through pinholes in the rim of the metal. He recoiled, dropping the flask. His hands and his robe were wet and sticky, and without thinking, he grabbed the nearest thing to wipe them clean, a T-shirt with a garish logo on it.

"Are you all right?" Gamal was at his side, a worried look on his face. "Did you open it?"

"I must have," said Azeem, dabbing himself down. The liquid had no odor, but it seemed to have gone everywhere. He found a bottle of water and used it to wash off his hands.

Gamal gathered up the hissing flask and put it back in the daypack.

"You're right," he told him. "Get rid of this."

"What do you think it is?" Azeem asked, his mind racing. "Some sort of practical joke?"

"That must be it," Gamal insisted. "Your cousin is making fun of you." He found a smile and nodded. "Next time, pay him half what he asks."

Azeem shrugged and tossed the daypack into the pickup's flatbed.

"I'll dump it later."

He stifled a catch in his throat. There was an odd medicinal taste at the back of his mouth.

Gamal absently rubbed his hands on his robe and moved back to the box of DVDs, nodding as he did.

"In the meantime, let me buy these to improve your fortune."

He held out a cluster of shiny discs, covering his face as he coughed.

Azeem nodded, as a vague wave of nausea washed over him.

In the back of the Toyota, the flask continued to emit a quiet, metallic whisper as its lethal payload emptied into the morning air.

Marc awoke slowly, degree by painful degree. A fitful sleep on the hard, cold floor of the cave had left him riddled with chills and aches, and his joints popped audibly as he rose and shook it off. Lucy crouched by the campfire, poking at the dead embers with a stick.

"How are you feeling?" she asked.

"Never mind me, what about you?" he countered.

They had spent the night wrapped around one another, preserving what fractions of heat they could, and the intimacy of the act felt awkward in the aftermath.

"I'm okay." That wasn't true, but Marc decided not to call her out on it. She nodded in the direction of the cave mouth. "Good news is, storm's gone."

Watery gray daylight leaked into the lava cavern and Marc gave a nod, looking around. In the pitch darkness of the previous night, it had been almost impossible to grasp their full surroundings, but now he saw how the ancient tunnel of rock curved away from them, disappearing deeper into the cold earth. Millennia ago, the cave had been a channel for volcanic magma, and the signature of the molten rock was still written on the craggy ceiling over their heads. A dirty silvery sheen marked where deposits of metallic gas had been locked into the rock.

"I'm going to one-star this place," he told her, gathering up the shotgun, starting toward the slope of rubble near the cave mouth. "Room service is terrible."

Despite herself, Lucy gave a hollow chuckle and followed him up, back out into the cold air of the morning. Cloud banks overhead extended off to the horizon in all directions and a light, fine rain was falling, but the visibility was good enough to see for miles. The previous night's violent wind had dropped to a steady, chilling breeze.

At the top of a low rise, Marc turned in a slow circle, getting his bearings, only to stop dead as he saw something that made him curse out loud.

"You are taking the piss!"

"What?" Lucy scrambled up the last few meters to his side, brandishing the stun baton. She followed his line of sight and then swore loudly along with him. "I do not fucking believe this."

Around a mile distant from where they had climbed down into the lava tube, there was a small prefabricated hut at the end of a hiking trail. A line of wooden spikes set in the frost-covered ground drew a course from the far side of the sinkhole entrance to the clearing around the hut.

"That was not there last night," Lucy insisted.

"Yeah, it was," Marc said, almost incredulously. "We just didn't see it in the pitch bloody dark!"

They trudged down the shallow incline and made their way across the moss-covered rocks toward it. As they came closer, Marc had to fight off the crazy impulse to reach out and touch the shelter, to be certain it wasn't some kind of hypothermia-induced hallucination.

"If this thing has a hot shower, steaks and coffee inside, I might be able to forgive it," Lucy muttered.

Marc circled the building, finding the front door. The hut's wooden exterior had been painted international orange some time in the distant past, but countless harsh winters had shredded the paintwork, exposing the planks underneath. He unlatched the heavy-duty weatherproof catches holding the door shut and ventured inside.

The hut's interior was damp and musty, but it was a palace compared to the cave. There were two beds with survival mattresses, an oil heater and a battery-powered UHF radio. Lucy wasted no time firing up the heater as Marc studied the radio set.

He reached for the handset, then hesitated.

"If we use this in clear and Verbeke's men are monitoring, they'll know we're still alive."

"They think we're dead. We almost *were*." She crouched by the heater, still shivering. "We have to take the chance. That, or we sit here, play cards and wait for the next tourist to turn up and jack their ride."

Lucy was right, and he knew it. Setting aside the sawn-off, Marc took a breath and keyed the mike.

"Break, break," he began. "To anyone copying this transmission. This is an emergency. I need to make contact with Inspector Andri Larsson of the SR. My name is Marc Dane, I am a private security contractor with the Rubicon Group and I have critical information for the police. Please respond, over."

Static hissed back at him.

"Look on the bright side," said Lucy, scanning the

sparse landscape out of the hut's windows. "We have good sight lines up here. Anyone comes with ill intent, we'll know it."

"Yeah, that makes me feel a lot better," he lied.

The radio crackled.

"*This is Ice-SAR,*" came the reply. "*What is the nature of your emergency, over?*"

"Get a pen," Marc told the rescue dispatcher. "You'll want to write this down."

— FOURTEEN —

By her estimate, Lucy was up by three hundred bucks when the helo buzzed the shelter. They dropped their cards and she snatched up the shotgun on the way out of the door, but Marc waved her off as the aircraft turned back and loitered, looking for a place to put down.

"It's Larsson," he told her, as the red and white Super Puma dropped to the ground and the hatch on the side slid open.

The Icelandic cop was first out, his coat catching the downwash from the rotors, and with him came four armed men in black tactical gear, each toting a Heckler & Koch MP5 sub-machine gun. Lucy had second thoughts about the sawn-off, holding it high as she followed the Brit out into the cold morning air. The tac-ops guys all saw the gun at once, and they took aim. Lucy tossed the weapon and did the smart thing, holding her hands up, palms open.

Larsson picked his way over the rocks to them, and he did not look happy.

"Let's go," he said, without preamble. "We'll get you to a secure location, and I'll be back to debrief you when we are finished at the Frigga facility."

"Wait, no." Marc grabbed Larsson's arm and the nearest of the tac-ops came over like he was ready to kick the Brit's ass. "You can't bench us, Andri. We were just in there!"

"You both look half-dead," Larsson shot back. "I warned you about coming out here unprepared. It's a wonder you're not corpses."

"Yeah, lucky us," Marc went on. "Mate, I didn't call you in so we could sit on the sidelines."

Larsson hesitated, weighing his options.

"Do you understand how much paperwork will be involved if you are injured or killed?"

"And do *you* want someone who can tell your men exactly where to go, or not?" Lucy shot back.

He gave a reluctant nod. "All right."

He called over one of the tac-ops guys and there was a rapid exchange. The men jogged back to the helo, and Larsson beckoned Marc and Lucy.

"Okay, it is already happening," said the Icelander. "Echo Squad is on approach to the complex. I had to miss out on the breach because I came to rescue you, so hurry up!"

They scrambled aboard the Super Puma and the aircraft pitched up into the air, taking off like a rocket. Lucy grabbed an intercom headset, looking over the nearest of the black-clad men in the seat next to her. His gear was squared away and in good order, and like the other masked operatives, he gave off the hard, steady focus of a career soldier. Lucy knew a fellow professional when she saw one. Wordlessly, he handed her and Marc spare jackets and gloves, which Lucy gratefully accepted.

On the jacket's breast, below a regulation police shield sigil, was a low-visibility black-on-black unit patch. It showed the face of a bearded Nordic warrior and a single word.

"*Víkingasveitin* . . ." She sounded out the syllables.

"I told you not to speak my language." Larsson's voice hissed in her ear through the headphones. "You

Americans always murder it." She looked back at him and he nodded toward the men. "Viking Squad," he explained. "Our equivalent of your SAS or Delta Force."

"Cool name," said Marc.

He shot the Brit a look. "Are you going to tell me the full story about why you came to Iceland? No more games, Dane. If my country is at risk, you need to come clean about it."

Marc glanced at Lucy, and she sighed.

"How long until we get to the facility?" she asked.

Larsson glanced at his watch. "Twenty minutes."

Lucy tapped her headset. "Can you patch me into a sat-com phone from this?"

"Yes."

"Call this number," she told him, and from memory she spooled off the SCD contact protocol details. "It's time we got everyone up to speed."

It took only a few minutes for the connections to be made, and then they were on a scrambled party line— Marc, Lucy and Larsson in the speeding helicopter, Assim in Singapore and Delancort in Monaco.

Marc gave up trying to work out what the time zone differences were. Unsurprisingly, everyone sounded strung-out and dog-tired. He chewed greedily on a ration pack offered to him by one of the helicopter crew, as if he could drag a little more energy from the gooey, tasteless bar.

He concentrated on the dull taste of it and the voices in his ears, ignoring the familiar, unpleasant tension building in the back of his head. Every time he climbed into a helicopter that he wasn't flying, his old fear crept back.

"This is Keyes," began Lucy. "Dane's here, and we have Inspector Larsson of the Icelandic SR on with us too . . ." Marc heard an audible intake of breath from Delancort over the encrypted channel, but Lucy kept speaking. "We're on the move, so I'll stick to the high points."

In short order, with keen military precision, she went through a blunt after-action report on their failed infiltration of the Frigga facility. Ji-Yoo Park's brutal murder was reduced to a clinical evaluation of the event, and Noah Verbeke's raging anger became a side-note to the issue at the core of everything.

Marc listened in silence, the guilt from his failure gathering in his chest like a ball of lead.

"We believe there are no biological agents on site," Lucy told them. "Everything they were doing there was at a distance. They faked us out. While we were busy tracking the Bitcoin transfers out here, they were shipping the bioprinters to other locations. We don't have a lead on those as yet."

"*Have you identified the biological agent that Park was being forced to work on?*" said Delancort.

"It's the Shadow virus," Lucy said firmly. "The weaponized fast-burn variant of Marburg developed by the DPRK."

"*Helvítis . . .*" Larsson muttered the curse, taking in this troubling new information.

"But I repeat, the weapon was not at the site," Lucy went on.

"Are you one hundred percent sure of that?" Larsson demanded.

He shook his head and began jabbing at a cell phone in his hand, sending out a series of urgent text messages.

"As sure as we could be," added Marc. "The Lion's Roar aren't stupid enough to bring something that lethal here. They have no reason to target this country."

"*All of this tracks with what I've uncovered,*" said Assim. "*I'm still teasing apart this web of financial transfers, but I did find a solid hit on a series of Bitcoin payments to shady characters in the Philippines. The transaction dates match up with an incident that took place in a biotech plant in Makati City near Manila. A disgruntled ex-employee came in and shot the place up—*"

"What does that have to do with this?" said Marc.

"*The plant in Makati manufactures biokits and seed materials compatible with the stolen bioprinters,*" replied Assim.

"*I authorized one of our pilots to fly one of Rubicon's security operatives to Manila,*" said Delancort, clarifying for Larsson's sake. Marc didn't need to ask to know he was referring to Ari Silber, the former Israeli combat aviator and the SCD's chief pilot, and Malte Riis. "*Our man is investigating the lead there as we speak.*" He paused. "*The Rubicon Group will, of course, cooperate fully with the Icelandic government and the SR with regard to this troubling turn of events.*"

"You should have done that first," Larsson said coldly. "Catch-up is a game we do not play here."

"*Yes, of course.*" Delancort's tone was conciliatory, but it swiftly turned flinty. "*Be assured any and all responsibility will be apportioned in full if our employees are culpable.*"

The last was clearly directed as a warning to Marc and Lucy. He would not put it past Solomon's aide to hang them out to dry if it meant protecting Rubicon's reputation.

They exchanged glances as Lucy spoke again.

"We'll provide whatever support Inspector Larsson requires."

"*Let me know how it goes,*" Delancort said curtly,

echoing Lucy's words to him from the night before as he cut the communication at his end. The point was not lost on either of them.

Marc's weary thankfulness for surviving the night on the ice melted away under the steady realization of the consequences he now faced. Park's death, Verbeke's cunning manipulation of them—the burden was his to shoulder.

I underestimated that bastard and I got cocky, he admonished himself. *Now we're paying the price.*

The pitch of the Super Puma's engine changed, and Marc felt the helicopter descending. The weight in his chest tightened a few notches more and out through the cockpit canopy he saw the valley they had surveilled the night before. Another white-and-red helicopter was already parked on the facility's landing pad, but there was no sign of the black Jet Ranger. Passing on a description of the aircraft was one of the first messages he sent over the UHF radio, but seeing it absent here stirred a growing certainty that Verbeke and his people were—once again—long gone.

Marc's fears were stoked as they approached the main blockhouse. Leaving the second helicopter grounded across the facility's entrance road, the Viking Squad team led the way with Larsson, Marc and Lucy bringing up the rear. The SR officer forbade them from doing anything more than observing, and he relayed Lucy's descriptions of the blockhouse's interior layout over a hand-held radio in gruff bursts of Icelandic.

Now the wind had eased, the steady white streamer emerging from the facility's steam pipes rose into the sky at a steep angle. In the stark daylight of the morning, the square buildings and silver domes glistened with hoarfrost, and the only sound was the crunch of the black gravel beneath their boots.

The door Marc had hacked the night before hung open.

Another bad sign, he thought. *They left in a hurry.*

Following the tactical squad inside the blockhouse, Marc was struck by the silence. He expected alarms, shouts, gunfire—but the ghost town nature of the place was, if anything, greater than it had been before. Two of the team broke off, likely to rendezvous with the second unit, while Larsson directed Lucy to show him where the server farm was located. Marc hesitated, seeing sets of drag marks on the scuffed flooring. Someone had hauled a heavy object down this corridor.

They rounded a corner and found their path blocked by a thick steel door, secured with an industrial padlock.

"This was open when I came through here," said Lucy. "The computer stacks are in the next room."

One of the troopers fingered the lock, giving it an experimental tug. Then he reached up and pulled a curved metal shape from a scabbard-holster on the back of his armor vest.

Lucy blinked "Is that . . . ?"

"An axe," Marc concluded. "Viking is not just a cool name, then."

The operative split the lock with a single downward blow of the black-anodized tactical blade, and the door swung freely. His teammate shouldered it open and the space beyond was revealed.

Marc looked in at dozens of server racks, the aluminum frames lining both sides of the room from the ground to the ceiling. On the floor there was a mess of discarded fascia plates and torn data cables, and where modular hard drives should have been there were only gaping spaces. More cables hung uselessly in ragged bunches, many of them stripped where they had been cut with knives in haste.

"Déjà *fucking* vu," growled Lucy. "Nothing in the damn box, same as before."

Marc stepped inside, crouching to peek into the frames.

"Bolts are sheared off on a lot of these." He smelled the faint whiff of burned plastic. "I think they pulled them without bothering to do a proper shutdown. They didn't want to leave anything behind."

"You assured me there would be physical evidence here," Larsson said firmly, and he tugged angrily at a cluster of cables. "This won't count for anything in a court of law!"

"They took them out," said Marc, pointing to the drag marks in the corridor. "Must have used a 4×4 to get the hard drives off site or loaded them on the chopper . . ."

One of the Viking Squad men nodded, and spoke up in English.

"Echo confirms two vehicles are missing, Inspector. Alerts have been issued."

"It's the Bitcoin heist all over again," grated Larsson, and he turned on his heel, marching out into the corridor. Marc and Lucy trailed after him as another voice crackled over the inspector's radio. He listened, his expression darkening, before he glared back at Marc. "The men sweeping the other buildings are reporting the same thing. No one on site. All computers have been cracked open and their hard drives removed."

"Andri, we didn't lie to you about what happened here," Marc insisted, seeing suspicion begin to form in the other man's eyes.

"I would welcome anything approaching proof of that," he retorted. "You may be certain that my superiors in Reykjavík will demand it."

Another Viking Squad officer marched up to them at the intersection.

"Found this."

He held up Marc's battle-worn Swissgear backpack. He shook it and broken pieces of equipment rattled inside.

Marc reached for it.

"That belongs to me."

"It is evidence now," Larsson told him, waving off the other officer.

"Andri—"

Larsson gave him a cold look.

"You will address me as *Inspector*," he corrected.

Whatever measure of openness the two of them had shared, it was gone now. Marc had burned through his currency with the Icelander.

The radio crackled again and spat out another terse communication. Larsson and the Viking Squad officer both stiffened, and the second man made a reply. Marc couldn't understand what was said, but the tone was clear: *Are you sure?*

Lucy saw it as well.

"What's going on?"

"A body has been found in the dormitory block. A woman."

Park.

Marc's gut tightened and he heard the echo of the scientist's tortured screams.

"I need to see her," he said.

Larsson's expressionless face studied him for a moment, then he nodded.

"This way."

*   *   *

The dorm rooms were an annex off to the south side of the main blockhouse, connected by a sheltered walkway. Like the rest of the buildings on the Frigga campus, it was a low, single-story prefabricated affair, divided into thirds. One section was a cafeteria, another made up of small rooms each with a single bed, but the largest was a combination changing area–locker room.

Park's body was lying on the floor of a shower cubicle, and breaths of hot steam fluttered in the air around her, dissipating into nothing.

She was still wearing the clothes she had been murdered in, the soaked-through lab coat clinging to her slight frame like a shroud. The dead woman's face, bloated and seared, was smeared with streaks of her black hair. Clasped in one hand was a kitchen knife, and there were vertical cuts on her bared forearms.

Lucy's jaw hardened as she took in the scene. This was a clumsy attempt to make her death look like a suicide, trying to hide the method of Park's murder beneath the boiling spray of the shower and the postmortem lie of the slashed wrists.

"When they came in, the water was running at full heat, full blast," said Larsson, translating the words of the men who had found the corpse. "It had to have been that way for hours."

"That's not how it happened."

Lucy looked back to where Marc stood a few meters away, staring fixedly at the body. Every mistake he had made in the past twenty-four hours was encapsulated in Park's murder. Seeing her again, so soon after witnessing Verbeke brutally end her life, shocked him into silence. She knelt by the body, forcing herself to stay focused.

"I'm sorry, Ji-Yoo," she whispered.

"This entire complex is now a crime scene," said Larsson, drawing himself up. "You two will return with me to the city, and we will attempt to unravel the mess you have presented us with."

"Are we under arrest?" Lucy asked the question without looking up.

Larsson held up his hand, the thumb and forefinger a short distance apart.

"You are very close."

Marc's head suddenly jerked up, like a machine reactivating. He crossed the room, moving to the lockers.

"The ring . . ." He glanced toward Lucy. "Her wedding ring. She doesn't have it on her, does she?"

Delicately, Lucy examined Park's pallid fingers.

"No. But she never had it on in the lab, before."

"What ring?" said Larsson. "Explain."

"We found her husband's wedding ring," said Marc, examining the line of lockers. "After Verbeke's people killed him and their son. They kept her working for them because she thought her family was being held hostage."

They wouldn't let me wear my ring. Park's words came back to Lucy in a rush. *It's safe in a locker in the other building.*

"Park knew where the bioprinters were sent," Marc went on, his thoughts paralleling hers. "She said she had that information in *a safe place*."

In a sudden flurry of movement, he spun toward one of the Viking Squad officers. Before the man could react, Marc snatched his tactical axe from the scabbard on his back and moved to the nearest of the secured lockers.

Lucy bolted to her feet as the operative brought up his gun to bear on Marc, but Larsson put his hand on the man's arm, holding him back.

The Brit used the razor-sharp head of the axe blade to cut through the deadbolt mechanism on the first locker, and wrenched it open. He rifled through the inside, then moved on to the next, repeating his actions.

"What is he doing?" Larsson demanded of Lucy. "Must I put you both in handcuffs?"

Marc was on to a fourth locker when he stopped suddenly.

"Here," he said. "Here it is!"

Thoughtlessly, he tossed the axe back to the Viking Squad officer, who snatched it out of the air with an angry grunt.

Lucy stepped in to take a closer look. In between the folds of the crumpled jacket Park had been wearing on the day of her abduction, there was a wad of toilet paper wrapped around a small object.

Marc picked the paper apart to reveal a silver wedding band, the twin to the one that Lucy had found in the bloodstained basement of a Singapore warehouse.

Larsson took the ring and sealed it into an evidence bag, but Marc was more interested in the paper that had concealed it. Carefully, he unfolded it to its full length. Writing in a shaky, hurried hand discolored the thin tissue, forming a string of symbols in *Hangul*, the Korean pictographic alphabet.

"Can you read that?" said Lucy.

Marc shook his head. "But I know someone who can." He turned to Larsson. "Andri, I need my pack."

"You are in no position to make requests," said the Icelander.

"Fucking hell, man!" Marc's frustration flared. "Take the bloody stick out of your arse and give me the pack!

SHADOW 303

I need my phone! Don't you get it? This is a lead. This is from her!" He pointed toward the body in the shower, and when he spoke again he was almost pleading. "Don't let her die for nothing."

Larsson frowned, but at length he beckoned over the officer holding on to Marc's gear and handed the backpack to him. He recovered his Rubicon-issue spy-Phone, laid out the paper on a bench and took a series of photos, before hitting the upload tab. The images would automatically be shunted through an encrypted satellite communications net directly to Rubicon's secure server.

"I'm sending a message to Assim Kader," Marc explained. "He can get a translation back to us. I'm betting Ji-Yoo kept this information because she thought she might be able to use it as leverage."

Lucy shook her head. "She didn't know what kind of people she was dealing with."

"No . . ." Marc agreed, and with it done, he handed back the phone and the daypack.

Larsson's gaze cooled.

"When were you going to tell me, Marc? At what point would have you revealed that a gang of right-wing terrorists were assembling a biological weapon in the middle of my country?"

The man's patience diminished with each word he uttered.

"There's no weapon here," Marc insisted, but the fight wasn't in him. "I told you, the Lion's Roar would gain nothing by launching an attack in Iceland. Europe is their heartland, that's where they are strongest. That's where they fight."

"Your judgment is not something I trust," Larsson replied. "Not anymore."

"We kept you in the dark because we had to." Lucy came to Marc's defense. "If we'd given you the full story, what would have happened? You would have stormed this place in full force."

She gestured at the Viking Squad officers.

"Yes, we would," Larsson agreed. "Because your approach was the wrong one, and this is the proof of it." He turned to his officers. "Take Dane and Keyes back to the city. Put them under house arrest. Do it discreetly."

The operatives moved up, flanking the pair of them.

"You're making a mistake," said Marc. "We have to keep after Verbeke!"

"I am not the one you need to convince," said Larsson, shutting him down. "When I return to Reykjavík, you'll be turned over to the National Security Unit for a full debriefing. And I advise you *not* to hold anything back this time."

The Arab had a nasal voice which Elija Van de Greif found distinctly irritating. When the man became agitated, his tone rose to a level that made Van de Greif wince with the utterance of every word. It was a struggle for the antiques dealer not to allow his contempt to show. He kept his expression fixed, allowing the Arab to rant about how long the delivery was going to take.

The great bronze Qing-era plaques the Arab had ordered for his Bahrain mansion had been held up at customs. It was a minor issue with the paperwork, but the man could not stop himself from immediately visiting Van de Greif in person to berate him. He stalked backward and forward in front of Van de Greif's desk, grabbing at the air and snarling. The dealer remained seated. Like many Dutch of his line, he was tall and thin, and when he stood next to his client he was forced to slouch in order not to tower over the other man.

The Arab's ranting was winding down, and Van de Greif decided to punish him for his crassness. He was already overcharging the grotesque little man with a huge mark-up, but on the spot he fabricated a story about how the delay was due to a backlog at the port.

"It could take *weeks* to clear," he said, faking a sorrowful look. "Unless we could consider arranging a priority transfer." He let his smile become a frown. "There would be an additional release fee, of course."

"Pay it," snapped the Arab, and he stalked out of the office without looking back.

I should send him fakes, Van de Greif thought, finally allowing his loathing to shine through once he was alone. *Let him whine about that, not that he would have the aptitude to know the difference.*

There was a tap on the glass, and Van de Greif's assistant Agatha hovered at the doorway. The elegant young blonde woman always kept out of sight around the Arab, affronted by his naked leering.

"Sir," she began, her open face lined with worry. "Your other guests . . ."

Van de Greif gave an offhand nod. "They'll be here in a couple of hours."

"No, sir," she corrected. "They're here now."

"What?" Van de Greif's blood ran cold. "Where?"

"In the storehouse."

He shot up out of his chair and waved a hand at her. "Close up. Do it now."

He stepped around his desk and dithered, pulling nervously at the cuffs of his gray Canali jacket. He wasn't ready. He wasn't prepared.

"No calls, no interruptions," he continued, walking

briskly across the gallery, toward the doorway in the far wall that led to the adjoining building.

"What should I do—" began Agatha, but he cut her off with a terse reply.

"Nothing! Just stay out of the way!"

Van de Greif paused to check his reflection in a glass cabinet. He reattached his professional half-smile once again, adjusted the shirt collar around his long neck and wiped a sudden sheen of sweat from his brow. Smoothing back his crown of graying hair, he attempted to project an air of cool astuteness. Inwardly he was grasping the edges of fear.

They came early to test me, he told himself. *That's exactly the sort of thing he likes to do. You stupid old fool! You should have anticipated this!*

Van de Greif took a deep breath, and stepped through the door in the wall. The connecting arch joined two skinny shopfronts along the downward slope of Lebeaustraat, a pair of five-story terraced buildings dating back to the eighteenth century that had been in the Van de Greif family for generations. One was the office, showroom and gallery space for VdG Acquisitions, and the other served as a storage facility for everything that wasn't on display, or was deemed too "sensitive" to be left in the company warehouse. The latter term was a convenient synonym for "unlawfully acquired."

The storehouse space was open from the basement all the way up to the third floor, fitted out with metal frames on which were stacked wooden crates, and pallets supporting ancient relics mummified in bubble wrap. The lowest level opened to a delivery bay, and that in turn to a narrow alley that emptied on to the nearby Boulevard de l'Empereur.

It was perfect for discreet arrivals and departures. It had served the Van de Greifs not only with regard to their business's myriad violations of customs law, but also in their support of certain political movements. These movements held views that were considered déclassé, if not completely abhorrent, by Belgium's bleeding heart liberals and their ilk.

Noah Verbeke looked up as Van de Greif entered and wound his way down a metal spiral staircase to the basement.

"Here he is, Elija!"

The big man was leaning on a marble statue from the Ming Dynasty, a snarling, ferocious-looking beast coiled like it was ready to leap off its plinth and attack. Van de Greif could not avoid the comparison with Verbeke himself. The swaggering, predatory brute exuded threat even when he was at rest.

The French woman Axelle stood nearby, keeping to the shadows and constantly scanning the alleyway. Cold-eyed and pale, Van de Greif had nicknamed her *de vampier*, although he would never have dared to utter the words in earshot of her. The third member of Verbeke's party was the morose thug called Duz, who hunched forward against the bonnet of the Nissan cargo van they had arrived in.

"It's good to see you, Noah," said Van de Greif, smiling his smile. "You're early."

"Are we?" Verbeke gave a shrug. "Afraid I would see you making nice with the raghead?" He chuckled. "I don't care, as long as I don't have to be in the same room with one of them. How do you tolerate the smell?"

He was holding something in his hand, slapping it carelessly from palm to palm, and Van de Greif stiffened as he realized that it was a valuable jade carving, a miniature version of the Ming statue taken from an open box on the floor.

"Hey, you will know the answer to this," Verbeke went on, bouncing the carving in the air. "These ugly dogs that the foreigners like so much, what are they called?"

"They are not dogs," Van de Greif said, automatically switching into a lecturing tone. "That is a common misconception. These are *shi shi*, Imperial guardian lions. They stand outside temples and palaces—"

Verbeke didn't allow him to finish.

"Lions?" He said the word as if he was gravely insulted, and grimaced at the jade form in his hand. "That is bullshit."

Without warning, Verbeke threw the ancient carving away, and Van de Greif had to scramble to catch it before it hit the concrete floor and shattered. The bigger man pulled open his shirt to bare the roaring, fanged maw tattooed on his chest.

"This is a lion." He prodded himself in the breastbone. "*We* are fucking lions. Do not forget that." He came closer and patted Van de Greif on the cheek, the angry outburst fading. "We had to move up the timetable a little. So I hope you have done your part for the cause."

Verbeke prodded him to underline each word.

"Of course." Van de Greif nodded, disengaging from the bigger man's grip.

Over the years, his association with the Lion's Roar had been lucrative. The network of shipping connections under the aegis of VdG Acquisitions ranged around the world, and his willingness to ignore legal barriers allowed him to move weapons and smuggle people wherever the group wanted them to go.

Van de Greif had been raised to believe in the fundamental supremacy of the white race, and of Europeans in particular, so a career built on plundering and reselling the antiquities of the Far East was almost a sacred calling. Partnering with the Lion's Roar allowed the man to feel as if he was doing something to beat back the tide of foreign mongrels without the actual need to get his hands dirty.

The most recent shipments from Manila and Singapore had moved into place without a hitch, he told Verbeke.

"The Philippine consignment was sent to your people at the warehouse by the canal, as you specified. The other one is here."

He put the jade carving somewhere safe and pulled up a dust cloth. A black lacquered cabinet in the Qing Dynasty style was revealed beneath it. The boxy shape was inlaid with gilt, faded marquetry and metal fittings.

"It was dismantled and reassembled around your equipment," he explained. "It passed through customs checks without detection."

Verbeke marched over to the cabinet and opened it. Inside, sheathed in plastic, was a machine that Van de Greif didn't recognize, a cube with a glass core containing nozzles and tiny metallic manipulators. The big man grinned.

"Good."

"I have the tools to take it apart," Van de Greif began.

"No need."

Verbeke put his foot on the frame and tore the door off with a single twist of his hands. Aged, tarnished brass buckled, and wood that had endured for two centuries splintered as the man ripped the casement to bits with his bare hands.

On the open market, properly restored, the cabinet would have been worth upward of ten thousand euros. Van de Greif gave an audible groan as he watched Verbeke willfully destroy it.

Axelle noted his discomfort and smirked.

"Sometimes there is elegance in the obliteration of a beautiful thing," she told him.

Van de Greif almost replied with the words he wanted to say. He *wanted* to tell her that Verbeke was an uncultured thug with the self-control of a backward teenager. He *wanted* to demand they tell him how their plan was going to proceed. But he did none of that. It was his curse as an educated man to understand the nature of his own timidity. He had never challenged the power dynamic of this relationship, and he was not about to start now.

He liked his money and his safety too much to ever overtly give voice to the hate in his heart. He loathed the refugee beggars on his streets, the arrogant foreigners in his gallery, the weakling politicians in his government—but not enough to sacrifice his comfort. Verbeke could do that for him. It was what he was good for.

Duz came over and helped Verbeke carry the plastic-wrapped machine from the wreckage of the cabinet to the cargo van, slipping it into the rear compartment. Axelle checked her watch, and Van de Greif suddenly felt extraneous, as if he were no longer visible to them.

"We can get it up and running in a couple of hours," said the woman. "We'll be ready for tomorrow."

"What about tomorrow?" Van de Greif felt the need to reassert his presence.

Verbeke paid no attention to the question and posed one of his own.

"On the way here, on the radio . . . I heard something about a demonstration taking place a few days ago. What do you know about it?"

Van de Greif scowled.

"Our spineless prime minister announced a partnership with an NGO this month. Something to do with that company, Rubicon. More refugees from Syria and Libya arrived." He shook his head. "We don't want them here! We should let them drown!"

"Brave of you to say so," said Axelle, meaning none of it.

"It's unacceptable!" he retorted.

"No," said Verbeke, walking to the van. "It's perfect."

— FIFTEEN —

Marc had expected the SR's "house arrest" to be a dingy room in some ice-cold industrial park on the outskirts of Reykjavík, but it turned out he was way off. Instead, the Icelandic security services put them up in a two-bedroom suite on the top floor of the 1919 Hotel, a decent place near the harbor, a few doors down from the Art Museum. It was positively civilized.

But as nice as the well-appointed, minimalist rooms were, they were also secure. To make sure the Rubicon operatives stayed put, two plain-clothes members of the Viking Squad stood sentinel out in the corridor, a pair of bearded, unsmiling muscular men, one blond and one dark-haired, whom Lucy had immediately nicknamed "Thor" and "Loki." If anything, they looked more intimidating out of their tactical gear than they did wearing it.

The early onset of darkness came rushing up over the sky, and for a while Marc sat on the bed in his room, killing time by hacking the hotel's network through the wireless keyboard tethered to the suite's smart TV. It was hard for him to concentrate on getting into the code. He ached all over, and the wounds on his chest were like steel bands constricting his ribcage.

Lucy appeared at the door to his room, swaddled in a heavy toweling robe.

"Bathroom's free," she told him.

"All right."

He didn't move, his hands clattering over the keyboard.

"What are you doing, ordering pizza?"

Her eyes widened as she saw the wall of computer code on the flat-screen TV.

Marc shook his head. "I can get into the outer layers of the room service system," he explained. "Access data on other guests, mess with the minibar settings, but not much else."

He blew out a breath and put the keyboard aside.

"So you *could* order pizza?" she said.

In truth, the Icelanders had already provided them with food and a change of clothes. Larsson's people were being good hosts, and in a way that made the situation even more annoying.

He shot her a weary look.

"I was trying to reactivate the suite's phones, but they've disconnected them at the switchboard, same with the internet connection on this floor. We can't call out, and they're not about to let us have our gear back." Marc waved angrily at the door, out in the main part of the suite. "If I had my RFID pinger, I could override the locks in a second."

"And then what? Ask the Viking brothers for a dance?"

"I don't know," he said, exasperated. "I can't stand this. Stuck in here, falling behind." Marc rose from the bed and winced at a jolt of agony from his chest. "We were on them, Lucy. We were close, and then I screwed it up. Now Verbeke's vanished and we are back to square one." He paced to the window. "No, actually, worse than that. Now we know *less* than we did a day ago."

"Hey, I don't like it either, but that's the way ops go

sometimes. We have to play the hand we've been dealt, Dane. And that means waiting it out." Lucy glanced around. "On the upside, this is by far the best accommodation we've had since we got here."

"How can you—"

He didn't finish his sentence. Another shock of pain constricted Marc's chest and he choked off the words in a grunt, clasping at his sternum. He unbuttoned his shirt, and to his dismay the T-shirt he was wearing underneath was lined with streaks of blood.

"You need to change those dressings," Lucy insisted, switching to what Marc had come to consider her "Army Voice."

He half-heartedly complained, but still allowed her to lead him into the suite's bathroom, where steam from the shower lingered and condensation collected on the picture mirror.

Fresh, stinging jags bit into him as he cautiously stripped to the waist. Marc sat on the edge of one of the double sinks and let Lucy remove the soiled bandages, piece by piece. The shrapnel wounds were a gooey mess of congealed blood and ripped skin. By rights, Marc should have rested up for a week or two to let them fully heal, but his exertion and exposure to the elements had reopened the cuts. Thoughtfully, the SR had provided replacement dressings and a first aid kit, and together the two of them cleaned and redressed the wounds.

Marc's frustration ebbed, and his skin prickled as Lucy ran her dark hands over his chest, setting the bandages into place. He became aware of how close she was to him, and the abrupt intimacy of the moment. Barefoot and wearing nothing beneath the hotel robe, the visible slivers of Lucy's athletic, ochre-toned body were suddenly very present in Marc's thoughts, and he swallowed hard, forcing himself to look away from the swell of her chest.

Lucy was staring right at him, and there was an expression in her eyes that was new to Marc. Something deep and needful, coming at him past that sleepy countenance she routinely wore.

He was still trying to figure out what it meant when she leaned in and their lips met. The first instant of the unexpected kiss was an electric shock, but that faded, changed.

Lucy tasted like cool, fresh water. Marc felt himself react, a flood of pleasant heat rushing to the surface of his flesh and down to his groin. His hand moved of its own accord, parting the robe to settle on the bare skin of her hip. Her body was warm, as if it was sun-soaked, still holding the heat from the shower.

He balanced on the edge of the embrace, ready to let go, ready to fall all the way into it. But knowing it was happening was enough to break the spell. He drew back, getting a last gasp of her breath in his as he disengaged.

"What?" Lucy's whisper was thick and husky. "We nearly froze to death out there on the ice. I want to remind myself I'm *alive*."

"How far are you going with this?" he asked.

"As far as we want."

The ghost of a daring smile played on her lips.

"I can't." He gave a faint shake of the head. "We shouldn't."

Lucy's smile vanished in a flash.

"Okay." She stepped back, flicking a look at his crotch. "Some of you sure seems interested."

"It's not . . ." He slipped off the edge of the sink, his color rising, fumbling for an explanation. "Not that I wouldn't . . ."

She eyed him, her gaze cooling by the second.

"You don't like coffee?"

"No!" Marc shook his head. "Oh shit, no. That's not it." His face creased in a scowl as the frustration came rolling back in. "I don't want to break . . . *this*." He gestured, taking in the two of them. "You and me . . . There's not a lot of people in the world I can trust, Lucy, and I don't want to complicate this."

The words spilled from him, and he knew it was coming out wrong. Keyes was an incredible, striking woman. Marc couldn't lie to himself and pretend that an attraction between them didn't exist—but crossing this line would put them in unknown territory.

He looked away, forcing himself to take a breath.

No, he told himself, *that's not true. I know exactly where this would lead, if I let it.*

And she knew it too—he could see it in her eyes.

"You know, technically speaking, my partnership with you has been the longest relationship I've had with a guy since high school. Less shitty dates at the mall but more getting shot at." She sighed. "You and me, that could be fun. It doesn't have to be a big deal. We're both adults. We both know where we're at and what kind of world we live in."

"That's precisely why not," he said, seizing on her words. "This 'world'? It took away one person I got close to. I don't need to go through that again."

He wanted to blot it out, but unbidden and unwelcome, Marc's memory showed him Samantha Green's face, her crooked and daring smile. In the clammy warmth of the hotel bathroom, he could smell stale canal water and burned flesh all over again.

"That's how it is?" Lucy stepped away, reading him like a book. "My mistake, I guess. You can't go past that moment when you lost Sam. You won't even take the first step down that road."

"Can you blame me?" he said quietly.

"Yeah," Lucy shot back. "I can. Because she's gone, but you keep trying to save her, Marc, and *you can't*."

"Not this again."

Months before, in the immediate aftermath of a near-fatal mission in South Korea, Lucy had called Marc out on his inability to move beyond the brutal events that had drawn him into Rubicon's orbit. It had put a distance between them that neither wanted to acknowledge, and now that gap was threatening to widen.

"Just let it go."

She wasn't the type to let anything drop.

"Before Special Conditions, you were a back-seater. The guy in the goddamn van. But not now. You might be cute, and fast, and you might be whip-smart, but you keep on throwing yourself at every long-shot risk like you have a death wish. And worse still if a woman's involved!" Lucy shook her head disappointedly. "Do you even know what you're trying to prove?"

"You do not . . ."

Marc was going to say *understand*, but then the telephones in the suite began to ring, and he lost his momentum.

"Saved by the bell," he muttered, and reached over to snatch up the handset near the toilet. "This is Dane."

Lucy walked out and picked up another receiver, as a familiar voice crackled over the line.

"*Marc? It's me, Assim.*" The young Saudi sounded hollow and afraid.

"How'd you get through here? SR told us the line to this room was cut off."

"*I had them reconnect us for this. I told them we were Rubicon's legal department, so they were obliged to let me speak to you.*"

"Good call," noted Lucy, from the other room.

"Did you get the translation from the Korean text on Park's note?"

Mentally, Marc was already boxing up and partitioning away the unfinished conversation with Lucy, snapping back to the mission.

"*Yes, but that isn't why I am calling . . .*" Assim gulped audibly. "*There's been a development. Turn on the television. Turn on CNN.*"

"Wait one."

Marc hung up the handset in the bathroom and marched back into his bedroom, activating the speakerphone in passing as he walked to the TV. With a few keystrokes on the remote, the flat-screen switched back to normal operating mode and the news channel flickered into view, the sound muted.

At first, he wasn't sure what he was seeing. The streets of a tumbledown, war-scarred city in the Middle East filled the screen. A cluster of ambulances bearing the Red Crescent were parked in the foreground, and behind them Marc could pick out figures in white oversuits struggling with injured people. A chyron ticker at the bottom of the screen said the location was Benghazi in Libya, and Marc tensed. Less than a week ago they had been off the coast of that country as their mission against the Bastion League reached its conclusion.

"What are we looking at?" said Lucy, standing behind him. "Missile attack? Suicide bomber?"

"No burned vehicles," said Marc, shaking his head as he studied the images. "No bomb crater."

"*The reports from on site are sketchy,*" Assim noted, "*but they're saying that there has been a massive outbreak of hemorrhagic fever in the center of the city. The Libyan government has already sent in the military to*" *enforce a quarantine zone. The World Health Organization has been alerted, but hundreds are already confirmed as infected."*

The images on the screen shifted to a different point of view—footage from another place, shot earlier in the day. The camera moved through a makeshift hospital ward set up in a dingy shopping mall, past lines of people lying on folding camp beds or on the floor. Every face was swollen and sickly, the young and the old struck down by the same awful malaise. Tears of blood streaked their cheeks, and some were racked by brutal coughs. Far too many of the bodies were hidden under shrouds, patches of dull red soaking through the material and pooling on the tiled floor beneath the beds. Medical staff in masks and bloodstained scrubs moved like wraiths among the dead and the dying.

"Damn," whispered Lucy.

The point of view switched again. Now it was out on the street, framing a group of young soldiers in the uniform of the Libyan National Army, clutching their assault rifles as they shouted at a crowd of fearful civilians, forcing them back past a line of barricades. Raw terror was writ large across the faces of the people. The camera panned up to an Mi-17 helicopter loitering overhead. More soldiers were visible on board, aiming heavy machine guns down toward the mob.

The program switched back to the studio and a pair of presenters, both of whom looked visibly shaken by the horrible sight of the deaths in Benghazi. Inset graphics on screen showed a map of the city and the surrounding area, marked with rings of crimson to indicate the areas that had been isolated.

"This is Shadow, isn't it?" said Marc, in a dead voice.

*   *   *

Lucy's gut twisted at what she saw on the screen, and her throat tightened.

The grisly manner of death was identical to the horrors she had seen on that miserable winter day when she changed Ji-Yoo Park's life forever. She knew that if she closed her eyes, she would relive it, recall the blood and the filth and the wretched victims she had witnessed.

Lucy forced herself to stay in the moment.

"There's nothing else it can be," she said, answering Marc's question. "The Lion's Roar did this. They took the legacy Park spent her life trying to escape and brought it back."

"*One fact is clear*," said Assim. "*CNN, Reuters and the other reputable news services are talking about this incident as if it is a medical crisis. There has been no suggestion that this outbreak is anything other than a natural disaster.*"

"They don't know?" Lucy took that in, the question tumbling into the churn of her thoughts. "But how would they—if no one takes responsibility for it? It could be months before anyone figures out this was a deliberate act."

Marc shook his head, trying to grasp the enormity of it.

"But why? What possible reason would Verbeke have to strike a city in Libya? And do it in secret?"

"*I am afraid Lucy's conclusion is probably the correct one*," continued Assim. "*The writing on the paper was difficult to decipher, but the first part I was able to determine with a high degree of certainty. It is a location, a street in the An Mursalhq district of Benghazi, near the coast road.*"

"That has to be where they delivered the bioprinters." Lucy followed the chain of logic, glancing at

Marc. "They shipped in what they needed and made the weapon on site, like you said."

He rounded on her.

"Why there?" He almost shouted the question. "The woman on the phone said four days, it hasn't been four days yet! This makes no sense!"

"No," she told him, "it does."

In the weeks leading up to the Bastion League take-down, Lucy had been inserted into North Africa under her "Aya" cover, and there she had seen first-hand the realities of daily life in that strife-torn region. Blending into the groups of refugees desperate to escape the chaos, she understood why some would risk so much to flee. These were the people dropping like flies in Benghazi, the people that the Lion's Roar and their kind considered subhuman and worthless.

"Verbeke's hitting his enemies where they live. He and his bullet-head Nazi pals, they hate them. They're killing them for daring to cross the sea to Europe. This is an attack on innocent civilians, pure and simple."

Marc gave a slow nod. "But what does that gain them?" He met her gaze. "If they're not taking responsibility for it, how does Verbeke get anything from this?"

"*Perhaps . . . it's just for hate's sake*," Assim said grimly. "*Done out of spite.*"

"Verbeke's a thug and a hooligan," said Marc, "but I think by now we know he's not stupid. He's cunning. He thinks ahead, yeah?" The Brit turned away from the screen. "He's playing a bigger game. This is one outbreak. There are two bioprinters."

"*Which brings me to my next point,*" noted Assim. "*The other text on the paper you recovered was unclear, but I was able to assemble a probable translation.*"

"Another location?" said Lucy. She had the grim

sense of events moving around her, picking up speed, as if she were a tiny cog in a much larger machine.

"*Yes. The address is Lebeaustraat in Brussels, Belgium.*"

"Verbeke's home town," she said immediately. "Motherfucker's gone back to his old turf. Makes sense, he's returning to the place he knows best."

"And hates the most," said Marc. "He's made no secret of his dislike of the Belgian government and the EU for their intake of foreign refugees. That has to be it. The Lion's Roar are going to launch the next attack there. Tomorrow." He went to the speakerphone. "We need to warn the VSSE, the Belgian state security service."

Assim paused before replying. "*That option is being considered.*"

"What the hell is that supposed to mean?" said Lucy.

"*Delancort went to the board,*" he continued, his tone dropping to a conspiratorial hiss. "*They decided that the first priority is for the Rubicon Group to insulate itself from any potential blowback in this matter. The bioprinters are MaxaBio property, and MaxaBio is a Rubicon subsidiary—*"

"In other words, they gotta cover their asses first," interrupted Lucy. "Meanwhile, people are dying!"

"Where's Solomon?" demanded Marc. "I can't believe he'd let this happen."

"*Mr. Solomon is in the process of directing assets from Rubicon's Disaster Recovery Solutions to Libya. The board has temporarily limited his involvement in all other matters and dialed back SCD operations. Technically, I'm not even supposed to be talking to you.*"

That explained the silence from the African. Lucy had

grown more concerned with every day that their employer was out of contact with them, and now she understood why. An unpleasant thought caught up with her.

"They're going to lock up on this," she said, almost to herself. "Roll out the lawyers, cut ties to MaxaBio before anything comes out to connect this whole mess back to Rubicon."

"And what happens in the meantime? We sit back and hope that the Lion's Roar don't release another Shadow infection in a major European city?" Marc's fury was building. "Verbeke is going to do it. You saw him—did he strike you as the type to choke out halfway?" He took a breath, centering himself. "He's going to be there, if he's not already. Verbeke's a vicious sod, he'll want to see his handiwork from the front row." Marc put his hand on Lucy's shoulder. "We have another chance to stop him. The last one we're going to get."

She inclined her head toward the door.

"Did you forget about Thor and Loki and their playmates? 'Cause if you wanna pitch another pull-it-out-of-your-ass plan to get us away from Iceland, I have to tell you . . . right now, you're oh-for-four."

"Is that a baseball thing?" Marc gave her a questioning look, and off her nod he shrugged. "You're right. My average has been in the shitter all week. I reckon I could spin up something, given time, but you know what? I'm not going to tempt fate. I need to bank the luck I still have, if we're going to stop everything from going to hell."

"So what's the play?" she said. "I'm open to ideas."

He didn't answer straight away.

"Assim, what's the quickest way to get us from Reykjavík to Brussels?"

Lucy heard the clatter of a keyboard down the phone line.

"*Okay. There is an Icelandair Cargo flight leaving for Frankfurt in two hours. I could arrange something, set up a connection from there to Belgium.*"

"Do it," said Marc. "We'll sort out comms and the rest on the way, call you back then." He hung up and gave Lucy a look as he marched to the door of the suite. "I am going to talk us out of this, that's my play." Marc banged loudly on the door and yelled. "*Oi!* Get Larsson in here! I need to speak to him!"

It didn't take long.

By the time Lucy had dressed, the key-card lock on the suite's door clicked open and Larsson stood in the hallway, flanked by the two Viking Squad officers.

"You pulled me out of an important meeting with my superiors," he told Marc. "This better be worth it."

Larsson entered the room, and Thor and Loki moved to come with him, but Lucy intercepted them.

"Just him," she said firmly.

It was a testament to her presence that the two men hesitated and looked to the senior officer for confirmation.

Larsson dismissed them with a weary shake of the head and they retreated, locking the door behind them. The Icelander walked to the suite's minibar and cracked it open. He picked through the tiny bottles inside, eventually choosing a miniature of the local Reyka vodka.

Marc didn't want to appear standoffish, so he grabbed a bottle of Brennivín for himself. Lucy declined a drink of her own.

"Someone has to stay clear-headed," she told him.

They sat across from each other in the suite's open lounge, sinking into square-cushioned armchairs. Larsson busied himself with the vodka.

"So speak," he said firmly. "What did your 'lawyer' have to say?" He made air-quotes with his fingers.

Marc committed himself to what he would do next, pulling up a mask of confidence that was mostly bravado. He swirled his Brennivín in its glass and looked across the rim at Larsson.

"By the time I finish drinking this, you are going to open that door and let me and Lucy walk. You'll even get the God of Thunder out there to give us a lift to the airport."

The corner of Larsson's lip pulled up slightly in amusement, and he nodded at the glass in Marc's hand.

"Have you had a few of those already? You should be careful. There's a reason why we call it the 'Black Death' here. Too much of it warps the brain."

Marc took a sip. The clear schnapps had a faint aniseed flavor and a strong, sustained burn as it went down.

"You've seen what's going on in Libya."

Larsson nodded gravely, staring into his vodka. "That's connected to this, is it?"

"It's just the beginning," said Marc. "It won't happen here. But it will happen again. We can stop it."

"Only you can stop it," said Larsson. "How lucky that it is in my power to assist you." He shot Marc a hard look. "Do you think that because I live on a frozen island in the middle of the sea, I am an idiot?"

"No," said Marc. "I think you're a pissed off SR inspector whose career has stalled because his superiors don't like the fact he's smarter than they are. I remember the work you did when I was with NSNS. I remember how you didn't get the credit you deserved for that investigation." The tensing in Larsson's face showed Marc had hit his point dead on. "Back in the Harpa, you talked about the men above you. People in the government . . . How did you put it?"

"Paying undue attention," offered Lucy.

"Yeah, that's right," Marc went on. "People invested in seeing the Frigga facility get a free pass. But now there's going to be an investigation."

"Starting with you," said Larsson.

"Maybe not," countered Marc. "See, if I was you, I would be wondering what those people who paid undue attention are doing right now."

"Calling their lawyers," Lucy suggested.

Marc gave a nod. "How close were they to the Lion's Roar? What did they have invested in an illegal Bitcoin mining operation? Did they know that the Frigga facility was being used for bioweapons research? And then there's the matter of the kidnapping and murder of an innocent woman."

He took another sip.

Larsson's cold blue eyes studied Marc, measuring him for artifice.

"Those questions will be answered. By the book. That is how we work here."

"Is it, though?" Marc gave a shrug. "Think how much faster this would move if you had the metadata for those Bitcoin transactions. Or the drives from those gutted servers. You'd have direct leads to the bank accounts of everyone who took some króna to look the other way. Email records, cash transfers, the lot."

Larsson tensed, and that was when Marc knew he had the man's full attention.

"Is this where you ask for a trade?" said the Icelander. "You give me the data and in exchange I release you on your own recognizance. Is that how you saw this going?"

"The thing I've always liked about you, Andri, is that you're quick to spot an opening. That's how we caught those ratbags smuggling the caesium, remember? Do you see this one?"

"I see someone attempting to play me. Poorly."

Marc leaned in. "Give me my smartphone, I know you've got it on you. Rubicon will get you the metadata. But the rest, that's with Verbeke. And we need to get to him, before more people die. So you have two choices. You cut us loose, we end this and we help you clean house at the SR—or you do nothing, and tomorrow Verbeke has his victory, and becomes the poster boy for every ultra-right-wing wanker on the planet." He downed the rest of the Brennivín in a single pull. "Make up your mind, mate. If we're staying, tell room service to send up some more of this, because I'm getting a taste for it."

Larsson took his time finishing his vodka, and when the glass was empty he reached into a pocket and produced Marc's spyPhone. He slid the glassy rectangle across the coffee table between them.

"Make me a believer," he said.

It took Marc less than a minute to send an encrypted message to Larsson's phone, giving him one-time access to a folder on a secret Rubicon data server. Inside the folder was Assim's work so far on tracking the cryptocurrency cash transfers to and from Iceland. Delancort would not be happy about sharing it, but Marc was past caring. Larsson's eyes widened as he skimmed the information.

"Good enough?" said Marc.

Larsson pocketed his phone and stood up.

"I am going to have to go back to the office. My dogs are going to wonder what has happened to me." He glanced at Marc, and patted his coat. "I could take this and leave. I didn't make any deal with you. I don't owe you anything."

For a moment, Marc didn't know what to say. A rip-off was the last thing he would have expected from the resolute Icelander, and it blindsided him.

"Yeah, you could," he admitted. "And that would prove that I was wrong about what kind of bloke you are."

"You were not wrong," Larsson said at length, and he walked back to the door.

Within the hour, an unmarked black SUV was speeding across the apron at Keflavík International, threading between the buildings toward the airport's cargo terminal. The driver aimed the vehicle at an Icelandair 757–200 package freighter aircraft undergoing final loading preparations, and drew to a halt under the Boeing's wing.

Larsson turned back from the front passenger seat to give Marc and Lucy a searching stare.

"I want to make something clear," he began. "This is not about me trusting you. This is about the information you will provide. Do not fuck me on this."

Marc blinked. It was the first time he had heard the Icelander curse.

"Never crossed my mind."

"The SR has a long reach. One call and every asset you have will be frozen. Rubicon will not be able to protect you."

"I like my assets warm," Lucy shot back. "Don't worry, we'll make good on our end."

They climbed out of the SUV and into the cold of the night. Larsson handed them back their gear and followed them toward the cargo plane.

"Your colleague has already cleared you on board," he noted, pausing to study Marc. "I have to admit, you've changed from the man I first met two years ago. That Marc Dane took far fewer risks than you do."

"Yeah," he admitted, throwing Lucy a sideways glance. "People keep telling me that."

"Don't get yourself killed before I have the information I need." Larsson shrugged. "Afterward, you can do as you like."

Marc extended his hand.

"Thanks, Andri."

Larsson looked at the outstretched hand but didn't accept it.

"Don't make the mistake of thinking we are friends, Marc. We are two men whose interests have temporarily aligned." He turned away and walked back to the idling SUV. "Work fast," he added, over his shoulder.

"So what's the count now?" said Lucy, as they climbed the crew stairs to the jet's open hatch. "I forget how many countries we've pissed people off in."

"Too many," he replied.

"You know there's no guarantee those hard drives are going to be with Verbeke in Brussels, right? You may have promised Larsson something we can't give him."

Marc nodded gravely. "We'll burn that bridge when we get to it."

The name of the skyscraper was Empire, but in typical fashion for those among Moscow's ultra-rich, it was uttered without a hint of irony. Originally known as the Imperia Tower, the sixty-story building rose high over the city's business sector, the aqua-green shades of its curved glass frontage catching the lights of the street far below and the glow from the strongholds of other oligarchs that flanked it. Empire wasn't Moscow's tallest skyscraper, but what it lacked in height it made up for with thick layers of opulence. Nowhere was that more true than in Pytor Glovkonin's rooftop penthouse.

Saito found the place soulless, for all its forced grandeur. There was no art to the décor, no truth in it. The objects within had been gathered to exhibit one man's wealth, but not his character. Saito recalled feudal castles and ancient temples from his native Japan, places that were rich not just in design but in spirit, heavy with meaning. Glovkonin's apartments were a monument to his bank balance and nothing more. The place was full, but it would always be *empty*.

Saito left the man he was escorting, designated on their helicopter flight plan as simply as *the guest*, in a luxuriously appointed anteroom beneath the Empire's helipad, while he walked into the main atrium of the apartments.

Misha and Gregor, the Russian's personal guards, surrounded Saito and checked him with a screening wand. He handed over his rod-like misericorde dagger and a USP Compact pistol without comment, placing them on a silver tray. Both men looked right through him with a cultivated air of disdain, and when the examination was over, they waved him on.

Outside, a heavy Siberian wind was muttering over the windows of the tower as the night drew in, but inside the penthouse was filled with the chatter of voices from a gargantuan television screen that dominated one wall.

Glovkonin sat before it with a glass in his hand, idly swirling the fluid within as he watched a financial report on a Russian-language news channel. G-Kor, the energy company that had made Glovkonin the man he was, had recently completed a lengthy series of takeover proceedings that netted them control of several media outlets. The opportune diversification of the company had come after the untimely death of the previous owner, Celeste Toussaint. The passing of the media heiress had allowed Glovkonin to add a new arm to his corporate machine, stepping into the breach when other bidders had mysteriously backed off.

All of this was engineered by the Combine, of course. Toussaint's death was murder, and the fog around the facts of her killing remained deep and obscuring. But the members of the Combine were not given to maudlin introspection. As Saito had learned in his service to their needs, individual members were transitory. With the woman's loss there were assets that needed to be made secure. Glovkonin, eager and driven, had presented himself as the ideal proxy through which the power brokers could maintain their continuity of control.

Saito, as the soldier, as the enforcer, could only ever glimpse these actions from the edges. That was his lot— to be in the service of a larger collective. The Combine existed to enrich itself, but in that enrichment there was stability.

So he believed. It was not something that Saito ever allowed himself to question.

At least, not until he had been tasked to serve the Russian. Now, questions were accreting in the back of his mind, and Saito was finding it harder to ignore them.

Who had really been responsible for Toussaint's killing? The evidence pointed toward an agent of the Rubicon Group, but Saito had met the man in question. He had a good sense for understanding killers, and the Englishman did not seem like a cold-blooded assassin. And if that was so, it set up many more possibilities that he could not ignore.

Glovkonin glanced up at him with a wry expression. The Russian made a point of looking him over, scrutinizing the slight limp that Saito could not excise from his walk. His judgment was silent, but obvious.

"What have you brought me?" said Glovkonin, muting the voices from the screen with a tablet device.

"Your guest is waiting," Saito reported.

"There were no issues bringing him back?"

Saito shook his head. "No one knows he is here."

Including the committee of the Combine, he thought, but kept that to himself.

"Khadir is quite efficient." Glovkonin nodded to himself, pleased with the prospect of a job well done. "The Chinese will believe our new friend is dead. Leaving us free to offer him a new purpose. How does he seem to you?"

"His condition is as expected. Some malnutrition. Scar tissue and internal damage from years of beatings. But he has strength. Lesser men would have died."

"How is he taking to his newfound liberty? Is he grateful to his rescuer?"

It came as no surprise to Saito that Glovkonin could find a way to make this moment about him. The Russian sat forward on the overstuffed leather sofa, still toying with the glass in his hand.

"He is interested in clarity," said Saito, picking his words with care.

In truth, the guest had spoken little to him in the hours after Saito took custody of the man at the Mongolian border. Khadir had handed him over with no formality, and Saito watched the Arab vanish back into the night.

The guest, though—the prisoner, as he had been—had the silent artfulness of a career spy, and a morose kind of hatred lurked behind his eyes like black fire, undimmed by years in captivity.

"I'll give him the clarity he needs, and more," said Glovkonin. "Bring him in. We'll toast his freedom."

Saito signaled to Gregor, and the bodyguard left the room for a moment. In the stillness that followed, he finally gave voice to the question that had been preying on him since that rainy day in Paris.

"What is special about this man? You have invested a great deal in tracking his location and securing him in secret."

Glovkonin nodded. "He has been an expensive project, without question. The money I paid to the Ghost5 hacker cadre to source his whereabouts was a high price alone. But I believe it will be worth it."

The Russian crossed to where Misha stood sentinel, and examined Saito's weapons on the silver tray. He picked up the thick misericorde dagger, balancing it between his fingers.

"This blade is made to slide through the gaps in a suit of armor where a sword could not, to go through chain mail and then into flesh." He made a slow stabbing motion. "To puncture the heart." He smiled again. "But you know that. You know how it feels."

Saito stiffened but said nothing. He had removed that same weapon from his own flesh, after Marc Dane had left it there during a fight in the bowels of a derelict gas rig off the African coast. And before that, Saito had buried the blade in the belly of Dane's colleague, the American woman Keyes. That it had found its way back to him convinced Saito that there was an ugly kind of balance to the universe.

"Victory comes down to a matter of using the right

weapon." Glovkonin put the misericorde back where he'd found it. "When you consider that, what does it matter how much the weapon costs?"

He looked up and his smile widened as Gregor returned with the guest.

Attired in a presentable blue Brioni suit and a white cotton shirt, the guest walked carefully down the stairs, taking in everything. His dark brown eyes searched the room as a soldier's would, looking for points of egress, cover and objects that might double as weapons if the need arose.

Like Saito, he hobbled a little, but the guest's limp was far more pronounced, forcing him to use a metal walking stick. The prisoner's age was difficult for Saito to determine. He was of Chinese extraction, anything between his early forties and middle sixties, the passage of time upon his face accelerated by his ordeals.

"You must be my benefactor."

The guest's voice was quiet and his words were chosen with care. He switched briefly to Glovkonin's language, and Saito followed along.

"My English is far better than my Russian," he said before switching back. "We will stay with that, if you don't mind."

"Of course." The other man opened his hands, playing the part of the generous host. "I am Pytor Glovkonin. You have no idea how pleased I am to have you here in my home, Mr. Lau. Welcome."

Lau. The identity meant nothing to Saito, connecting to no known alias that he was familiar with. But he knew it was a variant of *Liu*, the surname shared by the ancient warlords of the Han Dynasty, and that the word meant *to kill* or *to destroy*. An opportune name for someone the Russian considered to be a weapon.

"You have my gratitude," said the guest. "But I must

say, I do not understand why you have done so much."
Lau fingered the collar of his jacket. "Such fine clothes.
And so much effort made . . ." He shook his head rue-
fully, hunching forward, almost aging before Saito's
eyes. "For a man like me. I am grateful, but I am confused. Why would you do this?"

"A man like you." Glovkonin wandered away, toward
the sofa. "And what are you, Mr. Lau?"

"I was once a soldier for my nation. Overtaken by
arrogance, by the folly of youth. My reach exceeded my
reason and I was convicted because of it."

His head bobbed, as if he were repentant.

"A soldier." Glovkonin picked out the words. "But
not an ordinary one. An ordinary soldier in the army
of the People's Republic of China does not speak six
languages. Did not study at Oxford. Does not have degrees in economics, geology and finance. Did not train
with the Spetsnaz."

He picked up the tablet he had used to silence the
television and tapped at it, before making a flicking gesture that sent images directly to the bigger screen. Images fanned out over the display, prison records and
military documents, pages of text in close queues of
Chinese pictographs. Old photos of a much younger
man in a military uniform drifted past.

The eyes are the same, noted Saito.

But back then they were eager and daring. That had
been replaced with something else.

"I know all about you, Mr. Lau." Glovkonin weighed
the tablet in his hand, as if he were holding the sum total
of the man's life. "At first you were just a rumor caught
by my people, almost a ghost story. A man edited out
of history, forcibly forgotten by those who knew him."

Lau's body language shifted again. The appearance he
had given, that of a weakened and beaten-down man,

melted off him. Saito was impressed. Not once during
the flight from Mongolia had Lau's mask slipped. But
then, he had been given decades to perfect it.

"I've always liked mysteries, ever since I was a
boy," the Russian went on. "I found your story compelling, sir. The man who was once a hero to his nation, decorated and feted. Only to fall out of favor
because of hubris."

"I became poison," Lau said quietly. "It was my fault.
I believed I was far enough away from my masters to
make my own rules. They showed me how mistaken I
was."

"And yet, that story might have been different, if not
for a single betrayal."

With a conjuror's flourish, Glovkonin sent another
image to the screen. A photograph, washed out by age,
of two men in their thirties shaded beneath a skeletal
tree on some dusty grassland plain. Saito heard Lau
make a small noise in the back of his throat as he took
in the picture, not quite a growl but a murmur of animal sound. Something primal.

Lau was on the left of the photo. He wore tropical
combat fatigues, like the garb of a mercenary, and he
was staring out of the image as if daring the world to
challenge him. The man by his side was an African,
dark as polished teak, dressed in the same gear, with
his jacket open to his belly. Saito's eye was drawn to a
necklace the young African was wearing. A steel chain,
upon which hung an abstract metal object that could
only be the trigger from a rifle.

"I remember that day," said Lau. "We had such great
plans."

"This is why I have done so much for you, sir," said
Glovkonin.

"Yes." Lau nodded. "I understand now why I am

valuable to you." He paused, gathering himself. "What is it you want from me?"

"I need your knowledge." The Russian stared at the face of the young African in the image and Saito saw his expression harden. "I want you to help me destroy Ekko Solomon and everything he has built."

"Where do we begin?" said Lau.

─ SIXTEEN ─

Marc had a clear view down the descending curve of Lebeaustraat from the dust-filmed window of the empty office on the fifth floor, good enough to capture images of the front door of the VdG Gallery and anyone going in or out, but the angle was too oblique to get a direct look through the windows. He made the best of it, setting up a pair of Nikon digitals on tripods with overlapping fields of vision, one close-up and one wide-angle, to keep constant surveillance on the building.

He'd hooked up the HD cameras to a slimline Lenovo laptop and had everything working. The computer, like the camera and the other techie kit he was using, had come from a gadget store at the airport and he was doing his best to make it mission ready. The floor of the bare room was littered with boxes and plastic packaging, with Marc and Lucy's gear forgotten in a corner. Like everything else in the vacant space, the floor had a layer of brownish dust over it. The place had not been used in years, a testament to the high rents in the arty end of Brussels's Sablon district.

Their Rubicon-issue smartphones were the only tactical equipment the operatives had been able to bring with them from Iceland, so Marc had co-opted his to act as a temporary secure network hub. Through it, he ran a rapid download to the laptop's memory, filling the machine with any intrusion software he might need. It wasn't an ideal set-up, but circumstances had pushed the two of them into making do with what they could get their hands on.

He adjusted the focus on the cameras and shifted from foot to foot. Marc had followed Lucy's lead and snatched some rest on the flight in, but he felt as if he had been awake for days. He made a circuit of the room, leaving a trail of footprints in the dust. If he stopped moving, the fatigue would pounce.

A double-double knock sounded at the door and Lucy entered. Across her back she carried a heavy sports bag and in her hand was a paper sack from a local artisanal fast-food restaurant.

"Breakfast," she explained, and thrust the paper bag into his hands.

Marc delved inside and eagerly helped himself to coffee and a toasted baguette as she dropped the sports tote to the floor. It landed with an audible *clunk*.

"Anything?"

She jutted her chin in the direction of the window.

"A blonde girl entered about twenty minutes after you left." He ran a finger over the laptop's touchpad and brought up an image. "She's an employee, her photo is on the VdG website."

Lucy nodded. They'd used their time the night before, between changing planes at Frankfurt, to dig up what was publicly known about the second address found in Ji-Yoo Park's note. VdG Acquisitions maintained an austere web presence with some details of the gallery and the family that owned it, along with a digital catalog of their most crowd-pleasing procurements from the Far East. Their online security was good, Marc noted, better than average for a place that bought and sold million-dollar *objets d'art* on a regular basis. He was itching to take a run at their firewall, but Lucy had warned him off. Now was not the time to do anything to arouse suspicion.

For the moment, they had an advantage. Verbeke and his crew would assume that Marc and Lucy were dead, thanks to Andri Larsson agreeing to release a fake report stating that the Icelandic search and rescue had recovered the bodies of two missing tourists out on the ice. The lie would only last so long. They had to make the most of it.

That didn't stop Marc from doing some passive digital intelligence gathering, however. In the past couple of hours, he had researched VdG Acquisitions, its staff and its current owner Elija Van de Greif, combing social media sites, sweeping for anything that might raise a red flag.

From a distance, the gallery and the Van de Greif family appeared to be clean, but when viewed through the lens of what the SCD team had discovered, certain connections slotted into place. There was a small but certainly non-zero likelihood that the gallery had dealings with front companies owned by the Ang Soon Tong back in Singapore, and peering through the haze around the Bitcoin transactions Assim had uncovered suggested even more links. It wasn't a big leap to imagine that VdG Acquisitions didn't always acquire their items altogether honestly.

Being a link in a chain of black market smugglers made the gallery the perfect delivery point for one of the stolen bioprinters. But the connection faltered there. Marc couldn't find anything that directly linked Van de Greif to the Lion's Roar aside from the cryptocurrency.

Lucy nodded as he explained. "Could be they're a conduit, a way for Verbeke to get his toys into the country unnoticed. Or it could be more." She moved to the window, careful to stay out of sight of anyone down on the street. "For all we know, that bioprinter is in there right now and they're whipping up a bucket of virus as we speak."

"I don't think it works like that," said Marc.

"Yeah, well . . ." She stalked back to the sports bag. "We can't just sit up here and watch."

"I know that song." Marc gave a humorless chuckle.

"Last time we did it your way." Lucy unzipped the bag and Marc saw the matte black metallic forms of firearms inside. "This time we do it my way."

She handed him a plastic case, and inside he found a Gen4 model Glock 17, along with three magazines of 9mm Parabellum ammunition and a paddle holster. For herself, Lucy drew out a MP9 sub-machine gun, a compact and deadly weapon that was still small enough to fit under her baggy jacket. She made short work of checking it over, slamming a loaded mag into the well in the grip.

The bag also contained a folding assault rifle.

"What's that for?" said Marc.

"Just in case," she replied.

"Do I want to ask where you got this from?"

Lucy had been empty-handed when she left the office two hours earlier, heading out on an errand she vaguely described as "a shopping trip."

She made a face. "Oh, no. You certainly don't."

Marc gave a reluctant nod, checking and loading his own gun.

"So we're going for the . . . uh . . . *kinetic* approach to this, then?"

She countered with a question of her own.

"What time does Elija Van de Greif get in to work?"

Marc glanced at the dive watch on his wrist.

"Gallery opens at ten o'clock, an hour and five from

now. Company website says they take appointments from 10:30 on weekdays."

"He'll see us early," said Lucy, with a cold smile. "Guarantee it."

Marc's smartphone gave off a telltale warble signaling an incoming call, and he tapped the screen, activating the automatic encryption application to mask the conversation.

"This is Dane."

"*Hello,*" said Assim. The Saudi sounded weary and distant. "*What time is it there?*"

"Morning," said Marc. "What about you?"

"*I've lost track,*" Assim replied, with feeling. "*I've passed through tired and gone out the other side. Every time I try to go to sleep, I see . . .*" He halted, and Marc heard him swallow hard. "*You know, those pictures of the people in Benghazi. It's difficult not to think about them.*"

"I hear you, mate. Just stay on task, right? One way or another, we'll be done with this by the end of the day."

The last few words came out in a bleak tone that Marc didn't expect, and Assim heard it.

"*Yes, I suppose so.*"

"You have something for us?" said Lucy.

"*Oh, right, yes.*" Assim coughed and found his focus. "*We now have positive confirmation that seed materials and biokits for the printers were stolen from the factory in Manila. Check your email queue, Marc, I sent you a file.*"

"Wait one." Marc brought up a link to the SCD's secure email server and streamed the video to the laptop's screen. Grainy security camera footage unspooled as he watched. "What are we looking at here?"

"*I pieced this together from some video Malte was*

able to secure for us. Remember I said there was an incident, an active shooter at the factory?"

"Disgruntled ex-employee, right?" said Lucy.

"That's the popular narrative. The man was a security guard, fired for drinking on the job."

On the screen, a stocky Malaysian man carrying a shoulder bag strode warily into an office reception, and started yelling. An older woman behind the front desk tried to calm him down, but in the next second he dug both hands in the bag, and they came back out gripping a pair of silver revolvers. The footage had no sound, but Marc could see people in the office screaming and panicking. The stocky guy started shooting in random directions.

Something didn't track, though, and Lucy articulated the same thought.

"He's firing over their heads. He's not aiming at anyone." She tapped the laptop's touchpad to freeze the playback, pointing at the corner of the screen. "Look. That old lady is right there, hiding under the chair. He wanted to kill someone, he couldn't miss her."

Marc let the footage play on. The gunman emptied one pistol and advanced into the office, shaking out the spent cartridges on the floor, using a speed-loader to rearm as he walked. His movements were clumsy and frustrated, not the actions of a cold-eyed killer.

"This was cover for the theft of the seed materials," said Marc. "A distraction."

"Yes, got it in one," agreed Assim. *"And here's where it gets interesting."* The video feed suddenly blanked. *"That's the point at which the shooter entered the security office and pulled the plug on their recording equipment. There's no more video past that . . . But I spooled back a half-hour and I found something."*

The image returned: the same viewpoint, the same day. A group of people were milling around in the reception area, a mix of locals and Westerners. The lady from the reception desk was handing out visitor ID badges.

"A tour group?" said Lucy.

"*Yes. Some investors, in town to visit the plant. See anyone familiar?*"

Marc spotted her face immediately.

"Bottom right of the frame. The pale lady, in the flesh."

Axelle, the woman he had seen marching Ji-Yoo Park from her house, the one who had tried to kill them out on an Icelandic glacier, was doing her best not to be picked up by the security camera. But she couldn't avoid it totally, and as the group walked off with their guide, Marc raised an eyebrow at her choice of disguise.

"Is she wearing . . . ?"

"Fake pregnancy belly," said Lucy, with a scowl. "Big enough for twins."

"*The police report says eyewitnesses saw a pregnant European woman escape the building after the shooting started, along with dozens of other people.*"

"Let me guess," Marc broke in, "and then she disappeared."

"She walked out with what they stole under her dress." Lucy sneered. "Like a goddamn shoplifter."

"What happened to the shooter?" said Marc.

"*A police officer found him on the factory floor. Dead from a self-inflicted head wound.*"

"Self-inflicted," repeated Lucy. "Sure."

Marc put the narrative together. "So the Lion's Roar either paid or coerced the sacked bloke into doing his shooting spree and spiking the cameras. But Axelle goes in first to find what they need for the bioprinters. In the chaos she blows the poor sod's brains out so he can't talk, makes it look like a suicide."

"They've been planning this for a while," noted Lucy. "Assim, I bet you dig some more, you're gonna find evidence that VdG Acquisitions shipped out something small and fragile from Manila on the same day, to Belgium and Libya."

"*Already working on it.*"

Marc's attention was drawn back to the cameras and he moved to the window. A black Mercedes taxi with a yellow checkerboard trim halted in front of the gallery, and a tall, thin, well-dressed man climbed out, adjusting his tie as he was buzzed in through the front door.

"Van de Greif is in the building."

Lucy nodded. "If we had time and the resources, I'd say we snatch the guy and sweat him some, but we don't." She turned back to Marc's phone. "Assim. He's not going to be happy about it, but let Delancort know we're taking the direct approach on this. And for crying out loud, tell him we need to get the Belgians on board."

"*Understood.*"

Assim cut the call and then it was just the two of them.

"How do you want to do this?"

Marc checked the Glock pistol, then snapped the gun's paddle holster inside his waistband at the small of his back.

"High speed and low drag." Lucy looped the MP9's sling to hang from her shoulder, shrugging on her jacket to cover it up. "Follow my lead."

The apartment was tiny, it was cold, and it was always noisy. From the constant rattles and bangs of the bare pipes that ran up the walls to the other floors, Meddur had hoped hot water would flow through and give his family a little heat, but the opposite seemed true.

They had been here for weeks now, but this apartment, this city, this entire country was still cold to them. Not just from the gray rainy skies and the chill of the nights, but from a coldness that showed in the faces of the Belgians who looked at them with hooded, judgmental gazes. The icy manner wasn't limited to the Europeans, either. The other Middle Eastern immigrants who lived in the building's adjoining rooms, the hard-faced Sunni who owned the place, the people who ran the cramped little supermarket on the corner—all of them looked at Meddur and his family without an iota of warmth.

When they first arrived, the children were excited. It seemed like Brussels would be the end of their long odyssey from across the sea, arriving here after they had fled Khoms, down the Libyan coast from ravaged Tripoli.

Meddur knew he was one of the lucky ones. Many of their fellow immigrants had lost members of their family on the treacherous crossing, but he had managed, Allah willing, to keep his wife, Sakina, by his side, and his children whole and safe. Tadla, the eldest at twelve, had barely spoken during those hard months, while her brother, Aksil, had celebrated his eighth birthday sneaking out of the confines of a refugee center on the Italian coast. The boy refused to be frightened by his circumstances, embracing the changes in a way that made Meddur love him all the more. He had been the one singing songs as they drove through Brussels, in the back of a rusting minibus owned by the traffickers, the men who had taken his mother's and sister's gold bracelets as payment.

But then they crossed the bridge over the canal and entered Molenbeek, the borough that would be their new home. Aksil's singing trailed off as they saw the armed policemen patrolling and the locals with their haunted, distrustful faces. That first impression had never gone away.

Meddur had come far in search of a better life and a safe place to live, only to arrive here and discover the same grim reality his family were running from. In Khoms, the echoes of the civil war and the internecine conflicts between old enemies had made life there almost impossible. Every day felt like a gun was at their heads. Here, the constant dread was different but it was no less corrosive. Molenbeek might not be under threat from daily bombings, but another cloud of fears lingered amid the crushing poverty and the suspicions. He soon learned that the district was notorious for crime, and considered a no-go zone by many.

Meddur, Sakina and the children were illegals. They lived in terror of the strident knock at the door. The traffickers told them stories of how the black-masked Belgian *Politie* were ready to gun down anyone with a brown face unlucky enough to draw their attention. They told Meddur that ever since a gang of violent Islamists from Molenbeek had gone on a shooting spree in France a few years earlier, the Belgians saw everyone who lived there as a potential jihadi. When he tried to reach out to friends he knew who had made it to Antwerp, a city on the northern coast, the traffickers forbade it. They warned him never to use a cell phone, because government agents listened in on all calls.

We will keep you safe, they said, *as long as you pay us.*

Meddur had been a fisherman. A lifetime ago, he had captained his own boat. Now he was cleaning floors in a reeking warehouse for a pittance that barely kept his family fed. He wanted to find work driving trucks, but those jobs were jealously guarded. He would need to pay his way toward being considered for such a thing.

He rose and dressed, getting ready to go to the mosque. Through the ceiling, he heard the thuds and scrapes of movement from the people in the apartment above. They were an older family, and the husband argued constantly with the wife and the mother-in-law. Already, Meddur could pick out the man's hacking cough and the indistinct grumble of their peevish conversation.

Sakina brought him some tea. Like her husband, she had hoped to seek honest work here. Sakina was a trained nurse, but the traffickers had laughed at her when she told them. For now, she stayed in these three tiny rooms, looking after Aksil and Tadla, hoping for better days to come.

Sakina seemed uneasy, and Meddur reached up a hand to touch her face. Her deep brown eyes were troubled.

"What's wrong?"

The question seemed foolish. So much was wrong.

"Last night, while you were fast asleep, I found Tadla watching the television." She nodded at the aging black-and-white portable in the apartment's tiny kitchenette. "She saw the news from Benghazi and she was weeping."

Meddur let out an exasperated grunt.

"Did Aksil . . . ?"

Sakina nodded. "Yes, he knows about it too."

"I don't want them exposed to that," he hissed. "We left that behind us!"

"We can't hide it, husband. People on the street are talking, the others here . . ." Sakina gestured at the walls, indicating the other families living as they were in the rooms surrounding them. "It's all anyone is thinking about!"

A great weight pressed down on him, and Meddur felt the burden of every grave possibility on his shoulders.

"When are we going to be free of this?"

It was a moment before he realized that he had asked the question aloud.

Sakina blinked back tears and drew her husband into an embrace.

"We have endured everything put in our path," she told him. "We have love and strength. We will endure what comes next, *inshallah*."

The weight lessened, and Meddur felt a swell of affection.

"Without you my life means nothing, wife. You and the children are my world."

As if on cue, Aksil called out: "Father? Can you come here?"

The boy's voice filtered out of the narrow, box-like hallway that joined the room to the corridor beyond. He sounded frightened.

Meddur gave Sakina's hand a squeeze and crossed the room. The door to the hall was half shut, but as he opened it all the way, he felt a breeze. The front door was wide open.

Aksil stood rooted to the spot in the cramped space. Towering over the boy was a woman in a dark military jacket, trousers and boots. Two more men dressed the same way were standing out in the corridor behind her. Each of them wore a mask of soft black material that enveloped their heads, turning them into wraithlike, monstrous shadows. Close to their chests they held pistols with long barrels.

Meddur's instincts kicked in and he grabbed his son, snatching the boy up, putting himself between the intruders and the child. The woman's reaction was unhurried, raising a gloved finger to where her lips would be, the gun rising with it.

"What happens next," she began, with a cruel smile in the words, "is up to you."

The security door gave its characteristic buzzing hum and Van de Greif heard the heavy thud of the automatic bolts racking open.

Standing in the main floor of the gallery, he was in the middle of inventorying a series of brass castings, with Agatha dutifully taking notes, and the sound caught him completely off guard. The remote control for the door was up in his office, behind the glass partition, and the only other way to get it to open was with one of the gallery's RFID fobs. He had one, and the other was in Agatha's possession.

His first thought was that Verbeke had come back, that his oily, acne-scarred computer geek Ticker had somehow gained access to the building; but the two people who entered were unfamiliar to him. A scruffy-bearded white man in a baseball cap with a wary look in his eyes pocketed a cell phone as he entered, holding the door open for an athletic black woman wearing huge sunglasses that covered half her face. Both of them were quite ordinarily dressed and certainly did not display the fashion sense of his typical clientele.

"*Nee, nee*," Van de Greif said, in his nasal Dutch, wagging his finger at the new arrivals as if they were disobedient children. *Americans*, he guessed, *too stupid to read the sign*. He switched to English. "We are closed."

"Door was open, darling," said the black woman, with a Hepburnesque drawl. She made a show of looking around at a display of jade carvings. "Delightful. But a tad shabby. Where do you keep the good pieces?"

Van de Greif gave Agatha a dismissive look and she stepped away, moving toward the wide stairs leading to the office.

"Do you have an appointment?" he demanded.

"Darling." The woman pulled those ridiculous glasses down her nose so she could look at him over their rims. "Do I look like the kind of person who makes an appointment?" She shot the bearded man a look, pointing a finger at one of the larger bronzes. "That one for the villa in Tuscany." She looked back at the jade. "The fishy one is cute. That for the town house."

"I really must insist," said Van de Greif. "Your name, please!"

"He doesn't recognize me," said the woman, sharing the comment like a joke with the watchful young man. "But then this is Europe. So far behind the curve."

Van de Greif hesitated. Now he looked again, the black woman *did* resemble an actress he had seen in one of those noisy, brightly colored blockbuster films. Was it her? He couldn't be sure, but his innate avarice took over. Sales to Americans were always lucrative, and like the Arabs, they were too arrogant to admit they didn't know quality when they saw it.

"The mistake is mine," he said smoothly.

The antique dealer changed gears, affecting a cool smile as a part of him began to calculate by how much he would overcharge her.

She pointed at the office.

"Is that where you hide your best pieces?"

The woman didn't wait to be asked, climbing the

stairs. She kept her arms draped over her body, as if she were hugging herself.

Van de Greif followed her in quick steps, and her companion trailed behind him. There was something untrustworthy about the bearded man that the dealer immediately disliked. He kept staring, and it was becoming bothersome.

Inside the office, Van de Greif smartly stepped around the woman in the sunglasses and pulled out a chair for her, before taking his own seat on the far side of his desk. The woman didn't exactly sit, though, preferring to perch on the arm of the chair while her man stood in the doorway.

"What are you looking for?" he began, switching to his standard pitch for new clients. "Tell me the mood of the place you have in mind for these pieces."

"You have a storehouse next door?" The man spoke for the first time, betraying a British accent.

"Yes."

Van de Greif's reply was terse. He didn't like it when the hired help addressed him directly.

"Let's see what's in there," said the woman.

"It is not open to the public," Van de Greif replied.

"Oh, honey . . ." The woman pulled off her sunglasses and her voice hardened. "We're not the public."

With a flick of her thumb, she unzipped her jacket all the way open and her hand came back with a gun in it.

Agatha stifled a shriek and grabbed at the telephone, but the Britisher already had a pistol of his own drawn and he aimed it in her direction.

"Hands flat on the desk, where I can see them," he ordered.

His assistant let the handset drop and did as she was

told. The man pulled the entire telephone out of the wall, cord and all, before moving to Van de Greif's desk and repeating the act.

The salesman smile was immediately replaced by a fear-fueled but indignant arrogance.

"You come to steal? Do you know who I am?" Van de Greif snarled at the black woman. "I have connections! They'll cut your throat, you mongrel bitch!"

"Where have I heard that before?" said the woman, glancing at Agatha even as she lazily aimed her gun at his head. "Hey, girl. You know what kind of man your boss is? Who he runs with? Sure you do." She wandered across to the other desk. "Look at you. Blonde, all that farm girl firmness. Real Aryan queen material."

"I don't understand . . ." said Agatha, blinking tearfully.

"Not too bright, though."

The Britisher looked past the tray of expensive vodkas and single malts on the desk, to the security monitor screens mounted discreetly on the far wall's bookshelf.

"Here we go. Storehouse is through there." He pointed at the door in the arch. "Can't see anyone inside."

"Where's Verbeke?" The black woman tossed out the question, turning back to Van de Greif. "Listen, trust-fund, you do not wanna test me today. Where's he at?"

"Who?" It took an effort to show no reaction to the name.

"Is he in there?" The woman nodded in the direction of the storehouse. "Are you holding something for him?"

The man walked to a tower display of vases and carelessly pulled the top one off the shelf.

"I heard you can tell if these are the real deal by examining the cross-section of the ceramics." He bounced the vase in one hand, and it slapped against his palm. "Of course, you have to smash it first to check."

The vase came flying at Van de Greif and he barely caught it, a jolt of panic screaming through him.

"Clumsy oaf!" he shouted. "This is worth a hundred thousand euros!"

Hands shaking, he gently put the piece down on his desk.

"What about this one?"

The man grabbed another vase and tossed it heedlessly into the air. Van de Greif let out a pained howl and lunged, grabbing at the ceramic. It was slippery, and he lost his grip. Ice filled his belly as he fumbled, desperately trying not to drop it.

In the end, he found himself sprawled over his desk, both hands barely clasping the second vase. His heart hammered against his ribs.

"Stop it!" he yelled. "All right. I'll show you."

With a physical effort, Van de Greif calmed himself, and he pressed a brass button on a panel inset on his desk. Back in the gallery, the security door in the arch unlocked.

"There's nobody in there," he added, watching for the moment he needed.

And it came. For a fraction of a second, both of the intruders looked away, toward the arch. Van de Greif used their distraction to jab at another brass button on the panel. There was no sound, no indicator that the silent alarm had been sent.

The black woman saw his surreptitious movement from the corner of her eye and rounded on him. Her arm shot out and she grabbed his wrist, twisting it with enough force to make Van de Greif fold and fall to the elegant rug on the floor.

"Sneaky," she admonished, applying steady pressure to his wrist. It hurt so much he was afraid she was breaking it. "That for the cops?" She nodded at the button, then answered her own question. "Nah. Guy like you wouldn't want the police in here, would ya?"

Van de Greif was forced into a kneeling position at the woman's feet, and his anger finally won the struggle against his fear. He spat a string of venomous profanities at her in gutter Dutch. In all the years he had been secretly assisting the Lion's Roar in their activities, Van de Greif had rarely been anywhere close to the violence. Now he was, the sudden opportunity to drop his mask and show his defiance to this foreigner was too great to resist, and he snarled at her, baring teeth.

"You worthless animal! You and your race traitor are going to bleed for this!"

"You first," said the woman, and she cracked him across the face with the butt of her gun.

Van de Greif's nose broke with a sickly snap and hot blood spewed out of his nostrils as he fell to the floor.

"Where's the bioprinter?" she demanded.

He managed a shaky, defiant sneer.

"Long gone."

"We've got company."

Marc held up his smartphone, staring at the image on the screen. The cameras up in their temporary office hideout beamed a live video feed via wireless signal to Marc's device, showing a dark blue Renault Megane as it skidded to a halt outside the gallery. Three men boiled out of the car, clutching weapons, and a split second later they were pummeling on the front door across the room.

This time, the building's security was working in Marc's favor.

"Is there another way out?"

He shot the blonde woman a look and she nodded fearfully.

"Through the back of the storehouse!"

"Get out of here," Marc snapped, waving her away with the barrel of his gun.

She didn't need to be told twice, and the woman broke into a frantic run, discarding her high heels as she went.

"You let her go?" said Lucy, as she grabbed Van de Greif and dragged him to his feet.

"We don't need her, just this dickhead." Marc beckoned. "Come on!"

"You heard him." Lucy jabbed the antique dealer in the back. "Move your ass. Looks like we're doing a snatch and grab after all."

Van de Greif wailed something about his broken nose, but he stumbled forward as she shoved him toward the archway door into the storehouse. Marc followed, still watching what was going on outside through the remote feed. The men from the car gave up trying to shoulder open the door and one of them unlimbered a pistol-grip pump-action shotgun ending in a fat sound suppressor, working the slide to chamber a round. He fired into the mechanism as Marc, Lucy and their prisoner reached the other doorway.

Wood splintered and metal fragments scattered into the gallery as more shots blasted off the hinges. The front door fell in, crashing to the floor like a drawbridge.

Short of the archway, Marc ducked into the scant cover of a glass display cabinet as the three men burst in. They had that blunt-faced, always-angry look he associated with thugs and football hooligans, shaven-headed and heavy with inky tattoos.

The one with the shotgun came through first and saw Marc right away. The man had to rack a fresh round to open fire, and that bought him precious seconds. Marc brought his Glock up over the glass cabinet and squeezed the trigger. Both rounds zipped past the shot-gunner's head without connecting, but it made the man dive for the floor, giving Marc an opening. He rushed out of cover, sprinting toward the archway.

Ahead of him, Lucy pivoted, one hand holding a clump of Van de Greif's expensive suit jacket, the other aiming her MP9 at the men in the group. In the instant she fired, the antique dealer kicked her in the shin and hauled her off balance. The burst from Lucy's weapon went wild, stitching bullet holes up the wall and into the ceiling, missing the targets. Before she could react, Van de Greif punched her and snaked out of his jacket, slipping away in a flash of white cotton shirt.

The other two men had silenced pistols, and they opened up on Marc as he dashed across their field of vision. The guns chugged and glass shattered around him, hollow-point rounds echoing noisily off centuries-old brass castings. Marc blind-fired back, and a lucky hit caught one of the shooters in the shoulder, slamming the man into a table with the shock of the impact.

He got to Lucy and the two of them moved through the connecting vestibule between the buildings. Lucy fired another burst behind them to discourage pursuit, and Marc grabbed at the automatic sliding door, trying to pull it shut.

It didn't budge a centimeter. Whatever mechanism opened and closed it was locked in place, and the metal security door was too heavy to move by brute force.

"Forget it!" snapped Lucy. "Get him!"

She jabbed a finger toward Van de Greif, who was already clattering down the spiral staircase to the basement level. On the far side of the storehouse, the doors to the loading dock and the back alley beyond were hanging open, where the dealer's assistant had fled. Lucy instinctively aimed her MP9 to put shots into the man, but hesitated. They needed him alive if they were to find out where Noah Verbeke had gone to ground.

Marc took a shortcut around her, avoiding the stairs and vaulting over the cast-iron banister. He dropped the rest of the distance on to a fat sack of polystyrene packing peanuts resting on the basement floor. The bag exploded under his weight, spewing plastic nuggets in all directions, and his off-kilter landing threw him forward. Marc used the momentum to race after the dealer, who was almost at the door.

He caught Van de Greif as the man stumbled out into the morning air, grabbing his arm, yanking him back. His quarry spun wildly and clipped Marc in the temple with a closed fist, lighting sparks in his vision.

The roar of an engine sounded behind them as a second car, identical to the one up on Lebeaustraat, screeched to a halt and blocked the alleyway. Three more Lion's Roar thugs scrambled from the vehicle, and the first out was a narrow-eyed man carrying a cut-down Zastava carbine. The gunman reacted with instant violence, spraying a fan of 7.62mm bullets at waist level.

Marc was already throwing himself toward the doors the instant the M92's barrel turned in his direction. Untrained and unready, Van de Greif did not react in time and took rounds through the chest at close range, his white shirt suddenly marred with bursts of crimson.

Marc hit the ground and rolled into cover, firing again, his rounds sparking off the flanks of the car.

Inside the storehouse, Lucy's SMG was snarling as she fired up the spiral stairs, forcing the men who had breached the gallery to hang back. She saw Marc and her eyes widened.

"You're hit!"

"What?" He glanced down and saw red spatters across his jacket where Van de Greif's blood had marked him. "It's not mine."

Her face fell. "The dickhead?"

Marc made a throat-cutting gesture with his thumb. "*Shit!*"

To underline the dire turn events were taking, the Zastava kicked off again, bullets punching holes through the heavy wooden doors of the loading dock. Marc and Lucy returned fire, retreating deeper into the storehouse.

The Glock's slide locked open and Marc ejected the empty magazine, smacking in a fresh one.

"These guys must have been camped out around the corner, waiting for the word."

"Verbeke's smart," Lucy said, hissing in the sudden quiet between the gunfire. "He wasn't planning on letting Van de Greif live. We just moved up the timetable."

Marc cast around.

"No sign of the printer in here. He wasn't lying."

"Looks like," she agreed.

The men on the upper level tried to push forward again, and this time Marc and Lucy held their fire until the shotgunner was exposed on the upper landing. The storehouse was full of shadows and the guy didn't see them at first, as he panned around with his weapon.

Out in the alley, Marc heard the indistinct mutter of voices. The two teams were talking to one another.

"We don't want to be here when the cops arrive, and that won't be long," Lucy said in his ear.

She braced her MP9 on a wooden crate, holding the gun's fore grip tightly—and then fired. In the dimness, a jet of flame spat from the weapon's muzzle and bullets bracketed the shotgunner, sparking off the iron stairs. The man took hits and fell, and one of his teammates ducked low, dragging his body into the vestibule before Lucy could reload. Immediately, more shots came streaking in from the loading dock.

"Trying to keep us pinned," Marc called.

He dived flat on the concrete floor, and between the planks of a cargo pallet he saw combat boots shuffling forward, out in the daylight. Drawing a bead, he put a 9mm round through the broad side of the shooter's leading foot, and the man screamed, crashing to the ground. Two follow-up shots went into the torso and kept him down.

"Moving!"

Lucy broke cover and ran for the foot of the spiral staircase.

Marc sprang up and ran after her, catching sight of movement at the top of the stairs, at the entrance to the vestibule. Orange firelight flickered in the shadows, and one of the gunmen tossed two liquor bottles into the air, each with an improvised wick down the neck and already burning. He grabbed Lucy and pulled her aside as expensive Tanqueray and Belvedere firebombs shattered against the crates and piles of packing material. The alcohol exploded into blue flashes, instantly catching the dry kindling. Flames roared to life, ripping around the basement and sucking in air through the open doors. The rest of the contents of Van de Greif's pricey drinks tray came sailing down after, smashing against the walls and the floor.

Then the gunmen drew back, leaving Marc and Lucy to burn. If they made a break for it out the back, they would be cut down. Going up through the vestibule would channel them into a kill box. The flames gathered in a crackling knot near the far wall and began to spread. They had seconds at best before the fire surrounded them.

"Up!"

Marc pointed to a wooden service ladder mounted on the storage racks, and Lucy acknowledged with a nod and a stifled cough.

Above them, four stories high over the open drop to the basement floor, the canted roof of the storehouse had a square skylight. As Lucy began the climb, Marc pressed the cuff of his jacket to his face as a makeshift mask and fired into the window overhead, shattering the heavy pane. He dodged aside as jagged pieces of glass came raining down, and then started up the ladder after Lucy.

Gusts of heat, channeled by the stone walls, turned the open interior of the storehouse into a chimney. The fire rolled forward, consuming other crates as fuel, and Marc heard the cracking of ancient ceramics as the flames destroyed the gallery's secret stash. He had no time to lament the destruction, however. The lowest steps of the wooden ladder smoked as the fire lapped at them.

Somewhere outside, the rising-falling whoop of a siren was coming closer, but Marc concentrated on putting one hand in front of the other, pulling himself up rung over rung.

The black and pungent smoke made his eyes water and his lungs tense. He reached up and his hand grasped at nothing. Then he felt Lucy grab his wrist and she guided him over the top, on the highest level of the storage racks. Belatedly, the building's sprinkler system kicked in, but the spray was angled down and away from them. Marc wobbled on the slim, slippery ledge at the top of the racks, and looked down. The fire sputtered and crackled beneath the sprinkler deluge but it didn't die out.

"Last step," he coughed, lining himself up with the broken window. "Have to jump for it."

Lucy nodded. Neither of them needed to say that missing the sill would mean a fall that would kill.

Dwelling on the danger would only destroy his resolve, so Marc didn't wait. He pushed himself off the rack, feeling it sway alarmingly as he leaped. He hit the bullet-smashed frame hard with both hands, and hung on for dear life. Nubs of glass cut at his palms but he pushed the pain away, hauling his weight up through the broken skylight and on to the terracotta roof tiles. Rolling on to his front, Marc squeezed halfway back inside, and waved to Lucy, holding out his hands.

She leaped like a wildcat and their arms slapped together. Marc's heart almost stopped when Lucy slipped, but he held tight and so did she. In a mingled growl of effort, the two of them worked to get her out and into the cold air. Sprawled on the rooftop, they both fell into racking coughs as they cleared the smoke from their lungs.

"Need to move," he managed, crawling to the edge.

The next building was a story lower with a flat top, and he dropped down on to it. Lucy followed a moment later, and found him peeking over the edge.

"They're gone?" she guessed.

He nodded. "Two police cars down there. Fire engines will be coming."

"We need to move fast."

She pointed to the west, and Marc saw the bug-like shape of a white MD 900 helicopter vectoring in their direction from over Châtelain. She didn't wait for him to agree, and set off across the rooftops, fast and fleet-footed.

— SEVENTEEN —

When the thick sackcloth bag came off Meddur's face he flinched away from the bright light. Strong, gloved hands pressed him back into the plastic lawn chair he found himself in. The zip-tie holding his wrists together was cut off and he trembled.

He looked around desperately, searching for any sign of Sakina and the children. In the vehicle that had brought them here, Meddur had heard them crying and whimpering in the darkness, but each attempt he made to speak to his family had been rewarded with a kick in the head. Now he saw no evidence of them, and his blood chilled.

The lawn chair was sitting on the floor inside a large tent, the kind that rich people on television took into the woods for camping trips. The zip-flap door was closed, so Meddur couldn't see outside. In front of the chair, a set of industrial lamps on a stand seared him with punishing light, and he could make out a folding table next to it, with a computer atop it.

In the shadows behind the lamps, indistinct figures moved around, conversing in Dutch. Then one of them detached and came fully into view, a broad-shouldered white man with a shaven head and a grin like a shark's. He wore heavy boots, denim trousers and a black vest. Complex sleeves of tattoos ran from his shoulders to wrists, over hard planes of muscle. Meddur's terror grew as he realized that the people who had taken them were not the traffickers, not the police . . . They were something *worse*.

"You speak English?" said the man.

"Yes." Meddur nodded.

"The woman and the children, do they?"

"No." His first instinct was to lie, hoping to protect them. He shifted in the chair. "Please, where are my family—"

That earned him an open-handed slap across the head, almost hard enough to knock him to the ground.

"I ask the questions."

"Don't hurt them!"

The big man ignored his words.

"Someone else could have done this," he said. "I didn't have to get my hands dirty. But I wanted to take a look at you. To see what you're made of." He stalked around Meddur, prowling as an animal would. "Just to remind myself that I am right."

"I do not understand."

The man crouched down so he was at eye level with his captive.

"Why didn't you fight? When they came into your home, threatened your wife and children, why didn't you resist?"

A cold, judgmental hatred simmered behind the man's gaze.

"They had guns. They would have—"

"Coward!" He barked the word. "You're weak, like all of your kind. A man would have fought, guns or not." He leaned close. "A *white man* would have fought for his family, no matter the odds. But you gave up and let them take you. You people don't know what courage is."

Meddur shook, feeling hot tears course down his cheeks.

"No. No!"

His stifling fear was briefly swamped by a potent rush of shame, and he hung his head. The terrible humiliation of knowing he had been unable to stop the abduction made him sick inside. It was the responsibility of a father and a husband to protect his family, and he had failed.

The man spat at his feet.

"You come here, spineless and grasping, after ruining your own country, and you bring your weakness to my home." He jabbed Meddur in the chest. "*You corrupt everything.*"

"I . . . We . . ." Meddur gasped, trying to form the words, holding on to his last shred of defiance. "We are looking for a better life—"

Any reply he could make would have been wrong. The man slapped him again.

"You don't deserve that! This is our nation, not yours! You have no right to come here, begging for help when what you really want is to take what is mine!"

He cocked back his fists, and Meddur saw the raw rage about to burst its banks.

"Noah," said a female voice in a warning tone, from out in the shadows. "Don't break him."

Meddur blinked. He recognized the French accent. It was the hooded woman from the house.

"Get out."

The man she called Noah snarled at the woman, and another of the shadows broke away and moved off.

Meddur saw the tent flap open, glimpsing rusted metal walls outside before it closed again.

Noah hovered on the brink of unleashing his hate on his prisoner, and then slowly he took a step back.

"I'll give you a chance to show you have courage," he told him. "You can prove to your family that you are not a coward."

He snapped his fingers, summoning another man to step into the light. Meddur only saw the other one briefly, glimpsing an acne-scarred face with curly black hair, as he handed a sheet of paper to the bigger man. Noah studied the writing on the page as the second man moved something into view. A tripod, and atop it was a large camera with multiple lenses.

Noah dropped the paper in Meddur's lap.

"Can you read that?"

Cautiously, Meddur studied the document. His grasp of written English was adequate, but he had to work at it. His mouth moved silently as he followed the words with a finger.

"Out loud, stupid," said the other man, adjusting the camera so it aimed at the prisoner in the chair. He spoke with a coarse American accent.

Meddur shook his head. "Please, I do not know what any of this means."

Panic surged in his belly. The words on the page were meaningless to him.

Noah took his hesitation to be defiance, and with a swift movement he reached into the shadows, returning with a heavy, silenced pistol in his fist. He cocked the gun's slide.

"Which one do you care for the least?" He threw out the question. "The woman? The boy or the girl? Tell me, so the ones you love most will die last."

"No, stop!" Meddur bolted up from the chair, but Noah hit him in the sternum with the heel of his hand, and he crashed back, wheezing. "Don't hurt them, please, I beg you! Kill me if you must but not them! *Please!*" He sobbed out the words.

"Finally, a little bravery. I could kill you," Noah said, toying with the idea. "Perhaps as a lesson. I think if I did, your wife would obey me when she saw your corpse."

"I will do whatever you want," pleaded Meddur. "Anything you ask. Just spare them."

"Look into the camera," instructed the big man. "Read out the words."

Meddur took the paper in his shaking hands and did as he was told.

"*The . . . beige hue . . . on the waters of the loch . . . impressed all*," he began.

He was made to repeat the nonsensical English phrases over and over, until the acne-scarred American behind the camera was satisfied. Then they told him to remain in the chair while the camera was positioned in different places, to film Meddur from opposite angles.

While he sat there, he saw Noah move to the tent flap as it came open, revealing the woman standing outside. Unmasked, she was pale like a ghoul out of old myth, her lips as red as blood.

"Van der Greif just sent the panic signal," he heard her say. "Brewn is nearby, he'll check it out."

Noah grunted. "That poseur is nothing but a liability now."

"Agreed. Brewn will deal with the situation."

"We're finished here," called the man with the camera, detaching it from the tripod.

Noah whispered something else to the milk-pale woman, then walked back inside the tent, eyeing Meddur as he approached.

"Give him the watch," he told the acne-scarred man.

The American produced a thick, square wristwatch with a digital screen and snapped it into place on Meddur's arm. The device's display lit up with a rudimentary direction marker and distance counter.

"Don't mess with anything," he warned. "Take it off and . . ." He mimed a gun at his head. "Bang-bang, bye-bye wifey."

"Go get Kyun," Noah told him, and the American walked out of the tent, leaving the two of them alone for the first time.

Meddur couldn't take his eyes off the heavy pistol in the big man's hand. He didn't hold it like a soldier would. Instead, it dangled carelessly at the end of his arm.

"Here comes your chance," began Noah. "Show you have strength. Keep your family alive."

Meddur thought about the conversation he'd had with the traffickers—how the men who had smuggled them into Belgium wanted him to help them commit violent acts. An inexorable, gloomy familiarity settled on him as he tore his gaze away from the gun.

"What do you want?" His voice was broken and hollow.

"You're going to take a walk for me. Into the city, and then back to Molenbeek. You know the way."

"Why?"

"Because I wish it." Noah's expression became stone cold. "If you disobey me. If you talk to the police. If you do anything wrong . . . The boy dies first. Then the women will be raped and killed. I'll make sure your wife lives long enough to see it, and to know you are to blame."

Meddur gasped at the awfulness of the thought, his hand going to his mouth.

"How do I know you won't kill them the moment I leave?" he said, in a dead voice.

Noah shook his head. "You are my dog now. And to keep a dog in line, you need a stick."

He turned as the tent flap opened and a short, nervous-looking East Asian man entered, carrying a black nylon backpack.

"If you run away," he added, "it will only prove me right about your cowardice."

The new arrival beckoned Meddur to his feet.

"Stand up. Turn around. Arms down."

He followed the man's commands. The pack slipped on over his shoulders, and the Asian man adjusted the straps so it sat high and secure on his back. Meddur felt him working on something in the pack, feeling a dense weight shift around.

"It's ready?" said Noah.

"All set," came the reply.

The man stepped away and Meddur stood there, in the glow of the lamps, unsure what to do next. He wasn't a fool. There was only one thing the pack could contain.

"I am not a murderer!" he insisted.

He had seen first-hand the bloody carnage wrought by suicide bombers in Tripoli, and the notion that he might be forced to do the same was devastating.

"No?" Noah cocked his head. "Then your wife can carry the bag instead. It's your choice."

Meddur could do nothing but give a defeated nod.

Noah grabbed his arm, twisting it so he could see the face of the wristwatch.

"Get moving. Follow this."

Meddur took a cautious step, then another and another, walking out through the tent flap. Beyond it, he saw that the shelter had been erected inside a corroded, decaying warehouse, and he smelled the stale odors of diesel fuel, canal water and rust. The direction pointer aimed him toward an open roller door and the street outside.

Out on the cracked concrete floor beneath the warehouse roof, he saw a second tent and a pair of trucks, including the one that had brought them here. The pale woman stood at the cab. He thought he heard Aksil cry out from inside the back of the vehicle, but the woman glared at him when he dared to look in that direction.

"Keep moving!" Noah shouted out behind him, making Meddur jump. He twisted, and saw the big man behind him, standing by the tent. "We'll be observing you all the way!" he called. "So be a good dog."

"You think he'll actually do it?"

Ticker folded his arms over his chest as they watched the terrified mule walk away.

Verbeke cocked his head. "Axelle wouldn't have picked this one if she didn't think he'd obey."

"Hope she's right," grated the American. "All the work we put into this, and we leave the last step in the hands of a goddamn sand monkey." His lip curled. "Saw enough in the Gulf to know every one of them is as dumb as a box of rocks."

"You want to take his place?" Verbeke's anger had not fully subsided, and the hacker's habit of constant complaining tested his patience. "You look enough like one of them."

"Fuck off!" Ticker instantly reacted to the insult, but caught himself in time, before he said something he might regret. "Yeah, real funny."

He laughed it off nervously.

"Just do your part," Verbeke warned him.

"I will. I have," insisted Ticker. "GPS is gonna track mule-boy's location to within two square meters. Once he's on site, the nozzles will open." He made a spreading motion with his hands. "And then it's *adios muchachos*." The American nodded at Kyun. "He's the one you wanna make sure don't screw this up."

Verbeke watched the North Korean shakily lighting a cigarette.

"He'll stay in line. He saw what happened to that bitch in Iceland." His attention returned to Ticker. "Why are you standing around? Get the fucking video ready."

"I'm doing it!" Ticker bleated, retreating. "It's already compiling. Thirty minutes, tops. Then our little pet ji-hadi will say anything you want him to."

In the other tent, Ticker's portable mainframe was humming away. The same software that had allowed the Lion's Roar to create a credible simulation of Ji-Yoo Park's family would soon spit out another deepfake video. This one would have their erstwhile bag-carrier sitting in front of a black ISIS flag, decrying the powers of the West and taking responsibility for the virus outbreak in Brussels.

The release of the video would take place in time for the evening news cycle in central Europe, several hours after the weapon in Meddur's backpack would be spent, its lethal content carried along the man's route. Kyun had promised infection numbers in the thousands, and a firestorm of panic along with them.

Verbeke imagined the moment when the police eventually got around to kicking in the door of Meddur's dirty little apartment. He pictured them in hazmat gear, pushing through streets choked with immigrant corpses in body bags, a ghost town version of Molenbeek where the foreigners were dead or bleeding out. The cops would find the evidence Axelle had planted there. Cell phones with logs of dozens of calls directed to a certain garage in Benghazi, incendiary Islamic extremist books—all the expected detritus to be left behind by a fanatic militant.

The Lion's Roar would fan the flames of righteous

anger that came next. The outbreak in Libya had been designed to look like an accident, a slip of the hand from some overzealous terrorist. The connection would be inexorably drawn between the refugee infestation in Belgium and the rats' nest they spilled out of. Verbeke already had a plan of attack set up and ready to go, with other cells of Lion's Roar members across the continent standing by to firebomb mosques and stir up rage on social media. The ones he trusted the most would release false flag propaganda, pretending to be the enemy and praising the attack. The Combine promised that their troll farms in Russia would put their weight behind the disinformation campaign, amplifying it across the gargantuan echo chamber of the internet.

We will start an avalanche, Axelle had told him, that night in a field in Slovakia. As he stood there, with the adrenaline of the escape from the train fading away, he listened to her voice outlining the Combine's offer. And for all his hatred of those moneyed old whores, he hated the mongrels even more. *We will strike a blow for our race*, she said, and he smiled his predator's smile.

"The time is now," Verbeke said to himself, basking in the righteousness of his sentiment.

For years, he had watched as the idiotic fantasy of a unified Europe ate away at the sovereignty of nations. The only way to shock the system out of this self-destructive course was through violence, to reclaim their blood and soil, and eject the corruptive influence of all that was foreign. The nation was for its people, not for outsiders.

Lions and not sheep.

His stepfather's words echoed in his memory. The

sheep would see the death and disease and believe the immigrants were responsible for the outbreak. They would cry out for lions to rid them of this infestation.

His hands tensed into fists.

It will happen.

Walls would rise across Europe. Nations would be *strong* again.

He glanced at Ticker.

"Your little computer trick. You can do it with other languages? Arabic?"

The American nodded. "Sure, I guess. I have variations of the sampling text, the phonetic pangram."

He gestured at one of the trucks.

"The wife and kids are in there. Do the woman."

"Okay—but I don't have the bandwidth to render video of her. It'll be audio only."

"That's good enough. Program some generic replies in her voice, in case we need it. Begging her husband to help them. That sort of thing."

Ticker smirked as he walked away.

"Don't need the tech for that. I'll slap her around some." He leered at Axelle as she approached. "Lotta women love that shit."

Axelle treated the American as if he didn't exist, and crossed to Verbeke's side. She was holding a satellite phone in one hand, the thick tube-shaped antenna pointing up at the roof.

"Somebody wants to speak to you," she said.

"Now?"

He snatched the sat-phone handset from her and studied the screen. The display indicated a signal with a blocked sender.

"It's only to be expected," she said. "The Combine wants to check in on its new partners."

Verbeke raised the phone to his ear.

"I don't answer to you," he began. "Watch the news. You'll know when we are done along with the rest of the world."

"*I apologize if I have interrupted you at a busy time.*" The familiar, metered speaker on the other end of the line acted as if Verbeke had never uttered a word. "*But your attention is required.*"

He put a face to the voice. It was the Japanese, the one who had been waiting for him after the breakout from the train.

"You again? What is it this time?"

"*The same as before. I am here to provide assistance to you.*" In the background of the call, Verbeke thought he could hear the rumble of jet engines. The Japanese was aboard an aircraft. "*It would be in your interest to listen.*"

He chafed at the foreigner's irritatingly mild tone, and fought down an urge to throw the sat-phone across the concrete.

"So talk."

"*You should be aware that the Rubicon agents are in Brussels. They tracked you from Reykjavík.*"

"Bullshit!" he snapped. "They froze to death out on the ice. Axelle made sure of that."

"*Did she? The Frigga facility belongs to my employers. They have confidential sources embedded in the Icelandic government, in order to monitor it. We have learned that the reports of the dead bodies found on the glacier are false. A smokescreen.*"

Verbeke took a breath to moderate his surging annoyance, sparing Axelle a venomous glare.

"What makes you think they are here?"

"*An independent facilitator whom my employers*"

hold on retainer made us aware of this fact. One of the Rubicon agents made a purchase of several firearms from him a short time ago."

Suddenly, Axelle's earlier comments about Van de Greif sounding his panic alarm snapped into sharp focus. Verbeke's mind raced. The antique dealer knew the site of the warehouse by the canal, where the second bioprinter was set up in the back of the other truck. If he spilled his guts to Rubicon, there was a chance that this location was already compromised.

He muffled the phone's audio pickup with his hand. "Change of plan," he told Axelle. "We're not waiting until the dispersal is complete. Start the tear-down now. Ticker will have to finish on the move." He pointed toward the back of the warehouse, where a disused loading dock opened out on to the canal. "Get the boats here. Tell everyone, weapons free."

She saw the look in his eyes and knew enough to follow his commands without questioning them. Verbeke sucked in a breath through his teeth and returned to the sat-phone.

"*You understand*," the Japanese was saying, "*that this raises some concerns.*"

"It doesn't matter," he insisted. "What could they know? Not enough to stop us. So let them run around and panic. If they're in the city, even better. It would be fitting if they get to see the effects of Shadow up close." Verbeke grinned at the thought of that. "Let them die puking blood and knowing how badly they fucked up." When the man on the other end of the line didn't respond, he seized on the moment. "That's what those old shits holding your chain want, isn't it? Blood in the streets? A breakdown of order that they can exploit? At the end of it, we all get what we want, yes? Less of your kind, and each nation a fortress."

"*You paint a . . . singular picture,*" said the other man, masking his antipathy. "*I hope this information proves useful. My employers wish to see this endeavor reach its conclusion. They have invested a great deal in it.*"

"Don't expect me to thank you," snapped Verbeke.

"*I would not dare,*" came the reply, and the line went dead.

Marc found an unsecured window in the attic of a chocolatier that had yet to open, and he and Lucy made their way down the fire escape, through a back alley and to the street, a block away from the VdG gallery.

They were both dirty and stank of smoke, but the area was still relatively empty of foot traffic, and the few people who were on the street focused on the gallery in flames and the police presence. Stripping off their jackets to hide their guns in the folds, they walked unhurriedly in a wide loop that took them the long way around, back to the dusty office building. Lucy walked hand in hand with Marc as if she didn't have a care in the world.

No one stopped them. By the time they returned, fire units were in place and the police had the street cordoned off. The helicopter hovered unmoving overhead as if it was bolted to the sky, and both of them were careful not to look up, knowing that the aircraft's high-definition cameras would be recording everything happening below.

They slipped inside, secured the room and pulled the blinds. Marc sat heavily on the floor and ran back the footage from the cameras to watch events unspool all over again. It was only when he realized Lucy was deathly silent that he stopped and looked up at her.

"That could have gone better," he said.

Lucy fixed him with a glare that could have burned through an inch of steel plate.

"You think?" she spat. "We've lost the only lead we had."

"I know, I was there," he shot back, his temper fraying.

She started to change clothes, stripping off the smoke-tainted gear and pawing angrily through her bag for fresh garments.

"Only play we can make now is go to the local law and hope they don't throw us in a jail cell . . ."

She trailed off suddenly as a muffled warble sounded from the pocket of Marc's jacket.

He pulled out his smartphone.

"Delancort," he said, reading the caller ID off the screen.

There was an "urgent" flag next to the *incoming call* message. Marc shot a look at the smoke-blackened gallery across the way, where the fire was already out and emergency vehicles clogged the street.

"He can't know what just happened . . . ?"

"Answer it," she told him. "Don't give him an excuse to get pissy."

Marc tapped the speaker icon and put the device on the folding table next to his laptop.

"This is Dane," he began. "Look, this is a bad time, we're having a few issues here—"

"*We can discuss your issues later. I have someone on the line who wishes to speak with you.*"

Delancort talked over him, and the French-Canadian's manner was brittle and sharp. Lucy heard the tone of his voice and sensed the same thing Marc did. Something was wrong.

He expected the next voice he heard to be Ekko Sol-omon's—but the careful, cut-to-length words sparked an entirely different connection, to a man Marc had last seen caught under the guns of Somali pirates. A man Marc had personally stabbed through the shoulder with a six-inch-long steel dagger.

"*Mr. Dane*," said the man called Saito. "*There are matters we should discuss.*"

Lucy mouthed the words *what the hell?* but Marc's mind raced as he tried to process what he was hearing.

"I thought you were dead."

"*A mistaken assumption. I know why you are in Brussels,*" Saito went on. "*Your presence has not gone unnoticed.*"

Marc thought about gunfire and burning buildings and his lips thinned.

"Why are we talking?"

"*I have information you will find useful.*"

"How is this fucker even on our comms network?" muttered Lucy.

She pulled on a fresh sweatshirt and jacket, then set about jamming everything she could into a backpack, clearly intending to vacate the building as quickly as possible.

"*Ah, Ms. Keyes is there, of course. To answer her question, it was quite simple. The Rubicon Group's head office in Monaco maintains a public front desk. I contacted that number and made my identity known.*"

Marc almost laughed. The brass balls audacity of such an act was exactly what he would expect from the Combine's people. They believed they were untouch-able, arrogant enough to assume they could reach in and meddle with events any time they chose. The con-firmation that they were connected to the Lion's Roar and Verbeke's activities came as no surprise at all. Instead, Marc felt a grim sense of inevitability. There was no injustice, no hatred the group did not try to take advantage of for their own ends.

"*Your associate Mr. Delancort, who is doubtless monitoring this conversation, quickly understood the value of taking me seriously.*" Saito paused, and his tone shifted. "*I am heartened to see you are both alive and well.*"

"You stabbed me in the belly in Mogadishu and left me to bleed out," Lucy growled. "You double-crossed us. But that's SOP for the Combine, right?"

"*Please,*" Saito said coolly. "*I calculated that an operative of your caliber would be able to survive such a wound. Clearly, I was correct. And let me remind you, Mr. Dane returned the favor.*"

"So you got away from Ramaas's offshore rig in one piece." Marc glared at the smartphone. "Personally, I was hoping you'd gone to the bottom after the Russians torpedoed it."

Two years ago, in the headlong pursuit of a rogue nuclear device, Marc and Lucy had been forced to work with Saito and his Combine mercenaries. Their attempt to neutralize the weapon had ultimately succeeded, but not before Saito had tried to take control of it for his paymasters.

"*As engaging as this is, I did not contact you in order to reminisce about our previous encounters,*" said the other man. "*As I said, I am here to help you. I know your technicians are in the process of trying to trace this communication, so I will be brief.*" Saito read out the web address for an anonymous file transfer protocol server. "*You will find data there on a man named Meddur al-Baruni, a refugee from Libya currently living in*

Brussels. He will be at the Vlaamsepoort tram stop in under fifteen minutes, but after that time I have no intelligence on where he will go next."

"Who is he?" said Marc.

"And why should we care?" added Lucy.

"*On his own, he is a man of little consequence*," said Saito. "*An innocent dupe. His only crime is to be an undocumented immigrant. The man has a family. These factors have made him of use to certain people.*" Marc's gut tightened at the mercenary's next words. "*As we speak, he is carrying an aerosol dispersion device into the middle of the city. That device is loaded with the Marburg variant bio-agent known as Shadow.*"

"Oh man," Lucy whispered.

Saito went on, calmly and clearly. "*Mr. al-Baruni is being coerced into this act in order to preserve the lives of his wife and children. The data on the server will also give you their last known location. Act quickly. The validity of this information is time-sensitive.*"

"Why are you doing this?" Marc demanded. "What's the catch? The Combine helped the Lion's Roar set this whole thing up. You're responsible for those deaths in Benghazi! And now you offer up a way to stop a second attack, like it's no big deal? I don't believe a bloody word of this! You're setting us up, like you did in Somalia!"

"*It does not . . .*" Saito began to speak, then halted, as if he was trying to find the right words. "*It is necessary for Verbeke to fail today*," he said, abruptly rushing the reply.

"So stop him yourself," said Lucy, "if you've had a sudden attack of conscience?"

"*My conscience . . .*" Saito almost rose to the bait.

"*Using Rubicon is more efficient.*" Marc sensed something else behind Saito's words. The man's cool manner suddenly turned evasive, disquieted. "*The information is at your disposal. I suggest you use it.*"

The line fell silent, and then Delancort's voice issued out of the smartphone.

"*He has disconnected. We tracked the signal to an airborne source, somewhere over the Baltic Sea, but an exact fix was not possible.*"

"I'm pulling the data from the FTP site," said Marc. "Don't worry, I'll keep it firewalled in case there's some malware in there."

The data download took only a fraction of a second, and the content of the file was mostly surveillance photographs, images of a Middle Eastern man taken through a long-lens camera over a period of weeks. Some of the shots showed him going in and out of a mosque with a young boy by his side. In others, taken through the windows of a dingy apartment, the man and the boy were joined by a woman and a pre-teen girl in simple hijabs. All four of them had the cautious, beaten-down manner of survivors. There were also grainy, scanned images of documents in Dutch, rental agreements for a warehouse across the canal from the Molenbeek district.

Once Marc was satisfied the data was clean, he forwarded it to Rubicon.

"This makes no sense," he said, trying to reason it through. "Why give us the means to stop this at the last second? What possible benefit could the Combine get out of that?"

"*I gave up trying to figure out the nature of their games a long time ago,*" said Delancort. "*They are an opaque cabal. Laws unto themselves.*" He sighed. "*I have to take this to the Rubicon board. We have to decide on a course of action."*

The channel closed with a buzz of static.

"It's a trap," Lucy said flatly. "They're trying to drag us down into this mess. Pin the blame on us, or some shit like that."

The hands on Marc's Cabot dive watch showed fifteen minutes to the top of the hour, and he tapped out a search on his laptop, bringing up a map application.

"We're not far from that tram stop," he said. "I can get there in time to intercept this bloke."

"No," Lucy said firmly. "What we do is turn that file over to the Belgian cops and let them lock down the city."

Marc kept talking. "The warehouse at the canal, that'll be the harder target. More your speed than mine. It's probably where they have the other bioprinter too."

Lucy grabbed his arm.

"We are not doing this!" she snarled at him. "Goddamn you, Dane, have you been sleepwalking through everything? These assholes have been keeping us off balance since Singapore, now they're railroading us into acting without thinking, and you're letting them do it! You want to fuck up here like we did in Iceland?"

"The police won't get there in time," Marc said, pacing out his retort. "You know that. Even if they did, they don't know what Verbeke is capable of. We do. *We saw it.*" He ran out of impetus, and the last few words fell out of him. "We couldn't save Park. We couldn't stop the first attack. But we can try to stop this one."

"Saito—whoever is running him—they're manipulating us," she said, imploring him. "They're counting on us to get in the thick of this, because they know what

Rubicon is. They know who we are, they know what kind of people Solomon recruited for this team. Dane, anything they tell us is *tainted*."

"I know that. Of course I know." Marc put a hand on her arm. "They've used everything we have against us, and this is no different. But we don't have a choice here, do we? Inaction is action. We do nothing, and we may as well help Verbeke push the button ourselves." He closed the laptop and grabbed his phone. "I'm going. I need you to come too. If the guy with the device is being forced to carry it, he won't give it up unless his family is safe, so we need to rescue them."

"You don't get to make mission decisions," she told him. "That's my call."

"Yeah, that's right," he allowed. "I mean, technically you are my supervisor, and I am an employee of the Rubicon Group, Incorporated." He picked up the Glock, checking the slide before jamming it in his belt holster. "So if you won't help, as of now you can consider me resigned from the Special Conditions Division." He turned and walked away. "If I'm still in one piece by the end of the day, I'll put that in writing."

"You prick! Don't make me the bad guy!" she shouted at his back. "*Limey asshole!* Goddamn you for making me do this!" Lucy stormed over and grabbed the sports bag containing the folding assault rifle. "I cannot believe I actually thought about *screwing* you." Hauling it up over her shoulder, she marched back to his side, and that furious light was in her eyes all over again. "You won't make it an hour without me covering your skinny white ass! Send me the warehouse address."

"Thanks," Marc began, but she shoved her way past him, and set off down the stairs at a run.

* * *

Saito had rules for many aspects of his life. They helped him to maintain what the Americans called "compart-mentalization," the sectioning of his self into elements that could operate without conflict.

In one part of himself, he was a man who maimed and killed, a man who served the whims of a vicious elite. In another, he was a soldier with a duty. And in another, he was bound by obligation and the fear of what even the smallest disobedience might bring.

One of his rules was never to drink alcohol during an active assignment, but he did nothing to stop himself as he crossed the cabin of the Gulfstream G550 jet, and poured a measure of fine single malt whiskey from the aircraft's compact bar.

Further down the private plane's luxurious cabin, the man called Lau was sleeping in a reclining chair. His hands held a light blanket over his body, bunched up and pulled close. Despite his expensive suit, pricey haircut, and recent dental and medical work-overs, the man still looked like a prisoner. He slept afraid, some-thing that Saito could understand.

But Saito had trained himself too well to ever reveal so much of his inner truth, even in the deepest slumber. In Japan, there were accepted social-cultural concepts known as *tatemae* and *honne*. The former meant "fa-çade," and it was defined as the face that one would show to the world, the proper behaviors and actions that one would be expected to exhibit; the latter meant the "true sound" of one's spirit, the inner thoughts and impulses that could rarely, if ever, be shared. Often, *tatemae* and *honne* would be in direct opposition, but that could never be revealed. To do so would be to ir-revocably shame oneself.

Saito savored the whiskey, balancing on the razor's edge between the needs of his duty and the conflict against it. He knew full well the devil's bargain he had struck when he became an enforcer for the Combine. His only recourse was to silence his doubts, leave them behind.

The door to the Gulfstream's well-appointed bathroom slid open and Glovkonin stepped out, brushing a speck of talcum powder from the tailored cotton shirt he was wearing. Saito hid the glass in the bar, concealing his indiscretion, but not before the Russian noticed. The other man eyed Lau's sleeping form, then walked over to get a drink of his own.

"Is it done?"

Glovkonin found the same malt that Saito had sampled and poured some for himself.

Saito nodded. "There was resistance," he admitted. "But I was able to speak with Dane and the woman. I made the situation clear to them."

The Russian made a low, affirmative noise in the back of his throat.

"We may need to provide additional impetus, if they move too slowly."

"I do not believe that will be required."

Glovkonin raised an eyebrow. "How so?"

"You've met the Englishman."

"Briefly," came the dismissive answer. "He struck me as an insolent sort."

"True," agreed Saito. "But he has a code. Even against his own best interests, he will follow it."

As the words left his mouth, Saito realized that he could just as easily have been describing himself.

Did Glovkonin see that too? He smiled thinly.

"The details are open to interpretation. The only

variable that cannot change is Rubicon. Their hands must be on this." He walked away. "There are contingencies I can employ, of course, but it will be so much better if it comes from the African's little band of vigilantes."

Saito said nothing, holding back the questions that clamored for an answer.

The Russian sipped his drink, bending to look out through the oval window in the fuselage at the clouds passing beneath them.

"I have never believed in loyalty," he said, plucking the statement from the air outside. "What is it, really? It is too ephemeral to be the basis for a working relationship. But avarice? Fear? Those are solid. Men can be directed, trusted, relied upon, if you control those factors." He turned back to Saito. "I rely on you because I have control over what you fear."

Saito became very still, willing his face, his *tatemae*, to be as stone. He betrayed no sign of his *honne*, his inner truth.

"You look at what I tell you to do and you are conflicted," continued Glovkonin. "You and I work toward the Combine's goals, but here am I, undoing what they have put into motion. Sabotaging Verbeke's attack." He smiled and went on, as if narrating the moment. "*What must I do?* Saito asks himself . . ."

"I follow your orders," the mercenary said stiffly. "Without question."

"You don't see it now, but I am moving toward the betterment of all of us, including the Combine," said the Russian. "I am doing what others are reluctant to do." His glass empty, he put it back on the bar and met Saito's eyes. His gray, lupine gaze bored into the other man. "I do not need to appeal to your loyalty, your

sense of duty, or some abstract code to have you keep
your silence. You know what can be done. You know
what can be taken from you, yes?" Glovkonin did not
wait for him to answer. "Do what you do well," he went
on. "And perhaps one day your obligation will finally
be fulfilled."

— EIGHTEEN —

The black taxi deposited Marc at the intersection of Rue Antoine Dansaert and Boulevard de Nieuport, and he tossed the driver a fold of euros without waiting for any change, bolting from the back seat and out across two lanes of mid-morning traffic.

Narrowly avoiding a glancing hit from a passing car, he ignored the ensuing chorus of horns, and ran along the line of the canal. The tram route paralleled the boulevard and the waterway southward for almost a kilometer, but up from where the taxi had halted, the Vlaamsepoort stop was clearly visible. A handful of commuters and other locals sat or stood around open rain shelters, marking time before the next tram's arrival. Marc had to force himself to slow to an unhurried walk, trying to give the impression that he was some guy who didn't want to miss his ride, and not a man desperately searching the faces in front of him for Meddur al-Baruni.

He knew that somewhere further up the canal, Lucy was on her way to the warehouse that was mentioned in Saito's data-dump. Like Marc, she feared they were both walking into an ambush. He wouldn't put it past the Combine to lay a trap for the two of them, or run some game that would place the pair directly in harm's way.

That thought gave him pause. Marc had forced Lucy into this, and if something happened to her, the responsibility would be his.

But I can't do this alone, he told himself, dwelling briefly on the grim possibility. *The Combine like their schemes and gambits, they like playing chess with the lives of real people. I need her to even the odds.*

But this felt different from the previous encounters Marc had had with the agents of those shadowy power brokers. This particular game was authored by the Lion's Roar, with the Combine feeding money and opportunity to the ultra-right-wingers and their divisive, murderous ambitions. It was how the Combine always operated, one step removed from the dangers they unleashed on the world.

As he walked up the line of the platform, Marc saw the front page of that day's edition of *De Standaard* in the hands of a waiting commuter. He couldn't read the Dutch headline, but the images beneath it were from the tragedy in Benghazi, and it hardened his resolve.

A digital indicator board signaled that the next southbound tram was three minutes away. Marc pulled back his cuff to look at his watch. It was almost the top of the hour. Had he missed the man he was searching for? On the drive across town, he'd committed the target's face to memory, but now, as he swept his gaze over the people around him, the unsettling sense of something wrong crawled into his gut, threatening to become full-blown fear.

He was surrounded on both sides of the canal by four- and five-story buildings with countless windows, any one of which could hide a Lion's Roar gunman. Marc instinctively parsed his surroundings for escape routes, and his hand slipped under his jacket, to where his pistol was holstered.

Then a group of teenagers wandered away and revealed a man behind them, sitting alone on one of the shelter's benches. In a different city, in a different nation, the man was what intelligence analysts would call a "military-age male." Middle Eastern in appearance, dressed in shabby workman's jeans and a dark gray hoodie, he had a black nylon backpack cinched high and tight on his back. The man stared blankly at the weeds poking up around the tracks, his worried gaze turned inward.

Just as Saito had promised, Meddur al-Baruni was waiting for the tram. He didn't look like a killer.

Marc pretended to study a route map, watching the man from the corner of his eye. Now he had a line on his target, he was wary about closing in too fast. And then there was the possibility that the man might have Verbeke's watchers trailing him. None of the other people on the platform looked like the Lion's Roar type, but that wasn't a guarantee.

Marc's gaze was drawn toward the pack on al-Baruni's back. It was brand new, unlike the man's secondhand clothes, and when he shifted nervously, it moved like there was weight inside it. From this distance, Marc saw no signs of visible triggers, no wires leading into pockets or the like. Then the man pulled up his sleeve to look at his wrist, mirroring Marc's earlier action, and he saw something else that didn't match—a bulky smartwatch with an illuminated display. Was that the trigger, or something else?

One way to find out, he told himself.

Marc took out his smartphone, idly flicking at the screen as if he was swiping through a social media app, and wandered over to the bench where al-Baruni waited. Marc sat at the far end from the man, still absorbed by his phone. He had grown up in London, and he possessed the unconscious ability of all urbanites to be right next to another human being while completely ignoring their existence.

In reality, he was using the Rubicon spyPhone to send out experimental wireless pings to the man's smartwatch, and in a few seconds the scanning software in the phone registered that the other device was receiving incoming signals. Marc activated a mirror-effect program, a clever bit of code that he had stolen from a group of black-hat hackers Rubicon had tangled with the previous year, and the data going to the watch was paralleled on his phone.

The smartwatch wasn't a trigger; it was a control. The incoming information was a series of terse warnings: *Speak to no one. Do not raise suspicion. Avoid the police.*

The tram arrived, rolling to a halt, and the chatty gang of teenagers came back with the other commuters and crowded toward the doors, before stepping aboard. Marc's skin prickled as he became aware that the longer he sat on the bench and didn't move, the more suspicious he would appear.

Suddenly, the watch on al-Baruni's wrist let out a distinctive chime and the man flinched in surprise. He gripped the smartwatch as if it had shocked him, but a fraction of a second later the mirror program caused Marc's phone to emit the exact same noise. He'd been so quick to spin up the software, he had neglected to alter the alert settings.

The man shot him a frightened look. Reacting without thinking, Marc caught al-Baruni's eye and then it was too late.

The man shot up from the bench and shoved his way on to the busy tram car, even as the doors hissed closed. Marc was on his feet, but the tram was already moving, humming away toward the next stop. His target vanished into the press of the passengers and was gone from sight.

Marc had less than a second to react. There was no way he would be able to run and catch the tram at the next stop. The fitness regime that Rubicon's in-house wellness experts had imposed on Marc had done wonders for him, but he knew his limits. If he lost the target now, it would all be over.

He shoved his phone in his pocket, and as the last carriage of the tram rolled by, he jumped. Marc put one foot on the thick rubber bumper and his hands snatched at the single windscreen wiper on the rear window. The wiper was the only thing he could hang on to, and as the tram picked up speed, it bent out of shape and twisted in his grip. Marc drew himself in and hugged the bullet-nosed curve of the trailing carriage, hanging on for dear life as the boulevard flashed past on one side, and the waters of the Brussels–Charleroi canal ran deep on the other. Losing his footing would tip him into the path of oncoming traffic.

Marc saw a chubby face staring back at him through the rear window of the tram. All the other passengers were engaged in conversations, their newspapers or the screens of their phones. A baby girl in a sling over her mother's shoulder was the only passenger who seemed to notice Marc, and she stared blankly at the frantic determination on his face.

To Marc's dismay, the next station was closed for roadworks and the tram rolled right through it and kept on going. He could feel the wiper mechanism starting to part from the framework of the carriage, and for one horrible moment he visualized himself tumbling away to a messy end beneath the wheels of a cargo truck, with only that silent child seeing him go.

The tram juddered over a set of points and on to a

wide, tree-lined street before finally, mercifully, slowing to a halt at the next intersection. Marc dropped to the cobbles, massaging his hands, and ducked around the side of the carriage to get on board.

He saw the dark nylon backpack moving at the front of the tram, and tried to squeeze through the passengers embarking and disembarking to close the distance. He was four meters away when al-Baruni saw movement reflected on the inside of the windows, and he twisted, catching sight of his pursuer. The man burst into frantic motion once more, diving for the doors on the far side of the tram. He scrambled out into the street, and as Marc went after him, the doors began to fold shut.

Marc pushed up and caught the emergency exit button over the concertina-type doors before they could close, and they stuttered to a halt. He forced himself through the gap, trailed by irritable comments from the rest of the passengers, and hit the pavement a few meters behind his target. The man with the backpack was sprinting away down a side road, and Marc dashed after him, cursing inwardly.

All hope of a careful, controlled interception was blown. Meddur al-Baruni was a guided missile, and all Marc could do was try to catch the frightened man before he got to wherever the Lion's Roar had aimed him.

Indistinct, angry voices filtered out from the back of the parked truck, drawing Verbeke's attention. He could hear Ticker in there, yelling at the mule's wife.

The rest of the men working in the warehouse ignored the noise. They had seen and heard far worse from their brethren over the years, and not one of them would even consider lifting a hand to stop Ticker from slapping the foreigner around. All of them understood what these immigrants were worth. There were no soft hearts here, only stony glares where the mongrel invaders were concerned.

The phone in Verbeke's pocket rang and he raised it to his ear.

"Speak," he said.

Brewn's voice was rough and ragged with exertion.

"*The shopkeeper is dead,*" he began, using the group's derogatory codename for Elija Van de Greif.

"He won't be missed."

"*It wasn't deliberate. He was in the way. Call it a lucky bonus.*" Brewn gave a guttural cough. "*But there's been a fire. His place—it burned.*"

"You did that?"

"*Yes. Those two were there, the black woman and the English.*"

Verbeke frowned. Now he had confirmation that Saito had been truthful with him, he knew his first instinct to withdraw was right. He looked around. The tear-down would soon be complete, and out on the canal, a pair of fast boats had arrived and were in the process of mooring up.

"Are there police at the fire?"

"*Yes,*" repeated Brewn. "*We left before they saw us. What do you want me to do?*"

"Did you lose anyone?"

"*A couple of guys. We had to leave them there.*" There was a pause. "*The woman and the Englishman escaped.*"

His first thought was to berate Brewn for his failures, but he rode down the instinct, gripping the phone until his knuckles whitened.

"Listen to me. Forget the shopkeeper. I need you to locate the mule and shadow him. Keep your distance, understand?"

"*Why?*" Brewn seemed worried.

"If those two are still around, they'll be looking for the mule. Protect him until he gets to where he needs to be."

"*But . . .*" He could almost hear Brewn frowning. "*What about the . . . thing? If we're close when it goes off—*"

"You'll be safe," Verbeke lied smoothly. "Axelle has a cure. She's dosing everyone here. You'll get a shot when you get back." Before the other man could say more, he wound up the conversation. "Get to Place de la Bourse, to the Irish pub on the corner. Wait there. Follow the mule when you see him."

Brewn started to say something else, but Verbeke cut him dead and ended the call. Axelle stood behind him, drawn by hearing the mention of her name.

"There isn't any cure for Shadow," she said, cocking her head. "The Marburg virus doesn't work like that. You either survive it, or you don't. Mostly the latter."

"Brewn's not much of a reader," Verbeke replied, with a sneer. "He won't know any different."

Axelle gave a dismissive shrug.

"*Victimes de la guerre.*"

Verbeke rounded on her, irritated by her tone.

"The Japanese was telling the truth," he snapped. "Those Rubicon idiots are alive, and they're here. Van de Greif is dead, the gallery burned down." His hands opened and closed into heavy fists. "This is what happens when I delegate." He walked to her, looming over the pale woman. "You couldn't just fucking kill them . . ."

"I only did what you told me to—"

Axelle's words choked off in a high-pitched yelp as
Verbeke slapped her hard across the face, drawing a
curl of ruby blood from her lip. The blow had enough
force behind it that she almost stumbled to the cracked
concrete, but the woman held her ground, clutching at
her face.

None of the men paid even the slightest bit of attention to the casual violence. They, like Verbeke, knew the
worth of the woman.

"Don't ever talk back to me." He pointed toward one
of the trucks, as Ticker climbed out of the back. "I'll
give you another chance to do something right, and this
time don't screw it up."

"The wife and the children . . ." She gave a brittle
smile at the thought.

He nodded. "Get rid of what we don't need."

Some up-and-coming urban professional had made the
mistake of leaving their Piaggio MP3 unsecured, in a
side alley off the Sablon main drag. It was a mistake
Lucy was quick to exploit, and she had the reverse-trike
running in a matter of seconds, before gunning the motor and shooting out into the traffic. The moped wasn't
a patch on the Ducati racing bike she usually favored,
but current circumstances meant making allowances.

As the rush of the wind caressed her close-cropped
hair, she automatically leaned into it, reducing her cross-
section to cut down air resistance. The Piaggio was
nimble, and she threaded it between the larger, slower-
moving vehicles in her path. Every minute or so, her
eyes flicked to the smartphone clipped to the moped's
tiny dashboard, where a military-grade GPS mapping
application laid out a minimum-timeline path for her.
She wove down narrow side streets and around skinny

iron bollards, taking shortcuts along alleyways until
they spat her out back on to a main road. Soon the
character of her surroundings changed, the densely
packed tenement buildings replaced by the shells of derelict light industry and disused warehouses. Lucy saw
blinks of sunlight off the canal to her right and knew
she was in the right place. On the phone screen, the display told her she was almost at her destination. She
diverted into a turning and pulled up well short of her
target.

Stowing the Piaggio behind a clump of overgrown
bushes, she crouched low and dropped her bag off her
shoulder. There were no pedestrians around—in fact,
there was precious little sign of anyone at all, which
was likely why the Lion's Roar had chosen this as their
staging area in the first place. That was fine. If things
went sideways, having a background clear of civilians
would make Lucy's job a lot easier.

Working quickly, she unfolded the hinged metal
form of the XAR Invicta assault rifle in the bag, and
surveyed her target through the weapon's scope. The
body of the moped and the shade from the bushes kept
her in shadow, allowing her to glass the length of the
warehouse across the street.

The rusting corrugated metal walls supported a low,
sloped roof, and windows sprayed carelessly with black
paint were visible every few feet. The only angle inside came to her through an exposed truck entrance,
through a roller door that seemed to be jammed three-
quarters open. She could make out figures moving
around, in the process of loading gear into the back of
one of two weather-beaten Isuzu box trucks.

Lucy scoped their faces and she knew she was in the
right place. These men had the hard, cold manner of career thugs, and every one of them was dressed in simi-

lar fashion. Army surplus jackets in decade-old NATO camo, black jeans, steel-toed work books. Some had tattoos on their faces, most likely prison ink.

A charming bunch, she thought, *in town for the monthly lace-making circle.*

The grim smirk on her face faded when she heard a woman scream. From out of nowhere, a woman in a dark brown hijab came stumbling after a young boy as the kid tried to make a run for it. A similarly dressed girl trailed at her heels, her hands pressed to her face.

Lucy's whole body tensed as the scene unfolded. Some of the men dropped what they were carrying and jogged up to corral the boy before he could get too far. The woman cried out, screaming at the kid to run away. But he staggered to a halt, menaced by the men, and threw a panicked look out toward the open door. Lucy had a good look at the boy's terrified face. Then a tall, muscular man came into sight.

Verbeke.

The sneering brutish grimace on his face was the same expression he'd worn in Iceland, and Lucy let the XAR's cross hairs settle on his chest. For a second, she played with the idea of putting a shot through him, but held off. The scope on the folding rifle had not been sighted in, and at this range there was too great a chance of her shot going wide and clipping the woman or the girl.

The men surrounding the kid shepherded him back toward the trucks like he was an errant dog, and as Lucy watched, Verbeke rewarded the boy's mother with a punch in the gut, shouting at the girl when she tried to intervene. He shoved the three of them over to the truck and forced them inside with the threat of more violence, before moving out of sight behind the vehicle.

Marc had sent her the photos of Meddur al-Baruni's

family from Saito's FTP site. A woman, a teenage girl, a young boy. If the Brit was right, then Lucy was looking at the leverage being used to make the man carry a bioweapon for these vicious extremists.

Icy fury settled in her chest. All through the ride out here, the analytical, tactical element of Lucy Keyes as covert operative had been weighing the pros and cons of what she was doing. It felt like a set-up.

Hell, it *was* a set-up, because she had looked in Saito's eyes as the son-of-a-bitch put a dagger in her belly back in Somalia, and in that instant she had known exactly what kind of man he was. Calculating. Detached. Focused. And not the kind of man to do anything without a good reason.

Lucy thought she would be walking into a trap. But unless what she had seen was some elaborate bit of theater designed to kick her in the feels, she was fast coming around to the idea that this was a real hostage situation. One where the people with guns to their heads were not just Meddur's family, but the whole population of Brussels.

Through the scope she saw another face she wouldn't forget any time soon. Axelle, that Goth-looking bitch with the French accent and bad attitude, directed another pair of Lion's Roar meatheads to carry something hefty and dump it in the back of the same truck. It was a piece of industrial equipment, tightly wrapped in polythene and duct tape, and after a second Lucy realized she was looking at the second stolen bioprinter.

One of the thugs climbed into the box truck's cab and Axelle did a circuit of the vehicle, securing the doors before taking the passenger seat. Then it was moving, rolling up through the open doorway and on to the street.

Lucy dropped into a prone stance, willing herself

to vanish into the backdrop of the bushes. The truck ground gears and rumbled past her, heading northwest.

As a soldier, what had kept Lucy Keyes alive was the ability to make a split-second decision and commit to it; to negate doubt and embrace her choice without hesitation and trust fully in her training. The choice she *wanted* to make was to get into that warehouse across the street and kill everyone in there, starting with Noah Verbeke.

Ji-Yoo Park's grisly death still resonated in her mind, and Lucy couldn't help but dwell on what might have gone through the scientist's thoughts in those last agonizing seconds. Everything promised to her, every piece of her new and better life, Verbeke had destroyed. Lucy wanted to make him pay for that.

Fuck detachment. Fuck that warrior Zen controlled-emotion bullshit.

More than anything Lucy wanted to burn the thuggish murderer down for all that he had done.

Her odds were middling. She was a crack sharpshooter, even with a non-zeroed rifle. But given time and application, Lucy could put a world of hurt on those Lion's Roar pricks, maybe even put Verbeke down right here and now. Would that stall the release of the Shadow virus? She had no way of knowing, but a world without Verbeke in it was infinitely better than the alternative.

Of course, if she went in there, the wife and the kids in the truck would be dead by the time the smoke cleared. There was no doubt of that in Lucy's mind. Axelle was taking them away to be disposed of, three more innocents cut down as collateral damage in the twisted campaign of extremism that the Lion's Roar was fighting.

The deaths of Park, her husband and stepson were

marks on Lucy's butcher bill, they were her weight to carry. And try as she might to ignore it, the thought of adding three more to that tally made her sick inside.

No choice, she told herself.

The XAR rifle went back into her bag and Lucy revved the Piaggio's engine, hauling it around to speed after the retreating truck.

The target jackknifed around a sharp corner and Marc had to sprint across the street to get after him.

The man with the black backpack ducked into a narrow one-way street barely wide enough for a single vehicle, moving fast and low past lines of cars nestled in residential parking bays. Marc lost sight of him for a vital few seconds and when he rounded the corner, Meddur al-Baruni was gone, as if the earth had opened up and swallowed him whole.

Panting, Marc slowed his headlong run and tried to take in everything at once. Security doors covered every entrance spilling out on to the street and the windows he could see were closed. The street was full of apartments, and at this time of the day most of the people who lived there were out. He stopped, forcing himself to breathe evenly and *listen*. Filtering out the sound of traffic a block away, Marc strained to pick out a panicked stumble or the scuff of a boot on a cobble.

Faintly, in the direction of the far end of the street, he heard a digital chime and then the smartphone in his pocket made the same noise. Marc snatched at the device and looked at the screen. The mirroring software tracking the input to the smartwatch on al-Baruni's wrist was still working, but the range was limited. The display showed a directional indicator arrow, telling the man to keep moving northeast through the area around Avenue de Stalingrad.

If the phone was picking up the input, then it meant the target was less than ten meters away. Marc moved forward, stalking his prey, and spotted a likely place to hide. Building work was a constant throughout the city, and to the right of the street an old town house was in the process of being gutted. Wire fences kept it inaccessible from the pavement, but there were stacks of plasterboard and metal scaffolds waiting to be taken inside, piled high enough for a man to hide behind them.

He saw a shadow that looked like a crouching person and he slipped in behind it.

"Meddur!" he called, in a sharp, loud voice. "Don't move."

In the second it took Marc to realize he was actually talking to a black polythene bag full of builder's debris, a figure burst from cover behind him, swinging a short length of steel scaffold pipe.

Al-Baruni cried out and swung the pipe hard, but he timed his hit badly and struck Marc after having spent most of the momentum of the blow. Still, Marc took a hard hit that cracked his knee and he fell against the fencing, losing precious seconds as the other man took off at a run once again.

"Shit!"

Marc scrambled to his feet and staggered after him, jags of hot pain sparking down his leg. Al-Baruni slid over the hood of a parked car and into the next intersection, veering away around the base of a building with a giant comic art mural painted up along one wall.

The man was gaining distance. Turning the corner, Marc pulled the Glock from its holster and shouted al-Baruni's name again, swinging up the gun to take aim.

Could he shoot to wound, try for a leg shot and bring him down? The clearer play was to put a round in the middle of the man's torso, but that meant firing right at the backpack and whatever was inside it.

Al-Baruni twisted, throwing a look back, and he froze when he saw the pistol. He held up his hands, palms open. There was no dead man's switch, no trigger unit.

"Stop running!" shouted Marc, his voice echoing off the walls of the empty side street.

"I'm sorry . . ." the man called back, and his expression shifted between abject fear and terrified determination as he girded himself to flee again. "*I can't!*"

Marc's finger tightened on the trigger, but in the next second a loud crash sounded. The heavy wooden door across the entrance of an apartment house between the two men slammed open, and a group of laughing students spilled out on to the street. Marc immediately concealed the Glock in the folds of his jacket before anyone saw the weapon, and over the heads of the group he saw al-Baruni cut across into another alleyway and disappear.

The students flowed past him. They were dressed for fun, some of them carrying musical instruments, all of them happy and blissfully unaware of how much danger their city was in. He watched them go before limping back to the main street, scowling as he walked off the pain from the knee hit.

Wincing, Marc looked at his smartphone. The target was well out of range now, but the mirror program retained the last bit of data it had captured, the direction arrow pointing northeast.

A straight-up foot chase isn't going to get this bloke, Marc told himself. *Think smarter. Where's he going?* He opened a mapping application and zoomed out to get a bird's-eye view of downtown Brussels. *The bet-*

*ter question would be where are they sending the poor
bastard?*

The map suggested an unpleasantly large number of
potential target sites within a few minutes' walk. Shopping malls off Boulevard Anspach, a multiplex cinema,
a dozen different churches, and several métro stations.

The latter represented one of the nastiest options for
a bioweapon. Brussels and its underground rail system
was no stranger to terror attacks, having weathered a
bombing in 2016 that killed fourteen people, as part
of a double-header strike on the city and its airport by
the Islamic State. Would the Lion's Roar risk having al-
Baruni run the gauntlet of the increased security?

There was no way to be sure, but if Marc was right
about what the man was carrying, the weapon's discharge would be capable of killing hundreds, possibly
thousands more than the 2016 bombs. He felt a sickly
chill as he imagined the Shadow virus being propagated
through the métro's tunnels and air conditioning system, giving it a massive potential infection base.

The only way to stop al-Baruni would be to get ahead
of him, intercept him before he reached whatever arbi-
trary trigger point Verbeke had decided for the attack.
Thinking quickly, Marc plotted a route and hailed the
first taxi that passed him by.

"Take me there," he snapped, flashing his phone to
show the driver a point on Rue du Midi, less than a
kilometer north. "Do it in under two minutes and I'll
pay you double the meter."

"Seatbelt, please," said the young Kenyan behind the
wheel, with a grin.

The cab shot away from the curb and Marc watched
the streets flash past.

He was taking a big risk by breaking visual contact
with his target and hoping to reacquire al-Baruni in a

different location. If the follow had been set up by any conventional agency, there would have been a dozen agents in the field, cars on call and rolling coverage to ensure the subject never once knew he was under surveillance. All of that was an impossibility for Marc on his own, his circumstances forcing him to improvise.

There was a peculiar kind of excitement that came over him in moments like this one, when he balanced on the razor edge between success and failure. Was it wrong to admit that he felt energized by it? Marc's pulse raced. He felt alive, focused. He had purpose here, in this one instant, more than anywhere else in his life.

But beneath that surge of adrenaline lurked a black abyss. Marc Dane had pushed his luck more often than anyone had a right to, and this time he had crashed out. That terrible night in Iceland when Park had been murdered, when he and Lucy had been left to die of exposure—all of that spun out of his belief that he could roll the dice and come up a winner. Now he was in the same place, making the same kind of gamble, only the stakes were infinitely higher.

This time, if he failed, it wouldn't just be a handful of lives that were lost. The death toll would be catastrophic.

"Here we are," announced the driver, bringing the taxi to a sharp halt. "You know, if you're so eager to see the Manneken Pis, he's around the corner from here . . ."

The Kenyan pointed in the direction of the city's famous ornamental fountain.

"Sightseeing later."

Marc paid what he promised before scrambling back out on to the cobbles. He found a tabac shop with a broad glass frontage that mirrored the rest of the intersection in its window, and placed himself off the line of sight, standing in a half-shadow beneath an awning. And he waited.

Another two minutes passed before a familiar figure emerged from a side street. Marc felt a surge of relief; this time he'd chosen right.

Al-Baruni looked around furtively, but his gaze passed right over Marc's back without seeing him, and he kept on walking.

From the far side of the street, Marc watched him march dejectedly on his way, still heading northeast in the direction of the Bourse, the elegant Neo-Palladian building that was home to the Brussels Stock Exchange. Beyond that was the heart of the city's historic district, and on any given day it would be swarming with tourists.

Marc gave his target as much of a lead as he dared, and then set off after him. The gun in his waistband was heavy, and he felt the weight of every bullet in the magazine.

If I can't convince al-Baruni to surrender ... If I can't stop him in time ...

To prevent this day from becoming a nightmare, he might have to kill an innocent man.

Verbeke chose a Škorpion machine pistol from the gun case and loaded the weapon's stubby sickle magazine, ratcheting the side to make it ready. He cast around, watching Ticker and the others load the last of the gear into the rear of the remaining truck. The tents were being dismantled, and soon enough there would be little trace of the Lion's Roar in the decrepit warehouse.

Still, it was going more slowly than he wanted, and

his frustration warred with his need to get moving. He forced the Škorpion into a bulky pocket and glared at his watch. There was an overpowering appeal to witnessing the effects of his brutality up close, a fixation that Verbeke had never grown out of. He wanted to remain in the city's confines long enough to see the first immigrant mongrel coughing up blood on the afternoon news. But now that plan was being disrupted by Rubicon, forcing him to move up the timetable.

That same vicious instinct *wanted* them to come here, if he was honest with himself. He wanted the Englishman and the American to know it was him behind this, to see his face before he put a bullet through theirs. Anything less would leave him unfulfilled, his violent impulses swirling around, waiting to be spent on anyone who crossed him in even the smallest of ways.

When his cell phone rang, he barked out his answer. "What?"

"*Problem here,*" said Brewn. Street sounds and background traffic noise made it clear he was in the middle of the city. "*Got the mule zeroed, but he has company. The Englishman is following him.*"

"You're sure?"

"*See for yourself.*"

The phone pinged. Brewn had sent him a photo message.

The image was taken from across the road, but it clearly showed the male Rubicon agent walking by the Bourse's tiered steps. His face half-hidden beneath a dark cap, the Englishman was looking at his own smartphone.

"Has he seen you?"

"*Not yet.*"

For a moment, Verbeke toyed with the idea of having them drag the man back here, so he could have the enjoyment of personally ending him. But the operation was too important. He would have to find something else to take out his frustration on.

"*Orders?*"

"Kill him," said Verbeke. "Do it quietly, out of sight."

— NINETEEN —

The box truck swayed around a series of tight corners before veering down a curved concrete ramp. Lucy dropped back, slowing, holding the moped at a distance for fear of being spotted. The road they were on paralleled a long cutting where the city's métro lines crossed, but the ramp was off to one side, away from the main working tracks.

Pulling to a halt at the top of the incline, Lucy watched the truck push through a set of gates held shut with a weak chain, the metal splitting with a sharp shriek. The drifts of trash and windblown debris along the edges of the ramp made it clear this part of the métro system wasn't in regular operation.

Leaving the Piaggio on the road, Lucy moved down after the truck, staying to the shadows. The lurching vehicle reached track level, bouncing over the steel rails until it came to a sharp halt, half-inside a disused tunnel. Down there, with the only daylight coming in beneath concrete baffles and rusty wire fencing, it was difficult to get a good read on what was going on. But the moment the truck's engine died, Lucy heard the cries coming from the back of the vehicle, the sound of fists banging on the inside of the box frame.

She dropped to one knee and unfolded the XAR

rifle, bringing it smoothly to her shoulder and sighting into the gloom.

The truck rocked as the bearded, heavyset driver climbed out. He stood by the cab, reaching back in to gather something up, and around the front of the vehicle came the pale lady herself, a compact machine pistol hanging over the shoulder of her black jacket. Lucy tracked Axelle, evaluating the situation.

The woman walked over to where a dark tarpaulin had been draped over something large, and she whipped off the cover like it was a magic trick, revealing a pair of Yamaha SR400 street bikes and crash helmets that had been stashed there.

If they're changing vehicles, this has to be the end of the line for the hostages.

As if to confirm Lucy's conclusion, the guy with the beard walked along the length of the truck with a heavy jerrycan in his grip, throwing splashes of liquid from it up the side of the vehicle and over the tires. The banging noise from the cargo box grew frantic as the faint odor of gasoline reached Lucy's nostrils.

The man gave the can a final shake and discarded it below the doors to the rear of the truck. Backing away, he fished inside his coat and came back with the fluorescent tube of a road flare. Lucy put the XAR's cross hairs on him as he fiddled with the cap, hitting the flare's striker.

She let out half a breath and waited for her opportunity. The wrong angle, and the man would fall into the puddle of fuel and it would all be over.

The flare ignited with a pulse of bright red-orange flame, throwing jumping patterns of crimson over the concrete walls of the railway cutting, and in the same moment Lucy's finger tightened on the trigger. She sent a round through the joint in the thug's right knee, cutting his legs out from under him with the shock. He fell

screaming and the flare bounced away, spitting fumes
and infernal light.

Lucy traversed, swinging to aim at Axelle, but the
pale woman was faster off the mark than she expected.
Axelle's Škorpion pistol brayed on fully automatic fire,
a fan of .32 ACP bullets chopping up the dusty ramp
toward Lucy's position.

The rounds sparked off the concrete and Lucy leaped
away, moving and firing her rifle from the hip. She zig-
zagged, avoiding the burst from Axelle's gun, then
vaulted over the lip of the ramp's lower half and down
into the shadows of the métro rail siding.

Jumping into the dark was never a good idea. There
was no way to know what you would land on, and a
bad fall now would put Lucy down as cleanly as a bullet. Flat-footed, she hit the shingle piled alongside the
disused rails and the impact was jarring, almost enough
to knock her off balance. But Lucy was nimble and she
turned the momentum into forward motion, scrambling across the track.

The man Lucy had shot was shouting in pain, writhing
on the ground and calling out, but his companion did
nothing to help him. Axelle was more interested in killing
the interloper, and she didn't allow Lucy to find cover.

She came around behind the truck, still firing, brack-
eting Lucy with shots, and trying to keep her on the defensive. The snarl of gunfire echoed off the low roof
and down the shadowy métro tunnels.

It was a smart play, but Delta Force trained its operatives to work under live fire conditions and keep their
cool. Lucy Keyes was no different. Before Rubicon,
she had been a Tier One specialist in Delta's covert
all-female Foxtrot Troop, and the hard training that
had been drilled into her there was second nature. The
whine of bullets at close quarters was music she knew

well, and it didn't stop her from firing back. Her rifle chugged and Axelle ducked behind a set of wood and steel buffers. The woman fired once more, and there was an echoing *clack* of metal on metal as she finally emptied the Škorpion's magazine.

With the brilliant, blinding light of the flare ruining her low-light vision, Lucy could only see the jagged, moving shadows of the injured man on the ground and Axelle, half-concealed behind the buffer stand.

She had only precious seconds to exploit the lull in the firefight. Lucy dashed forward, swinging the XAR rifle back over her shoulder on its sling, drawing her Glock semi-automatic. She put down a few rounds to keep her attacker in cover, the sound reverberating off the walls, and broke into a run.

In the quiet between bursts of gunfire, the hostages inside the truck continued their cries for help. Lucy heard the piercing wail of a terrified child, and knew it had to be Meddur al-Baruni's son, the frightened little boy she had seen earlier. Every second they remained trapped inside there was a second closer to a grisly death, and that she could not allow.

Not this time. Not again.

On the far side of the rail siding stood a series of rectangular support pillars, and Lucy used them as concealment, slipping from one to the other, breaking Axelle's line of sight so the pale woman wouldn't know where to aim. Moving deeper into the tunnel, the hellish illumination thrown out by the hissing road flare turned everything into a two-tone world of flickering red and fathomless black. She moved slow and steady, careful to spread her weight as she walked over the wooden sleepers between the rails and the heaps of loose stone chippings around them. The jumping motion of the flare's flame threw moving shadows on the walls, threatening to distract Lucy from any real target.

She circled back toward the truck, the stink of gasoline hitting her again. The wounded man was on the far side, making an attempt to drag himself away. Snarling in pain with each movement, gravel rattling as he hauled his ruined leg after him, he continued to call out for Axelle's help. Wherever she was, she continued to ignore him.

Lucy stopped and peered into the wavering shadows, looking for something that made a human shape.

Loose stones clattered behind Lucy and she pivoted, fast and graceful. It wasn't fast enough to avoid Axelle flying at her from the dark, like a pale-faced vampire bursting from a grave.

The woman had her crash helmet in one hand and swung it like a wrecking ball, cracking Lucy hard across the cheekbone. Her head snapped back with a flash of sharp pain at the base of her skull and she staggered. There was no sign of Axelle's machine pistol, but with her free hand the pale woman grabbed Lucy's gun arm in a vise-like grip, razor-sharp nails biting into her wrist.

By sheer reflex, Lucy's finger twitched on the Glock's trigger and a shot went wild, sparking off a far wall. She pushed through the disorientation from the blow to her head and tried to turn into the other woman's attack, but Axelle was quicker than she expected, nimble and sinuous. She threw out a punch, but she might as well have been fighting smoke. In the half-dark, the pale woman got behind Lucy and snared the XAR rifle where it still hung over her shoulder.

Axelle fought to pull her off balance again as they still struggled for control of the pistol. The razor nails dug into nerve points beneath Lucy's flesh, drawing blood, and her hand jerked unexpectedly. The Glock barked twice more, this time the bullets going into the frame of the box truck. The cries of the captives inside became screams.

Then the rifle's two-point sling snapped up and caught Lucy across the throat. The webbing pulled painfully tight and she felt Axelle's shoulder in her back as the woman began to strangle her with the gun strap.

Lucy tried to pull in a breath, but nothing came.

Marc kept his Rubicon spyPhone clasped tightly in one hand, holding it inside the pocket of his jacket. He drew in, his body language deliberately low-key, keeping his baseball cap down over his brow as he walked along the cobbled street.

Up ahead, on the far side of a knot of German tourists, Meddur al-Baruni continued his dejected, fearful trudge, moving off the main streets and toward the historic quarter. The man hung on to the straps of the pack on his shoulders as if it contained the weight of the world, and every few dozen steps he cast a furtive look at the bulky smartwatch on his wrist.

Marc felt his phone vibrate each time the man received an update on his directions, as the software intercepted the same signal. This time, he had switched off the audible message cue, for fear that it could alert his quarry once again. But for the moment, al-Baruni seemed to think he had lost his tail, and Marc wanted to keep it that way.

He felt sorry for the man. He had to be overwhelmed by everything that was happening to him, trapped in this foreign city and forced into this act by those without conscience. But unless Marc could find a way to reach him and get his lethal payload away, Meddur al-Baruni would go down in history as the lynchpin of the worst terrorist atrocity to strike continental Europe.

He would have to act soon. It was late morning now, and the streets were filling up. Shoppers, locals, tourists, and people dining out at curbside cafes were everywhere Marc looked. Again he saw more students like the ones he'd encountered before, these ones carrying guitar cases and passing out brightly colored flyers. Marc took one and studied it. There were similar posters around advertising a week-long music festival at numerous venues around Brussels. Any one of them would be an ideal place to trigger the Shadow device.

As he tucked the leaflet in his pocket, Marc's target passed the mouth of an alley, and a man stepped out and came to a halt in the middle of the street. He glared straight at Marc as al-Baruni walked on, oblivious to the man's appearance. The guy had a face like a clenched fist, hairless and tracked with scars, and he was wearing what Marc had now come to consider the Lion's Roar "uniform"—work boots, army surplus trousers and a dark jacket in a military cut.

He was staring Marc down, challenging him to react.

They must have made me when I caught up with al-Baruni, he thought. *And if there's one of them . . .*

His gaze flicked left and right, before it zeroed in on another figure captured in the reflection of a shop selling tacky souvenirs. A second man with stringy brown hair in the same kind of outfit was trailing Marc, just as he had been following al-Baruni.

Too busy watching your target to check yourself, Dane, he admonished silently.

When he had been recruited to MI6, the instructors at Fort Monckton had trained them in dozens of scenarios like this one, and the rule was: if you were spotted by your target or by enemy operatives, you disengaged immediately.

That wasn't an option here. If he lost al-Baruni in the crowds of tourists, there was a good chance he would never be able to find him again. But he couldn't get caught by two of Verbeke's bruisers in broad daylight either.

To Marc's right was a shabby indoor shopping mall with kiosk-like compartments selling cheap imported goods. He pivoted smartly toward it, and stepped through the entrance. The instant he was out of the eyeline of Verbeke's men, he broke into a run. The cramped mall was a far cry from the posh arcade of the Royal Galleries a few blocks away, with its fancy chocolatiers and ritzy perfume stores. This place was gloomy, packed with stalls selling knock-off designer handbags, noisy plastic toys or paraphernalia for those who liked a little ganja. What they did have in common was multiple entrances and exits, and Marc turned a corner down one narrow passage toward what he thought would be a way out.

His path was blocked by a wall of temporary metal fencing that rose to the low ceiling, cordoning off part of the building that was under construction. The unpleasant possibility that he had made a serious mistake started to form in Marc's thoughts.

He headed back the way he had come, this time cutting across a silent food court in front of a shuttered burger bar, and the reason why the mall was so ill-lit quickly became clear.

Apart from a handful of kiosks near the entrance, manned by bored-looking shopkeepers, the rest of the complex, tiny precinct was closed up. Roller doors were down on every alcove, and the overhead lights were switched off. Despite it being broad daylight outside, the only illumination was what leaked in from the entrance vestibule. More of the metal fences were visible down another corridor, and Marc heard the thud and bang of workers busy on the floors above as they knocked down walls and carted away rubble. Half the place was being rebuilt, it seemed. The smell of plaster dust and fresh concrete hung heavy in the air.

Staying low, Marc looked back toward the entrance and found the balding thug standing sentinel just inside the door, like a bouncer at a dingy nightclub. His comrade was following the same path Marc had taken, peering into the dead-end passage.

The only other route was a fourth corridor that led around to the far side of the building, and Marc went for it. He gave his smartphone a quick look. The device had gone silent. With no line of sight to al-Baruni, the mirroring software had nothing to track, and he hoped that didn't mean the target was lost for good. Marc stuffed the phone in his back pocket and turned the corner, hoping to find another way out of the darkened mall.

Another temporary fence was waiting for him across the locked doors, a sheet-metal portcullis that was far too heavy for one person to move.

Had this been the plan all along? He wondered if the Lion's Roar thugs had chosen this moment to reveal themselves, because they knew they could herd Marc in here and deal with him out of sight.

I don't want to stick around to find out.

Searching about in the dimness, he found a shopfront with a shutter that didn't quite reach to the sloped floor. There was enough room for him to get his fingers underneath and he pulled it up, giving it all he had. The roller door let out a pained creak and rose half a meter, enough that Marc could get beneath the lip and shoulder it open a little more. The shutter finally jammed in its runners at a steep angle, but there was room enough to squeeze under.

The noise was going to attract the thugs, but at this point there was nothing else Marc could do. The distinctive smell of freshly cut leather hit him inside the cluttered little shop. Crammed in there were dozens of black plastic showroom dummies, decked out in long rigs, biker gear and jackets of every hue and design. Marc had to push through the unmoving throng, past a glass display counter filled with matching spiked bracelets, sculpted collars and zircon-covered chokers. In the gloom, he picked out a door that he hoped would lead to a back alley, and a way out.

He kicked the lock off the door and it opened halfway, revealing a space beyond that was filled from floor to ceiling with bags of unsold goods. If there was an exit in there, it was buried under half a ton of poorly made bolo jackets and studded chaps.

Out in the corridor, heavy footfalls were coming closer. Marc shrank back into the crowd of dummies, peeling off his baseball cap and setting it on the head of a male mannequin in a long coat. He grabbed a dark red racer jacket off a rack, and held it in front of him like a shield to break up his silhouette.

Letting out a breath, he froze, blending into the ranks of human-shaped shadows. For a moment, he thought about the Glock semiautomatic holstered inside his waistband. The gun would make short work of this, but using it in here would bring the police in moments. A single shot would echo like a thunderbolt, and Lucy had neglected to pick up any sound suppressors along with the weapons.

Last resort, then, he told himself.

The younger of the two thugs swung in under the

half-open shutter, his head swaying right to left as he peered into the darkness. His right hand was clamped around the grip of an ugly-looking combat knife. The weapon had a wickedly curved guard and a spiked spine that glittered in the gloom, looking more like something from a Hollywood action movie than an actual fighting tool. Still, the broad, polished blade had a keen edge that would go right through flesh.

Marc took advantage of the man's momentary distraction and nudged the stand holding up one of the dummies. The figure rocked and the thug instantly went for the decoy, shoving the other mannequins out of the way.

He was looking in the wrong direction when Marc came at him, leading with the jacket bunched over his fists.

Marc's Krav Maga teacher—a tough young Bosniak Muslim with an easy grin and a take-no-shit attitude—had always extolled the virtues of getting in one's retribution early, and while Dane had never been a top student, that lesson stuck. Marc fired a series of short, sharp punches into the thug's head before the man knew what was happening, the racer jacket acting like makeshift boxing gloves. He whipped it around, smacking him with the flapping sleeves, trying to keep him from regaining his balance. Marc stepped inside the thug's reach, shoving the jacket at his face, briefly blinding him.

The knife came up in a rising cut that Marc felt more than he saw, the low hum of its passing making him flinch backward. It was all the brown-haired man needed to turn the fight back his way and he advanced, making diagonal cuts in the air that caught on the leather, slashing it into red ribbons.

The blade was designed to intimidate, to make an opponent back away and give control of the fight to the wielder, but the thug was overextending his stance with each downward sweep. Still gripping the ruined jacket, Marc threw out a block and the knife bit into layers of leather, sawing through. It was a cut that would have gone straight to the bone through nerve and vein, but the jacket gave Marc some temporary protection, and the chance to score a shin kick and a follow-up punch to the ribs. The man grunted in pain and tried to pivot, but he collided with another of the mannequins and lost his footing.

Marc saw that and helped him along, shoving him face first into the clear-topped counter. Glass shattered and the thug reeled away, losing his blade in the dimness, desperately clamping his hands to his neck. He let out a wet, sucking gasp and Marc saw a jagged spar of plate glass protruding from his throat. Blood jetted from the fatal wound and the man tumbled back out into the darkened corridor, gurgling and choking.

Marc followed him, still clutching the torn jacket. The thug managed two or three steps down the tiled corridor, his blood spattering the dusty floor, before he toppled at the feet of his hard-faced comrade. The second man had come to find his buddy, but he didn't stop to give him any help. Instead, the older thug stepped over the dying man, letting a weapon of his own slide down from where it had been hidden up his sleeve.

The *Rambo* knife had been bad enough, but the scarred man had gone one better. He gripped the handle of a fat-bladed agricultural machete that was easily as long as Marc's forearm. The attack came fast and angry, in downward diagonal swoops that crossed over one another. What remained of the shredded jacket was cut in two as one slash connected at the collar and ripped it open. Marc threw one ragged punch at his assailant, desperately trying to extend the distance between the tip of the blade and his own throat, but he knew he didn't have anywhere to go.

He twisted toward the blocked entrance behind him, snatching at the Glock in his belt. *Last resort time* had come quicker than he expected. Marc heard the machete come down, skin-crawlingly close, the edge slashing open the jacket and shirt on his back.

A line of fire lit up across his shoulders, and Marc let out a cry. The shock of the pain made him stumble, even as his fingers found the butt of the Glock and pulled it free of its holster. Time turned fluid, slowing as fresh blasts of adrenaline shocked through his system.

The balding thug was still on the attack, both hands on the machete's handle now as he brought it down like a shortsword, aiming to plunge it into Marc's chest.

Marc jammed his pistol into the folds of what was left of the racer jacket and mashed the trigger. The torn crimson leather muffled the gunshot, and the bullet cut a gory divot out of the scarred thug's thigh. He cried out and faltered before he could make his killing blow. Marc didn't wait; he put two more shots into the man's chest and down he fell. The searing exhaust gases trapped in the torn jacket stung his hands and he shook the torn material away, hissing at the burn.

The stink of cordite, blood and burned leather hung in the air, and in the aftermath, the enclosed space of the dark shopping arcade felt close and oppressive.

Marc realized that the noise from the floors above had stopped.

Did someone hear the shots?

He stood up, and his fingers came back stained red when he probed the cut on his back. The steady burn of the wound pulsed as he moved, but he had been lucky. The cut was shallow, the brunt of the damage taken by his clothes, but he had nothing to dress it with.

Walk it off, said a voice in his head that could have belonged to Lucy Keyes.

Scrambling around, Marc recovered his cap and took another racer jacket, leaving the dead men where they had fallen.

Emerging back in the daylight, he saw some of the stall owners outside in a worried bunch, one of them speaking quickly into a cell phone. Marc pulled his Rubicon-issue device, working urgently at the touch-sensitive screen as he set off in the direction al-Baruni had been taking.

The copycat program duplicating every input sent to the smartwatch had caught one last thing before the connection dropped out. An audio message. Fearing the worst, Marc tapped the *play* tab and held the phone to his ear.

It was a woman speaking in Arabic, and she was terrified. Marc didn't understand the language but the tone was clear as day.

Help us.

It had to be the wife, he reasoned. The voice continued for a few seconds, and divorced from the ability to comprehend the actual words, Marc listened to the pace and rhythm of them. He looped the playback, losing himself in the sound.

Back at Six, one of Dane's sharpest skills had been his ability to "see the music" when confronted with a wall of intelligence data. There was a knack to it, being able to look at the big picture and see the spots where the notes didn't ring right. That same sense was being tweaked right now, as the panicked message played out. The shape of it seemed . . . *artificial*.

Like the video of Ji-Yoo Park's family, he thought. Dead for days but faked back to life by the Lion's Roar in order to make the scientist do their bidding.

Meddur al-Baruni was carrying a virus bomb because he believed his family would be killed if he didn't. But they might already be dead.

The dark, shadowed edges of the subway tunnel began to contract around Lucy, and the bloody color from the flare faded to gray.

Her brain was being starved of oxygen, the life being choked out of her by the thick gun strap tightening about her throat. Within a couple of heartbeats, Axelle would tip her over the edge into semi-consciousness and then Lucy would be at the mercy of the pale woman. And she would die down here, in this stale dead-air tunnel, left behind for the Belgian cops to find days or weeks from now . . .

No.

Blindly, Lucy snatched at the rifle strap and slid her fingers down it until she grasped the quick-release lock on the two-point harness, snapping it open with a flick of her wrist.

All the strangling tension around her neck vanished in an instant as the XAR rifle came loose and clattered to the ground. Color flooded back into Lucy's vision and she choked down a lungful of much-needed air.

Acting on angry impulse, Lucy struck out blindly at the assailant behind her with a reverse shoulder jab and cracked Axelle on the jaw. The blow was hard and direct, and the other woman gave a choked wail.

But still the pale woman held on to Lucy's gun hand, digging in her nails to draw blood, the fluid flowing freely from the new cuts. She hissed in pain, but didn't let up.

They spun about, coming together into a chaotic dance, skidding off the flank of the box truck. Trading blows, battling for control of the pistol, each of them tried to twist the weapon toward the other. Lucy's boot splashed in a pool of spilled gasoline as Axelle forced her back against the truck.

Neither woman held the clear physical advantage over the other. Lucy had the build of an Olympic runner, firm muscle and toned limbs married to stamina and core strength. Axelle was more like a dancer; hers was the illusive and willowy form of a ballerina with zero excess body mass. She was supple, but wire-hard with it, never putting a foot wrong.

Using her whole weight as a lever, Axelle curled around Lucy and forced the Glock back in the direction of her opponent's face. Lucy's finger was still locked on the pistol's trigger and before it passed a point of no return, she pulled hard. The gun barked, shooting a 9mm round uselessly into the concrete ceiling in a blink of muzzle flash. Lucy kept on mashing the trigger, the report of the shots elongating into one constant thunder, cordite stinging her throat, brass shell cases flicking away into the gloom. In the dimness, at such close range, the bright discharge from the barrel dazzled them both. Then the Glock's slide locked back and the gun was empty.

Axelle gave Lucy the opening she was desperately

searching for, a fractional, momentary relaxation of pressure as her opponent shifted weight. Lucy took the opportunity with a vengeance. Putting all the force she could muster into it, she jabbed across with the empty pistol, smacking the metal frame of the handgun into Axelle's head.

It was a good hit. The pale woman let out a pained, animal cry and reeled away. Lucy went on the offensive, spinning the Glock around to use it as a knuckle-duster, landing a punch that glanced off Axelle's arm, tearing a rip in her leather jacket. Blood streamed from a cut there, and more of it was drooling out of the pale woman's mouth, making her look demonic in the red light from the sizzling flare.

Hits and blocks passed between them, one after another, and Axelle swayed, briefly losing a beat. Another opening was too good to pass up, and Lucy leaned in, swinging for it.

Axelle's error evaporated. It was a feint, a deliberate misstep to draw Lucy in, and she had taken the bait. The woman fired off two brutally pitched sideswipe kicks that landed on Lucy's shin, exactly at the point where her stability was weakest. She lost balance and fell, down to the loose-packed gravel, hands splashing into the spilled fuel.

The pale woman used her momentum to pivot into another attack, coming in for the kill. Her leg snapped up into a spin kick, a lethal neck-breaker aimed straight at Lucy's throat.

Lucy threw up her bleeding, lacerated arm and caught the leg before the hit could connect, trapping it and twisting it with a wet crackle of fracturing bone. The motion tore Axelle's poise to shreds and she was forced into an uncontrolled tumble, slamming into the ground.

The pale woman's head struck the corner of a steel rail and she jerked as if she had been hit by an electric shock, but only for a moment. A low, long gurgle escaped her blood-colored lips and then she was still.

Wincing from the pain in her arm and her leg, Lucy dragged herself up into a crouch and took a shaky step toward Axelle. Her opponent stared blankly at the ceiling above them, dark blood seeping out into the shingle from her cracked skull.

Lucy clasped her wounded wrist, limping back toward the rear of the truck as the red flames from the flare abruptly shifted, throwing new voids of shadow across the walls. She heard heavy footfalls crunching on the gravel chippings and came face to face with the man she had shot through the knee.

"*Godverdomme doos!*" he spat.

He was red-faced with exertion and anger, supporting his ruined leg with a metal spar as an improvised walking stick. He brandished the crackling flare at her like it was a dagger.

"Sorry, don't speak needle-dick," she shot back.

"You can scream!" His English was thickly accented and sputtering. "I burn you alive!"

"Fuck."

Parts of her jacket and trousers were soaked through with gasoline. If a spark from the flare came close enough to ignite it, she would be a torch in seconds.

The guy saw the understanding in her eyes and he showed his teeth, revelling in the moment.

But then a piece of the shadows came alive behind the man and swarmed over him. Lucy glimpsed a dark-haired guy in a black hoodie come from out of nowhere and snake his arms around the thug's neck, dragging him away from her.

Caught by surprise, the thug panicked and flailed, but Lucy's silent rescuer pulled his arms into a lock and from a sleeve came the dull flash of light off a blade. The knife slid up through the soft flesh under the thug's jaw, and that was pretty much the end of it.

Twitching his last, the thug dropped in a heap, and the figure in the hoodie gathered up the flare before throwing it as far down the tunnel as he could.

"Uh . . . *thanks.*"

In the silence that followed, Lucy's eyes darted around, looking for anything she could use to defend herself. The Glock had gone, lost in the fight with Axelle.

The man in black rolled down his hood. A hard, Nordic face with a soldier's watchful eyes looked back at Lucy, and then she placed him. The last time she had seen this guy, they were in an unmarked police SUV on the tarmac at Keflavík Airport.

"Loki," she said, raising an eyebrow.

"That's not my name," he told her, but he didn't volunteer a correction.

The Viking Squad officer knelt by the body of the man he had killed and checked the thug's pockets.

"What the hell are you doing here?" Lucy demanded. "Don't get me wrong, happy to have the assist, but—"

"Did you really think that Larsson would let you and the Englishman leave, without some sort of assurance?" He didn't look up. "We are not stupid. We concealed a tracking device in your bag. I was on the first flight to Brussels after yours."

"Just you, or did you bring the God of Thunder as well?"

"Just me." He paused. "This is low profile. Viking

Squad has no authority to operate outside of Icelandic territory."

"And yet you did just kill someone."

"Arguably, a wanted terrorist responsible for crimes against my country," he corrected. "And you are welcome. For the record, I was told to keep my distance unless civilians were directly at risk." He found a set of keys and tossed them to her, nodding at the truck. "Here. Get them out."

Lucy walked back to the vehicle. The sounds from inside had gone ominously silent during the shooting.

"You didn't think about stepping in earlier to help out?"

Loki—she couldn't think of him any other way now—gave a non-committal shrug.

"I followed you into the city. Kept you under surveillance. When you split up from Dane, I chose to monitor you, as you are the more dangerous."

"I'll take that as a compliment."

"We need to inform the local police about this," he went on.

"Be my guest." She unlocked her smartphone and threw it to him. "But just stick to the basics."

As he worked the phone, the latch on the back of the truck opened with a squeal of hinges, and Lucy had to duck back to avoid being hit in the face by a blunt piece of wood wielded by a terrified woman in a hijab. She yelled rapidly in her native language, cursing them with every damning epithet under the sun.

"Whoa, sister!" Lucy held up her hands in surrender, catching sight of the teenage girl holding her little brother tightly in the shadows at the back of the cargo space. "I won't hurt you!" she called. "We're here to save you! I want to get you away from here, you understand? We're going to get you safe and find your husband!"

"Meddur?" The woman let her makeshift club drop, and spoke in halting English. "Where is he?"

"Someone I trust is looking for him right now." Lucy offered her hand. "I know you're scared, but you have to trust us. Please, come with me." She dug deep to recall the name of the wife from the data Saito had dropped on them. "You're Sakina, right? The kids are Aksil and Tadla? My name is Lucy." She jerked her thumb at the Icelandic cop. "You can call him Loki, like in the movies."

Sakina gathered her children to her and climbed out of the truck without any help, but then she stopped and took Lucy's arm, giving it a quick once-over.

"You are bleeding."

"It happens," she agreed, glancing in the direction of Axelle's body.

"God will judge her for her sins," said Sakina, her expression hardening as she saw the dead woman. Then she looked away, back to Lucy. "Your wrist, it must be bandaged. I am a nurse, I know this."

"We need to go," insisted the Icelander. "The police are on the way. I have a car up on the road. If we stay, there will be many questions which none of us want to answer."

He crouched in front of the little boy, offering to carry him and smartly distracting the kid from the sight of two dead people behind him. On a nod from his mother, Aksil climbed into Loki's arms and the five of them made their way back up the ramp.

"Where is Father?" said the wide-eyed girl, trailing along on her mother's arm. "Did they kill him?"

"I'm going to make sure that doesn't happen," Lucy

said firmly, even as stone formed in her chest, accreting around the words.

Another promise made, said an acid voice in the back of her thoughts. *Can you keep this one?*

"They sent him away to die," said the teenager, tears streaking her face.

"That is not true," said Sakina, putting on a brave face for the girl. "These people are going to help us, Tadla. They will bring him back."

A sudden thought occurred to Lucy as they reached a rented Nissan SUV parked on the curb.

"Sakina . . . do you know where Meddur is going?"

"No." The woman ignored the Icelander as he beckoned them into the vehicle, instead grabbing the Nissan's first aid kit to dress the cuts on Lucy's arm. "Those animals, they think we are stupid because our skin is a different color than theirs." She hesitated, holding back tears as she relived those moments. "But I saw something . . . The pale one had papers on her. A map."

Lucy didn't wait, and she bolted back down the ramp, the half-done bandage on her arm trailing off in streamers of white.

"Keyes!" The SR officer shouted after her. "There's no time! I hear sirens!"

Lucy heard them too, distant but getting closer by the minute.

"Don't wait for me!" she called. "Get on the road, I'll catch you up!"

Loki muttered something irritably under his breath and he jogged away. She paused briefly to haul one of the stowed SR400 bikes on to the railbed between the tracks, and then crouched by Axelle's body.

Lucy searched the dead woman. Just as Sakina had

said, there was a folded-up tourist map in her inside jacket pocket, the kind that sat in leaflet racks in bars, hotels and restaurants. She flicked it open, revealing a color-coded plan of central Brussels. Pre-planned exit routes from the city via road and canal were marked in red ink, along with three street intersections. One was the location of the waterfront warehouse, the second the disused métro tunnel.

The third was the target.

— TWENTY —

The first grasping claws of raw panic scraped over Marc's chest as he cast around the cobbled pedestrian street. He tried to look in every direction at once, feeling the cold run up through his veins. Wasting time dealing with the Lion's Roar thugs back in the shopping arcade had taken too long.

Marc swallowed hard, feeling sick inside at the thought of the horrors that would unfold if Meddur al-Baruni carried his deadly payload to its ultimate destination. The death and pain that had been unleashed on the streets of Benghazi would be repeated here in Brussels.

An awful paralysis threatened to engulf him.

Did I buck the odds one time too many? Is this fate balancing it out? Marc shook his head, angrily dismissing the bleak thought. *No. There's still time. We can still stop this.*

He threaded around the back end of the shopping arcade, past more fenced-off areas where construction was still under way on thick concrete pilings sunk into the ground. The narrow street opened out into a wide avenue, and the sound of jaunty music came up on the breeze. Somewhere ahead, a band was playing and people were clapping along.

Marc remembered the students he had seen before with their instruments, and the brightly colored leaflets being handed out. The festival taking place today was a freestyle celebration of the city's musical heritage, past and present. He followed the tune toward the growing numbers of a large crowd moving in the same direction, and those razor claws around his chest gripped tighter.

It became starkly obvious where Verbeke intended to trigger the second Shadow device. Before Marc was the perfect target—Grand-Place, the venerable old city square where temporary stages had been set up for bands to play their songs, where hundreds of people thronged together in close proximity. It was an ideal ground zero for a germ warfare attack.

Marc pushed through, weaving around the slow-walking tourists and the relaxed locals, entering the square from Rue Charles Buls on the southern side. On one axis, the city's town hall thrust a baroque tower toward the sky, rising from an arcade of arches and ornate windows. Along the other flanks of the square, guildhalls dating back as far as the 1600s shimmered in the sunlight. Intricate gold detailing and elegant statuary stood out on every frontage, designating houses dedicated to carpenters, bakers, brewers and other trades. It was an elegant and beautiful space, but that was lost on Marc in this moment. He saw a vast kill box, a corral enclosing countless more potential victims for the Shadow virus.

The square was thick with people. Around the edges, busy cafes and pubs spilled out on to open-air benches, and in the center a crescent-shaped dais formed the locus for the music festival. The band currently at play were blasting through a pacy jazz-fusion number and the crowd around them clapped along enthusiastically. The vibe in the square was crackling, positive energy, but for Marc it drummed into his skull like the pressure wave before a deafening crash of thunder.

He jumped up on to the edge of a vacant bench to look out over the heads of the crowd, but there were too many people for him to see across Grand-Place from one side to another. A police officer in a blue jacket looked in Marc's direction with a questioning stare, and he dropped back down before he drew too much attention. The Glock pistol was in the leather satchel he had snatched from the arcade, and the last thing he needed was to have some dutiful cop come and take a look.

Marc ducked into the closest of the old guild houses. The ground floor was a Starbucks and it was busy, with a thick line of people queued up for their coffees and pastries. Marc strode quickly past them to the toilets at the rear of the building. He made a smart turn through a door marked *ALLEEN WERKNEMERS* and found himself on a landing with stairs leading up and down. Taking the steps two at a time, he reached the second floor and shoved a pile of spare chairs out of his way, finding his way to the windows.

From up here, the span of Grand-Place was visible, and Marc scanned the crowd, looking for al-Baruni and the dark shape of the pack he carried.

His smartphone buzzed and Marc seized it. *Another message.* The mirror program had picked up the signal being sent once more, which meant the man had to be close at hand. Marc was right on top of him.

The directive on the phone screen was chilling.

"Take off the pack," Marc read aloud. "Carry it to the town hall."

His head jerked up and he stared into the crowd.

There!

The man's worried aspect briefly appeared in a gap among the other faces, and Marc watched him set off in the direction of the old building, slipping the black nylon daypack off his shoulder.

At a full-pelt sprint, Marc raced back down the stairs and bolted through the coffee shop. Emerging into the bright daylight again, he made a split-second choice to go around the edge of the square rather than press through the crowd after al-Baruni. The satchel over his shoulder banged against his back as he took the pace, moving as fast as he dared. The police officer who had spotted him before was still in the area, and if he ran, Marc's profile would stick out a mile.

As he approached the arches of the town hall, Marc caught sight of al-Baruni once more, shuffling slowly through the crowd. The man's face was fixed in a morose cast, his shoulders hunched as if an impossible weight was bearing down upon him. Around them, people were singing along as the band on the stage approached the high point of their performance.

Now or never, Marc told himself, and he stepped out in front of his quarry.

"Meddur al-Baruni!" he called, loud enough for the man to hear him. "I just want to talk."

The other man saw him and jerked to a halt. He turned deathly white as the color drained from his face.

"No . . ." he began, desperately looking around. On all sides, locals and tourists sang along, unaware of the drama unfolding among them. Al-Baruni put the black backpack down at his feet and held up his hands. "Please, don't get in my way."

Marc came closer, until he was almost within arm's reach. He kept his hands at his sides, but the satchel was open and if he needed to, Marc could have his pistol out in under a second.

Don't make me do it, mate, he thought.

"You know what they want, right?" Marc nodded at the pack. "You know what that is?"

The other man blinked. "I think so."

"I need you to give it to me."

"No!" Al-Baruni shrank back, shaking his head, snatching up the pack and holding it close. "They will know! I can't . . ." He wiped a sheen of sweat from his brow with the heel of his hand. "Please, my family—"

"He took them." Marc concentrated on maintaining a level, moderated tone to his voice, even though his heart was hammering in his chest. "Noah Verbeke. He made you do this. He told you he would hurt them if you refused."

"Yes!"

"Meddur, I am here to make sure that doesn't happen. Let me help you."

"How?" The word was almost a sob.

Cautiously, Marc removed his smartphone.

"You want to be sure your family is okay, yeah? If I can prove that to you, will you give me the bag?"

The man eyed him with suspicion.

"I heard them. Through this." He showed Marc the smartwatch around his wrist. "They are his prisoners!"

"Maybe not."

Marc tapped the speed-dial icon for Lucy's smartphone and held his breath. He had no way to know if she had been successful in her part of the plan, and the fact Lucy had not already contacted him to confirm that was a bad sign. Everything was happening so fast, Marc could only hope that they could still make it through this day without more loss of life.

He held the phone to his ear. Each *buzz-buzz* of the ringtone seemed to take forever, and Marc let his hand drop to rest on the satchel.

If this doesn't work, there's only one other way this is going to end.

The phone clicked as the line connected and Marc let out a held breath.

"Lucy! It's me, do you have them?"

"*Is that Dane?*"

A man's voice asked the question, and the shock of hearing him brought Marc up short. The accent sounded familiar, but Marc couldn't place him. The close background noise indicated the man was inside a moving vehicle.

"Who the hell is this?" he demanded.

"*I am Officer . . .*" The man on the other end of the line gave a heavy sigh and began again. "*You do not know my name. You called me Loki. From the Viking Squad.*"

A dozen questions crowded into Marc's thoughts.

"You're here? Larsson sent you after us?"

"*Yes, and—*"

"Doesn't matter!" Marc cut him off with a sharp retort. "Explain later! Where's Keyes, where's the hostages?"

"*I am following your colleague to Verbeke's staging area. The woman and the two children are in a vehicle with me—*"

Again, Marc didn't give the Viking Squad officer a chance to finish the sentence.

"Put the wife on, do it now!" He tapped the speaker icon on the phone and took another step closer to al-Baruni. "Meddur, listen. Sakina and the kids, they're okay."

A woman's plaintive voice, the same one Marc had heard earlier in the intercepted message, issued from the smartphone. She was crying, sobbing through her words. Al-Baruni looked shocked and shook his head.

"This is false—you are doing this!" he insisted. The

man clutched at the bulky watch on his wrist. "She spoke to me before! She told me they would kill her!"

"*Husband, that was a lie!*" said the voice on the phone, in faltering English. "*That was not me!*"

"No . . ." Confusion and fear warred across al-Baruni's features. "It's not true."

"What you heard before, *that* was the fake!" Marc held out the device to him. "Take it, man. Talk to her! Ask her something only your wife would know." He jabbed a finger at the smartwatch. "That thing is what's feeding you lies!"

Marc was aware that some of the people in the crowd around them had drawn back, sensing the tension in the air. He took the last step and pressed his phone into al-Baruni's trembling hand.

"Take this," he repeated, "and give me the bag."

"Sakina?" The man held the phone to his ear. "Is it you?"

"*I love you*," said the woman. "*We love you.*"

Marc didn't wait any longer. Al-Baruni made no attempt to stop him as he snatched the backpack away, cradling Marc's phone as if it was the most precious thing, naked and unashamed relief turning into tears down his cheeks.

Dragging the bag with him, Marc dropped down behind a metal crowd barrier in front of the town hall and pulled open the zip. Packed inside, the fat silver bullet of a thermal flask was aimed up at him. Aside from the cap, which he wasn't about to mess around with, there was no visible triggering mechanism, no timer. Warily, Marc leaned in and put an ear to the metal canister. He heard thick liquid gurgle inside, stirring as if it was coming to life.

Marc looked up as the band on stage finished their

number and the crowd exploded into loud applause. They pressed forward, calling for an encore, and suddenly it seemed like there were twice as many people in Grand-Place as there had been only moments before.

Everyone here is going to die.

Marc's breath shorted in his throat as the dire thought struck. He blinked and rubbed his sweating hands on his stolen jacket, looking right and left, searching for somewhere to take the weapon before it activated.

Inside the hall?

He had no way of knowing how many people were in there, or if that would be enough to contain the discharge.

Down a manhole, into the sewers?

Introducing the toxin to a water supply would be even worse.

He needed somewhere he could seal it in, some way to smother the release. His mind raced, desperately reaching for and discarding one possibility after another . . .

And then he had it.

Marc snatched up the backpack and broke into a run, holding it close to his chest as he stormed through the crowd, back in the direction of Rue Charles Buls, back the way he had come. He shoved onlookers aside and leaped across barriers and café tables, knocking over steins of beer and scattering people as he went.

Someone cursed angrily and a sharp, hard shout followed. Marc saw the flicker of a blue police jacket in the corner of his eye, but he didn't break his pace. Adrenaline flashed through his veins. This was his one and only chance to get the weapon away from its targets, and if he failed Marc Dane would be the first victim it would claim.

He dashed around the corner, the crush of pedestrians thinning as he hit the cobbled side streets, and ahead Marc saw the plastic-clad exterior of the shopping arcade.

"*Halte!*" came a shout at his back. "*Politie!*"

Marc ran at the metal fencing walling off the construction around the outside of the arcade and leaped at it, snatching at the chain-link mesh. His momentum got him halfway up, and he hauled himself over the top, the pack jangling across the wire. The racer jacket caught and ripped on the bare wire, and he tugged, freeing himself. Marc landed hard on the dry, bare concrete on the other side of the fence, and his feet scraped as he regained his pace.

The police officer from the square, a stocky older guy with a blue forage cap atop his thin face, was right behind him, starting his own climb up over the fence line. Nearby, construction workers in hi-vis vests were moving closer, drawn by the commotion.

Marc ripped open the backpack to expose the silver flask inside.

"It's a bomb!" he bellowed. "Run! All of you, get the fuck out of here!"

The police officer dropped off the fence in shock and backed away, and the workers bolted, leaving Marc alone amid the chattering cement mixers and diesel generators. He saw the Belgian cop go for cover, snatching at his radio to call in an emergency. Marc moved deeper into the building site, searching for the unfinished concrete pilings he had seen before.

He found a deep pit going ten or more meters down into the earth, lined with precast plates reinforced with metal rebar. In the shadows at the bottom, he saw what he needed, a pool of drying liquid cement. With both hands Marc threw the backpack, flask and all, into the gray mud-like mix.

The pack landed with a dull splat and sat on the surface, resolutely refusing to sink. Over the grumble of the mixer's motor, Marc caught a new sound. The thin squeal of fluid under high pressure.

He looked up. Fat droplets of cement drooled from the mouth of a hopper hanging suspended over the open pit, and Marc reached out for it, clawing to grab the handle that would open the valve. He put his hand on it and pulled hard. The motion made the hopper swing away on its chain and Marc felt himself go with it, his feet slipping off the lip of the pit.

The latch clanked open and the hopper ejected a torrent of fresh cement, but now Marc was hanging on to it, his legs dangling over the open space. Beneath him, the new flow of thick slurry covered the pack and buried it, drowning the cylinder with a wet belch before its lethal payload could spread.

Marc's hands, still smarting from clinging to the back of the tram, could not maintain purchase on the slippery metal handle, and gravity began to reel him in. The fall wouldn't be enough to kill him, but suffocating in a pit full of toxin-laced liquid cement would do just as well.

Then someone grabbed his jacket from behind and Marc's weight shifted back toward the edge, toward safety. He finally lost his grip, but it didn't matter. He fell back, landing with a grunt on the unfinished floor of the construction site, and rolled over.

Meddur al-Baruni stood over him, offering Marc a hand up.

"Are you all right?"

"Thanks, mate." Marc gratefully took the man's hand and pulled himself to his feet. "You came after me."

"I had to help you." He pulled Marc's smartphone from his pocket, handing it back. "And return this."

"No worries." Marc nodded, a rough laugh escaping

with the words. He cast a look back into the pit, and al-Baruni did the same.

"It is down there?" said the man.

Marc nodded, then reactivated the phone, calling Lucy's number once again. The Icelandic cop she'd nicknamed Loki answered on the first ring.

"*Dane?*"

"Where is she?" Marc beckoned al-Baruni to follow him through the construction area, away from the fence and over to the gutted fascia of the shopping arcade. "I need to talk to her. The second device has been neutralized, but we don't know if Verbeke has any more of this poison."

"*Keyes went on ahead. She's going after Verbeke on her own. The woman is willful.*"

"And then some." Marc shook his head. "You're at the warehouse by the canal? I'm not far away. I'll come to you, just hold off."

"*It may be too late for that.*"

"Police are here," said al-Baruni, pointing back the way they had come.

Marc cut the call and threw a look over his shoulder. Sure enough, the cop from the square now had backup, as he and two more uniformed officers scrambled over the fence.

"I've got to get out of here," muttered Marc.

"I will come with you," insisted the other man. "Take me to Sakina and the children."

"Can do, yeah."

Through a nearby archway, Marc saw a man stepping off a swift-looking Suzuki scooter parked outside a bakery.

"I'll get us a ride," he added.

*   *   *

"Boats are ready," said Ticker, shifting nervously from foot to foot on the warehouse's debris-strewn floor. "All my kit is on board, plus the hard drives." He threw a nod in the direction of the canal. "So, we going?"

Verbeke gave him a narrow-eyed look.

"What are you afraid of?"

The other man showed an insipid smile.

"We don't need to be here no more, do we?" He waved at the rest of the men. Two of them were closing up the last truck, and the other was setting a fire to burn the tent where the Korean had done his work with the bioprinter. "Let them finish up."

That shark's grin unfolded on Verbeke's face. The hacker was a weasel of a man, of use only because of his skills with computers. In any other circumstances he would never have been inducted into the ranks of the Lion's Roar. He reeked of fear, and Verbeke wanted to punish him for it.

"Have you seen how someone dies from Shadow?" He made a mock-retching noise. "Black blood gushing from everywhere. You die shitting out your innards. It's not pretty."

Ticker paled. "It's what they deserve, right?" He forced out a weak smirk. "Fucking mongrels."

"You look a little sickly. Sure you didn't get too close to it?"

The hacker's smile faded.

"No. I'm good." He swallowed hard. "I just wanna know why we're still waiting around."

Verbeke shot a look at the open doorway leading out to the street. Axelle should have been back by now. It didn't take that long to torch a truck. But as each minute passed, he wondered if something had gone wrong. Had the cops caught up with them? Or was it Rubicon?

He gave a low, derisive grunt. It didn't matter. Axelle knew the plan. If she wasn't here, that was her problem, and he had places to be.

"Start it up," he told Ticker. "We're out of here."

The hacker didn't wait to be told twice, and he ran across the disused warehouse to the loading dock near the water, where the two boats were moored. Verbeke called out to the others and gestured at the truck. It was time to go.

The Korean came jogging up to him, running a worried hand through his hair.

"I will come with you?"

"No," snorted Verbeke, snidely amused by the foreigner's presumption. "Get in the truck. I don't want to look at your face any longer than I have to."

"We had an agreement," Kyun insisted. "I have delivered on everything you and the Combine asked of me."

Verbeke turned angrily on the other man and prodded him hard in the chest, suddenly seething at the mention of the Combine.

"This is my game, not theirs. You get that? We run it how I say!"

He was about to give Kyun a hard shove to underline his point, but then the nasal snarl of a motorcycle engine rose out on the street, and a bike came curving around, bouncing up the ramp and into the warehouse proper. A woman in an all-encompassing black helmet was in the saddle, and Verbeke's shark-smile flickered.

She made it back.

But the thought was only half-formed when he realized that the figure on the bike wore a different jacket, and had one hand on a pistol laid over the handlebars.

He grabbed at Kyun as the biker pulled the trigger, and dragged the Korean across him, into the line of fire.

Kyun twitched and danced, crying out in agony as the bullets struck him. Verbeke discarded the man and broke into a sprint, hauling out his own gun to shoot back at the motorcycle as he ran.

Shots struck the wheel and the bike skidded. The rider kicked off and landed in a tuck-and-roll. The other men had been caught unawares, and only now were they reacting. The woman used their laxity to her advantage and put rounds into the two by the truck, dropping them.

Verbeke fired again as he moved, and one round clipped the biker's helmet, skipping off the curved surface and knocking her back. He reached the loading dock as she tore off the damaged dome and tossed it away.

"Bitch," he snarled.

It was the black American, the one that was supposed to be a frozen corpse on some Icelandic hillside. He kept firing, forcing her to stay down behind the fallen motorcycle.

Behind him, Verbeke heard the roar of an outboard engine, and he pivoted toward the sound. Ticker had cast off one of the speedboats, and like the coward he was, the hacker was saving his own neck. The boat left the dockside in a spray of foam and bounced across the swell behind a passing cargo barge, before zooming away up the canal.

Verbeke grimaced and darted out to the dock where the second speedboat was moored. Lines held it to rusted iron cleats, and he holstered his gun, exchanging it for a tactical knife to cut away the ropes. Back inside the warehouse, more shots sounded, then nothing. He slashed through the first line and crouched by the second, sawing through it with the blade.

"Where d'you think you're going?" said a voice. "Stand up, asshole, and turn around."

Verbeke halted, then slowly rose to his full height. He took a step and came about to face the American. The woman was a head shorter than him, her dark face filmed with sweat and marred by cuts and bruises. She had a semi-automatic pistol in one hand, aimed directly at his chest. The barrel didn't waver as she stepped out of the warehouse and on to the dockside.

"Lose the blade," she told him.

He gave a shrug and tossed the knife into the canal. It didn't matter. The second line was cut nearly clean through, and one sharp pull would snap it.

"What do you think is going to happen here?" Verbeke cocked his head, looking her up and down. "You believe someone like you can stop me?" He laughed at her.

"Get on your knees," she told him, each word spat out like it was a piece of broken glass in her teeth. "Show me your hands."

He sneered at her audacity. "You don't have any authority over me. I don't take orders from your kind."

"I'm the one with the gun," she retorted.

"So shoot me!" He advanced a step toward her and she tensed. "Go on!" he snarled. "Or I'll take that from you and force it down your throat! Beat you with it until you beg me to stop!"

Verbeke savored the rush of blood racing through him at the thought of such violence. He imagined punching her, kicking her, saw her bleeding and crushed in his mind's eye. She wouldn't be the first he had beaten to death with his own hands, and she wouldn't be the last.

"But you don't have the strength, do you? Americans always want their hero story. You want me to surrender so you can feel righteous!" He spat on the concrete, his stepfather's lessons rising in his thoughts. "Never! This is war. Never submit. Never yield. Death first."

"You have it backward, Jean-Claude Van Dumbass," she replied. "Right now, it's taking every fucking ounce of my strength not to put a bullet in your belly and let you die screaming right there. One time, I never would have hesitated. Now . . ." She showed her teeth. "Now I wanna see you dragged out in chains for the world to laugh at." Verbeke's towering rage stoked higher as the woman smiled and steadfastly refused to rise to his goading. "You got no war, no cause, nothing but an excuse for that hate-filled shithole you call a personality. You're gonna go to jail, motherfucker. You'll pay for what you did in Benghazi. And everyone is gonna see it happen. All the people you terrorized, the scumbags who funded you, all your fascist boyfriends. They'll see you pay for what you've done. Count on it."

For a long moment, he teetered on the edge of attacking her, heedless of the gun in her hand. Then he shackled his anger and spread his hands.

"You want to take me in? You are welcome to try."

Marc guided the stolen Suzuki through the backstreets of Brussels, tracking away from Grand-Place and into the network of alleys and avenues. In the saddle behind him, al-Baruni hung on for dear life, muttering a prayer under his breath as Marc gunned the engine and pushed it to its limit.

Weaving around trams and other vehicles, taking

risky lines against the flow of the traffic, he brought them out on Quai de Willebroeck. The dual carriageway paralleled the canal and Marc pointed the Suzuki north along it, speeding through red lights across intersections, closing on the warehouse as fast as the scooter could take them there.

Once or twice, he had seen the flash of strobes and heard the skirl of sirens, but so far the police were still off his pace, unable to follow him over pedestrian streets and down passages too narrow for cars.

Even then, it seemed to take forever to cross the distance to the warehouse, and as they ate up every meter, Marc's pulse raced.

I never should have sent Lucy out here alone, he told himself. *If anything happens to her . . .*

He shut down the traitorous thought with a shake of the head and leaned into a turn, bringing them down a shallow incline leading toward the canal. There, on the street in front of the warehouse, he saw a car skewed across the street and a dark-haired man in cover behind it. A woman in a hijab, a boy and a teenage girl were close by, under the man's protection.

"Sakina!" Al-Baruni saw his wife and called out her name.

Marc hit the brakes and they skidded to a halt on the intersection. The man didn't wait for the scooter to stop, and he leaped off, running into an embrace with his family. At once, they were crying, holding each other, their stark relief overwhelming them with emotion.

But Marc's attention was elsewhere.

"Where is she?"

He shouted the question at Loki, who came up and out of cover, brandishing a pistol.

"Inside," said the Icelander, pointing at the warehouse. "There was a firefight. The local police will be coming."

"Have no doubt," Marc retorted, and he revved the engine.

The Suzuki surged forward, up the vehicle ramp and into the derelict warehouse. Dust kicked up and Marc tasted acrid burning plastic. He saw glimpses of the chaos around him—a heap of burning fabric, an idling truck, a discarded motorcycle and bodies on the ground—before coming to a screeching halt just before the loading dock leading out to the canal.

He dumped the scooter and ran out into the sunlight. Out on the dock, Marc saw Verbeke with his hands raised and Lucy drawing down on him. She had a set of zip-ties in one hand.

"Ah, the race traitor is here," called Verbeke. "Good timing."

"Shut up," Lucy snapped, never taking her eyes off her target.

"The cops are right behind me," called Marc. "I got to your mule, pal. It's over."

"You're lying," snarled Verbeke. He made a show of pulling up his sleeve to look at his watch. "The device has activated by now." He leered at them. "Shadow is out there. It's loose—and this city is going to learn the price of opening its doors to foreign scum."

"Actually," said Marc, with a shake of the head, "your toxic little toy is buried under a ton of wet cement."

"Another lie!" Verbeke barked, but there was a moment of hesitation, an iota of doubt.

"Step away from the boat," Lucy ordered. "And get on your damn knees. I won't tell you again."

Verbeke paused, then gave a nod. He stepped forward, coming closer to Lucy.

"It doesn't matter. There's always another way. Always another weapon."

Marc saw something metallic glitter in the daylight, a slim tube that Verbeke had slipped out of his cuff, and shouted a warning.

"Lucy, he's got . . . !"

What happened next came in a flash of motion, almost too swift for Marc to follow. Verbeke's hand came up and the tube shrieked, firing a jet of fluid straight into Lucy's face. With a cry, she reeled back as if she had been punched, her hand coming up to claw at her eyes and nose.

As she stumbled to the ground, Verbeke dived into the idling speedboat tethered to the dock and he slammed the throttle forward. Marc pulled his gun and started firing, his bullets skipping across the back of the boat as he unloaded the magazine. He saw a splash of red as Verbeke jerked against the wheel, but the boat didn't slow and continued on its course away down the churning canal.

He spun, finding Lucy sprawled on the concrete quay, her body shaking as she pawed at her skin. A gluey, pinkish fluid coated her hands and face. Marc felt hollow and cold inside as a medicinal smell reached his nostrils.

"Stay back!" Lucy shouted. "Shit. *Oh shit!* This is Shadow! Marc, stay the hell away from me. Oh no."

She gave a racking cough and spat up thin bile.

A flood of fear charged through Marc and he fought it down, tearing off his ripped racer jacket.

"I got you," he said, folding the leather over her torso and around her head, wrapping her in it.

"No," she said, wheezing. "Don't."

Marc ignored her and hauled Lucy up on to his shoulder in a fireman's carry. He could feel her trembling as the bioweapon hit her system, and he moved as fast as he could. That terrible sense of time running out tightened in his chest.

Loki, al-Baruni and his family were still there as he emerged on the street, but Marc warned them away.

"Keep back, she was hit by a dose of the virus!"

"What . . . virus?" said Sakina, her eyes widening.

"Marburg variant," Marc panted. "Same thing they released in Benghazi."

"Let me see." Sakina came forward, and her attitude shifted, becoming firm and businesslike. "I am a nurse. Show me."

Marc put Lucy down on the hood of Loki's car and Sakina peeled back the jacket around her. The dusky color of the American's face was already taking on an ashen pallor, and she gasped with each painful breath she took.

"She's going into shock," said Sakina. "We have to get her to a hospital right away. Every moment she is here, her chance fades."

As Sakina spoke, her last few words were drowned out by howling sirens. A trio of white Federal Police cars emerged from the intersection and screeched to a halt. Uniformed officers burst out, drawing pistols and extendable batons.

Marc had lost his gun somewhere on the dock, and he turned to the Belgians, his mind only registering Lucy's condition, and the desperate compulsion to save her life. The weapons they pointed at him seemed insignificant.

He advanced on the closest of them.

"We have to get this woman to a hospital right away!" he shouted. "She's in critical condition, do you understand? She will die!"

"Put up your hands, sir!" called the closest officer. "Stay where you are!"

Marc ignored him, reaching for the driver's side door of the closest police car.

"I'll get her there, we have to get her there . . ."

Nothing else mattered. It was as if the entirety of the world had dropped away from him, and the only thing remaining was to get Lucy Keyes to safety, to keep her alive.

I can do it. I can save her.

This time, I can save her.

"Raise your hands!" shouted the policeman. He moved up, his drawn gun at Marc's head. "Stop!"

"I can't!" Marc roared, and spun about, unleashing a wild punch that caught the police officer by surprise and knocked him down to the road. "I have to—"

From out of nowhere, an ASP baton cracked Marc across his shoulders and he felt the world turn sharply around his axis. The ground came up to meet him and Marc's vision blurred, becoming hazy and indistinct.

"You are under arrest!" said a voice.

Marc didn't hear it.

"Help," he breathed, forcing out the words. "*Help her!*"

— TWENTY-ONE —

The battery of tests included half a dozen blood draws, skin samples and invasive swabs from Marc's mouth and nostrils, leaving nothing to chance. Gloved hospital technicians in plastic smocks and full-face masks worked around him, talking in swift snatches of Dutch that he couldn't follow.

What parts of the conversation were in English were impenetrable medical jargon, and when it became abundantly clear that they were not going to answer his questions, Marc gave up and sat there on the end of the bed in the secure infection unit, letting them poke, prod and pull him around.

After a while, the technicians left him alone and he sank back on to the bed, his mind turning in a cycle of dread. In the end, it had been Loki—whose real name was actually Björn—who flashed his badge and forced the Belgian cops to listen to them. The Icelander had convinced the locals to get everyone to the nearest emergency ward and that had been the last Marc had seen of anyone else.

He fixated on a fleeting image of Lucy lodged in his thoughts, shivering on a gurney as doctors ran her away down a corridor. Marc dreaded the possibility that this would be the last thing she left him with. Lucy was the strongest person he knew, and it tore him up inside to think that she might go out in so much pain. The weight of that notion was iron on his shoulders; it was tight around his chest, making it hard for him to breathe. Marc leaned up, found a jug of water and poured himself a cupful.

On the other side of the isolation room's door, he could see the back of a uniformed policewoman standing guard. Marc sipped the water and took in his surroundings, trying to turn his fear into fuel, to give it purpose.

If they were not going to tell him how Lucy was, he would have to find out on his own. The first step toward that was to make it out of here. He looked down at the pulse rate sensor attached to his finger, trailing a wire to a medical monitor behind him. The moment he removed it, someone would be alerted. He needed a plan, and then . . .

And then?

All at once, the energy fell out of him. Wasn't this how he had got into this situation? The fool rushing in, risking everything on his wits.

"What's that done for you, Dane?" He asked the question to the empty room, staring morosely at the far wall.

A shadow appeared at the window in the door and the policewoman stepped aside. Marc drew back and weighed his options, as in came an unsmiling man in his late forties, walking with difficulty on a carbon-fiber stick. The guy had a craggy look about him and a manner that immediately connected to *military* and *veteran* in Marc's mind, but he was dressed in a police windbreaker with a rank tab on his breast and an ID pass around his neck.

The new arrival gave Marc a sideways look and then aimed his stick at a chair in the corner of the room.

"I'm going to sit," he said, in accented English.

"Doctors tell me I shouldn't even be back at work for another month or two, but what do they know?"

The man lowered himself on to the seat with a grimace. He moved like he was wounded, favoring his right side. When he saw Marc watching, he gave a shrug and tapped his belly.

"I had a pair of .38 slugs go through me. Lived to tell the tale, though."

Marc gave a nod. "I know how that feels."

"Yes," agreed the man. "The doctor who examined you said she found some interesting scars. Perhaps later you can find a moment to explain where you got them." He propped himself up on the stick, leaning on it with both hands. "I am trying to fathom this out. My name is Inspecteur Nils Jakobs, of the Belgian Federal Police."

"Martin Dale," said Marc, recalling the name from the Canadian passport he had used to enter the country.

"That is what your documents say," agreed Jakobs. "They're very convincing." He went on, before Marc could say more. "But let's treat each other like two professionals and dispense with the usual bullshit, yes? You and your lady friend are extralegal, non-official cover operatives working for a transnational security contractor."

"I need to see her."

Marc looked into the other man's eyes, trying to gauge him.

"She's with the doctors now. They'll do all they can, be certain of that. But you can't help there." Jakobs showed a flicker of compassion, his tone softening for a moment. "You are close?"

"Yeah." The words seemed hollow and broken. "You could say that."

"The other woman, the wife . . ." Jakobs nodded in the direction of the doorway. "You're lucky she was there. She told the clinicians what to look for. Gave them vital information. Every second counts with something like this." He looked away, frowning. "My soul shrivels up when I think about what might have happened today."

Marc said nothing, aware that he had already let on more than he should have. He wondered what al-Baruni had told the police. If their roles had been reversed, Marc would have given up everything he knew if it meant saving his family.

"They're not part of it," he said. "Sakina, her husband, their kids—they're innocent."

"That's not for you to decide." Jakobs considered his own words for a moment. "Their blood tests came back clean, no infection. Same with your associate, the Viking." He studied Marc. "You haven't asked me about your own health yet."

Marc gave a shrug. "I'm not bleeding out of every orifice, and you're not wearing a noddy suit, so . . ."

He trailed off. Thoughts of his own survival had been a distant second to everything else.

"Fair point," continued the other man. "From what I understand, this thing is quite horrendous when it gets its hooks in you." He paused again. "Four city blocks around the town hall have been quarantined. We're telling the media it is a gas leak." Jakobs shifted uncomfortably, making a low grunt as he moved. "So far, no reports of any infections have come in. But you have left quite a few bodies in your path, you and your colleague. I know them all."

Again, Marc held his silence. Before, he might have hoped that Rubicon's heavyweight legal team could swing into action and intervene on his behalf, but with everything going on in the upper echelons of the company, he couldn't rely on that. If anything, there was a good chance that the board of directors might go the other way and totally disavow any knowledge of Marc and Lucy's actions.

"You have brought a mess into this city, my friend," continued Jakobs. "I will be honest with you, because it will save time. As we speak, a group of men with ranks much higher than mine are trying to unravel what took place, and most of them want to find a way to pin it on you and those immigrants." He spread his hands. "After what has happened in Brussels in the last few years, do you know how the rest of Europe sees us? They think Belgium is a breeding ground for terrorists, run by apathetic and spineless politicians."

"It's not foreigners who did this," Marc said, the words slipping out. "It's one of your own."

Jakobs gave a rueful nod. "More than you know." He shifted again in his seat and gripped the handle of his stick. "I had a long conversation with the Icelander," he said, changing tack. "And his boss. In exchange for some latitude for his man, Inspector Larsson was quite forthcoming about your identity and that of Ms. Keyes."

"*Shit!*" Marc cursed quietly.

"Indeed. And quite deep it is too, Mr. Dane. Interpol has a thought-provoking file on you. You are a person of interest. Your name comes up in all kinds of places. The Royal Navy, the British intelligence service, the United Nations Office of Nuclear Security . . . You get around."

"Travel broadens the mind," he offered.

"I was particularly drawn to your possible connection with a murder in St. Tropez last year. Celeste Toussaint, the television baroness. But that investigation has stalled. Lack of actionable evidence."

"I don't know anything about that," Marc replied, which was more or less true.

He knew full well who Toussaint was—he'd even been part of a mission to tie her to the Combine and their dealings with right-wing extremists in France.

Was that connected to the Lion's Roar?

But the true circumstances behind Toussaint's death were not known to Rubicon.

Marc blew out a weary breath.

"Look, mate, if you're going to arrest me, let's just get it over with, yeah?"

"Do you read?"

"What?" The question wrong-footed him.

"Books," added Jakobs.

Marc nodded, then felt the need to clarify.

"Well. Not literary fiction. Beach reads, mostly."

"*Moby-Dick*," Jakobs added. "Ahab and his white whale."

"'From hell's heart, I stab at thee.'"

"That's the one." The other man leaned forward on his stick. "I have a nemesis of my own. Noah Verbeke. A week ago he tried to kill me, and that wasn't the first time. Almost succeeded, too." He patted his torso, and his voice turned grim. "He's out there now because of me. I thought I had the angles covered, but the Lion's Roar outplayed me. People are dead because I made the wrong choice, Mr. Dane." Jakobs looked up and Marc saw his own remorse in the other man's eyes. "I have been hunting him for years. But I let him slip through my fingers, and now my commanders are going to throw me under the bus, as the Americans say." That bleak look in the older man's gaze glittered and turned fiery. "Verbeke and everyone like him are a cancer. He cannot be allowed to get away with what he has done."

And at once, Marc realized what this conversation was actually about.

"You want Rubicon to help you."

"We are both in a similar situation." He nodded to himself. "Rubicon has deniable resources that a man like me cannot access, yes? The Icelanders are willing to cooperate, but our window of opportunity is closing quickly. The boats Verbeke used were abandoned upriver, and we believe he has gone to ground in Antwerp. Best estimate, we have less than a day before he jumps the border to the Netherlands or gets away on a ship. Antwerp is a port city with dozens of vessels coming and going all the time, so he could vanish and resurface anywhere in Europe." Jakobs slowly rose to his feet. "I believe you are as motivated to stop him as I am."

"I'm in." Marc gave a nod. There was no hesitation in his answer. "One condition. I want to see Lucy first."

For one terrible moment, he thought she was already lost.

The nurses wouldn't allow Marc to enter the biosafe room where Lucy lay unconscious, and he was forced to make do with the view through a wire-reinforced window in an observation anteroom. He watched a medical technician in a hazmat suit take a blood sample from Lucy's arm, and the shade of her skin seemed wrong. She looked lifeless and dull, as if the energy had been sucked out of her body. The slow shock of it rolled over Marc in a steady wave.

Marc had seen death before, through violence, through misadventure, and the unhurried, inexorable

kind of ending brought on by disease, and he felt the
aura of it looming here. In every sense of the word, a
shadow was hanging over the life of Lucy Keyes, and
all Marc could do was watch.

Her chest moved in shallow, stuttering breaths. The
doctors had intubated her, snaking a pipe between her
pallid lips and down her throat, and plastic bags of fluid
solution hung above her bed, thin lines leading down
to her arm. Tears of pinkish-red marked her face and
her eyes were closed. The slight movement of her chest
and the steady peaks of the heart monitor were the only
signs of life.

The Marburg virus and its weaponized Shadow variant had no miracle cure to be given to her. There was
no magic bullet vaccine, only therapies and medications
that could try to ease her pain and strengthen her body
against the poison coursing through her veins. She
could only hope to *endure* this, to battle through and
make it out the other side.

The next twenty-four hours would be critical. If she
could hold on until then, her odds would improve dra-
matically.

"You are the strongest person I know," Marc told
her, willing his words to carry through the glass, to find
their way to her. "You'll beat this, Lucy. I know it."

He stepped back from the window, but it was hard to
turn away. A compulsion kept holding him there, as if
he believed that as long as he stood in this room, keeping watch over Lucy Keyes, nothing more could happen
to her. The feeling was old and familiar. Once before he
had stood in the same place, watching his mother suc-
cumb to the slow march of illness. The helplessness of
it was stifling, and in the end, it took a physical effort
for him to walk out, back into the corridor.

The room where she was being tended to was one

of a cluster in the hospital's secure wing, behind airlock
doors and layers of screening to prevent the spread of
any contagion. Some of Jakobs' cops were stationed
nearby, all of them wearing surgical masks over their
faces as they stood guard. They watched Marc with
calm indifference, and he wondered how much they
knew about what had really taken place earlier that day.
If events had played out for the worst, this ward would
have been filled to capacity, with every visitor to Grand-
Place a victim of Verbeke's false-flag attack.

"Dane."

Marc turned to see Loki—he still couldn't think of
him as Björn—in an examination room, finishing up
his conversation with a doctor. The Icelander was in
the process of shrugging on a shirt, and Marc saw a
band of black tattoos across his broad chest. Norse
symbols, the same kind of icons he had seen on Noah
Verbeke.

"How is Keyes?" asked the Icelander.

The doctor pushed past him and Marc stood there,
unsure what to say next.

"She's a fighter," he said, at length. "She's not going
to give that bastard another victory."

Loki nodded, running a hand through his dark hair.
"I should have gone in there with her."

"Then you'd both be in the ICU," Marc replied.
"Right?"

The Icelander paused, sensing something unspoken.
"What is wrong?"

Marc moved so he was blocking the doorway, and
nodded at Loki's chest.

"That ink. I've seen it before."

"Ah." The other man halted. "Of course." He opened
his shirt again and tapped his chest. "You are afraid this

makes me like Verbeke, yes? Because of the runes? Because I have respect for Odin and the old gods?"

"You said it, pal, not me."

Anger flickered across the other man's face.

"I am proud of my heritage. Viking blood runs in my family. But never tell me I am like that man. That insults what this means." He drew a line across the spindly runes over his skin. "Men like Verbeke have taken the meaning of these words and twisted them. Corrupted the beliefs of others and clothed themselves in it." He shook his head. "They have no right. No honor. His kind would see me dead." He reached in his pocket and pulled out a wallet. "Let me show you something."

He removed a photo and handed it to Marc.

The dog-eared picture showed the Icelander and another man, both of them dressed in snappy tuxedos. They were holding hands, showing off wedding rings and grinning. It reminded him of Ji-Yoo and her husband.

"Cute couple," Marc offered, handing it back. "Sorry. It's been a tough day."

"Understandable," said Loki.

Marc shook his head. "That's no excuse. Sowing division is what the Lion's Roar does. That's what this whole thing has been about, trying to turn one group of people on another."

He glanced over his shoulder and saw the al-Burani family gathered in a waiting area. They stayed close to each other, unwilling to go beyond arm's reach.

He walked across to them, throwing the husband a nod.

"How are you holding up?"

"They won't tell us anything," said Meddur. "They say we will not become sick, but nothing more. I think they're going to deport us."

Marc remembered the faces of the refugees the Rubicon team had rescued from the waters of the Mediterranean, back before this had started. They had the same haunted, desperate look in their eyes, that fearful sense of events beyond their control moving around them.

"None of this is your fault," he said. "You'll be okay."

Meddur looked away, shaking his head.

"I will accept any punishment. I understand my responsibility. But my family . . ." He grasped his wife's hand and squeezed it. "I only want them to be safe."

"I work for a man who might be able to help," Marc told him. He turned to Sakina. "I want to thank you. You didn't need to stay to help Lucy, you could have run before the cops arrived. You put yourselves at risk for her when you didn't need to."

"She came to save us," said Sakina. "I could not pay that back if we fled." She gave a shaky smile. "I couldn't let her die. And if we did flee, where could we go? We've been running since we left our home."

Marc's smartphone buzzed in his back pocket and he sighed.

"Excuse me, I have to take this." He stepped away, pressing the phone to his ear. "Dane."

"*I have something for you.*" Assim sounded distant and strung-out, and Marc's first thought was to ask him how much sleep he'd had in the last few days. "*But, ah, can I ask . . . ?*"

"She's not out of the woods yet," Marc told him, knowing the question before he asked it. "But you know Lucy. She's tough."

"*The team at Rubicon's private clinic in Zurich are on standby,*" he went on. "*I've been trying to route a med-jet to Brussels, but it is taking too long. I might be able to arrange something else . . ."* He faltered, running out of steam.

"The board will let you do that?"

"I didn't ask the board. Mr. Solomon authorized it personally. We protect our own, he said."

"Yeah, we do." Marc nodded to himself. "Don't worry, she's in good hands here. They can't move her until she's out of critical condition anyway." He straightened, pushing his own fears aside for the moment. "You said you had something. Did you get a hit in Antwerp?"

After his conversation with Jakobs, Marc's first instinct had been to send a message to Assim with an emergency action request. The digital currency transactions they had captured days earlier had been their best source of intelligence for tracking the finances of the Lion's Roar, and Marc's instincts told him that there was still more they could learn from it, if only they looked in the right place.

"I sifted the metadata for any hits corresponding to that city and there's a cluster of payments from a month ago."

"Tell me you've found a location."

"Yes and no." He could hear Assim frowning from half a world away. *"I was able to narrow it down to a postal area in the city, the 2060 district, but that's all."*

"2060 . . ." Marc repeated the number, rubbing the tiredness from his eyes. "All right, send me everything you have."

"I'm sorry, Marc." The Saudi hacker sounded defeated. *"Verbeke has covered his tracks here. He must have planned to use this as his escape route right from the start."*

"We can still get him," Marc said firmly. "Start digging into Bitcoin brokers on the dark web, look for anyone in Belgium in the market to exchange crypto-currency for hard cash. Verbeke's going to need ready money to get out of the country. We might be able to use that to tighten the noose."

"*Will do.*"

Marc saw Meddur approaching and added one more thing.

"And do us a favor, see if you can get someone from that Emigrant Aid NGO up here."

As the call ended, Meddur gave Marc a questioning look.

"Forgive me, but I heard you speaking to your colleague. You spoke about the 2060 . . . In Antwerp, yes?"

"You know it?"

Meddur nodded. "I have friends there, men I knew from our town back in Libya. It was where we hoped to go, when we first came to Belgium, but the traffickers who brought us into the country gave us no choice and forced us to settle in Brussels. The 2060 is like the Molenbeek here, it is the ghetto for people like us, from North Africa."

Marc felt a tingle in the back of his head, the sudden flash of hope.

"The man we are looking for—Verbeke. He's gone into hiding there."

"Are you sure?" Meddur's expression shifted, a new determination appearing there. "If that is so . . . someone would know."

"These friends of yours." Marc offered the man his smartphone. "Can you contact them?"

"I can," he said, catching on quickly.

Meddur took the phone and began to pick meticulously at the keypad, dredging up a number from memory.

Marc called out to the Icelander. "Oi, Loki!"

"My name is Björn," he replied wearily.

"Don't care," Marc shot back. "Find Jakobs, will you? We just got back in the hunt."

The shabby apartment at the top of the three-story block was barely decorated, with only a couple of beds, some chairs and a folding table. In the corner of the living room–kitchen area, a television played a newsfeed with the sound muted, showing footage of the chaos still unfolding in Benghazi.

The room reeked of stale, over-spiced food, and Verbeke wanted nothing more than to fling open the windows and let in some of the rainy air outside. He had to remember to stay away from the windows and keep his face hidden behind the thick blackout drapes hung across them. He had no choice but to sit there and seethe, breathing through his mouth as every passing second dragged by like an hour.

The belongings of whatever foreigners had lived here before he arrived were piled up into a heap of rubbish in the corner of one of the bedrooms, but even stripping the place of their traces wasn't enough for him.

He hated being here. He hated hearing the mongrels chattering endlessly through the paper-thin walls. Hated the smell of the place and the cooking stink constantly wafting up the stairwell, from the grimy fast food shop on the ground floor. He hated how these immigrants strutted around down on the street below, back and forth past the métro station across the way, as if they had a right to be here. He hated the Arabic scrawl on the signs over their squalid little storefronts.

He hated, and hated, and hated, and there was no end to it. Noah Verbeke's enmity was depthless and dark.

It was the ultimate ignominy to be hiding here among

those fit only to be his prey. The safe house was prepared and secure as promised, but to get there through
the streets of Antwerp he had been forced to disguise
himself. Hiding the wound from the glancing shot
across his arm, the scratchy fake beard and the prayer
cap had been enough to stop him drawing too much
attention among the swarms of Muslims infesting this
part of the city. Once inside and out of sight, he tore
them off and spat on them, furious at the shame of it. To
be forced to pretend to be one of *them* made a mockery
of everything the Lion's Roar stood for.

Ticker was already there, of course, planning his own
escape. The coward had been shocked to see him still
alive. The hacker tried to frame his abandonment of
Verbeke as some clever move on his part, but it was
exactly what it seemed to be. When push came to
shove, the rat-faced man could not be trusted to follow
the cause. Ultimately, he was only interested in self-
preservation, and Verbeke had already decided that he
would kill Ticker once they were safely away, when he
didn't need him anymore. Hackers were greedy children at heart, and it wouldn't be difficult to recruit another.

"What?"

Sitting at the table, Ticker had stopped hammering
away at his laptop and was watching him suspiciously.
Verbeke realized he had been staring at the other man,
his hands clasping as he imagined crushing his throat.

"Get back to work," he growled.

"I'm doing it," Ticker whined, and pointed at the
screen. "The 3G here is for shit, but I have word from
our contact. Van's gonna come pick us up after sun-
down, take us to the docks. Got a freighter to take us
up the coast."

Verbeke considered that. Once they reached the North Sea, Ticker could be disposed of and that would be the end of it.

"Course, that won't mean shit if we don't get the cash crossed over first, but I have a line on that." Ticker hesitated before adding something more. "I told them there was just the two of us . . . right? I mean, Axelle, she—"

"She *what*?" Verbeke rose and crossed the room to him. "Go on. Say it."

"She didn't come back, which means—"

"It means she's dead. Can you get that?" Verbeke prodded him in the chest. "She gave her life for the Lion's Roar—do you understand the courage that takes?" Ticker said nothing, as the storm of Verbeke's fury filled the room. "This is a fucking war, you piece of shit." He waved at the walls and the city outside the window. "We are deep in enemy territory, surrounded by these animals! You look out there and you see what they want, to swarm over everything and steal it from the whites. It takes courage to fight that. You don't have what she did."

"I'm sorry about your woman," Ticker managed, uncertain which reply would be the right one to give.

For the briefest moment, a tiny ember of actual regret burned in Verbeke's chest, the first tiny spark of an emotion that could have been sorrow, an acknowledgment that the woman had meant something to him. It brought a physical reaction with it, a twist of pain worse than the bullet wound.

He stamped it out mercilessly, destroying the moment without compunction before it could fully form.

That is weakness, he raged at himself. *That is corrosion.*

"She's dead," Verbeke repeated, reining in his rage. "If you don't want to end up the same way, do your job."

He turned away, without waiting for a response. His dark mood deepened as he glared at the images on the television.

"This isn't over," Verbeke continued, jutting his chin at the scenes of horror and degradation unfolding on the screen. "We can make more of the weapon. We can keep striking back. It won't end here." His hands contracted into fists. "I will make sure it *never* ends."

In an alleyway off Van Stralenstraat, a few blocks south of the Lion's Roar safe house, a panel-sided beer truck was parked in the shadows cast by the fading day. Any passing observer would not have given it a second look, but if they had, they might have noted that no delivery was taking place.

In reality, the truck belonged to the UCT, the undercover operations unit of the Belgian Federal Police's counter-terrorist division. In the back, Marc sat across from a command and control console under the watchful eye of Nils Jakobs and the men from his command. It was cramped in there, along with the Icelander and Meddur al-Baruni, who rocked gently in his seat. The refugee was visibly nervous, surrounded as he was by armed police officers, the people he had been told would hunt him down like an animal.

"Don't worry," Marc told him. "This'll be over soon."

Loki shot him a questioning look. The Icelandic cop knew that was not a given, just as Marc did, but he wasn't about to correct him in front of the civilian.

"This is as close as we can get," announced Jakobs.

"Verbeke was trained in counter-terror operations. He knows what to watch for, he knows our playbook. I'm reluctant to send anyone in while it's still daylight."

"It won't be dark for hours," said Loki. "Do we want to wait that long?"

Marc glanced at Meddur. The man had been as good as his word, and used his contacts in Antwerp to ask around, looking for any sign of new arrivals in the 2060. Sure enough, there was mention of two men taking up residence in an apartment where the previous family had suddenly been evicted with no explanation. The men had arrived a couple of hours after the incident in Brussels.

"They said they looked like converts," noted Meddur. "Both Europeans. One of them large, the other with dark hair."

"Ticker and Verbeke," said Marc, "hiding in plain sight. Cheeky bastards."

He removed a hard-side case made of gray armored plastic from his daypack, and spoke into a voice-activated lock on the side. It snapped open and from within he recovered a ruggedized tablet computer. Assim Kader had arranged for the gear to be in Brussels when Marc and Lucy had flown in from Germany, but aside from the pistol, he'd had little opportunity to use most of it. As the computer booted up, Marc was struck by a moment of cold familiarity.

Back in the van again, he told himself. *Some things never change.*

For a long time, this had been his posting in OpTeam Nomad, working as a field support officer for MI6's strike teams, monitoring from a distance while others went in harm's way.

But that past Marc Dane seemed like a stranger—the

man who had chosen not to take any risks, the one who had kept on what seemed like the safer path. He wasn't that person anymore. Marc had learned to his dire cost that there was no safe path.

Risk wasn't something you could hold at bay, not if you lived in this world. Now it was something that he sought out, a phantom from his past he felt compelled to confront over and over again.

The shadow at my heels, he thought.

"I would welcome any input from our observers," said Jakobs, resting heavily on his stick.

"I have some new intel," said Marc, reading off his screen. On the drive north from Brussels, he had been busy coordinating with Assim, trawling through the illegal money-changers of the dark web, looking for a telltale spike of digital traffic. "Ticker's set up a meeting with a buyer. He's going to exchange one of the Bitcoin drives for a bag of euros."

"Where and when?" said Jakobs.

Marc showed a crooked smile.

"Right here. Right now."

Ticker couldn't stop himself from throwing a look back up at the top floor window as he stepped out on to the street. A dark shape moved in the depths of the room and he knew it was Verbeke glaring down at him.

It had taken every bit of his persuasion to convince the man not to come after him. Ticker cited the fact that his contact would walk away if he saw a face he didn't recognize, along with Verbeke's ready notoriety to the Belgian law enforcement community.

You're a liability, he'd told him, expecting to take a punch for saying it. *Come out on the street and you put everything in jeopardy.*

In the end, that was how he'd convinced him, leaning hard into talk about *the cause* and *the mission*. Ticker gently reminded Verbeke that showing his face was what had got him arrested back in Slovakia.

The big man had relented, but not before he promised the hacker that he would hunt him down and slice off his cock if he tried to double-cross him.

Ticker adjusted the grubby white kufi cap on his head and pulled up the hood of his sweatshirt, burying his hands in the belly pocket. He wore a pair of glasses in his one other attempt to modify his appearance, but it was a poor disguise that wouldn't stand up if the police took a hard look. Lucky for him, most of the time the Antwerp cops tended to keep their distance from the 2060 district. Within its borders, the area was dominated by Turkish and North African immigrants, and he didn't see a single white face as he marched up the street.

He felt Verbeke's eyes on his back all the way up to the corner, before he turned out of sight of the apartment and headed toward the café on Diepestraat where the meet was set to take place.

He thought about running. Verbeke had always been a terrifying force of nature in the Lion's Roar, yo-yoing between smiling insincerity and violent anger, but that stuck-up French witch had always been there to give him something to aim at. With her gone, Verbeke was searching for a new target to unleash his endless anger on, and Ticker knew that sooner or later he would lash out at the closest person. He didn't want that to be him.

There was a look that Verbeke got, a mad distance in his eyes, a kind of blankness that came over him just before he blew his stack. Ticker had seen it more than once, even cheered it on when the man had been kicking a foreigner to death in some dank back alley.

The thought of being on the receiving end of that torrent of rage made his gut clench.

Sure, he could run. In his back pocket he had one of the hard drives from the server farm they'd been running in Iceland. It was loaded with Bitcoin data worth hundreds of thousands of euros, and even with the conversion discount the buyer was going to give him, he'd have enough to get out of Belgium, even back home to the States. He had people there who would take him in.

But Verbeke was a vengeful son-of-a-bitch. He wouldn't let Ticker get away with leaving him in the shit. That was why he had demanded the hacker leave his gear behind in the apartment, except for a phone, knowing that he would have to come back. If he ran, he would be looking over his shoulder for the rest of his life. His *short* life.

Mongrels and foreigners were scum, race traitors little better. But the weak bred a special kind of hatred in Noah Verbeke, and Ticker was terrified of being labeled as that.

Just get the money, he told himself. *Do that, and he'll see he still needs you.*

Ticker was trying to carry his stride with a little more confidence when a dark-haired guy in a black jacket stepped out in front of him. The word *cop* flashed up in Ticker's head and he pivoted away, pretending he intended that all along.

From the corner of his eye, he saw more movement as another figure came out of a side alley, and he looked before he could stop himself.

"Hello, ugly."

The scruffy-looking limey he'd first seen in Singapore was right there, one hand under his jacket in a way that made it clear he had a weapon beneath it.

The dark-haired man shoved Ticker into the alley,

where there were two more men waiting. Both were in heavy raincoats that just about covered the police tactical rig-outs they wore beneath them.

"You're nicked," said the Englishman, and he grinned. "Always wanted to say that."

The dark-haired cop searched Ticker, finding the hard drive and the phone.

"You don't wanna hold me," Ticker snapped. "If I don't make a call on that in five minutes, another can of Shadow goes pop." He showed his teeth. "We put it in the train station," he added, making up the threat as he went.

One of the cops immediately stepped away to talk into his radio, but the Englishman leaned in, giving him a withering once-over.

"I might believe that, if I didn't know what a lying little tosser you are."

"Verbeke has the rest of these?" broke in the dark-haired man, holding up the hard drive.

"Nah, I sold them to your fat-ass momma."

"Rude," replied the other man, and he pocketed the device.

"Let me make this clear," continued the Englishman. "No one is coming to meet you. The Belgians already intercepted the buyer you hooked before he made it to the 2060. We've been ghosting you through the net since you left Brussels." He made a disappointed tutting noise. "I told you before. Your info-sec game is sloppy, mate. You give black hats a bad name."

"Fuck you!" Ticker retorted, but it was half-hearted. Everything was coming apart and he couldn't stop it. "Five minutes," he insisted. "Let me go!"

"I have a better idea," came the reply, and the Englishman nodded toward the café, giving him a hard shove in that direction.

Across the street, through the window, Ticker could see the place was busy. There were a dozen or so men in there, all Muslims, all watching the television up on the wall. Even from here, he could see it was tuned to the same news channel Verbeke had been watching. The men looked solemn and angry.

"I'm willing to bet that everyone who lives around here knows someone from Benghazi," said the Englishman. "What will they do if we walk you in there, tell everybody who you are and what you've done, then close the door and leave?" He paused to let the threat sink in. "Your choice. Talk to us, or talk to them."

— TWENTY-TWO —

He paced the room, prowling as a tiger would circle a cage. Alone in the apartment with only the silent television for company, Verbeke's short fuse was burning down, moment by moment.

There was no news from Brussels of any terror attack, no word of the weapon he had sent out to murder his enemies, and spread discord in the city he had come to loathe. He knew well enough not to reach out to any of the group's other cells, to check in with them and see if they knew any more, but the inaction irritated him. He pawed at Ticker's laptop, looking over alt-right blogs and nationalist websites, searching for anything of note. But it was the same as it ever was, the legions of keyboard warriors throwing directionless spite and bile, all sound and fury with no core to it. These people were useful to the movement, Axelle had often said, but on an operation out in the real world, their value was far less. They were no use to him now.

He tossed the laptop back on the table and stalked away to the window, pawing at the bandaged wound on his upper arm. The woman's words continued to return to him as he stood there in the quiet. Verbeke could never admit to himself that he needed her, and with each hour that passed it became more likely that she had died at the hands of the enemies of the Lion's

Roar. The alternative was that Axelle had allowed herself to be taken prisoner by the police, and that he would never accept. He could not accept the possibility that she would surrender.

The Lion's Roar had no lack of soldiers and casualties of war. The fallen deserved to be remembered, and more so one who had become a martyr in the name of the conflict. This was the closest Noah Verbeke could ever come to showing care toward her, to rank her alongside the dead men upon whose backs the group was built.

But even that moment of regret still smacked of frailty. He could find another woman. They were venal and easily bent to his will. His needs would be serviced and Axelle would be forgotten. There was no place for attachments in this war. A man could only be the perfect weapon if he were in command of such needs. As Verbeke looked down at the street, watching the foreigners wander aimlessly through their pointless lives, he reminded himself that this was a truth lesser peoples could never grasp.

We will show them, he thought. *If not today, then tomorrow. And the day after, on and on until we rid ourselves of them.*

He caught sight of a figure in a familiar black hoodie, hunched forward as he walked, face lost in the depths of the raised hood. Ticker was on his way back, but the hacker was acting oddly, staying close to the edge of the street, taking the most direct route back to the apartment block.

Verbeke sneered.

Idiot.

It didn't matter how many times he tried to train these fools in counter-surveillance techniques, when they were under pressure they acted like the amateurs they were. For all his digital skills, Ticker was inadequate in the field. He couldn't stand up in a real fight, could barely handle a gun. Outside the internet, he was a poor specimen who otherwise would never have passed muster in Verbeke's brotherhood.

Then he looked again and a nagging suspicion pushed into the front of Verbeke's thoughts. The way Ticker was walking seemed wrong. The purpose in his pace was different from before.

He tried craning his neck to get a better look, but short of opening the window and leaning out, there was no other angle from which he could observe.

Heat tingled along Verbeke's nerves. The innate predator's sense that had always been in him came alive, the raw instinct sounding a warning. It was too soon. Ticker had barely been gone a few minutes.

Why would he come back so quickly?

He looked up and down the street, searching for other warning signs. A dark-haired man, a Westerner, was walking in the same direction. Aside from the other man, the foot traffic seemed to have suddenly reduced.

Then it came to Verbeke that the figure in the hood wasn't actually Ticker at all. The uneasiness he felt snapped into place. Back at the warehouse, that American bitch had got the drop on him by disguising herself with Axelle's helmet, buying herself enough time to get close to him. He wouldn't fall for that trick again.

In a bag at the foot of the window there was a Škorpion machine pistol with a lengthy sound-suppressor mounted on the muzzle. Verbeke snatched up the weapon and racked the slide, then kicked over the table on to its side and pulled it to the center of the room. He dropped into cover behind it and gripped the Škorpion with both hands, settling the iron sights on the door leading into the apartment. He flicked the fire selector lever to the "20" mark for fully automatic, and waited.

He strained to listen, catching the sound of quick footsteps coming up the concrete stairs to the third floor. They approached the door and then there was a hesitant knock, the pattern a one-two-three.

On *three* Verbeke squeezed the machine pistol's trigger and the Škorpion bucked in his hands, as he unloaded the weapon into the door and whoever stood beyond it. He wrestled down the recoil as the gun brayed, the sound resembling the noise of a drill bit chewing through dense wood. An extended burst of rounds punched through the cheap door, gouging out divots of it and splintering the frame.

As the last casing spun away from the ejector port, Verbeke was already on his feet and storming to the ruined door. He kicked it open and the whole thing came apart in pieces, collapsing into the gloomy hallway landing outside.

He strode out, ejecting the spent magazine in favor of a fresh one. The landing was ill-lit and the air was laced with the smell of spent cordite and seared plywood.

Verbeke registered the gloom. Pools of darkness lay where the weak illumination from the grimy skylight overhead failed to fall, the shadows reaching down past the chipped iron balustrade to the levels below.

The bullet-riddled body Verbeke expected to find sprawled on the landing was absent. Even as he registered that, from the corner of his vision he glimpsed a figure in a black hoodie burst out of the shadows at a full-tilt run, one arm coming down in a falling arc.

A silver-black rod glittered in the attacker's hand and it cracked hard across Verbeke's arm where he had been shot, lighting a storm of agony that made him drop the

Škorpion's reload before he could jam it into the magazine well. A rain of rapid-fire blows from the metal baton hit the exposed flesh of his neck and his face, opening cuts on his cheek, his brow, splitting his lip.

He threw up his hands to deflect the attacks, trying to snatch at the baton as it swept back and forth, snarling as he was forced on to the defensive.

The face beneath the black hood belonged to Dane, the Englishman, and in the man's eyes was the kind of rage and hate that Verbeke knew like an old friend.

At the last second before he rapped on the apartment door, Marc changed his mind and used the extended ASP baton to do the knocking. As much as he believed that Ticker had given him the right address, he feared Noah Verbeke enough to take that extra precaution.

The instinct had saved his life, and the spray of bullets ripped the door to pieces. Marc had no time to dwell on how Verbeke had known something was wrong, and instead he turned the adrenaline shock of his survival into motive power. His fight instructor always told him to divorce himself from anger when the blows started flying, but he couldn't do that. Not here, not now.

As the big man came stalking out into the hallway, all Marc wanted to do was hit him as hard as he could, to see blood and hear bone break. The bleak dread in his heart, that Lucy Keyes would never get out of the hole Verbeke had put her in, ignited in the rage.

Keeping one hand up high to protect his head, Marc used the baton on a rapid series of falling strikes, cracking the bigger man across the brow, the bridge of the nose, his forearms and hands.

Marc had borrowed the collapsible steel tube of the ASP and a couple of other party tricks from the Belgian cops who arrested Ticker. He still had the Glock pistol in the back of his waistband, but as furious as he was, his first instinct was still to take Verbeke alive. Marc believed Ticker was lying about his five-minute deadline and the possibility of another Shadow dispersal device in the Antwerp Central rail station, but there was a chance he wasn't. Verbeke's capture was the priority, as Jakobs had insisted over and over again. Dead, he would become a fallen hero for his followers. Alive and imprisoned, he would be a warning to them.

Down on the street, the Icelander was watching the front entrance, and Jakobs would have his men racing in to block off rear access from the apartments. Marc had drawn the short straw, going in to entice Verbeke to where he could be isolated and captured.

At least, that was the idea. The hits he landed were good, but Verbeke didn't slow down, and belatedly Marc was wishing he still had the dart gun he had used infiltrating the Frigga facility.

Verbeke managed to grab the tip of the baton and twist it. Marc had to make a split-second choice, to either have his arm bent the wrong way or to lose the weapon entirely. He picked the latter and the baton flew out of his hand, pinging off the balustrade and spinning away into the open light well leading down to the ground floor.

A hammer blow whooshed past Marc's head as Verbeke closed the distance between them. He avoided it and fired back a couple of punches, but that was just what the other man wanted. Verbeke snagged Marc's arm and trapped it, grimacing through the blood that oozed from the cuts on his face. All at once he was on him, shoving Marc into the iron rail.

"*Shit!*"

Marc's feet slipped out from under him and the small

of his back smacked into the top of the balustrade. It went wrong so fast. He was going over, losing his balance. Verbeke would pitch him into the air and there would be nothing to break his three-story fall, down to the cracked black and white tiles in the hallway below.

Clawing wildly at Verbeke's face with his other hand, Marc grabbed at one of the metal spindles along the rail and held on as tightly as he could. The momentum of the two men shifted awkwardly as Verbeke tried to shove him the rest of the way over.

For one horrible second, he balanced there, his body from the waist up flailing out into empty space. Then Marc got a good grip on his opponent's jacket and did the exact opposite of what Verbeke expected. Instead of trying to scramble back over the rail to safety, he pushed off, hauling the other man over the edge with him.

There was a giddy swell of vertigo and Verbeke shouted out in alarm, failing to stop himself. His greater mass did the work. He and Marc toppled over the rail.

The fall didn't come. Agony exploded down the length of Marc's arm as he took his own weight and Verbeke's together, clinging to the iron bar. They hung there for a fraction of a second, but it felt like an eternity. Marc yelled in pain as his shoulder joint extended and twisted. He felt sickening pain as it began to dislocate, felt the raw burning in his hand as the rusty metal lacerated his palm.

He struck out blindly, jabbing with his fingers, and connected with Verbeke's face. Scratching at his eyes, Marc jammed his thumb into the right socket and the big man howled.

Suddenly, the agonizing weight was gone and Marc's other arm was hanging free. Shaking with pain, he snatched at the edge of the stone landing and gripped it. Then, with slow and aching motions, Marc dragged himself up, hand over hand, back over the rail.

Panting, he supported himself on the thick balustrade and cast a look over. On the tiled floor below, Noah Verbeke lay face down in an unmoving sprawl. Marc probed his shoulder as he eyed the body. Everywhere he touched it there was burning and stinging, the memories of past conflicts written into the meat of him coming back with a vengeance.

Satisfied that the thug wasn't going anywhere, Marc pitched through the broken door and into the apartment beyond. Stiffly, he finally drew the Glock and panned it around the rooms, making sure there were no other surprises waiting for him. He found no sign of any kind of triggering device, or any evidence of another metal canister like the one he had smothered back in Grand-Place. The only items of note were a shop-new laptop, and a sports bag lying under a table.

The bag contained a dozen rectangular metal ingots, each one the size of a paperback book. Marc picked one at random, looking it over. Hard drives, commercial high-density solid-state units, a few of them scratched and dented where they had been stripped from the frames that had held the devices in their servers. It was the Bitcoin bounty from the Frigga facility, hundreds of thousands of dollars' worth of digital ghost money.

Marc opened the window and yelled down to the street.

"Oi!"

Loki emerged from the doorway and looked up, frowning.

"You found him?"

"He found me," Marc corrected. "Got something for you."

He stuffed the laptop in the bag, then hefted it up

over the windowsill and waited a count before letting
it drop. The Icelandic cop stepped up smartly to catch
it as it fell.

"Merry Christmas," Marc added.

He walked back out on to the landing, feeling flashes
of pain in his arm with each motion. A few apartments
along, doors were open and some of the other residents
clustered worriedly on the threshold, afraid of what the
commotion in the hallway might presage.

"It's okay." Marc tried to wave them away, wincing
as the movement sent stabs of new agony through his
shoulder. "I'm . . . uh . . . with the police. Go back inside. Everything is okay . . ."

When he reached the balustrade and looked down,
he realized that everything was *far* from okay. Where
Noah Verbeke's body had been lying only moments ago,
there were a few spatters of blood and nothing else.

Marc descended the stairwell in quick jumps, cannon-
ing from corner to corner, keeping his pistol close to his
chest. Reaching the ground floor hallway, he skidded
to a halt, panting hard, peering into the shadows. It
was noisier down here, with a steady burble of Middle
Eastern music coming through the door that led into
the takeaway fast food joint adjoining the apartment
building. Across the way, the hall narrowed into a
short corridor that ended in a heavy security door at
the front entrance.

He started toward it. If Verbeke had gone that way,
he would have run straight into Loki. Marc looked
back in the opposite direction. The doors over there
opened out to a narrow back alley filled with rubbish
bins, a path that would only lead to where Jakobs and
his men were waiting.

Which had to mean that the target was still in the building.

Marc heard a huff of heavy, labored breath behind him and whirled around. There was a trash chute in the corner of the hallway that he had missed on his way in, and in the shadows it cast there was more than enough room for a man as big as Verbeke to hide.

The thug was injured and he was moving slower, but still he had the drop on Marc. A savage blow came out of the gloom and struck him broadside across the chest. It was like being hit by the branch of an oak tree. Marc's own forward motion supplied most of the force and he crashed to the ground.

Verbeke swept in and stamped on his forearm, ripping a cry from his lips. The blow didn't land straight, so bones didn't break, but it was enough to jolt the Glock out of Marc's grip. Scrambling, Marc rolled away, trying to find his way back to the gun.

The other man wasn't about to let that happen. His combat boot connected with Marc's hip with enough force to lift him off the floor and flip him over. Marc sucked in a breath, turning to shout out toward the front door, hoping he could project it enough to get Loki's attention. Verbeke kicked him again, knocking the air from him in a rush. Pain-fires lit up along his side and he lost a moment to the rippling agony down his torso.

Then Verbeke dragged him off the floor and Marc swung a punch, hitting his attacker in the head. The bigger man's face was a mess of scratches and contusions, his eyes wide and wild, his teeth bared and pink with his own blood. With a wordless snarl, Verbeke threw Marc against the wall. He deflected off the frame of a door and struck wood. The door swung open under him and Marc fell backward into the clammy, brightly lit interior of the takeaway. He tasted stale air, heavy with the odor of sharp spices.

Marc slipped over a cracked vinyl table, knocking aside squeeze bottles of ketchup and mustard, before his stumble was abruptly halted as he fell against the glass frontage of a food counter.

The fast food place was empty except for a skinny Moroccan man in a grubby white smock, who stood in shocked silence behind the counter. Marc barely registered him as the cook shook out of his surprise and set off a string of invective in his direction, complaining vociferously over the loud music on the radio.

Verbeke was right there, never giving Marc a moment to catch a breath, storming toward him, charging in.

Marc brought up his hands in a boxer's defensive posture, twisting to avoid another rain of hammer-like blows from the bigger man. Verbeke missed with one shot and put his fist clean through the glass of the counter, spilling shards over the tubs of food behind it.

The guy in the smock snatched up a lengthy chef's knife and turned his ire on Verbeke, waving the blade in his direction and saying something about "*Polis, Polis!*"

Marc took the distraction and backed off, but he had no way out on to the street, and with the braying music filling the air, he could fire off a shotgun and the sound of the blast would have been lost.

Verbeke sent a punch across the top of the counter, the blow machine-fast and unstoppable, hitting the cook squarely in the head. He fell down and disappeared behind the counter, but not before Verbeke snatched the grimy knife out of his hand. Then he turned and stalked after Marc, flipping the blade about to present it in a fighter's grip, the cutting edge out.

Searching for something to put between them, Marc

grabbed the back of a chair and pulled, but the plastic seat didn't move an inch, the feet bolted right into the floor.

The knife glittered dully as it came at him and he jerked back, flinching away as it slashed the air. The blade was sharp enough to open his throat if it came close enough, and Verbeke palmed it from hand to hand, making shapes in the air with the tip. He was wheezing through the pain of cracked ribs and stinging lacerations, but grinning that feral grin all the way. The bastard was actually *enjoying* this.

Verbeke backed Marc into a corner, cutting off any avenue of escape. The blade flashed again and Marc ducked, bolting for a door at the back of the takeaway that had to lead to a kitchen, and another way out.

The chef's knife came at him as Verbeke came in for a stab and Marc twisted his body. He felt the tip pull at the baggy material of his hooded sweatshirt, barely missing his flesh as it pinned the hoodie to the door behind him. The blow was so forceful the knife passed through the wood and stuck there.

Marc lashed out with a vicious double-hit, first a rabbit-punch to the wound in Verbeke's arm and then a strike with the heel of his hand into Verbeke's blooded nose. The two men were so close, it was impossible to miss his target, and the kinetics of the blows forced the kitchen door open behind him. Marc pulled away, the hoodie ripping open as he tore from the blade and retreated into the preparation area.

If it was hot and close in the grubby little café, then the kitchen was ten times worse in half the space. The galley-sized area was home to a hissing, oil-smeared oven and hot plates filmed with years-old layers of grease. Stacks of dirty pots and pans were heaped on drying racks around a stained metal sink. A large walk-in refrigerator, too big for the tiny area, had been retrofitted into one corner. There was a heavy fire exit door on the far wall, but Marc's heart sank when he saw it was held shut with a bicycle chain-lock.

He'd trapped himself in a dead-end space, and the only way out was through the man trying to kill him.

Marc grabbed the first thing that could serve as a weapon—a saucepan with a heavy copper bottom—and used it like a bludgeon. He slammed the flat of the pan into Verbeke's head with a satisfying crunch, reeling it back for a second blow.

Blood gushed in free flow from the other man's ruined nose, over his mouth and chin, a red spatter collecting on the front of his jacket and the T-shirt beneath. He resembled some mad-eyed Dark Age berserker, a comparison that Verbeke would doubtless have relished.

The man had been given the opportunity to escape, but once more the truth of who he was became apparent. Noah Verbeke was brutal for brutality's sake, and whatever grand plans he might have for inflicting greater pain on his enemies, he liked the taste of blood above everything else. The abstract way of killing—of bombs and deadly infections, of death inflicted from distance—would never be enough. He wanted to get his hands dirty, to kill up close.

Marc hit him again and Verbeke shrugged it off, cuffing the pan away and out of his sweat-slick fingers. With a weighty backhand, the bigger man knocked him into a pile of plates and Marc's head rang like a bell.

Verbeke wiped red spittle across his sleeve and tilted his head, eyeing his opponent.

"You should have shot me dead from a mile away," he said thickly. "Flattened this place with a drone strike.

Stormed it with a hundred jackboots. Instead you came on your own."

"I'm not on my own," Marc retorted, around a wheezing breath.

"You *are*," Verbeke insisted. "Your mongrel bitch will be dead by now. Those chems she sucked down, it's a bad way to go." He laughed wetly. "But you know that. You watch the news. One more animal corpse. Send it back to Africa, eh? Burn her with all the rest." He spat on the floor. "We'll make this continent *pure*, you'll see. Purge it. Become the fortress we used to be. And then we'll sit back and watch the rest of the lesser races die off. The weak perish and the strong survive. How it should be." Verbeke's eyes shone at the thought of it. "How it *will* be."

For a moment, the fury that had been pushing Marc through faded like the wind changing direction. He felt empty and dejected at the prospect of a man like the one standing before him.

"You—your kind. There's no end, is there? No bottom to the well. Just hate and fucking bile going on forever."

Verbeke showed his shark's smile.

"It's glorious, isn't it?"

Marc's anger came back in a hot wave, instantly rekindled by the sneering, hateful contempt on the other's man's face.

Right about one thing, he thought. *We should have killed him.*

He moved before Verbeke could stop him, bringing down his fist on one of the scattered plates, breaking it into jagged wedges of ceramic. Marc snatched up the biggest piece and launched himself at the other man. He jammed the makeshift dagger into his chest, feeling the tip pierce flesh and glance off his ribs.

Verbeke howled and retaliated, hitting Marc so hard that for a second he almost blacked out, feeling the floor move under him and the dizzying sense of the room spinning. He slammed into the door of the refrigerator, and barely ducked out of the way before a fist slammed into the metal. The broken shard of plate was still stuck in him, but Verbeke kept on going, each blow he didn't land putting a massive dent in the door plate.

Marc snagged the handle and pulled hard on it. With a gust of freezing cold air the refrigerator door creaked open, and he put his shoulder to it, swinging it wide to slam the corner of it into Verbeke's face. He let go and stumbled away, trying to gain some distance, but the floor around the overfilled sink was slippery and he fell down on one knee.

"Enough . . . bullshit . . ." gasped Verbeke.

He pulled a meat cleaver off a rack on the wall and advanced on Marc.

In the damp, slimy space beneath the sink there were dozens of plastic bottles and battered aerosols. Marc snatched up a dirty orange can and mashed the nozzle, spraying an acrid haze of oven cleaner into the air.

With his face covered in dozens of open cuts, the fine mist burned Verbeke like acid and he let out a strangled scream. He slapped at his face, the cleaver dropped and forgotten.

Marc rose, bracing his hands on the sink and the cleaning rack on either side of him, enough that he could swing both legs up and plant a double-kick squarely in the bigger man's gut. Verbeke toppled backward and fell into the open walk-in refrigerator, crashing down through wire shelves and frost-slick boxes of frozen meat.

Marc charged at the door, reaching into the torn

hoodie's belly pocket for his last-ditch weapons, the other party tricks he had taken from the Belgian cops. Back in Iceland, Verbeke and his cronies had used something similar on him and Lucy, and now Marc was going to return the favor.

He pulled the pins on the two knurled black cylinders in his hand, letting their spring-loaded trigger plates fly away. Verbeke was already hauling himself back to his feet, as Marc threw the M84 stun grenades into the cold store and slammed the door shut. He jammed the latch closed as the big man charged the door in desperate panic, making the entire thing rock on its mountings.

Then the grenades detonated inside the cramped space, with brilliant flashes of million-candlepower light and roaring screams of hundred-decibel sound.

Delancort stepped off the launch and on to the deck of the *Themis*, his brow furrowing as he saw that he was not the only person who had been summoned to the yacht. Beneath a folding pergola over the aft of the vessel, seats had been arranged for the members of Rubicon's board of directors and their aides, and he was the last of them to arrive.

Gerhard Keller gave him a wan salute with a glass of sparkling water and smiled.

"Ah, Henri is here." The German financier glanced around at the others. "Perhaps now we can get some answers?"

"Where's Ekko?" Esther McFarlane sat as deep in the shade as she could get, frowning at him from behind dark glasses and a sun hat. As usual, the woman didn't waste time with any preamble. "If he wanted to talk to us, we could be doing it in a nice air-conditioned room."

She waved dismissively at the blue waters where the *Themis* was anchored, a short distance off the coast.

Delancort looked back in the direction of the Monte Carlo skyline and the Rubicon tower in particular. Bringing them out here was a theatrical gesture, something that Ekko Solomon was not known for. Delancort's employer was far too direct for that kind of thing. He clearly had something else in mind.

"I know as much as you do," he replied, finding an empty seat next to Victor Cruz. The Chilean was the only member of the group who seemed comfortable being there, and he basked in the bright Monaco sunshine.

How much of that is a false front?

Since the board's arrival and the delivery of their ultimatum, Solomon had barely spoken to Delancort. It felt as if things were coming to a head. Delancort had tried several times to rein in Solomon's desires to pursue dangerous challenges and risk Rubicon's involvement in increasingly perilous extra-legal situations, but with little effect.

It wasn't that he didn't believe in Solomon's cause. Delancort understood that the world was a harsh place where the disenfranchised and the unfortunate were continually victimized, and he was willing to do all he could to help. But step by step, Solomon had shaped Rubicon's Special Conditions Division into a task force that operated above the law, and done it without any oversight.

Solomon's vessel, named after the Greek Titaness of justice, was an example of his crusade made manifest. The gigayacht was all smooth-lined luxury, but it also contained a compact crisis center on the lower decks and enough military grade hardware on board to outfit a special forces unit. He glanced at Cruz, Keller and McFarlane, wondering if they knew about that.

How much of what the SCD have done has he kept from them? The thought bled into another, more cutting question. *How much has Solomon kept from me?*

Delancort knew there were operations that had not been documented, missions from the earliest days of the SCD that left no trace. Despite the warmth of the day, he suppressed a shiver. Being on the inside of the circle of Solomon's trust had made it easier to overlook those possibilities, but his brief experience of being outside it sent his thoughts back to the matter of exactly how much he *didn't* know.

The glass doors at the back of the yacht's lounge opened and Solomon stepped through. It was rare to see him in anything other than an impeccably tailored Savile Row suit; however, today the man was dressed in a short-sleeved cotton shirt, tan trousers and deck shoes. His eyes were hidden behind mirrored sunglasses, and despite his casual attire, his manner was stiff and formal. In one hand he carried a tablet computer, one of the military-specification portable units from the crisis room.

"Thank you for coming," he rumbled. Solomon did not sit at first, taking them in with a measuring look. "Before we get down to business, I wanted to inform you that our assistance to the humanitarian effort in Libya is going well. We coordinated with United Nations medical teams and *Médecins Sans Frontières*. The disaster relief units shipped to Benghazi have made a great difference there."

"The outbreak has been contained, then?" said Keller.

"Indeed," replied Solomon. "The situation is fluid, but it appears that the spread of the contagion was far less than first expected."

Delancort saw McFarlane nodding.

"This is the kind of work the Rubicon Group should be seen to be doing. In the public eye, in the light of day."

Solomon stiffened. The Scottish woman's comment immediately changed the tone of the conversation.

"You have completed your review of the Special Conditions Division," he said.

Cruz frowned. "Well, there are still some areas that need—"

"You have completed your review," Solomon repeated, making it clear the statement was not a question. "This has gone on long enough. If you have issues to bring to me, now is the time. Speak plainly."

McFarlane, Cruz and Keller exchanged glances, and the German was the one to reply.

"Ekko . . . we understand what you have built here. And the board accepts that the SCD was created with the best of intentions. But each time you green-light an operation, you put all of Rubicon at risk. You have spoken before of how small actions can effect great changes, and no one sees that better than I." Keller made a turning gesture with his hand. "I have watched a one percent shift in a stock price turn into a catastrophic nosedive that bankrupted a Fortune 500 company overnight. I have seen how one tiny investment can help a whole nation to bloom. But those are acts within the law. What the SCD does takes place beyond that framework. It goes past any gray area and deep into the black."

McFarlane removed her glasses and scowled into the sunlight.

"You brought us here where no one can listen in on us, so let's say the words, shall we? There's evidence that your SCD operatives have broken dozens of international laws, resisted arrest, *killed* people. How can we allow that?"

Delancort cleared his throat.

"Our military contractors and security staff have mandates to use lethal force if required."

"Depending on contracts, local laws and dozens of other variables." The woman silenced him with a withering look. "There's a world of difference, Henri. Don't insult my intelligence by suggesting otherwise." She looked back at Solomon. "If this information were to become public knowledge, it could ruin us."

"We keep our secrets for a greater good." Solomon glanced down at the tablet computer in his hand. "A few hours ago, our specialists, working in concert with the Belgian counter-terrorism division and officers of the Icelandic financial crimes unit, assisted in neutralizing a terror cell, and stopped a biological attack in the city of Brussels." Everyone else on the sundeck fell silent. "This is being kept from the media, as is the truth behind the horror you have seen unfolding in Benghazi."

"What do you mean?" said Cruz.

"The outbreak in Libya was deliberately engineered by the same terrorist group. Those behind that attack sought to duplicate their atrocity in the heart of Europe." Solomon took a breath. "This is what the SCD does. We oppose these threats. You may challenge my motives and my methods as you see fit. But know that today, lives were saved and justice was served. I will never apologize for that."

"It's not our job to protect the world, Ekko," said McFarlane.

"With respect," came the calm, implacable reply, "I

disagree. And while I remain in my position with this organization, I will . . ." Solomon paused, reframing his words. "*Rubicon* will do all it can to balance the scales of the world." He looked away, out over the sea, and repeated a mantra that Delancort had heard many times before. "I believe in responsibility. The responsibility of the rich to see that the poor do not starve. The responsibility of the strong to see that the weak are not preyed upon." He turned back again. "Rubicon has power, and we have an ethical imperative to use it to do right. We cannot be afraid to travel to dark places in order to do so." Solomon's gaze settled on McFarlane. "If there is anyone here who does not wish to be a part of that, I will respect their choice. But as of now, I am ordering the SCD to be returned to full operational status." He gave Delancort a nod and stepped away. "My chef has prepared a light lunch. Please enjoy it. The launch will return you to Monte Carlo afterward."

Delancort followed him, blinking as he passed from the dazzling light of outdoors and into the shady interior of the *Themis*.

"Sir," he began. "Is there any update on Lucy's condition?"

Solomon nodded once. "She is stable."

He chewed his lip. "Sir, if my support has not been clear over the past few days, I—"

"To do what we do," said Solomon, speaking over him, "I need my people operating at the best of their ability. I need to trust in them. That includes you, Henri."

Delancort gave a slow nod. "Of course."

Solomon was going to say more, but then the doors slid open again and Esther McFarlane entered, clasping her hat and glasses.

"If it's all the same to you, Ekko, I'll skip the lunch and go ashore now."

─── TWENTY-THREE ───

Her dreams were filled with shapeless, formless things. Walls of rippling color and motion, sounds that made no sense. And pain-laced fear shimmered underneath it, gripping her with iron claws.

Lucy rose gradually out of the ocean of sensation and drifted back toward awareness. The lights and shapes of the hospital room took on solidity, and she saw the patient monitoring machines by her bedside, the reinforced window on the far wall. A sudden, desperate need to see the outside world, to have daylight on her skin, caused a half-sob to form in her chest, and she caught it before it could escape.

Still here, she told herself, insisting on the truth of it. *Still alive.*

With one shaking hand, Lucy reached up and touched her face. She remembered the sickening, burning sensation across her mouth and her nose when Verbeke had dosed her with the bioweapon, and in her half-awake state she was afraid it might have left her permanently scarred. Her flesh was hot to the touch, raw and swollen, but otherwise undamaged. She took a breath, and the smell of chemical antiseptics and the odor of her own tainted sweat were heavy in the air.

The door slid open and a figure in a blue biohazard oversuit walked in, the boxy see-through helmet catching the light. Through the plastic faceplate she saw Marc staring back at her. He looked haggard, forcing a smile.

"Hey," he said, coming closer.

"Hey," she repeated.

The word sounded like the creak of a broken hinge. Lucy realized her throat was desert-dry, and she made a drinking motion.

"I got you," said Marc, bringing her a squeeze bottle of cool water ending in a hooked tube she could draw on. He handed it over and sat on a metal stool next to the bed. The oversuit was comically big on him, and the thought made her smile.

"That get-up, look like you oughta be in a cartoon," she said. "Spaceman."

He reached out and took her hand.

"You look okay."

"You're a liar," Lucy retorted weakly, and managed a gruff chuckle.

Marc's tired eyes narrowed.

"Is it stupid to ask you how you feel?"

"I'm . . ."

Terrified.

She wanted to say the word, but it was hard to drag it up and put it out there.

"I'm here," she managed.

"You're going to get over this," Marc insisted. "You made it through the most critical phase of the infection, and it's already burning out of you. I told the docs you're a tough one, they said *yeah, we know.*"

"Flatterer." Lucy sifted his words. "How . . . is that? Marburg's not . . . quick."

"The Shadow variant is different," Marc noted. "Park said it was designed to be programmable. High infection rate, fast burn through. But this thing is dying off way quicker than anyone expected it to. I think she might have messed with the matrix before it went out to the bioprinters."

"Huh." Lucy thought back to the woman she had known, the strong-willed soul who had risked certain death to flee the North Korean police state with her, and she knew what Ji-Yoo Park had done. "She sabotaged it."

Even in the midst of her world coming apart around her, Park must have altered the viral model to weaken it and radically truncate the bioweapon's lifespan. A despairing, desperate attempt to do what she could to negate the attacks she knew would happen. Far more victims would survive a fast-burn infection than exposure to Shadow at its fullest potency.

"They're going to move you tonight," Marc was saying. "Silber is flying in the jet to take you to Rubicon's biomed clinic. They'll get you better."

Lucy shook her head. Right now, the last thing she wanted to do was think about the state she was in and the road ahead of her. She held her fears at bay and looked Marc in the eye, asking the question that she had to have answered.

"Did you get him?"

Marc's head bobbed inside the confines of the helmet.

"Oh yeah. You know the Belgians really hate that bloke?"

"Wasn't easy?" She reached up and touched the faceplate. Marc had nasty purple-yellow bruises on his cheek and popped capillaries in one eye. The careful way he had sat down on the stool told her that he was hurting in lots of different places. "You seen a doctor?"

"Later." He dismissed the comment. "You just worry about you. Meantime, the rest of us are chasing up the loose ends."

Marc told her that even though Assim had passed on the full take of the Bitcoin transaction data to Larsson and the SR, he still wasn't sure that the Icelandic government would forgive them.

"Loki has the hard drives from the servers," he continued. "Interpol secured the bioprinters. The Belgians have Ticker's computer, after I made sure to delete all trace of the Shadow viral model from it before they got their hands on it. Anything they can use on there will go toward rolling up more of the Lion's Roar."

"Sakina?" she whispered, pausing to take another sip of water. "Her family?"

Marc nodded. "I called in a favor with Emigrant Aid. They're going to help them in their case for asylum. That's going to be an interesting discussion. But Meddur helped us isolate Verbeke, so they have to take that into consideration." He sighed, the sound echoing inside the helmet. "They can't send them home. It's still bad in Benghazi. Rubicon is helping out with transport and medical supplies. But it could have been a lot worse."

"Yeah."

Without Park's intervention, the Libyan city would have become a living hell, but still the death toll would be considerable. Dark, forbidding memories of sickened bodies in rusting metal cells pushed at the horizon of her thoughts and Lucy turned away from them, trying to concentrate on something else.

"We still have one unanswered question."

"Saito." Marc rose and paced the room. "I keep coming back to him. Didn't have the time to weigh it up when the shit was hitting the fan, but now I've had a while to process it . . ." He paused, staring into space. "I go over that phone call again and again in my head, trying to figure him out. It doesn't make any sense. He gave us the Lion's Roar, when all he needed to do was *nothing*, and the Combine would have made big on their investment."

"Maybe . . . they bet against him," she offered.

Talking was tiring her out, but she needed to know.

"Saito wanted us to deal with Verbeke for him, so he could keep his hands clean," Marc went on.

"If it was Saito," Lucy managed, "you gotta know it's really Glovkonin pulling the strings. And I don't like . . . not knowing what that Russkie son-of-a-bitch is up to."

Marc nodded his agreement. "No argument here. One thing's for sure. Glovkonin never does anything without a good reason." He dwelled on that thought for a moment. "Somehow—in some way—we helped him."

Lucy barely caught the last few words he spoke. The fear and the darker memories haunting her had crept closer as they talked, and she couldn't hold them back any longer. A faint gasp escaped her and she felt tears on her face.

Marc sensed the change in her and came back to Lucy's bedside.

"What's wrong?" He took her hand. "I'll get the nurse."

"No," she told him. "It's not that."

Vulnerability was not a word that Lucy Keyes ever applied to herself. It was a quality that she sought in her enemies, the chinks in their armor, the holes in their defenses. They had burned it out of her in the army, or so she had believed. But in this room, the lie of that became clear.

"Marc, I did a terrible thing." Her voice was low and breathy. "Broke my promise to that woman. I said I would get her to a better life and I failed twice over. I've shed so much blood, I wanted to have one good thing on the right side of the scales. Just one."

The fear that she would not survive this gripped her, that her end would be marked only by what she had done in the darkest of her days.

"That's not on you," he told her.

Lucy looked down at her hand, seeing the chalky cast to her ochre skin where the IV line entered her arm.

"You know, they trained us to die like heroes. Like Aunt Dani, rushing into that tower when the sky was falling in," she rasped. "But I'm not ready to go out like this. Like a victim."

Like my father, she thought, *cut down by something he never saw coming.*

"You won't." Marc pulled the metal stool closer and put himself on it, leaning close until the blue plastic of his oversuit touched the bare flesh of her arm. "I'm not going to let that happen." His long fingers clasped hers. "Back there, all I could think about was keeping you alive. You always have my back, Lucy. You're what keeps me going."

The simple words and the honest, human contact made the memories and the horrors they held draw back and fade.

"You saved the girl after all, white knight," she told him, her smile coming back. "Glad it was me."

"Just paying back what I owe. Look at us." He gave her a wan smile in return. "All worn out and beaten up. But like you said, we're still here, yeah? We're not done yet." He shook his head again. "Not by a long way."

She didn't have to ask him to stay, and he didn't make it a question. Lucy's head sank back into the pillow and her eyelids fluttered closed. She felt the gentle press of the oversuit helmet resting against her shoulder, and as she listened their breathing slowly fell into sync.

After a while, the two of them surrendered to the inevitable and drifted away, toward silent shores of sleep.

* * *

"Wake up."

The words were fuzzy and muffled, and they came with a splash of freezing water over his face, shocking him out of his doze.

He blinked, remembering where he was, and instinctively rocked forward in the metal chair bolted to the floor in the middle of the room. Restraints around his thick wrists and muscular ankles bit tight, forcing him back into the seat.

"You are not dead," said an unpleasantly familiar voice, "as good for the world as that might be." The speaker turned to another figure in the gloom, beyond the pool of light falling from the caged lightbulb overhead. "Can he hear us?"

"The discharge from the flashbangs cost him the hearing in his right ear," said another man. "But he knows what you're saying."

Nils Jakobs stepped into the light, and for a brief moment he showed the glimmer of a smile.

"Good."

Seeing the older man's face ignited the anger in Noah Verbeke, and he bellowed like an enraged animal, once more straining wildly at the chair. But it was an impotent, directionless fury, and the sound rebounded off the concrete walls of the cell. Going nowhere, meaning nothing.

"Did that make you feel better?"

Jakobs gave him a sideways look when he reeled back, panting and spent.

"It did." The sounds in the room had a muddy quality, and even his own voice seemed to be coming to him from a great distance. "Nils. I knew I should have slit your throat."

"Another failure on your part," said the police officer.

Verbeke's eyes still ached from the burning flares of white fire that had temporarily blinded him, and his skull throbbed incessantly. Even his sense of balance was damaged, making his stomach lurch with the slightest motion of his head. But all this he ignored, unwilling to show even the smallest sign of weakness to his enemy. He gave a derisive snort and made a show of glancing around.

"This feels familiar. We've been here before, haven't we? It wasn't enough for you to have your men on the train killed? Fine. We can do this again."

"No one is coming to rescue you this time," said Jakobs. "By the end of the week, anyone who ever cared about your wretched existence will be in prison or on the run."

"You think so?" Verbeke shot back.

"I know it." Jakobs came closer, leaning heavily on a walking cane. "I'm going to remember you every day of my life, Noah. Every time the wound you gave me acts up. Every time I take off my shirt and see the scars where they dug those bullets out of my gut." Verbeke grinned at that idea, but Jakobs kept on talking. "But it is *worth* it to know that you are finished." He nodded at the door. "You should have picked better people to work for you. The American—Ticker? He willingly turned over your entire operation to save his neck. We're going to give him a deal, and in return he will open up the Lion's Roar to my department. We will eradicate your repugnant horde of racist shits, and salt the earth behind us."

"He doesn't know anything," Verbeke sneered, convincing himself as he threw out the lie. "You might score a couple of arrests—so what?" He chuckled. "We are legion, Nils. We are everywhere. We do what others are too afraid to! You can't stamp out the truth!"

Jakobs gestured with the cane, taking in Verbeke with the motion.

"This is the problem with people like him," he said, addressing the other person standing in the shadows. "They cannot conceive of the fact that anyone else thinks differently from them. They believe that every man is as hateful as they are. They think that everyone dissimilar to them wants to destroy them." He paused. "It is because they are afraid."

"I'm not afraid of you, you old prick." Verbeke laughed at the idea.

"That's true."

Jakobs beckoned the other figure into the light. A man with Middle Eastern features became visible. He wore a uniform in dark blue urban camouflage, and he glared at Verbeke with naked, seething hatred.

"This gentleman is an officer with the Libyan Judicial Police, invited here by Interpol. It has been decided, in the interests of international cooperation, to expedite your transfer to a military prison outside Tripoli, so that my colleague here can interview you about certain matters." Jakobs let those facts sink in. "I am sure someone like you will be able to look after themselves in such a dangerous place."

"You're going to turn me over to those animals?" said Verbeke, in a low growl. "I have a right to be tried by my own kind!" He pulled uselessly at the restraints again. "You told me you would put me in prison for the rest of my life!"

"I did," agreed Jakobs. "And you *will* be in prison for the rest of your life." He turned away, and limped toward the door. "However brief that is."

* * *

Pytor Glovkonin schooled his expression as he entered the white anteroom, arranging his features into what most closely resembled a remorseful attitude, and waited by the window, looking out into the Parisian evening.

Contrition was an alien concept to him. Even as a child, it was not an emotion he had ever engaged with, but he could fake it well enough when circumstances demanded it, and he did so now. On some level, it amused him to play at humility. However, he couldn't quite grasp how lesser men dealt with it on a daily basis.

He sensed someone else enter the room and saw the Asian woman with her austere dress and calculated manner, reflected in the glass.

"They're ready for you," said the committee's aide.

He suppressed a smile. This time, the Combine committee did not play games with him. This time, they wanted him standing in front of them for judgment over a failure.

But not mine, he thought. *Theirs. Had they listened to me at the start, had they shown me the respect I am due, none of this would have happened.*

Now the arrogant fools would be manipulated into an endgame they would never see coming.

But first I have a play to perform, Glovkonin reminded himself.

Straightening his jacket, he stepped through the doors from the anteroom as the woman announced his presence. She closed the door behind him and he halted at the end of the long, ornate table.

Two of the three seats at the table were occupied. The Italian magnate lounged in one of them, toying with a cut-glass tumbler of rum. The dour Swiss banker sat stiffly in the other, leaning over the table with his hands in a steeple. The American was absent in the ruddy-faced flesh, but his visage was displayed on a screen on the far wall. From the way the image's point of view moved, he appeared to be communicating via a hand-held device. Over his shoulder, Glovkonin saw the sands of a white beach and bottle-green waters lapping at the shore.

As he expected, none of the men offered him the empty chair.

"Good evening," he began, "I came as quickly as I could."

In fact, he had flown in from Moscow two days earlier, but made sure to keep that piece of information secret.

If they knew he was lying, they didn't mention it.

"This group has weathered many storms, many setbacks," said the Italian. "For all our successes, there are the inevitable failures. This is a fact of life. But we have kept these issues to a minimum. When something goes awry, it is contained."

"This is not one of those times," snapped the Swiss.

His tone was so strident, so challenging, that it almost made Glovkonin forget his act and sneer back in reflex. He caught himself and studied the man as he went on.

"We expected much from you, and this fresh disappointment leaves the committee questioning our choice to advance you so swiftly."

"*This thing is falling apart*," added the American, scowling out of the screen at him. "*I mean, I reckon we can salvage some elements of it, but the core plan is a goddamn bust.*"

"Yes," Glovkonin said solemnly. "Well put. I will have information leak out to the media, suggesting a cover-up in Brussels and pushing the narrative of immigrants as potential disease carriers . . ." He gave a theatrical sigh. "But I'm afraid without the central event in Belgium to underscore that, it will be seen as a fringe conspiracy theory. It will only feed the prejudices of those already aligned with those views."

"The point of this operation," said the Swiss, tapping the table with a thick finger, "was to move that into the mainstream. To demonize one group and empower those we can influence."

"I am aware of the stated goal," said Glovkonin.

Again, he tamped down his irritation. After his last visit here, he had set to work digging into the backgrounds of these three men and learned much about the financier from Switzerland along the way. He had been amused to discover that, in the past, this man's bank had made several attempts to buy up controlling shares in Glovkonin's company G-Kor, only to be thwarted in their efforts. When the opportunity arose, he would punish him for his temerity. But that lay in the future.

"You let Verbeke have too much freedom." The Italian sounded bored. "You knew he was a violent thug. Why didn't you hold his leash a little tighter?"

"I did as the committee asked me to," Glovkonin replied. "I remind you, it was you who told me to monitor, but not to deviate from the plan." He stared at the older man. "Your exact words. When I previously petitioned to take more direct control, I was censured."

The American snorted.

"*You know, for a second there, it sounded like our buddy here was blaming us for his mistake!*"

"I only wish to present the facts," Glovkonin continued, seeing his opportunity. "We stood in this room and I warned you that the Rubicon Group were a threat to the Combine's operations. You disagreed with that assessment. And now Ekko Solomon's people are responsible for disrupting the Shadow project."

The banker's lined face creased in annoyance, but he said nothing. This was the moment, if it were to happen, that Glovkonin's plan would go awry. If they suspected what he was doing, if they knew he had deliberately leaked information to Rubicon's agents.

If Saito talked . . . he thought. *But no. That kind of disloyalty is impossible for him, even if he detests me. His duty is his life.*

"*There was the Al Sayf thing in Washington,*" said the American, his sour expression filling the screen. "*Then that shit with the suitcase bomb, then Toussaint's assassination and now this. Rubicon's been getting in our way for a while now and we keep letting it slide.*" He shook his head. "*Have to say it, the new guy has a point.*"

"The Combine has many enemies," said the Swiss. "Rubicon is just one of them."

"True, true," allowed the Italian. "But unlike the FSB or the CIA, we can't buy them off or suborn them." He looked into the depths of his glass. "We always intended to deal with Ekko Solomon one day. In the light of recent events, perhaps we should re-evaluate our timetable."

Glovkonin nodded. "It can be done."

The other men continued as if he hadn't spoken.

"A termination, then?" suggested the banker, brisk and dismissive.

"*That won't be enough,*" said the American. "*We gotta burn him down to the ground. Make a lesson out of it for anyone else who thinks about crossing us.*" He jutted out his chin, as if squaring up to an unseen enemy. "*It's a matter of reputation now.*"

"So we break him." The Italian gave a nod, then

looked back at the Russian. "Our friend wishes to support us in this."

Glovkonin removed an encrypted smartphone from his pocket and speed-dialed a number.

"It's time. Bring him in," he said.

"We do not use those in here!" snapped the Swiss. "We have a procedure!"

Glovkonin gave an insincere smile.

"Forgive me. The exception will be worth the lapse this once." He walked up to the table, deliberately finding a place at the head of it. "I am happy to be of assistance in this action. You see, I have a unique weapon at my disposal . . ." There was a knock at the door and his smile grew. "Well. Let me introduce you." He called out "*Enter!*" and the door opened, revealing Saito on the threshold.

Saito gave a nod, never meeting the gazes of the men in the room, and stood aside to allow a new arrival to step in.

"What is this?" demanded the Swiss, growing incensed at the continued breaches of committee protocol.

"Gentlemen, this is my guest, Mr. Lau." Glovkonin made a sweeping motion. "I have brought him a long way to meet you."

"And who are you to us?" said the Italian, raising an eyebrow.

Without waiting to be asked, the Chinese man in the expensive suit made his way to the empty chair and sat down in it.

"I am the man who founded the Rubicon Group," he told them. "The man that Ekko Solomon abandoned and left for dead." His hard, battle-worn eyes took them in with a glance. "I am what you need to destroy him."

ACKNOWLEDGMENTS

Once more, much appreciation must go to all at my agents and publishers, without whom these books would not be published; my thanks to Robert Kirby, Kate Walsh, Amy Mitchell, Hannah Beer, Margaret Halton, Steve O'Gorman, Jonathan Lyon, Zoe Ross, Margaret Stead, James Horobin, Stephen Dumughn, Nick Stern, Jennie Rothwell, Sophie Orme, Kate Parkin, Francesca Russell, Imogen Sebba, Felice McKeown, Christopher Morgan, Marco Palmieri, and everyone else who has worked so tirelessly to make the Marc Dane series a success.

Any errors in this work are mine, but every attempt was made to be accurate! In the pursuit of that, thanks to the following people for moral support, advice, and invaluable research assistance: Peter J. Evans, Ben Aaronovitch, Lisa Smith MSc, Kin-Ming Looi, Jan Blommaert, Clint Emerson, John Dwarka, Alex Hern, Xan Rice, Doug Saunders, Sigga at Tröll Expeditions, and Collette at *Writing with Color*.

And as always, much love to my mother, and my better half, Mandy.

Forge

Award-winning authors
Compelling stories

· ·

Please join us at the website
below for more information
about this author and other great
Forge selections, and to sign up for
our monthly newsletter!